The Folks
At
Fifty-Eight

Michael Patrick Clark

Copyright © Michael Patrick Clark, 2012

All rights reserved

MDB Publishing

ISBN: 9780957248908

For Pam

AUTHOR'S NOTE

Set in the aftermath of World War II, ***The Folks at Fifty-Eight*** is a Faustian tale offering all the lust, violent death, intrigue, suspense and pace you might reasonably expect from a conventional espionage thriller.

Here you will find former OSS agent and handsome archetypal loner-hero, Gerald Hammond, estranged from his wife, socially outcast and haunted by the guilt of so many deadly sins committed.

In keeping with many examples of the genre, you will also find a femme fatale in the guise of young, beautiful, mercurial and utterly amoral Catherine Schmidt.

Within these pages lurk the glamorous and ugly, misguided and devious, patriots, traitors, shameless hedonists, evil manipulators, erotic sirens and sadistic killers.

So, all straightforward adult thriller stuff then. . .

Or is it?

Perhaps I should also mention that this tale was inspired by actual characters and events of the time.

I leave you to draw whatever lines you deem appropriate between fact and fiction, historic event and later interpretation, innocent mistake and sinister conspiracy.

Enjoy.

MPC

BACKGROUND

It is spring of 1946. To the east of a chaotically-partitioned Germany, the Red Army continues to wreak a vengeance that began at Stalingrad. Summary execution is commonplace, expulsion to the Gulag a constant threat. For the women there is additional fear. In the twelve months since the Soviets stormed Berlin, conservative estimates put the number of rapes against German women in excess of one million.

In Washington the intelligence community is in disarray. OSS is disbanded, the fledgling Central Intelligence Group under-resourced and hamstrung by bickering rivalries.

In New York City the celebrations continue, but while the ticker tape rains down, sinister men in grey are already planning for the next confrontation.

In Moscow a paranoid Joseph Stalin summons Lavrenti Beria, his chief of espionage and state-sponsored terror. Both men believe the Soviet Union must rapidly develop an atomic weapon or be forever subservient to the West.

They also believe that, in espionage terms, the West will never be more vulnerable.

1

When a keen-eyed Marcus Allum first spotted the weather-beaten face and broad shoulders of Gerald Hammond he was almost eighty yards away, casually strolling along on the far side of Washington's Connecticut Avenue. Allum hurriedly turned away and then ducked into a convenient coffee shop, where he threaded his way through the busy seating area, selected a table at the back, and then hid behind his newspaper.

Not that Marcus Allum imagined for a second that Hammond hadn't seen him. When you have been trained to scan a sea of faces for a single nervous look, you don't miss something as obvious as an old friend avoiding an embarrassing reunion; you don't miss anything. And when your life has so often depended on you seeing them before they see you, you make damn sure you see them first.

However, as Gerald Hammond wandered past the frontage, his attention didn't shift from the sidewalk and his face betrayed little of his thoughts. He seemed preoccupied and distant, almost to the point of morose. He obviously hadn't noticed Allum duck into the coffee shop, or seen him watching from behind his newspaper. Given Hammond's well-publicized problems, Marcus Allum could fully understand why.

Allum ordered a black coffee and sat moodily remembering, as the doubts began to nag at what little conscience he possessed. Two years ago Hammond wouldn't have missed him. Two years ago Gerald Hammond was the best in the business. Two years ago he would have seen Allum at least fifty yards before Allum saw him.

Maybe returning from the war in Europe to find OSS disbanded and his wife sleeping with strangers had jointly conspired to blunt all those finely-honed skills that had once set Gerald Hammond apart from other agents. Maybe all those rejected applications to join the State Department had dented the ego and sedated all those extra senses. Maybe loved ones and circumstance at home had succeeded where a deadly enemy and war overseas had failed.

Had he suffered anything more than a minor twinge of conscience, Allum might have resolved to look up his old Princeton friend and former OSS colleague, but Marcus Allum wasn't the type to allow distraction. These days the State Department's Head of Occupied Territories had more important problems to wrestle than the disastrous marriage and sudden career nose-dive of Gerald Hammond.

Nonetheless, it disturbed him.

Allum vigorously stirred his coffee and stared into the resulting vortex as the memories swirled and his mood deepened. He was thinking back to Princeton and those early days, when they had both been young enough to believe in naïve pledges of loyalty and honour and friendship.

But that had been long before London, and even longer before Rouen.

Gerald Hammond always said that Marcus Allum was never the same after they made him London Station Chief. Marcus Allum always said that Gerald Hammond was never the same after Rouen. Both accusations held more than a grain of truth.

In Allum's case the reason was simple. His all-consuming ambition, political chicanery and lack of any moral code merely confirmed Hammond's assertion that the quest for power can sometimes corrupt as absolutely as the power itself. With Gerald Hammond the reasons were more worthy and more complex, but neither man was ever the same.

"Excuse me, sir. . . Mr Allum."

2

The interruption jolted Marcus Allum from his thoughts. He let go of the memories, and looked up from his coffee. An immaculately-suited underling stood before him, impatiently shifting his weight from one highly-polished brogue to the other.

"I'm sorry to disturb you, sir."

"What is it?"

"It's the girl, sir. They've found her."

"Where?"

"In Magdeburg, sir."

Uncharacteristically, Marcus Allum allowed his surprise to show.

"Magdeburg? Are they sure? Not Berlin?"

"No, sir. They say she's definitely in Magdeburg." The young man furtively scanned the surrounding area and then lowered his voice to little more than a whisper. "The Sovs are already out looking for her, sir. They say it's just a matter of time."

The thunder on Allum's face deepened.

"Shit! All right, tell Alan Carlisle I want to see him as soon as I get back."

"Yes, sir."

The young man turned to make his way out of the shop. Allum stopped him.

"Just a minute. . . How did you know where to find me?"

"Uh, I ran into Mr Hammond, down the street, sir. He told me."

The young man stood nervously watching, uncertain as to whether a conversation with Gerald Hammond might be construed as fraternization. He needn't have worried. The look of thunder on Allum's face fell away and previously scowling features suddenly broke into a grin.

3

"Did he now? I bet he even told you which table I was at?"

"Yes, sir, he did."

"All right. Tell Carlisle I'll be back directly."

****

A casual ten-minute stroll away, Gerald Hammond had returned to his office and was thinking similar thoughts to those that had troubled Marcus Allum, but Hammond's thoughts were blacker than any of those that Marcus Allum might have conjured from his coffee. Hammond was thinking of London and OSS, but mostly he was thinking of Rouen.

The assault on Rouen had happened two years earlier, a little over six weeks before D-Day, when a reckless bureaucrat with the token rank of Major had flown a solo reconnaissance mission over Occupied France. A lone Messerschmitt intercepted the Lysander, and his resulting capture threw Allied plans for invasion into chaos.

The Normandy Resistance discovered his location. They radioed London with the news. The Gestapo were holding him in Rouen, not in the infamous tower, but in the headquarters opposite. A highly-skilled team, with a lot of luck, just might get him out.

A frantic Allied command immediately dumped the problem into Allum's lap. He just as quickly dumped it into Hammond's. The orders were clear: Make sure you get to him before they realize who they've got and transfer him to Gestapo headquarters in Paris. Oh, and bring him back safely if possible. The obvious question had received a chilling answer.

"It is essential to the successful outcome of the war that he does not reach Avenue Foch or the rue des Saussaies alive. How you achieve that is your decision."

Hammond's team hit the Rouen Gestapo Headquarters at four-thirty the next morning, in those muddled few minutes between night and day, when darkness retreats into shadow and the eyes can so easily deceive.

They began the carnage, not with the crash of grenades and the rattle of small-arms fire, but with stealth and skeleton keys, suppressed Sten-guns firing subsonic rounds, and a silent bullet that shattered the skull of the only external guard.

From there, they moved noiselessly through the building, killing as they went, leaving no room unvisited in their search for a reckless bureaucrat, and no one alive to raise the alarm. Few of the victims woke in time to see their killers. None put up any kind of fight.

It took almost fifteen minutes of searching and killing before they found their objective, locked in a top-floor bedroom, guarded by a single SS trooper.

A minute after that they were out of the building and away.

Whenever Hammond thought of Rouen, and that was often, he would recall the disgust and shame he had felt at the need for so many cold-blooded killings, so many that the heat of the Sten's suppressor had blistered his hand. He would then go on to recall each briefly-illuminated face of each slumbering victim, and finally bring to mind the look of terror on a reckless bureaucrat's face as the torchlight searched him out.

That same bureaucrat went on to help plan the invasion of mainland Europe and the downfall of Adolf Hitler. The powers that be may have privately called him a reckless fool, but they publicly feted him as a hero and awarded him the Silver Star.

Those same powers that be had also recommended Hammond for a medal, someone even mentioned the Congressional Medal of Honour, but then someone else whispered something about 'handing out gallantry medals for killing people in their beds' and that idea was quickly shelved. Gerald Hammond hadn't cared. The last thing he had wanted was a further and tangible reminder of that night.

And so Hammond's reward was a curt nod of thanks and a hearty slap on the back for having killed so many and saved just one, before another Marcus Allum order saw him loaded on to a night flight and dropped back into Occupied France with Operation Jedburgh.

After attending the Rouen debriefing, Hammond never again spoke of the horror and carnage that he and his team had wreaked in the early hours of that innocuous spring morning. He never spoke of the accusing faces that visited him every night, and he never spoke of the shame and disgust that remained lodged so vividly in both conscious and subconscious minds.

Nowadays he spent his nights alone, in a cold sweat, and his days sitting behind a desk among the labyrinth of streets and avenues that sprawl in all directions from Washington's Dupont Circle; the land of ambition and greed, where the fortunate few come to rule and the aroma of power and privilege hangs in the air like perfumed smog.

Sadly, for Hammond, there were no windows in his office to invite that wonderful aroma, just a softwood door and wafer-thin partition wall between him and the typing pool outside; no intoxicating whiff of power and privilege, just the stench of tedium and failure.

"God Almighty, save me."

Suddenly there was only silence. The petty gossip, cackling laughter and constant tap, tap, tap of the typewriters had all stopped. For a splendid moment he sat quietly appreciating the silence, idly wishing it could always be like this, before suddenly realizing why it was.

He had spoken his blasphemy out loud and they had heard. He smiled a cynical smile. Perhaps God had heard, too.

Moments later, normal activity resumed, assuming that such an ugly racket could ever be described as normal. The gossip, the cackling, the tap, tap, tap; it had all returned to irritate him, and it had fetched the sadness with it.

It was now just after three o'clock in afternoon, and he was sitting with his head in his hands and his eyes closed. In the two hours since returning from lunch he had managed to collate just four items of correspondence from a stack of a hundred. He opened his eyes to view the unfinished work, piled up in his in-tray and felt even more miserable. He hated every aspect of this job.

A knock at the door interrupted the gloom.

"What is it?"

"It's Alice, Mr Hammond. I've got someone here who wants to see you."

A portly figure pushed her aside and a face Hammond remembered well smiled warmly.

"Gerald, it's good to see you after all this time. How long has it been now?"

The man was short in stature and long in self-importance, with slicked and thinning hair receding from a well-padded face and small grey eyes. He wore a dark blue three-piece suit and a starched white shirt, with a gold pocket watch and chain that looped its way across a well-padded midriff. To complete the immaculate presentation he wore a blue and white diagonal-striped silk tie that said, 'If you don't know this is Yale, you don't matter'. Should an ignorant world still fail to realize just how important this man was, he carried a monogrammed black calfskin briefcase and a rolled-up copy of the *Wall Street Journal,* presumably for swatting lesser beings.

Gerald Hammond knew how long it had been: twenty-three months and two weeks. Hammond remembered precisely, because he would never forget his previous encounter with Davis Alan Carpenter. Today the features looked bloated and supercilious, but two years ago they hadn't looked like that. Two years ago, in the torchlight's beam, they had been thin and drawn and contorted in terror.

"May I come in?" Davis Carpenter ambled through the doorway without waiting for an answer. Hammond clasped the outstretched hand and gestured to a chair. The portly bureaucrat sagged into it. He fished in his pocket for a handkerchief and then mopped at his brow. "God, it's hot in here." He replaced the handkerchief and began rummaging through his briefcase, talking as he searched.

"You know, Gerald, I never got the chance to thank you properly for that bit of business in Northern France. Perhaps I can do that now."

"I'm sorry, what's this all about?"

"They tell me you're looking for work with the State Department."

Hammond nodded furiously and rifled through his desk drawer for a résumé. He found a dog-eared copy and offered it to Carpenter, who grinned and waved it away.

"I already know what the résumé says, Gerald."

Davis Carpenter produced a pack of cigars from his briefcase. He took one, lit it, and offered the case to Hammond, who shook his head.

"And what else do you know?" he asked.

"That you're a small-arms and unarmed combat expert, but perhaps a little rusty. You like to drink scotch, but only in moderation. You're employed here, as a grade-three manager, with the Washington office of The Mutual and Equitable Insurance Company of Beaumont Texas, but despise the job. You're bored and in a rut, but don't see a way out. You want into the State Department, but have run out of any contacts who might sponsor you. . . Did I miss anything?"

"Not much. Now tell me what you don't know."

Davis Carpenter took a moment before answering. He seemed almost embarrassed.

"I know you've got ability, Gerald, and I know you had a heart big enough to take on an army. I should know that better than most. However, and let me be candid here, all that cloak-and-dagger stuff is a young man's game. You're forty years old."

Hammond tried to interrupt. Carpenter held up his hands in mock surrender.

"I know. I know. It's not two years since you pulled me out of Rouen, and there's none of us getting any younger, but I'm not gonna pull punches here, I've got too much respect for you to do that."

There was clearly a more aggressive side to the portly and pretentious Davis Carpenter.

"I think you're one of the good guys, Gerald, but let's face facts. You've taken some knocks recently; some pretty serious knocks. You've no friends, or none that could do you any good. You've no immediate family to speak of, or none that could give a damn. Your wife screws her way all round Washington, and rubs your nose in it at the same time, and whatever's left of a once-promising career is now well on its way down the toilet."

Hammond watched Carpenter watching him, seeing the clumsy attempt to incite and understanding the reason for it. If Davis Carpenter wanted to spark a reaction, wanted to see if the heart was still there, Gerald Hammond was only too happy to oblige.

"If that's true, then what's a high-flyer like you doing, taking the time to visit a washed-up wreck like me? Deskbound bureaucrats like you don't need the aggravation."

Carpenter's answer was equally candid.

"Because I saw you in Rouen, and you were magnificent. You were, you know. I honestly thought I was dead until you came along. We bet everything on you then and you didn't let us down. Problem is, we don't know if we should do it again. We don't know how badly these domestic problems have affected you, or how much remains of that big heart of yours."

Sensing the approach of yet another disappointment, Hammond pushed back.

"There's more than enough heart in me, and you owe me."

"That's true. As a friend and a colleague I owe you more than I could ever repay. But as the man who has to decide whether an emotionally damaged, forty-year-old former OSS agent can still serve and protect the country we love from those who seek to destroy it. . ."

Carpenter shrugged and left the point unfinished. Hammond frowned.

"What is all this, anyway? I thought this was about a post with the State Department?"

"Oh, it is, and I'm pleased to tell you that, as soon as I put in the paperwork, you'll report directly to me. However, there was something else we rather hoped you'd do for us in the interim. You do speak German, don't you? That is one of yours? Oh yes, and Russian, of course?" Hammond frowned again, and then slowly nodded. Carpenter nodded back and once again began rummaging through his case. "Yes, that's what they told me." He explained as he searched. "You see, Gerald, we've something in mind for you that's a little more up your street, as they say; a little more involved. Now where did I put that file? Ah yes, here it is."

2

At one minute before dusk they said it was safe to use the streets, but then safe was a relative term in Berlin's eastern sector, as was dusk, for that matter. At one minute after that they would shoot you without hesitation or warning, and that was a Soviet guarantee.

There were many who believed the curfew was just another Bolshevik excuse for furthering Stalingrad's vengeance. They said the average Red Army soldier didn't care about the time. They said he couldn't even tell the time. They said if he ever got a clear shot on a dull day, he'd kill you just for the meanness of it. Others went further. They said the average Red Army soldier would open fire under the mitigating shade of a drifting cloud. All fat Martin Kube knew was that dusk had fallen thirty minutes ago, and he was still on the street.

He had been at the rendezvous point on time, but the contact had failed to show, and so he'd waited there for over an hour, crouched in the alleyway, silently cursing from the shadows, allowing the sweat to slide, the panic to calm, and the breathing to quieten. He shifted position to ease the cramp and mopped at heavy jowls with a grime- and sweat-stained sleeve. Then he shuffled his uncomfortable bulk back into deeper shadows, to wait a little longer.

As dusk became darkness he gathered his courage and peered out from the alley, panning the grim silhouettes of bombed-out buildings and crater-strewn streets dotted with piles of rubble and fallen masonry. He was looking for hidden snipers and approaching patrols, listening for the sound of a voice, or the clatter of boots on the cobbles. Praying they wouldn't see him there, crouched among the shadows; praying, too, for salvation.

For a moment of curious bravery he peered around the corner. Narrow-set eyes squinted through the gloom as he mentally gauged the distance from where he now hid to the single yellow light at the street's western end. It acted as a beacon for returning Red Army foot patrols and a killing field for the machine-gun nest they'd hidden in the ruins beyond. He judged the distance from his current position of safety to that SG43 and certain death to be around three hundred meters. He decided this was as close as sanity allowed.

He racked his memory and made a further calculation. Assuming he could somehow negotiate the foot patrols and the killing fields, the distance from that solitary light to the back of the burnt-out Reichstag building was a matter of five hundred or so meters more. From there a desperate man could work his way around to the front of the building. Then it was only a brief, albeit terrifying, dash across the rubble to the safety of the American sector.

Unhappily for Martin Kube, the proximity of sanctuary only mocked at his cowardice. It was less than a kilometre away. It might just as well have been a million.

"Where the hell are you, you bastards!"

The oath echoed around the alley and out to the street. He ducked down and mentally cursed his own stupidity, while frantically scanning the surrounding gloom for any sign of other's awareness. There was nothing he could see or hear, or was there?

It was then that he saw it, to the rear of the building across the street: the faintest of lights for the briefest of instants. It had momentarily glowed out from among the piles of rubble and tangled metal. He peered harder and silently mused. Broken glass perhaps, reflecting a passing light from the street beyond? But then the glow was there again, and the scuff of footsteps on rubble carried through the night. It was obviously the light from a cigarette, but who was on the other end?

He clutched at a breath, and held it, while a bolt of adrenaline surged from somewhere to nowhere. Then he remembered the Radom and fumbled in the coat's right-hand pocket for the pistol's reassurance. After that, he kept his place among the shadows and gripped the butt in blunt fat fingers and a palm that was slippery with sweat.

He could see them now, three of them, shadowy figures moving slowly through the rubble, slipping and sliding as they searched.

They paused and he heard them muttering. A flame briefly flared in the darkness as someone lit another cigarette. The muttering stopped. They began moving again. Then they altered course and started towards him.

The shapes were clearer now. They were undoubtedly Russians, a lone patrol with three at the front, and three more a few paces farther back. They were obviously searching for someone, and more than likely him. He wondered if they had seen him, crouched there in the alleyway, or if their sudden change of direction was just another slice of the same bad luck that had dogged him since Prague.

He wiped the sweat from his palm, then pulled the Radom and aimed it at the nearest Bolshevik, feeling the pulse thumping against his temple and knots of fear gripping at his stomach.

"Put the gun away, Herr Linz, before you get us all killed."

The voice had come from somewhere behind him. Despite the even tone, it made him start and almost drop the gun. He swivelled around to see who had spoken, but saw nothing in the alleyway but blackness. As he peered into the gloom the voice spoke again, the accent clipped and precise, the instructions delivered in the same low and even tone.

"Stay low, keep quiet, move slowly. There is a gap in the wall, ten paces back and left. Get into it." As he started backing up, his foot dislodged a brick. The sound echoed around the alleyway. The voice stopped him. "Keep calm. Turn around. Look to where you are going."

He slid the Radom back into his coat and did as ordered, turning on all fours and then slowly creeping his way back along the alley, with the sweat running and his limbs trembling. The voice had told him the distance to the gap was ten paces. Expecting to feel a bullet in his back at any moment, it felt more like a hundred.

But then fear suddenly turned to panic as he heard the sound of another voice. It was startled and agitated and shouting in Russian. It came from behind him and alerted the rest of the patrol. It told him that whatever luck he'd had to this point had just run out. Then another voice shouted at him in broken German. It ordered him to stay where he was. When he pulled the Radom and began to move, a shot cracked into the night. He heard the bullet whine as it passed overhead, before ricocheting off the wall to the right.

Now the whole patrol was shouting and running. He could hear them, excitedly calling to one another as they clambered across the rubble. Another shot cracked. Another bullet hit the same wall in the same place. Terrified, he lay still and dropped the Radom.

It was over.

He held up his hands to show they were empty and began clambering to his feet.

That was when the roar went up and the building across the street suddenly exploded before his eyes. It lit up the night sky and briefly illuminated every street and alleyway and jagged outline for a thousand meters. Almost immediately the blast hit him, and then it was raining concrete and rubble. He dropped to the ground, then lay still and covered his head with his hands, while the rubble continued to rain and the dust and smoke began choking his lungs. Then he felt hands clutching at his arms. They lifted him from where he lay cowering and hauled him to his feet. Someone told him to follow. Someone else told him to run. They said the place would be full of Bolsheviks at any minute. Then he heard the sound of boots, clattering away down the alley.

He wiped his eyes with the heel of his hand, and then coughed up some dust-laden mucus and spat. He picked up the Radom and peered around in fear and confusion. The Russian patrol had disappeared, as had the building across the street where the patrol had been sifting. Kube turned in the opposite direction and peered down the alley. He could just make out three figures at the far end. One of them called to him through the gloom and smoke and dust. The voice shouted "Linz!" and then swore at his dithering and told him to get a move on. Despite being out of condition, with his eyes streaming and his lungs clogged with smoke and dust, despite being grossly overweight and disoriented, Martin Kube started running for his life.

He reached the far end of the alley, and looked again for his saviours. At first he couldn't see them, but then he spotted the last man, around fifty meters away, running along the far side of the street. Kube followed at a lumbering canter, with his breathing laboured and his legs drained of energy. Up ahead, he saw them duck into a building. He reached the same place and ducked through the same hole in the wall. Then he stumbled through a maze of bomb craters and rubble and ruined buildings, across the street beyond and through more ruins, then across another street and through more ruins still.

He didn't look for machine-gun nests and hidden snipers. He didn't look for foot patrols or Russian check points. He just ran blind and prayed that his luck would hold.

Up ahead they kept running and calling out to him, and he followed as best he could. He reached the next derelict block and stopped to retch. Then panic drove him on and he started running again, following the disappearing shapes through the rubble and along the next street, then down yet another alleyway and into yet another building. When he reached the far side of that he stopped and gasped for breath, then looked around in rising exhaustion and wild-eyed terror.

His saviours were gone. They had disappeared into the night and he was alone in the blackness with no idea of where he was or how far he'd run. He thought he heard a noise and swivelled left and right, pointing the Radom at anything and everything. Then a door opened on the far side of the street. The same familiar voice called to him. He staggered across and through the open doorway, then dropped to his knees in exhaustion. The door closed behind him. He started retching again. His lungs ached and his eyes still streamed from the dust. He felt weak and the nausea wouldn't clear, but at least he was safe.

There were four of them in the room. They stood in the light from a kerosene lamp, watching while he spluttered and choked, saying nothing as they waited for the coughing to stop and the breathing to calm. Someone passed him a canteen of water and he greedily drank. Then he saw the Luger pointing at his chest.

Somebody reached out and took the Radom from his hand, then searched the rest of his pockets and found his papers. The man with the Luger fired a question.

"Where is Horst?"

"I do not know anyone named Horst."

"We sent him to meet you; him and a colleague. They did not return."

"I know nothing about that. All they told me was to wait in the alley. They said someone would meet me half-an-hour before curfew. No one came."

One of the men walked to the lamp and scanned his papers. Kube watched the brow furrow.

"These belong to you? You are Martin Linz?"

Kube nodded. The questioner studied the papers for a while longer.

"These papers are in order. Why did you not use them? The Bolshies would have let you through during daylight. You had no need to use us. Why did you?"

"That is my business."

The man with the Luger spoke again.

"No, Herr Linz, it is our business. We lost two good men tonight. I want you to tell me why."

He nodded.

"They think I killed a Russian, in Prague; an agent, an infiltrator, one of their best."

"And did you?"

"Yes."

The man with his papers studied him for a while and then nodded to the gunman, who pocketed the Luger. He returned the papers and then held out his hand with the palm up.

"You owe us five hundred American dollars, Herr Linz."

He blurted a refusal.

"No. . . Not until I get to the American sector. . . That was the agreement."

"You are in the American sector. Now give me the five hundred."

"This is it? I am here?" A nod confirmed the truth. Kube smirked in triumph. He unbuttoned his shirt, exposing a grey cloth money belt fixed around an ample waist. He pulled a wad of American dollars from one of the pockets, counted out five bills and passed them to the speaker. Then he replaced the balance, rebuttoned his shirt and posed a question that had bothered him since the alley. "What happened back there?"

"You mean with the explosion?" He nodded. The speaker smiled grimly. "You are a lucky man, Herr Linz. I would have to guess that someone woke a sleeper in all the commotion. You should thank the Woolwich Arsenal and the Royal Air Force. Tonight they saved your life."

"A sleeper?"

"An unexploded bomb. The whole city is littered with them, the whole country probably. Anyway, that is six less Bolshies we have to worry about. Serves the bastards right."

"I need to get away from here, out of Germany, out of Europe. Do you know anyone who can help?"

"It will be expensive."

Kube patted the money belt. The speaker nodded.

"Very well, Herr Linz. For now, though, you had better find yourself a corner and get some rest. I will take you to meet someone in the morning."

"What about my gun?"

"You can have it in the morning."

The questioner studied his uncertainty and offered a reassurance.

"Herr Linz, we are former SS officers, gentlemen of the Reich. We are not thieves. You and your money are quite safe."

Kube again patted the belt.

"Maybe, but this is a lot of money."

"Get some rest, Herr Linz. I will take you to meet someone who may help, but only when it is light."

Kube saw the determination and nodded a weary acceptance. He looked around for somewhere to rest and found a blanket on the floor in the corner. He wrapped it around himself and then sat on the floor, warily studying his aggressive-looking saviours until someone turned down the lamp.

He didn't much like them, and he certainly didn't trust them. He ought not to fall asleep, but what difference would it make? They had guns. He had nothing but his wits. Anyway, he couldn't keep his eyes open.

Ten seconds after that he was asleep.

****

"You lied to us. Why did you do that?"

Kube woke with an ache in his body that went all the way from his neck to his knees, and the glare of the Berlin early-morning sun hurting his eyes. He squinted hard at the figure towering above him, while his eyes accustomed themselves. Then he stalled for time, while his brain raced to understand what had suddenly gone wrong.

"I do not understand. What do you mean?"

He could see the speaker now, tall and gaunt, with the Radom in his hand and a look of loathing distorting weathered features. He hadn't seen him clearly the previous night, but now the light was streaming in and he could see every pore and nuance. The face was familiar, and that wasn't good. He vaguely remembered it; from Warsaw, or was it Prague? He didn't remember the name, but he never forgot a face. His accuser spoke again.

"Your name is not Linz. Your name is Kluge, or Kluber, or something like that. I remember you. You were on Heydrich's staff in Warsaw. You were Gestapo."

By this time the rest had gathered to listen. Kube got to his feet and tried a bluff.

"You are mistaken, my friend. My name is Martin Linz and I was a Stabszahlmeister. I worked in the Ogrodowa headquarters for a short while, yes, but I was just a Stabszahlmeister; in charge of the cipher section."

His accuser looked again, seemingly less certain following that well-delivered and entirely plausible denial. Kube sensed the possibility of a reprieve and held the pose of outraged nonchalance, but then his accuser spat a confirmation and he knew that he was in trouble.

"Kube! That was it. Your name was Martin Kube, and you were a Gestapo chief in Warsaw. I knew I had seen you before. I did not recognize you at first without that black trilby hat, and I did not realize just how bald you were. But I remember you now. Fat Martin Kube. How could I have forgotten? You were there, in Warsaw, with Heydrich."

Kube looked from one set of accusing features to the next and persevered with the lie.

"I have never heard of Kube, and I never spoke to Heydrich. I was Wehrmacht. For a short time I was in Warsaw, you are right, but then I was posted to Prague. My name always was and always will be Martin Linz. Now stop all this nonsense and give me my gun back."

It was never going to fool them and he knew it.

The leader who had questioned him the previous night stepped forward and reached into his coat. He took the papers belonging to Martin Linz and tossed them aside. Kube offered no resistance, but protested when the man then began fumbling for the money belt. A vicious punch to the solar plexus halted the protest and sent him to his knees, where he remained groaning and massaging the pain. A pair of hands pushed away his and snatched at the money belt. He sneered through the pain.

"SS officers and gentlemen of the Reich? Huh! You are all traitors, nothing more than snivelling cowards and common thieves. Do you have any idea who I am?"

The leader sneered back at him.

"We do not care who you are, and we do not care what you did. In war we each had our tasks; SS, Wehrmacht, even Gestapo pigs like you. You could have been on your way to Bremen, and then Bari, and from there to the Americas. Instead you chose to lie to us."

Suddenly fearing for his life, Kube babbled his mitigation.

"You do not understand. I had to lie for the Children, for the Reich, for the Führer."

He only succeeded in angering them further.

"How dare you use his name to save yourself, you filthy Gestapo scum!"

A single punch to the jaw toppled him from his knees. Then they started kicking. A boot connected with his genitals. He screamed in agony. Another thumped hard into his belly. He gasped for air and begged and groaned and tried to cover up. A savage kick bruised his ribs. Another broke a bone in his forearm. He heard and felt it snap, and screamed again. Then a steel toecap caught him across the temple and he mercifully passed out.

****

When Martin Kube regained consciousness the sun was still shining, but the face looking down on him was altogether friendlier than the last he'd seen. She was a nurse, middle-aged and bustling, dressed from head to toe in white, with a benevolent smile and caring features. He muttered a question in German.

"Where am I?"

"You are in Stubenrauch-Krankenhaus, Herr Kube."

That didn't make sense.

"The SS Hospital?"

She smiled and shook her head.

"It used to be, but now it is Station Hospital Number 279; an American army hospital."

He breathed a sigh of relief, and looked around to find he was in a small side ward with two beds. The second was empty. Someone had drawn the curtains to shield the sun's fierceness. A glass and water jug sat on his bedside cabinet. A white-coated doctor, engrossed in a chart, stood to one side. Kube looked up at his nurse.

"How did I get here?"

"Some men brought you in. They gave us your name and said they found you lying in the street. They said a street gang had attacked you. Do you not remember?"

He shook his head, but then she bustled away and he found himself looking up at an American army captain, who spoke to him in English.

"Good afternoon, Herr Kube. I trust you are feeling better."

He suddenly remembered his cover.

"My name is Linz, Martin Linz. Why are you calling me Kube?"

The captain looked surprised, but then smiled and apologized.

"Oh, I'm so sorry, Herr Linz. I thought that was the name they gave us. In all the commotion somebody made a mistake. I will make sure everyone knows."

"They took my money and my papers."

"Yes. We'll sort all that out when you're better. You rest now, and we'll talk later."

The captain wandered over to talk to the doctor. Kube sank back into the pillows and assessed the damage. There was a plaster cast on his broken arm, and heavy strapping around his ribs, but that apart, his injuries seemed no more serious than some stitched cuts and colourful bruises. He'd lost all his money, and that was a serious setback, but on balance he'd been lucky once again.

But then a man in a charcoal-grey suit came to the door and stood watching him. When the captain left the room to speak to the man, the door swung wider. That was when Kube saw the military police standing guard. That was when he looked more carefully around the room and saw bars at the window, blocking the sun's rays and leaving tell-tale shadows on the curtains.

That was when he knew the captain had lied.

3

Proud Ukrainian Ivan Stepanovich Levitsky thought Sergey Brusilov just another murdering bandit from Georgia. Stalinesque to a fault, with those same brutish manners and that same unfeeling stare, Brusilov was everything Levitsky despised. Brusilov had married Nikki, a beautiful nineteen-year-old Russian girl from Leningrad, but beat his young wife regularly and slept with Germans and whores. Or he did according to the unhappy Nikki, and the jealous and infatuated Levitsky.

Why they had ordered him to undertake guard duty in the company of such a man, Levitsky had no idea. Uniformed Red Army guards usually escorted prisoners, but this time they wanted MGB men in plain-clothes. They had only told him the prisoner was important and the order had come from the highest level. Levitsky hoped it wouldn't be too long a journey. Transporting a dangerous and important prisoner across occupied Europe was a difficult enough assignment, without having to rely on a man such as Brusilov.

Levitsky didn't speak to Brusilov as they sat waiting for their prisoner. He sat at the opposite end of the bench, studiously ignoring him and glaring at passers-by. Then they brought the prisoner up from the cells below, and surprise overcame hostility.

Flanked by two Red Army soldiers, the prisoner was a woman, young and slender with exquisite features, piercing blue eyes and soft blonde hair that fell across petite shoulders. She was wearing a full white cotton and lace skirt that flowed as she moved, with long black boots that finished immediately below the knee. A close-fitting leather jacket to match the boots had the lapels turned inward and was fastened to the neck, an acknowledgement of circumstance that did little to detract from her beauty or disguise the figure beneath.

Levitsky studied her in wide-eyed admiration. He didn't know who she was. He didn't care why she was in handcuffs. He only knew that she was beautiful.

A low whistle from the other end of the bench told him that Brusilov must have also seen the girl. Levitsky tore his eyes from her and scowled his disgust at the uncouth Georgian. The Red Army captain in charge of prisoner escort barked an immediate warning.

"The state will not tolerate the abuse of prisoners, without orders. Do you understand, Brusilov? You are to escort the woman from Magdeburg to Leipzig by train, and then hand her to our comrades from Prague; nothing more. Comrade Levitsky will go with you. He will ensure you obey your orders."

Levitsky snapped to attention and nodded his agreement. It would be his pleasure to protect such a beautiful creature from the crude ambition of that chekist thug.

Brusilov shook his head.

"I am MGB. I do not take orders from the army."

"This order comes directly from Comrade Colonel Paslov."

At the mention of the notorious regional head of the MGB fear momentarily disrupted Brusilov's sneering features, but it was gone in an instant. He slowly and lasciviously looked the girl up and down as he snarled a question.

"This is her? This is the German whore who murdered all those Red Army officers?" In answer to the officer's nod of confirmation, he said, "They say she fucked them as she killed them. I say there are worse ways to die."

Levitsky listened to Brusilov's crude commentary and suddenly realised who the girl was. He remembered hearing about her from some of the guards. At the time he had thought their description of the girl and their graphic tales of her lust and savagery exaggerated. Now he could see they had spoken the truth, at least as far as her beauty was concerned.

The guards had told him that her name was Catherine Schmidt, and she stood accused of murdering and horribly mutilating a string of army officers. They had gone on to describe her alleged crimes in lurid and graphic detail.

But as Levitsky studied the girl, he found himself unable to fathom how one so young and stunningly beautiful could have committed such dreadful acts of violence and depravity. She looked so petite; so dainty, so delicate. He couldn't imagine her being guilty of anything, least of all that. There had to be a mistake.

The officer clearly held no such reservations. He snapped an order to the two soldiers.

"Make sure you do not leave her alone. And leave the handcuffs on."

Levitsky felt unhappy with the order.

"What if she has to. . . ?"

"She can piss and shit in her pants. You keep her handcuffed, and you stay with her."

"Yes, Comrade Captain."

****

Although barely one hundred and sixty centimetres in height, Kurt Meissen cut something of an imposing figure as he strode along the platforms of Magdeburg railway station. As with the Saxony porcelain that shared his family name, the pint-sized stationmaster believed precision paramount and perfection a pursuit. He similarly believed the punctual departure of those many converging trains that briefly stopped at Magdeburg's platforms to be a personal responsibility.

On this particular morning, however, the pint-sized perfectionist was less than happy with his Russian masters, because the train to Leipzig should have left fifteen minutes ago. With the clock ticking and his passengers frowning, there was still no authority to send the train on its way, nor any official reason given for the delay.

A woman in a fur-collared coat glared at him from her place on the train. Meissen glared his authority back at her. He'd been about to march over and tell her to keep her mouth shut and her stares to herself, when three Opel Blitzes drew up at the station entrance. Both angry woman and indignant official stopped glaring and watched as two full platoons of Red Army soldiers piled out of the back of the trucks and ran along the platform.

With long-barrelled Mosin-Nagant rifles held at arm's length and parallel to the ground, the first dozen soldiers formed a cordon and began shepherding Meissen and his fellow spectators away from the train. The balance of the two platoons formed a line of defence between the entrance and the front carriage. As stationmaster, and therefore person temporarily responsible for the stationary train and its passengers, Kurt Meissen felt aggrieved at such an affront to his authority. He wisely decided not to argue the point.

Meissen and his fellow spectators looked on as a Red Army captain jumped down from the front passenger seat of the leading truck. He selected three soldiers, who then marched to the front of the train and began herding passengers out of the front carriage.

One of those ejected was the superior-looking woman in the fur-collared coat. She glared her special glare of superiority at the captain and began loudly objecting.

"You have no right to do this. Who do you people think you are? I happen to be. . ."

Protest gave way to anguish as the butt of a Mosin-Nagant hit her hard across the back of the head. The woman cried out and sank to her knees, while the captain looked angrily at the soldier responsible and halted any further assault with a curt word of command. Cowed by the captain's anger, and following a second command, the soldier slung the rifle over his shoulder and helped the stricken woman to her feet. He linked his free arm around her waist and then began manhandling her along the platform. Opening a compartment farther down the train, he pushed her up the steps and through the doorway. Somebody reached out to help her up, but nobody spoke and nobody else moved.

With the front carriage now empty, the captain took a long look around the station, and then signalled towards the entrance. A man clambered from the back of the second Opel. Intrigued, Meissen studied him as he turned and glared at the gathering. The man looked squat and solid, belligerent and dangerous. He looked like MGB. Had he been any closer, Meissen would have quickly averted his eyes, but he was far enough away to risk a further look.

A woman followed the man from the truck. She was young and she was beautiful, and she was handcuffed. Meissen's heart immediately went out to her. She jumped down from the open back and then staggered before regaining her balance. The squat-looking man caught her. He had held her close and grinned as she squirmed against the hold, before passing her to the two Red Army soldiers who had followed them from the truck.

Meissen watched the trio as they hurried their prisoner along the platform, and then climbed into the front compartment of the now empty carriage. He wondered what she could have done to warrant such specialist treatment. He shuddered to think of what lay in store for her. Then his eyes caught the movement of another man clambering out of the truck.

As with the first man, he was dressed in civilian clothing, but unlike the archetypal MGB thug who had preceded him, this man was tall and slim and stylish. He strode arrogantly along the platform, but instead of joining them in the first compartment stepped up and into the last compartment of the same empty carriage. It seemed his job was to ensure the quartet at the front of the train remained undisturbed during the journey to Leipzig.

The captain signalled again, and the train slowly pulled out of the station. Kurt Meissen looked on with anger in his eyes; that had been his responsibility. The captain suddenly noticed him standing there and nodded a cursory acknowledgement as he waved the platoons back on to the trucks. Meissen thought of speaking, but said nothing and nodded back.

After a final glance at the departing locomotive, the captain turned and walked back along the platform before climbing back into the passenger seat of the lead Opel. He gave the order and they all headed off, presumably back to barracks for a well-earned glass of vodka.

As he watched them go, Kurt Meissen's glare fluctuated between the distant locomotive and the disappearing trucks. Then he spotted a discarded cigarette packet lying on the platform and roared at one of the porters to pick it up. With platform once again immaculate and ego thus salved, he puffed out his chest and marched smartly back to his pristine office at the end of the concourse.

****

Catherine Schmidt sat in the far corner of the lead compartment, quietly studying her motley assortment of guards. She was looking for weaknesses, anything with which she could divide and conquer; or in this case, divide and escape. The two uniformed soldiers seemed harmless enough. They were typical Bolshevik cannon fodder from the Sixty-Second Army. But then she recalled that same fodder had trapped the German Sixth Army in Stalingrad for two and a half months and cost The Axis eight hundred thousand lives. She also recalled the words of her father. He had told her that Bolsheviks fought without fear of death, because a life under Stalin was a life without joy and a life without hope. He also said that any enemy who fights without fear is worthy of respect.

The Stalinesque thug who had mentally undressed her at the detention centre and then mauled her at the railway station was a different matter. His name was Brusilov, she had heard that at the detention centre, and he obviously kept what few brains he boasted between his legs. That was exactly where she liked her Bolsheviks to keep their brains. Even now he was sitting opposite her, leering at the intentional exposure of a naked upper-thigh beyond a hitched hemline and intentionally-widened knees. He was the obvious weakness, she thought. He would be the target.

The fourth man wasn't with them. He would be farther down the train; the last line of defence, or the first. Nobody had spoken while they were in the truck, but she remembered him studying her at the detention centre. He was smitten with her looks, she had seen that immediately, but there was wisdom in his eyes that belied the façade of an infatuated dupe. He would not be so easily fooled. If the opportunity to escape arose, she hoped he would remain at the other end of the carriage.

It was time to turn up the tension.

She released the upper fastenings on her jacket, restored each lapel in turn, and then slumped back in the seat and left her knees spread. Brusilov studied the increased exposure and rewarded her effort with a smile of lechery.

She suddenly stretched out a leg and kicked at his.

"Hey, Bolshevik pig! Stop looking up my skirt."

She saw him glare at the kick, and then frown as he listened to the words. That was good. He obviously didn't speak German. She could use that to her advantage. Although she spoke enough Russian to get by, she had feigned ignorance of the language throughout her arrest and interrogation. There was a reason for that.

One of the guards obviously did speak German. He laughed and translated.

"She called you a Bolshevik pig. She said to stop looking up her skirt."

Brusilov snarled back at the guard.

"Ask her why not? They say half the Red Army has had their cocks up there."

Laughter faded to a smirk as the guard again translated. She feigned indignance, snapped her thighs together, sat upright, and then answered the insult with a toss of her head.

"Tell him he is not important enough, or good-looking enough. Tell him he is just ugly cannon fodder." Mischievously, she added, "I expect he has a tiny cock anyway."

The guard started laughing again, but wisely stopped when Brusilov demanded a translation. When the man from the MGB heard, he scrambled to his feet, snatched a cruel handful of long blonde hair, and dragged her head back.

"We will see how small it feels when it is fucking you in the ass."

This was better than she could have hoped. He was clearly a thug and a lecher, and that was good, but it was the aggression and obvious lack of any self-control that made him ideal for her purpose.

Earlier, she had deliberately staggered against him after jumping from the truck. When he had grabbed at her and pulled her close, it confirmed her initial appraisal of him, but it also confirmed something else: the bulge she had seen on the left front of his inside jacket pocket; it was caused by a Tokarev automatic pistol.

That confirmation had pleased Catherine Schmidt a good deal more than the crude mauling of her young body could possibly have pleased Sergey Brusilov.

As he stood towering over her, oafishly asserting his masculinity, the guard again translated. She winced, and then bravely spat a question at the interpreter.

"Is this the only way he can do it? From the back, with the woman handcuffed?"

If she was going to get to the Tokarev, she would need to be facing him when he took his pleasure. If her hands were free, it would make the task all that much easier. She held out the handcuffs in mute testament. Again the guard translated. That was the beauty of needing a third party to translate. It allowed her to manipulate one comrade by using the voice of another. She knew the mocking laughter of a comrade would wound his machismo more deeply than a sneer from her ever could. By pretending ignorance of the language it also allowed her more time to think, more time to plan, and more time to compose the next barb.

Just as she had anticipated, Brusilov listened, snarled, and held out his hand.

"Give me the keys."

But then a setback, as the guard stood his ground and shook his head.

"No, Comrade. I have orders not to do that."

She privately cursed the guard's obstinacy, then turned to study the red-faced Brusilov, and sneered, silently mocking his apparent impotence and hoping to further enrage. It had the desired effect, because he dragged her up by her hair, spun her around, pushed her face-down on the seat, and then growled an order at the guards.

"Get out of here, both of you."

Now she could feel the heat of his breath on her neck and smell his sweat on the air. Now she could hear his breathing over the rattle of the train, short heavy grunts of uncontrolled lust that came and went as he mauled at her flesh and dragged her knickers down. Now he was clearly out of control, and that was what she had hoped for. Now all she needed was privacy.

He duly obliged, between grunts.

"If you two are not out of this compartment in two seconds, your next train-ride will take you to the Gulag. Now get the fuck out."

The two men studied her apparent helplessness with shame in their eyes, before turning away and slowly filing out of the compartment. She felt the elation rise as she watched them shuffle along the corridor. Now she could concentrate solely on him. One-on-one, this ignorant Bolshevik pig would be no match for her. One-on-one, she would flatter and deceive, gasp and writhe in helpless acquiescence, feed his ignorance, fuel his lust, and gently coax him between her thighs.

Once he was there, she could get to the Tokarev.

But then the compartment door slid back and everything went wrong at once. The groping hands and probing fingers suddenly withdrew. The grunts of animal lust subsided. The heat of his breath and the smell of his sweat receded. All she could feel was the swaying of the carriage. All she could hear was the rattle of the train.

There could only be one reason.

She cautiously turned her head and saw him there, the tall and elegant-looking one, with a look of thunder on his face, and the snout of his seven-six-two millimetre Tokarev gouging into Brusilov's temple.

The man reached into Brusilov's coat and collected his Tokarev, then backed into the corridor, where the two soldiers stood watching. He motioned for Brusilov to follow, and then turned to where she sat covetously studying the automatic and silently cursing his interference. He spoke to her in German.

"Cover yourself, woman. You move one millimetre from that seat and I will shoot you in the head. Do you understand?"

She nodded meekly and began restoring modesty, then watched as a sullen-faced Brusilov followed him out of the compartment. He snapped at the two soldiers.

"You two get back in there and stay with her. And this time obey your orders."

The two uniformed men nodded their contrition and shuffled back into the compartment. Brusilov stood before him in the corridor. She sat quietly listening to their conversation and planning her next move. Both men sounded angry, but there was a nervous edge to Brusilov's voice as she heard him ask,

"What is it, Cossack? Want her yourself, do you? Is fucking my wife not enough for you?"

The tall man's anger and contempt were obvious.

"I have never touched your wife. I have the utmost respect for Nikki. It is a tragedy that you do not. As for the German woman, we have our orders, and I will ensure you obey them."

"So what now, Cossack? Are you going to shoot me?"

"The only reason I have not already done so is out of fondness and respect for your wife. But I warn you, Sergey Brusilov, you touch that woman again and I will kill you. Now get back to the compartment and obey your orders."

"What about my automatic?"

"You do not need it. The soldiers have their carbines. When we reach Leipzig, I will hand the weapon to Comrade Colonel Paslov and tell him why I took it from you. Now get back in there, and remember what I have said."

A sullen Brusilov returned to the compartment. Catherine Schmidt, with modesty restored, watched him sit down in the far corner.

"What is the matter, Bolshevik pig? Did somebody just teach you some manners, or is your cock so small you did it without me knowing?"

Brusilov didn't ask the guards for a translation, and the guards didn't volunteer one. Instead, he sat sulking in the corner, while they stared out of the window at the passing countryside. Catherine Schmidt sat outwardly gloating and inwardly seething. She'd expected that fourth man would be trouble. Now, it seemed, he had just ruined her only chance of escape.

****

When Ivan Levitsky returned to his compartment at the end of the carriage, he found a man sprawled across the seat with an all-but-empty bottle of schnapps in his hand. Levitsky studied the man for a few moments. He was a middle-aged drunk, who must have staggered into the carriage and was now sleeping fitfully.

Whenever the man began drifting into a deeper sleep, his fingers would relax their hold on the schnapps. Then he would wake with a start and grip the bottle tighter before returning to his stupor. It was a classic alcoholic daze. Levitsky had seen it, or something like it, too many times before not to recognize the symptoms.

He'd been about to rouse the man and tell him to move to the next carriage, but thought better of it. The last time he had seen a man in such a condition at such an hour had been two months earlier, just before his father had died. Instead of moving the man on, as Levitsky knew he ought, he sat down by the door and quietly watched him snort and groan. He was remembering his father, recalling the pain of an alcoholic, the heartache it had caused the family, and the shame of a life so tragically wasted.

He watched the town of Schönebeck come and go, and then Köthen after that. The train would soon be stopping at Halle, and then it wouldn't be too long after that before Leipzig. He wondered how the great and terrible Stanislav Paslov would react to the news that one of his most trusted MGB agents was a common rapist. Perhaps Paslov would do nothing and put it down to high spirits, but then why issue the order? If Paslov was anything like his psychotic boss, Lavrenti Beria, he would probably make Brusilov a Hero of The Soviet Union and send Levitsky to the Gulag.

He was still pondering the possibilities when the train pulled into Halle. A couple of civilians tried to get into the carriage. Levitsky sent them farther down the train. He continued guarding the carriage access until the train pulled out of Halle, waiting until they reached the city outskirts before returning to his compartment and the drunken interloper.

"Who the hell is that?"

He hadn't seen Brusilov move along the corridor. He'd been too engrossed in painful memories. Neither had he seen the 1938 carbine in Brusilov's hands, until its shortened barrel pointed at the drunk on the seat. Ivan Levitsky shrugged his shoulders and raised his hands. So much for Red Army comrades.

"Just a drunk passed out. I did not see him as a threat. But for a man who beats his wife and has to handcuff and sodomize a helpless girl, you may see him as a danger."

Brusilov sneered.

"Keep laughing, Cossack, and they will bury you with that smile still on your face. Now move to the far side. Oh, and I will take my thirty-three. . . and yours."

Levitsky removed the two Tokarev automatics from his jacket pockets. He placed them on the seat and then backed away to the other side of the compartment. He watched Brusilov pick up the first, and then lean the carbine against the door before picking up the second. The Georgian sneered in triumph as he pocketed one and levelled the other.

"Sorry, Cossack, but I cannot have you telling your tales to Paslov."

Levitsky shrugged a nonchalance he didn't feel.

"I am fascinated to know how you intend explaining all this. . . my death, the violation of the girl. I assume that when you are done with me you are going to finish what you started. And then, of course, you have our two uniformed comrades to consider."

"They will keep their mouths shut, and who is going to listen to a murdering Nazi whore?"

"And what about my death? How will you explain that?"

Brusilov's face fell, but then the malevolent smile reappeared and he nodded to the drunk.

"I think I will let our friend here take the blame. I came to check on you and found him standing over your body, with your gun in his hand. . . Of course I killed him."

"Do I get any say in that?"

Levitsky turned, to look at the drunk and gave a start. The hand that had previously held the bottle now held an automatic pistol with a suppressor. The suppressor's one-inch-diameter barrel was pointing directly at Sergey Brusilov's head.

Less than a second later, two slugs, fired in rapid succession, hit an astounded Georgian almost precisely between the eyes.

Levitsky stood watching the lifeless body of Brusilov in open-mouthed shock, but then found his voice and addressed that same one-inch-diameter barrel.

"If those were point two-two LR rounds, I would have to assume that is a Hi-Standard HDM and that would make you OSS?" A smile confirmed the truth, but the killer failed to answer. With stomach churning and heart thumping, Levitsky tried again. "Am I next?"

"Not necessarily, and OSS disbanded in forty-five. Did they not tell you at MGB school?"

It was Levitsky's second surprise in under a minute. It hadn't initially registered, but the man with the HDM spoke perfect Russian. The Ukrainian quipped back bravely.

"I went to NKVD school, not MGB. Showing my age, I suppose."

The killer picked up the automatics and carbine and tossed them on to the luggage rack. The smile reappeared as he waved Levitsky towards the corridor and then stood back.

"Time to move, old man."

Levitsky smiled politely and made his way toward the corridor, believing he was a good ten years the junior of the man with the HDM.

It was the last thing Ivan Levitsky remembered.

****

Catherine Schmidt sat watching the two Red Army soldiers with one eye and the passing countryside with the other. She didn't know precisely how far they'd travelled, but they couldn't be far from Leipzig and a second opportunity to escape had not presented itself. She listened to the soldier who had given up his carbine to Brusilov. He didn't seem happy.

"Where the hell has that MGB bastard got to with my carbine? He said he would only be a minute. We are nearly in Leipzig."

The other soldier seemed less concerned.

"Stop complaining. You gave it to him. It is your responsibility."

"You heard what he said about the Gulag. I had no choice."

"So, go and get it back."

"Forget it; he will be back any minute."

"Well, if he is going to have the woman before Leipzig, he had better get a move on."

She suddenly saw Brusilov's leather coat and heard a voice calling the soldiers out to the corridor. Maybe there would still be time to get to the Tokarev before they got to Leipzig. She doubted it, but maybe. The soldier's relief was obvious.

"He is back, thank God," he said. "What does he want now?"

The soldier got to his feet, slid open the door and took a pace forward, but then suddenly grunted and fell back into the compartment. He lay sprawled at her feet, his eyes wild with terror, his hands covered in blood and clutching at the gaping wound in his throat.

The second soldier panicked. He stood up and grabbed for the carbine. A foot kicked it away from shaking hands. An arm clamped around his neck. It lifted him up and spun him around, before the point of a flat-bladed knife punctured his right kidney. The soldier groaned and continued struggling. The arm moved from his neck. A hand grabbed at his hair. It pulled his head back to locate the blade, and then thrust it forward while another drew the lethal edge through his windpipe.

The second soldier's body slumped alongside the first. Stunned, Catherine Schmidt looked blankly up at the killer as he fired a question.

"You are Catherine Louise Schmidt?" He had spoken in German, but the accent wasn't German. It was North American. Still handcuffed, she nodded and got to her feet. He spat another question. "Which one has the keys?" She pointed to the second soldier, but still didn't speak. The stranger rummaged through the soldier's coat pockets before finding the key. He unlocked the handcuffs. She massaged the ache in her wrists as he drew the blinds and barked an order. "We have to get out of here now. Do you speak English?"

"Yes, but what are you doing here? Who are you?"

"They sent me to get you. My name is Hammond."

She meekly followed him to the carriage door and then watched as he threw it open and held it against the force of the rushing air current. He shouted to her above the noise.

"There is no time to wait for the train to slow, so we have to go now. When you hit the ground, you roll, and then you stay still. Got that?" She nodded, not understanding who he was or what was happening, only knowing that he was getting her away from the train. He continued issuing instructions. "Don't look up, don't get up, don't move, and whatever you do don't look back at the train. You stay where you land until I tell you to move. Got it?" She nervously studied the open doorway, but said nothing. He grabbed her arm and pulled her to the opening. "Good." He held the door wide and, with the briefest glance at the onrushing countryside, threw her into the abyss.

She heard the howling wind suddenly quieten, and felt as if she had been falling for ever, but then hit the ground with a thump that jolted the wind from her lungs. She cartwheeled once and jarred her shoulder, and then began rolling down the slope at the side of the track.

She hadn't felt the pain of impact, she was too excited for that, not until she had lain where she stopped rolling for a full twenty seconds. She lay still as ordered, feeling the adrenaline ebb and hearing the train disappearing into the distance. Then she heard Hammond's voice shouting at her.

"Right, you can get up now. Come on, on your feet. Now we run. . . and I do mean run."

Suddenly her shoulder hurt like hell.

****

As the nine a.m. train from Magdeburg to Leipzig was passing some fields to the south of Wiederitzsch, a haughty-looking woman in a fur-collared coat stood in the corridor and stared out of the window. She watched two people jump from farther up the train, and then saw them rolling down the embankment. One of them looked like the drunk who had staggered against her in the corridor. The other was the girl she'd seen handcuffed at the station. The woman in the coat was sure of that. For a moment of indecision she thought of sending for help, maybe even stopping the train.

But then she remembered the feel of a Mosin-Nagant rifle butt in the back of the head. She gingerly rubbed at the bruise and smiled quietly into the passing countryside.

4

Alan James Carlisle wasn't every girl's dream, but he was smart enough, good-looking enough, incorrigible enough, and, at thirty-seven, still just about young enough to charm his way into a few. Carlisle was tall and rangy, his hair black and thick, his eyes dark and soft, his voice a seductive bass-baritone. Like so many lotharios before him, Carlisle took great pride in his appearance. He kept himself physically fit, well-groomed and permanently doused in cologne, and wore only expensively-tailored suits and shirts and handmade shoes.

When he wasn't chasing women, and sometimes even when he was, Alan Carlisle worked for the U.S. State Department, under the rapidly expanding remit of the Office of Occupied Territories. His published brief was to aid America in better understanding European cultures and traditions. His unpublished brief was an altogether different and less worthy one.

A product of privilege and Princeton, Alan Carlisle was something of a State Department rising star. Those who worked with him thought him the Office of Occupied Territories' proverbial rough diamond: undeniably flawed, but with the potential for brilliance. Those who slept with him, however, and that included a fair number of their wives, found themselves only able to recount the flaws.

Carlisle spent his working hours commuting between glamorous locations along the U.S. eastern seaboard and a dour-looking building in U.S. occupied

Germany. The glamorous locations included upmarket addresses on New York City's Manhattan Island, a multi-millionaire's sprawling estate in Connecticut, and the corridors of power in Washington D.C.

The dour-looking building was the main debriefing block at Camp King, a U.S. military base to the north-west of Frankfurt. Before the war, Camp King had served as a Wehrmacht detention centre. It was now one of America's most secret military establishments.

Carlisle was making his third visit to the base in less than a month. Pacing the floor of interview room two, in reality a euphemism for a holding cell and not a particularly pleasant one at that, he gathered his thoughts.

Interview room two's walls were soiled and defaced with all manner of graffiti. Its ceiling had been stained yellow with nicotine. Its air was damp and stale and thick with cigarette smoke. An electric bulb, surface wired and out of reach, was its only source of light. A wooden desk, two wooden chairs, and an iron bed with an enamel chamber pot beneath were its only amenities.

Carlisle finished pacing and sat down at the table. He briefly scanned one of the documents laid out in front of him, and then boomed an order to the prisoner, who had only recently arrived from Berlin and now stood waiting outside.

"Come along in, Herr Kube, and tell me some interesting things about Prague."

Two military policemen brought in the shackled and prison-suited Martin Kube. Carlisle assumed an air of arrogance and indifference while he studied the overweight Gestapo chief. Finding nothing remarkable, just another overweight and underwhelming Gestapo thug, he told the guards to wait outside and gestured for Kube to sit.

The guards stepped out. The door swung closed with a thud that shook the walls. Kube slumped on to the chair. Carlisle tried a disarming smile.

"My name is Alan Carlisle. I work for The U.S. State Department. My brief is to identify suitable candidates, who might aid America in better understanding European cultures and traditions. We think you might be one of those people, Herr Kube."

Kube shook his head and spoke in a voice heavily laced with exasperation.

"My name is Linz, Martin Linz. I told them at the hospital."

Carlisle held the smile as he read from his notes.

"Now that is strange. It says here there's a warrant out for Martin Linz, issued by the Nuremberg Tribunals people; something about war crimes in the Prague and Warsaw ghettos." He looked up, and the smile was gone. "Are you sure your name is Linz?"

Carlisle was lying. He had no knowledge of anyone called Linz, but he knew the man sitting before him; knew who he was, and what he was.

Kube's eyes shifted left and right.

"That must be some other Martin Linz. I was only a clerk."

Carlisle abandoned the lie and pronounced the most terrible of indictments.

"Your name is not Martin Linz. Your name is Martin Kube, and you were one of the most senior Gestapo agents in occupied Europe. In the Warsaw ghettos you were responsible for the deaths of hundreds of innocent civilians; in Prague many more. We know you reported directly to some of the most senior members of Adolf Hitler's regime, firstly to Oberführer Josef Conrad Schmidt, and then to Reichsprotektor Reinhard Heydrich's successor, Karl Hermann Frank. We also know that at one time you reported directly to Heinrich Himmler."

Kube met the accusation with a vehement denial.

"But, that is simply not true. My name is Linz, Martin Linz. I was a Stabszahlmeister. That is a hauptmann; a captain with the administrative corps. I was the most senior cipher clerk in Wehrmacht headquarters Prague, but I was only a clerk. I remember Kube. I knew him quite well. He was Gestapo, you are right, but now he is dead. They say he died protecting the

Führer's bunker, slaughtered, like so many others, slaughtered by the bloody Bolsheviks."

It had been a good performance, maybe even a great performance. Carlisle was suitably impressed, or he might have been if he hadn't already known the truth.

"If that is so, then what happened to his body?"

"Check the records. They burned his body and scattered the ashes to the winds."

"And what happened to your documents?"

"Bandits stole my money and papers, probably the same bandits who gave me up to you. Cowards and deserters and the scum of mankind."

Alan Carlisle took a cigarette from the packet on the desk. He lit it, inhaled deeply, then tilted his head back and slowly exhaled. Kube looked longingly at the open packet. Carlisle saw, but didn't offer. Instead, he began a carefully-rehearsed speech.

"Herr Kube, you have the time that it takes me to finish this cigarette to start telling the truth. After that I will order your immediate transfer to the tribunals at Nuremberg. Make no mistake, this is your last chance to save yourself from the hangman, and that chance is literally going up in smoke as I speak. Do not try my patience any further. Tell me something interesting, and tell me now, or I do promise that your overdue appointment to burn in hell will be sooner rather than later."

Carlisle could give a good performance, too, when it suited him. He watched the German stare straight ahead and knew exactly what he was thinking. Kube was waiting for a further comment, some sort of inducement to give up what he knew. Carlisle wasn't about to provide one. He stared blankly back, watching nervous perspiration gathering along Kube's temples and forehead before running slowly down. It trickled into the German's eyes. He blinked away the intrusion, and held the stare. Carlisle quietly watched, and waited, and smoked his cigarette.

The cigarette was almost done now. He lifted the remnants to his lips, and. . .

Suddenly, there it was. Kube's eyes briefly flickered to the rapidly-dwindling stem of that vital cigarette and Carlisle knew that he had him. All he had to do was wait.

When the German slowly nodded his head, it came as no surprise.

"Most convincing, Herr Carlisle. I believe you would do exactly that, and so I will tell you what you want to know. I only hope that I am dealing with a gentleman. . . ?"

Carlisle read the pause, but refused to provide the answer that Kube was obviously hoping for. He took a last long drag on the cigarette and moved to stub it out. When Kube hurriedly continued, Carlisle held the smouldering remains hovering theatrically above the ashtray, while he waited for the German to place his head all the way into the noose.

"You are, of course, correct. My name is Martin Kube, and I was a Kriminaldirektor with Section Four of Reich security. And yes, I served in both Warsaw and Prague. However, what you obviously do not know is that I was also head of all counter-intelligence, and foreign surveillance, for the Reich Protectorate of Bohemia and Moravia."

Carlisle had already known that. He allowed himself a fleeting smile of triumph, finished stubbing out his cigarette, and fired a question.

"Why should I believe you now, after listening to so many lies?"

Martin Kube's sneer of confidence told its own tale.

"Oh, you believe me. I can see it in your face. And you need me. I can see that, too."

So far so good, but Carlisle didn't want Kube getting too comfortable.

"We already have Gehlen. Why should we need you?"

"You have Reinhard Gehlen?"

When Carlisle nodded, a look of puzzlement disrupted the German's flabby features. It seemed the enormity of that statement was taking time to register. Then a look of excitement replaced the confusion and an animated Martin Kube began babbling.

"But that is even better. Gehlen only ran the eastern front. He had no responsibility for Bohemia and Moravia. You need me, Herr Carlisle. You need me more than ever. Consider the geography. With my networks you have a wedge to drive right into the communist heartland, a wedge to divide the puppet states and link with Gehlen's eastern front. Between the two operations they will put you ten years ahead of Lavrenti Beria. . . You know they will."

Alan Carlisle knew exactly what combining the two operations would mean. He had known it long before fat Martin Kube had fallen so conveniently into his hands. Until now it had been just another pipe dream; it still might be. To this point, Kube had only confirmed information that Carlisle already held. The most important question was next. Its answer would either fulfil that pipe dream or send Martin Kube to the gallows.

"And you can simply remember all of this, can you? All the contacts, all the details?"

"There are also documents. I have them hidden. They contain all the detail you require."

Whether or not Kube was aware of it, he had just saved himself from the hangman. Carlisle wondered if he knew.

"And where can I find these documents?"

"All in good time, Herr Carlisle. We have much to agree before that."

It seemed he did.

Carlisle was now in touching distance of what he had worked towards and dreamed of for so many months: an entire dormant Nazi spy network, running right through Czechoslovakia. Once reactivated, it would be like a dagger plunged into the heart of Soviet state security. Now he needed to get the news back to his masters in Washington and New York. The haggling could wait. That seamier side of things had always bored him.

He collected his papers, picked up his briefcase and made ready to leave, but not before he had fired a passing shot to disrupt the German's fragile arrogance.

"Don't be too confident, Herr Kube. You haven't evaded the hangman's noose just yet."

Carlisle banged on the cell door. It opened immediately. He left the room without looking back, threaded his way between the guards, and then stood quietly collecting his thoughts as the door slammed shut behind him. Moments later, he strode along the featureless corridor to an office at the far end. Two more guards stood outside that. He nodded as they snapped to attention. The sign on the door read: Colonel H. H. Strecker, OIC Briefings.

A token knock served both to announce his arrival and accommodate etiquette.

"No, don't get up, Colonel."

He wandered in, slammed the door shut with his foot, and waved Howard Strecker back into his seat. Then he picked up the telephone and began tapping at the cradle.

An apologetic female voice answered. He gave his name and asked for hers. She answered with a delightful lilt that told him she just might be open to giving up more than just a name. She said it was Melody Strand. He smirked. This sounded promising.

The name was twinkling and catchy, and the twang pure Louisiana. To a spoiled and silver-spooned rich-kid from New Hampshire it conjured images of nineteenth-century southern plantations and submissive doe-eyed slave girls. Alan Carlisle's sexual proclivities were many, but if he loved one thing more than any other, it was the erotic contrast of a smooth-skinned ebony beauty, lying sprawled and ready for him on a crisp white cotton sheet.

He made a couple of double-entendres. She responded with suitable gasps of maidenly outrage, but the laughter in her voice had remained. She apologized and said she had to go. America was waking up, and the switchboard was busy. He asked her to get him his home number, then replaced the receiver and turned to face the waiting Howard Strecker.

"Hope you don't mind, Colonel, but the hotel's a little too public."

"Of course not, sir. Would you like some coffee?"

Strecker was a bland, forty-something career soldier, who disliked his job and resented his current orders, disliked the need for political expediency and resented being away from his wife and family. Carlisle knew all this. He also knew that Strecker disliked and resented him. The dislike was mutual. Carlisle viewed Strecker as a sycophant and puritanical hypocrite, and tweaked his resentment at every opportunity. But Howard Strecker also had his uses.

"Coffee won't cut through the bad taste I've got in my mouth."

Strecker moved to the stationery cupboard, where he kept the essential booze.

"Scotch or schnapps? Or I could rustle up some bourbon? You want something to eat?"

He shook his head and pointed to the scotch. Strecker poured out two measures.

"So what did he have to say for himself?" he asked.

At that moment, Carlisle had a more pressing matter to address.

"Before we get into that, I need to know if you've heard from Hammond."

Strecker handed over the glass and shrugged his ignorance.

"Hammond? I don't quite. . ."

"Hammond, Gerald Hammond. The man we sent after the girl."

"Ah yes, him. My mind was on other things for some reason."

Carlisle wasn't in the mood for sarcasm, especially not from Strecker.

"Well, get it off other things and concentrate on this. This is important."

The smirk on Strecker's face faded. Now he looked confused.

"I don't understand. What do you mean, important? Carpenter didn't stress any special importance. He just said she was a good-looking young woman and we were rescuing her from Beria's clutches. He said it was a favour to someone. Beria being Beria, I assumed it was to save her from the obvious fate."

Alan Carlisle knew the public persona of Lavrenti Beria, as the head of Soviet state security: a sadist, rapist, and mass murderer, who terrified the Soviet Union from his third-floor office in the Lubyanka. But, unlike the rest of the world, Carlisle also knew Beria as a spymaster without equal, an espionage genius, who was taking maximum advantage of America's unpreparedness for the rapidly-approaching cold war.

He up-ended his glass, and passed it to Strecker for a refill. The phone rang. He picked it up. Melody had the number he'd asked for. He thanked her and waited, and then said,

"Hello?"

A youthful male voice crackled out from the receiver.

"Yes, what is it?"

"Mathew? It's your father. What are you doing home? You should be at college."

"I got bored."

"Bored? You're studying at one of the finest universities in the world, or you should be."

"I told you, I don't like politics and I can't stand economics."

"You're not there to like them. You're there to secure a future for yourself." A lengthy silence followed before he spoke again. "Is your mother there?"

"No."

"So where is she?"

"Out, thank God."

"Whad'yer mean, out? It's only just gone seven a.m. in Washington. Out where?"

"How the hell should I know? Drank too much at one of her boring charity dinners, I expect. Why would you give a damn? Look, I have to go. There's someone at the door."

The line went dead. He replaced the handset and tried not to show the anger as he spoke.

"Kids, huh! Who'd have them?"

Strecker looked embarrassed. He moved to top up Carlisle's glass. Carlisle persevered.

"You got any kids?"

Strecker poured his own freshener, then returned to his chair and nodded happily.

"I've got two, one of each. Jane's twelve, gonna be a stunner. Peter's up at Yale."

Carlisle stared moodily into his glass as he considered the limited merits of his only son.

"I've just got the one. Mathew. He's up at Princeton, or he should be. Pulled some serious strings and got him into PIA. For some inane reason, I always figured PIA stood for Public and International Affairs; didn't realize it stood for piss it away."

49

He took another drink, and changed the subject to a more interesting one.

"Girl on the switchboard. Melody, is it? Sounds like she could be fun. Not black, is she? Name sounds black?" Then, in response to the answering frown, he said, "Don't get me wrong. No finer sight than a well-rounded pair of glistening ebony buttocks thrusting back at you."

Alan Carlisle knew that his comments would outrage the puritanical Howard Strecker. That was precisely why he made them. He stifled a smile as he watched and listened to Strecker, clearly struggling to keep any hint of censure from his answer.

"Part African, part Cajun, I believe; beautiful girl, lovely smile, hour-glass figure. But, I should warn you, she's happily married. One of my former lieutenants took one look at her and was instantly smitten. That was less than six months ago. Sorry to disappoint you."

Strecker didn't look sorry. He looked disgusted. Carlisle shrugged and feigned indifference, but the interrogator in him had heard something interesting, and he wasn't about to let an opportunity like this pass him by.

"I'll live with it." And then, when he saw Strecker's look of disgust turn to one of relief, he said, "Did you say, one of your former lieutenants? Am I to assume he's no longer here on the base?"

Strecker's face suddenly fell.

"Uh, no. Transferred him to VA last month. We're winding Europe down, consolidating our experienced teams over at Fort Hunt. But then, I have to presume you already knew that?"

Carlisle ignored the question and feigned concern. He was thoroughly enjoying this.

"And she didn't go with him? What a shame. Poor girl must be so upset. . . and lonely."

Strecker hurriedly rustled through his in-tray.

"Young Melody requested an immediate transfer, of course. Couldn't approve it, because of staff shortages, but I've told her, I'll sanction it just as soon as we get some replacements."

Strecker finally found the document. He waved it in the air, like a trophy. Carlisle held out his hand.

"May I see?"

He took the form, studied the information and grinned.

"Only twenty-two, huh? All seems so unfair. Look, why don't I see if I can pull some strings when I get back to the department? Send you someone and get her stateside."

"Sorry, sir, but I can't let you do that. Regulations, I'm afraid."

Carlisle wasn't about to let him get away with that. He waved away the objection.

"Not a problem, Colonel. I'll deal with it. Least I can do. Unless, of course, you're determined to make an issue of this?"

If it came to a conflict between the two men, there could only be one winner. He knew it, and he knew that Strecker knew it. He watched him squirm, and heard him say,

"They're all someone's daughter, you know, and they all have feelings."

"You just concentrate on the sons and leave me to worry about the daughters. Now, what do you suggest we do with our fat little Kriminaldirektor in interview room two?"

Strecker's failure to protect the vulnerable Melody Strand had hurt; it showed.

"If it were up to me I'd ship him straight down to Nuremberg, let them deal with him. The more I see of these murdering bastards, the more they make my skin crawl." Carlisle frowned, and then stifled another smile as

Strecker hurriedly back-pedalled. "No disrespect intended, sir, but strictly speaking, these people are war criminals. They are on the list."

"That all depends on whose list you use, Colonel, and your precise interpretation of Article Six. But no, that can't happen. Kube's too important to throw to the wolves." He thought about his own level of political exposure and decided that escalation was the safest option. "I'll call Marcus Allum, see what he wants to do. That is what they pay him for."

He picked up the phone. She answered immediately. "Get me Marcus Allum at the State Department, would you, Melody? Oh, and I may have some news about your transfer. I'm tied up this afternoon. Perhaps you could drop round to my hotel this evening, around seven. We'll discuss it then."

"Uh, uh, yes, sir."

Alan Carlisle gave a self-satisfied smirk as he replaced the receiver. Then he saw the look of disgust and dismay on Howard Strecker's face and roared with laughter.

5

Gerald Hammond crouched low at the edge of the copse and scanned the road in both directions. He turned to ensure the girl was safely hidden from view, and found her as he'd left her, waiting a few paces farther back and looking anxious.

They had been lucky in their leaps from the moving train, landing on soft ground and suffering little more than minor cuts and bruising. Then, in a frantic effort to escape the early search radius, they had run until tired legs could run no more. They found a wooded area and rested for ten minutes, knowing the train would soon arrive in Leipzig and their head start limited. After that they walked quickly for the rest of that day and all through the night, staying out of sight, or close to cover, until they neared their primary objective.

Hammond had purposely chosen to head for the safe-house in Dessau. He reasoned the Soviets would expect them to make a run for the western-alliance sectors, and concentrate most of their search effort to the south and west. He obviously couldn't take her south and east, because that way lay Leipzig and a large contingent of the occupying Red Army. North was the only sensible option, and north meant the safe-house in Dessau.

Dessau, and more precisely its Junkers aircraft factory, had been the objective of heavy allied bombing during the war. As a result, the proud capital of the former Principality of Anhalt had suffered badly. However, it was not to the rubble-strewn centre that Gerald Hammond and his young charge were headed, but to one of the few undamaged buildings on the town's northern outskirts.

Hammond scanned the road and countryside again, just to make sure, then called and beckoned for her to join him. She crept forward, and he heard her ask,

"Are you married?"

The question took him by surprise. Of all the questions he might have anticipated her asking, about who he was, why he had rescued her, or if it was safe, she had asked that. It was only when he saw the admiring look in her eyes that he suddenly realized.

He was her saviour, her gallant rescuer. It was a natural and understandable reaction, particularly for one so young, but it was a reaction that, nonetheless, needed careful handling.

"Yes."

He wasn't good at that sort of thing. She looked disappointed. He smiled benevolently and gently teased her.

"Sorry about that. Would you like me to take you back to the train?"

She smiled back at him.

"We've probably missed it by now. We could wait for the next one."

She had a sense of humour. That was good. He smiled again and returned his attention to the road below.

"Tell me about your wife,' she asked. 'What's she like? Is she beautiful?"

"Yes."

"Do you live in New York?"

"No."

"One day I'd like to go to New York. I want to climb right to the top of the Empire State Building. They say it's over a hundred stories high and you can see all over the city."

As he listened to the lilting voice, speaking English with the merest hint of an accent, he found it enchanting. Her constant chattering was obviously an unconscious release of nervous tension, and that was good too. Victims of brutal interrogation sometimes found it difficult to conduct even the most basic conversation. She had obviously suffered no such trauma. Hammond knew something of Soviet interrogation techniques. She had been lucky.

She continued chattering. He happily indulged it.

"And I want to go to Los Angeles. I want to see Hollywood and all those famous film stars. I want to see Ray Milland and Clark Gable and William Holden. Oh, and especially Cary Grant; he's lovely." She paused for a well-earned breath, and then began again. "Oh yes, I want to go to Chicago, too. I want to see where all those gangsters live. Do you live in Chicago?"

"No."

"So, where do you live?"

"Washington."

"State or D.C.?"

"D.C."

"Have you ever met the President?"

"No."

"I met the Führer once, when I was a little girl. We were invited to Berchtesgaden. Everybody there was very important. He came across to us and asked my name, and then he gave me a kiss and said I was very pretty. Everybody was looking at me and smiling. I'll always remember that. Have you ever met anyone really famous?"

"No."

"You don't say much, do you?"

He smiled a smile of warmth, and gently chided her youthful garrulity.

"I think you say enough for both of us. C'mon, let's move."

They left the copse, climbed over a wire fence and scrambled down to the road. He crouched by a drainage ditch at the roadside. She crouched alongside and continued firing questions.

"Back there on the train, when you said 'they' sent you, did you mean the Americans?"

"Yes."

"So why did they. . . ?"

"Be quiet."

Hammond had just seen a convoy. It was still some way in the distance, but travelling quickly and heading straight for them.

He shoved her into the ditch, and followed immediately after, then pulled her against the roadside bank and crouched beside her in the stagnant water. When she tried to peep over the top, he pulled her down and held her close, then clamped a hand over her mouth and hissed a second instruction for her to be quiet.

He peered out from behind a convenient tuft of grass as the convoy neared and then rumbled on by. There were four Opel Blitzes, commandeered from a defeated German army. Stragglers, he guessed, from the larger convoy that had passed by a few minutes earlier. Each was straining to make up time, and each was packed with Russian troops.

He again scanned the road to Jessnitz, or he hoped it was the road to Jessnitz. It was a tactically poor position, but they'd had little choice. They had to get to Dessau before dark. That meant leaving cover and negotiating a large expanse of open farmland.

Hammond cast his gaze over the road and across the farmland to the safety of the woods on the far side. He calculated they could make it in eight or ten minutes, but that meant eight or ten minutes of exposure to prying eyes.

He looked again. The Russian convoy had gone. Now there was nothing moving for miles. He thought of making a dash for it, but caution told him to wait a little longer. From where they crouched, the flat and uninspiring terrain allowed them an advantage. They could see the enemy from distance. However, once they left the safety of cover and started running across that field, it would offer the enemy a similar advantage. A few more minutes wouldn't hurt.

As Hammond searched for signs of further Soviet troop movement, he thought back to the last time he'd undertaken a rescue mission on mainland Europe. His mud-spattered face smiled grimly as he compared the two missions and found nothing in common between them.

The previous rescue effort had been that hastily-organized dash to Rouen, and he'd been in uniform: a night-time assault with a team of professionals alongside, and surprise in his favour. In Rouen the main German army had been miles away, up on the Pas de Calais, peering nervously into the mist of the English Channel.

In Rouen, he'd had the assault and exit planned, the French Resistance to spirit them cross-country and a British Royal Navy submarine waiting offshore to ferry them home. He'd also had a fallback plan, which would not have been good news for Davis Carpenter, but would probably have given Hammond's team a chance to escape with their lives.

Carpenter's rescue from Rouen had been conventional combat, subject to the rules of war and the Geneva Convention. Magdeburg was anything but that.

In Magdeburg he was a rogue agent, working unofficially and alone. Not only that, but he'd killed three Soviet officials. He had no fallback position, no rules of engagement, no Geneva Convention, or even any official acknowledgement of his existence. In Magdeburg he was deniable, and they would deny.

Which all led him to one inescapable question: why the hell had he agreed to do it?

He considered the question, and compared the two individuals who owed him their lives.

The girl who crouched alongside him was a beautiful young German, innocent and helpless and easy on the eye, but in reality little more than a child.

In stark contrast, Davis Carpenter was an overweight bureaucrat, who had taken a stupid risk without consideration for others. A desk-bound strategist, who happily sent others on missions that all too often resulted in their deaths, without any empathy for the courage needed or sympathy for loved-ones left behind. He was a man for the bigger picture and the larger stage, the end and not the means; the greater good rather than the individual tragedy.

He thought back to that afternoon, when Carpenter had arrived out of the blue and explained the deal. He had jumped at it. A State Department appointment, in exchange for 'another minor bit of business in Europe'; there was no decision to make. Carpenter said it was a long-overdue reward for Hammond saving his life in Rouen. Hammond couldn't believe his luck.

He nodded a furious agreement and signed on the dotted line, then shook Carpenter by the hand and thanked him for remembering. He had been so desperate for a chance to join the State Department and escape the drudgery of that insurance company, he would have agreed to anything. At the time he'd considered rescuing and wet-nursing a good-looking young woman a small price to pay.

Three days after that he had set out for Europe, in good humour. They sneaked him onto a prototype Stratofreighter, ostensibly running long-range tests out of Andrews Field. The tests went well. The following day the plane touched down at Wiesbaden. From there he made his contacts in Frankfurt without problem or incident. They in turn contacted their people to the east of the country, and arranged his overland transport to Magdeburg. Everything, it seemed, was going according to plan.

But then he reached Magdeburg and the price suddenly soared, because in the early hours of the morning, on the day he arrived, the Soviet authorities discovered Catherine Schmidt hiding in an attic. They took her into custody and questioned her at length about the gruesome murders of three Red Army officers. She shook her pretty head and claimed she knew nothing about the killings. Stanislav Paslov, the head of the Soviet MGB in southern Germany, drove over from Leipzig specifically to question her. He hadn't believed a word she said.

Fortunately, the local Saxony-Anhalt cell boasted an informer in the Leipzig headquarters. He gave them details of her interrogation, and told them of MGB plans. They told Hammond.

The authorities in Magdeburg planned to transfer her to their counterparts in Prague, for further questioning about a similarly-gruesome murder there. After that, they intended taking her up to Moscow, where the Mingrelian Monster himself, the great and terrible Lavrenti Beria, awaited her arrival.

By then Hammond had long since stopped smiling. In the space of five hectic days his part in an unofficial back-scratching exercise had graduated from a covert walk in the park to something bordering suicidal.

"When can we go?"

The girl was clearly impatient. An older and wiser Gerald Hammond was more cautious.

"Not just yet. When I'm sure it's safe."

"Where are we?"

"On the floodplain, to the south-east of Dessau, I hope. Don't you know? This is your country."

"It was my country, but not any more. Now my people have no country. Barbarians have taken it from us. Anyway, I only know Berlin, and a little of Prague, I suppose."

"Well, I'm betting the River Mulde is on the far side of those woods. If it is, we should be able to follow it all the way up past the town."

As she peered across the fields to the woods beyond, following the tip of a grubby finger, he quietly studied the girl beneath the layers of caked-on dirt. She was more than easy on the eye, she was stunning, with classically beautiful features and clear blue eyes that laughed and sparkled through the fear.

Crouched low in the stagnant water and peeping over the rim of the ditch, she reminded him of an impish tom-boy, with her face and limbs streaked with dirt, and her long blonde hair hanging in damp and matted strands. The white cotton and lace skirt she wore was now torn, stained with grass and embedded with grime, but the body that so beautifully distorted the mud-spattered jacket was not that of an impish tomboy but a fully-formed and exquisitely-proportioned young woman.

As he quietly watched her, he found himself inexplicably drawn and wanting to believe in her innocence. She was obviously young and beautiful, but she was also deceptively strong; agile and athletic and mentally tough.

"Can't we risk it? I'm getting cold."

She had posed the question without any hint of complaint. Hammond studied the empty road and the fields beyond. He knew they needed to make the northern outskirts of Dessau before dusk, but there was still that large expanse of open ground to cross before they could make the cover of the woods. He decided they had no choice. They had to chance it.

"I suppose we have to. We can't stay here forever. We'll head for the woods over there, but if you hear anything or see anybody, you drop immediately and lay still. Got it?"

She nodded. He clambered out of the ditch and pulled her after him.

Then they ran; over the road, into the field and across the open farmland; eyes scanning the surrounding countryside, lungs gasping for breath, progress hindered by the cloying mud that grabbed at their feet and wearied their legs.

Ten minutes later, they made the woods on the far side of the fields, and paused to rest exhausted limbs. He checked to see if anyone had spotted their frantic dash for cover. He saw no one.

"I think we're safe, for the moment anyway. Now let's find the river."

6

Around four thousand miles to the west of where Hammond and the girl were making for the River Mulde, 1946 Washington D.C. saw J. Edgar Hoover and 'Wild Bill' Donovan continue their high-profile battle for control of the new Central Intelligence Group. The battle would continue into the following year, when the initials CIG would be changed to CIA, but while the two political heavyweights wrangled, another faction of former OSS members quietly made their move.

Posing as Wall Street lawyers, State Department officials, and government advisers, these grey-suited men began building espionage networks in Europe with neither approval nor knowledge of President or Congress. They met and plotted in New York City, at the Council on Foreign Relations, in a building on the corner of East Sixty-Eighth Street and Park Avenue: a building numbered fifty-eight.

This day, however, two of those same grey-suited individuals could be seen strolling together in the unusually public arena of Washington's National Arboretum. With collars turned high and hats pulled low, Marcus Allum and Daniel Chambers walked as they talked, stopping only occasionally to allow passers-by to move out of earshot before resuming both stroll and conversation.

"So where are we on this Magdeburg business?"

The pretentious and sombre Daniel Chambers was the more senior and sinister of the two. Thin of face and narrow of mind, Chambers was a grey man in every sense of the term. From the charcoal-grey suit and silver-grey hair to the sombre thoughts that inhibited his being, Chambers was colourless. A graduate of Harvard Law and a name partner at the Wall Street firm of Cartwright Chambers and Kent, Daniel Chambers treated those around him, and particularly his State Department counterparts, as intellectually inferior. It was a trait that sometimes amused, but more often infuriated, his current companion and co-conspirator, the manic-depressive Marcus Allum.

Loathed by some and mistrusted by many, two distinct Marcus Allums ruled the Office of Occupied Territories. One was a taciturn and uninspiring Deputy Assistant Secretary, who'd sit alone in his office with a look of thunder on his face while the grey clouds gathered and the grey schemes hatched. The other was a charismatic and charming Princeton graduate and Ivy League athlete, the life and soul of any party, and the lifeblood of Occupied Territories.

On good days Allum was the State Department's political chameleon: tall, slim, fair-haired and sharp as a whip, flattering and seducing the ladies who lunch with a ready smile and an instant quip, and blending into any scenario from the sleaziest bar to the Oval Office.

On bad days he was best avoided, and today was fast becoming a bad day.

"It all went pear-shaped; someone talked."

"Someone?"

"It's the only explanation. We had her well hidden. They found her too easily."

"Someone in Germany?"

"Had to be. Everything here's watertight."

"You're sure about that, Marcus?"

Allum wasn't at all sure. He was privately worried about his own department, and the distinct possibility that it had somehow been infiltrated by a Soviet mole. For all of that, he wasn't going to allow the arrogant and pretentious Daniel Chambers any reason to initiate a purge of his office, or to see just how worried he was.

"I have to believe it."

"So where does that leave us?"

"We still haven't heard from Hammond, but there's still time."

Marcus Allum held the confident façade. Chambers frowned.

"Well, you recommended him, Marcus. This goes south, and you'll go with it."

"Yeah, well, don't worry about me. What was it Twain said? Reports of my death, and all that exaggerated shit. Anyway, I don't see a problem; or at least, not yet. Hammond's one of the best. He may even be the best. I know I never saw anyone better. He's been in tough spots before. He'll pull this one out. I'm certain of it."

"I hope so, Marcus. I hope so for your sake. I spoke to Conrad yesterday. He's not happy. If we lose this girl, he just might blame me, and then guess who I'm gonna blame?"

Allum gave a humourless grin. He knew the game as well as anyone could, and he knew how ruthless Chambers could be. Chambers wouldn't hesitate to feed him to the lions, if it meant saving himself. Allum was under no illusion about that.

"So tell me something I don't already know." They strolled for a while before Allum spoke again. "Conrad Zalesie's nobody's fool. Anyway, I briefed him this morning. He knows we're doing everything we can. It wasn't our fault the silly bitch got herself arrested. I mean, who the hell asked her to start carving up half the Sov army? Anyway, my money's on Hammond."

"You'd better hope you're right. I get the feeling Conrad's taking this one personally."

"Yeah, I kinda got that feeling, too."

Despite his assurances and the undoubted skills of his old Princeton friend, Marcus Allum was a good deal less certain than he sounded. Daniel Chambers asked about Hammond.

"Gerald Hammond? The name's familiar."

"He was OSS, with Jedburgh. Before that, he was the one who pulled Carpenter out of Rouen that time. I think he was one of a handful who could have done it."

Chambers looked puzzled.

"I don't follow. If he's as good as you seem to think, why did you wait until now to bring him on board? Why didn't the State Department snap him up straight after the war?"

Allum smiled as he recalled the belligerent and artless Hammond.

"Nobody trusts a man you can't corrupt, Daniel. You should know that better than most, and Gerald Hammond's incorruptible. He has a moral compass that points six degrees west of self-righteous; it never varies. He's straight, and he's as belligerent as hell. It's a shame. With a little flexibility, he could have gone all the way."

"But you still trusted him for this?"

"I didn't have a lot of choice. This business with the girl happened too fast. I had to move, and I didn't have time to worry about the fine points. But do I trust Gerald Hammond? Yeah, I trust him. Out in the field I trust him a hundred per cent. It's when he gets back to Washington and resets that moral compass, that's when I have to put him on a short leash. That's when the real headaches begin." He took the opportunity to change the subject. "So, how'd it go with the president?"

Chambers appeared even more sombre than usual.

"He still won't sanction any covert activity, and the rest are still on the fence."

Despite his bluster, Marcus Allum was already on the raggedy edge. News of this latest set-back almost sent him over the top.

"But he has to sanction it. Jesus! This isn't a game. Don't they understand the position we're in? They set up a Central Intelligence Group to counter Sov expansionism, tie one hand behind their backs, and then expect them to take on Beria with a fucking water pistol. And lest anyone forgets the reason we're in all this shit, the reason we had to use Hammond for Magdeburg was because Truman wouldn't sanction covert ops."

"I'm sorry, Marcus, but it's still not going to happen; not in the short-term, not officially."

Allum's mood was deepening by the second.

"For Christ's sake, Daniel. I'm not asking for any great advantage here. Beria may have pissed away most of the old NKVD in the shake-up, but he's still running more covert crap out of the Lubyanka than you can shake a stick at. I can beat him. I know I can. All I'm asking Harry Truman for is a level playing field."

The response was sympathetic, but unyielding.

"I know that, and so does the president, but give it time, Marcus, give it time."

"So what the hell happened this time?"

"You tell me. What always happens?"

"Hoover."

Daniel Chambers nodded moodily and continued walking. To the uninitiated and those few passers-by who ventured out on a chilly late-spring afternoon, the men's stroll would have appeared innocuous enough. The pauses, frequent features of that same casual stroll, similarly appeared as innocent gaps in conversation, rather than any need for confidentiality.

66

They could have been regular businessmen discussing sales strategies or their favourite baseball team, but the reality was anything but that. Daniel Chambers explained the latest setback.

"Hoover's still looking to steal a piece, no matter how small. Since he lost out on CIG he's been claiming all sorts of nonsense about the Soviets, and Truman's been buying it."

"I don't see why he doesn't just back off and get on with his own damn job."

"You mean, apart from having an ego the size of Washington?"

"It can't just be that. He's lost before."

"Not this big, he hasn't."

Allum could see the truth of that. He moved the conversation along.

"How's he doing with the White House sweep?"

"Morton Simmonds is still viewing the world through the bottom of a glass, and Hoover still hasn't got a scrap of worthwhile evidence. Pretty much business as usual."

Allum smiled malevolently as he thought of J. Edgar Hoover's massively-expensive and on-going operation to purge the Federal Government and White House of communist sympathizers. He was also thinking about the man Hoover had picked to head up the 250 agents assigned. Allum chuckled as he recalled his old adversary, the philandering and hard-drinking FBI senior agent, Morton Simmonds.

"So you're saying, despite all this time and expense, the only thing Hoover's got that's guaranteed to hold firm under the spotlight of a grand-jury investigation is Morton Simmonds' dick."

Even the prudish Daniel Chambers smiled at that. He said that was why J. Edgar Hoover had needed to distract Truman. Hoover had picked on Soviet expansionism and the inability of the CIG to combat it, because it offered a distraction from his own failings. They couldn't argue their case by telling

Truman about the European networks, because he had already forbidden any such covert activity. Once again, J. Edgar Hoover had played his hand to perfection.

Allum nodded. Suddenly it all made sense.

"Of course.   That's what all this is about. We don't get covert ops approved, because Hoover screwed up on his bid to run CIG?" He saw Chambers nod, and vented his fury. "He lost, for Christ's sake. We all did. What the fuck's the point of kicking at a corpse?"

Marcus Allum's hatred of Hoover was almost as obsessive as his hatred of communism. He raged on. "That's the trouble with these fags; they get so damn bitchy when they lose."

Daniel Chambers seemed more positive.

"Don't let him get to you, Marcus. We're still in good shape. We keep building the networks, quietly and efficiently, and we keep Hoover so busy he won't have time to draw breath. When I get through with Mr John Edgar Hoover, he'll have commies coming out of the White House woodwork; even Harry Truman's gonna be checking under his bed every night before he turns out the light."

The uncharacteristic fire in Chambers' eyes slowly dulled.

"Anyway, what was so important we had to meet like this?"

Allum gave him the good news.

"Strangely enough, it was on that very subject. Zalesie just approved the funding on a new Czech network. Carlisle's in Frankfurt now. He says we just need to line up a couple of ducks and we're all set."

"Who's doing the horse-trading?"

Allum didn't want Chambers knowing everything, at least not yet. He talked briefly about Kube, but didn't give any specific details. Chambers looked straight at him.

"You're not going to say Gestapo, are you? Tell me you're not going to say Gestapo?"

Marcus Allum hated these stupid mind games. If Chambers already knew the answer, why ask the question? He shrugged his indifference and held his anger.

"It's the nature of the beast, Daniel, and we've taken worse."

Neither man spoke for a while as they continued their stroll. They stopped to admire a well-tended bed of azaleas in full bloom and allow a passing couple to wander on by before resuming both afternoon stroll and clandestine conversation.

"OK, Marcus, let me have the figures, and I'll transfer the funds. Have you called Carlisle?"

"Yeah, called him earlier. He'll run with this, and keep us briefed on the situation with Hammond and the girl. He's due back here Wednesday. Hopefully, Hammond will have come through by then. We'll organize a meet in Connecticut for Thursday."

For the second time that morning, the sombre Daniel Chambers smiled.

"So Carlisle's in Frankfurt over the weekend. God help the fräuleins."

****

Later that day, on the other side of the Atlantic, Alan Carlisle sat in the deserted lounge of his Frankfurt hotel. He had chosen an intimate corner and told the waiter not to disturb him unless called. He was now sipping at a scotch and waiting for his guest to arrive.

Following Marcus Allum's telephoned approval, Carlisle had sealed an agreement with the fat Gestapo spymaster. Further progress would have to wait until Monday, or at least progress on that particular agreement.

For Alan Carlisle weekend stopovers in Frankfurt consisted of extravagant room service and crude indulgence, in the company of working fräuleins. However, on this particular weekend an unprincipled rogue had more devious entertainment in mind.

"Mr Carlisle?"

He studied her as she stood before him, and smiled inwardly at her coyness. Howard Strecker had been less than forthright. The doe-eyed and statuesque Melody Strand was exquisite.

"Melody, I presume?"

"Yes, sir."

"Come, come and sit."

He patted the seat next to him. She sat down.

"You wanted to see me, sir? Something about my transfer?"

He smiled his usual disarming smile.

"Yes, that's right, I did. Can I get you something to drink?"

"No, thank you, sir."

Carlisle shrugged and produced the form.

"I'm afraid the Colonel wasn't able to approve your transfer. I'm sorry, my dear."

He watched anxious features fall.

"Why not? He told me he would."

Carlisle nodded. A devious plan was progressing nicely.

"Yes, but since then they've changed the rules. This is a top-secret base. Everyone has to be checked, double-checked, and positively vetted. We can't just transfer people in and out. Nowadays, it needs State Department approval for unscheduled transfers. I'm so sorry."

Her face fell further.

"But you're with the State Department. Couldn't you approve it?"

Within seconds Carlisle had feigned surprise, deliberation, reluctance and indecision.

"Well, I could, I suppose, but I shouldn't really interfere. I mean, you seem like a charming girl, but I hardly know you. I couldn't. . ."

"Please, Mr Carlisle. Please say you'll help me."

"Well, I suppose we could get to know each other a little better. I am stuck here until next week. Perhaps we could have dinner, discuss it over a bottle or two of champagne."

He looked for a reaction, and got it as her brown eyes widened in shock.

"Mr Carlisle, if you're suggesting what I think. . . I'm a married woman."

"Who loves her husband?"

"Yes, of course."

"How much?"

"I'm sorry?"

He grinned and qualified the question.

"How much do you love your husband?"

An expression of shock suddenly turned to one of outrage.

"You're saying, if I have sex with you, you'll approve my transfer?"

He answered with feigned nonchalance.

"I wouldn't put it so bluntly, but, yes, I suppose I am."

She stood up to leave.

"You go to hell, you bastard!"

It was a bluff. Carlisle could tell. He could see she was intrigued by the suggestion; perhaps a little outraged, too, but definitely intrigued. He tried a bluff of his own.

"No doubt in time, but right now I think I'll have a lie down before dinner." He finished his drink and made ready to leave. "Goodbye, Melody. Pity about that transfer."

"God, you're a bastard. The other girls were right. They told me about you. They warned me not to come here. They said what would happen."

"Perhaps you should have listened to them."

As he spoke, he watched her watching him. She was obviously considering his offer. He could almost read her thoughts. Then he saw her shrug and felt the elation rise.

A moment after that, she sat down again.

"All right, you bastard. Just this once, and then you'll approve my transfer. You swear?"

Carlisle felt that old familiar rush of sexual adrenaline as he sat down alongside her, this time sitting closer, much closer. He began stroking the small of her back, and, when she didn't flinch or protest, reached down with the other hand to squeeze and fondle her knee.

Still she didn't resist or complain, and so he inched his fingers all the way beneath the hemline, and then began idly stroking a path along her inner thigh.

"Just this once, did you say? Good god no, my dear. I've got the whole weekend to kill."

He saw her mouth open as his fingers slid higher. It described a gasp, but made no sound. He tugged her thighs a little wider, teased a little more, and watched her brown eyes struggling to focus. A low groan of lust and despair confirmed the guilty pleasure as her thighs relaxed and her eyelids fluttered. When she finally spoke, it was in whispered syllables that lacked conviction.

"No, not here, please."

A hand clutched at his arm, a slim and dainty hand, with trembling fingers and crimson nails. It tried and failed to deny the intrusion, but then gripped a little tighter and guided him higher, encouraging him beyond the stocking's perimeter, to where his fingers toyed and caressed before worming their way beneath that final flimsy barrier.

A suddenly jolt greeted the first electric contact. Another groan announced a helpless young beauty's erotic dilemma and increasing arousal. He tormented for a while, and explored for a while, and watched her fighting the urge to respond. He found himself whispering disgraceful thoughts of lust, and crude predictions of pleasure, intending to compound her confusion, knowing she was almost ready.

"What is going on here?" And then. . . "Herr Carlisle. This is a respectable hotel."

Despite instructions to the contrary, the waiter had come in from the bar, under the pretext of checking to see if he needed another drink. The waiter was a bumptious individual. Carlisle remembered him from a previous visit and a situation not entirely unlike this. He scrambled to his feet and began to bluster a pointless and ridiculous explanation. It was then the waiter saw the extent of young Melody's dishevelment. He wagged an index finger and scolded her.

"And as for you, fräulein. . . you should be ashamed of yourself."

When Melody Strand pulled down her skirt and stood up, she didn't look in the least bit ashamed of herself. She calmly patted her hair into place, carefully straightened the seams of her stockings and looked deep into Carlisle's eyes.

"Room number?" she asked.

He swallowed hard as he processed the words, then rediscovered his voice.

"Uh, one-o-five."

"Key."

She held out her hand. He fumbled in his jacket pocket for the key, found it, and dropped it into the open palm. Her fingers closed around the fob. She smiled briefly and enigmatically, then turned to the waiter.

"Frau, not fräulein. Do try to remember. Does the restaurant have oysters?" The waiter nodded mutely. She looked concerned. "We're almost into May. Are you sure they're fresh?"

"Of course."

The waiter both looked and sounded insulted. He seemed to have momentarily forgotten the circumstance that caused his intervention. She haughtily studied him as she gave her order.

"Send a dozen to room one-o-five, with a bottle of decent champagne and two glasses. In about an hour, not before."

"Certainly, Frau. . . uh. . . ?"

She failed to answer the unasked question and returned the stare to a delighted Carlisle.

"Well, you talk a good fuck. . . Let's see if you give one."

Carlisle's mouth hung open, but his mind was racing. Could this possibly be the same vulnerable young newly-wed described by the over-protective Howard Strecker; the same helpless and innocent beauty, who had so naïvely fallen into his dastardly trap?

He followed in rapt attendance as she sashayed her way towards the foyer, then saw her stop, turn back to the still open-mouthed waiter and cheekily amend the order.

"On second thoughts, perhaps you'd better make that two dozen."

She smiled a wickedly mischievous smile and nodded to where Alan Carlisle stood silently marvelling at the sheer audacity of her performance.

"You see. . . he has the whole weekend to kill."

7

Gerald Hammond crouched low, on the far side of the street from the former guesthouse and primary rendezvous point. He was peering through the half-light of dusk, studying each darkened room in turn. He wasn't sure it was safe. He wasn't even certain he had the right house. He did know they had to move now or spend another night in the open.

He turned and gestured for her to join him. She crept forward, then looked nervously up at him as he handed her the compass and whispered,

"Wait here and stay low. If I'm not back in ten minutes, get out of here. Get back to the river. Then head south until you're clear of the town. After that, start heading south-west. Stay away from built-up areas. Get to the American zone and tell them what's happened. Tell them you need to speak to a man called Davis Carpenter in Washington."

"I don't have a watch."

"So count. No, wait. Here, take mine. I'll do the counting."

Hammond handed her the wristwatch and then slipped quietly away. He crossed the road and moved towards the house, staying low and keeping to the shadows, before working his way around to the back.

He reached the first darkened window and gently tapped on the pane, peering through the blinds for any sign of movement and waiting for an answer. When neither came, he moved farther along and tapped a little louder at the next window. The sound carried through the late-evening stillness. He prayed it wouldn't attract unwelcome interest. He prayed, too, for an answer.

A figure appeared at the doorway and stood in the light from the kitchen. It was a woman, elderly and frail and slightly hunched. She was wearing worn and threadbare clothing. Her hair was white and brittle, gathered and pinned into a bun. Her face was lined, the complexion wizened by hardship and time, but the eyes that picked him out in the gloom were both clear and alert. On the third finger of her left hand she wore a plain gold band. In the skeletal fingers of her right she held a walking stick, but didn't use it for support. Instead she waved it at him as she returned his look of uncertainty with a glare of hostility.

"Who are you? What do you want?"

"My name is Hammond. You are expecting me?"

She nodded briefly, and answered in English.

"Come along in. Quickly, before someone sees you."

The door opened into an oversized kitchen, with a log fire flickering in the grate. A large coffee pot and battered kettle stood side-by-side on the blackened surface of a huge wood-burning stove.

Despite the reassuring warmth and welcome, Hammond drew the automatic. He glanced around the kitchen before continuing into the hallway, past a dining room, and toward the front of the house. He paused at the foot of the stairs and listened for any sound from above. He wondered if he should check, but it was clear there was no one else in the house.

When he returned, he found the old woman sitting by the fireplace in an old varnished rocking-chair, seemingly unconcerned and nursing a cup of coffee. He looked to the table, where two more cups of steaming coffee wafted a welcoming aroma.

The old woman explained.

"They said there would be two of you."

He suddenly remembered the girl.

"I'll get her."

He returned with the girl in tow and ushered her into the kitchen. The old woman nodded a greeting but didn't get up. Instead, she sat quietly rocking back and forth, nursing her coffee and studying the girl. She seemed lost in thought; memories perhaps. He interrupted.

"I'm sorry, but my friend needs to rest."

The old woman nodded and shuffled off into the hallway. She returned carrying some towels and a nightgown in her arms. She handed one of the towels to Hammond, and passed the remaining bundle to the girl.

"Give me those clothes, they're filthy. I'll wash and clean them, and hang them by the stove. They'll be dry by morning. You, too." The old woman nodded at Hammond and then gestured to the girl and the torn material of her skirt. "I'll see if there's some thread for that. The kettle's hot. You can wash in the sink."

Hammond stood in the centre of the kitchen, uncertainly eyeing the two women. She couldn't possibly mean for him to undress and wash, not in front of them. He looked, first to the old woman, who stood waiting for the clothing, and then to the girl, who showed no such compunction. She eased off each boot in turn, and then began separating the jacket fastenings. She paused, for a provocative moment and looked up at him through long seductive lashes, then smiled a mischievous smile when she saw his flustered reaction.

Hammond, captivated, had watched her pout at him and wilfully provoke his embarrassment, but then suddenly remembered his gallantry and lost his nerve. He blurted an excuse about checking the upstairs rooms, then turned and fled.

He allowed a full fifteen minutes to pass before deeming it safe to return. The girl had finished washing and climbed into the comforting warmth and shapeless security of a heavy nightgown. She was brushing and drying her hair by the fire.

Cutlery and plates were set out on the table. The old woman was cooking eggs on the stove. She scooped the eggs on to a plate and carried them to the table, then shuffled over to a cupboard and returned with a loaf of bread.

Hammond thanked her and sat down. He was suddenly ravenous. Other than some chocolate carried for emergencies and a few apples he'd stolen from an orchard, neither he nor the girl had eaten for two days

When they had finished their meals, the old woman pointed to the sink.

"And now I'll take those clothes and you can get over there and wash that dirt off. I've refilled the kettle. The water will be more than hot enough by now."

Hammond flushed red and mumbled a refusal.

"I'll clean up in the morning."

The old woman was insistent.

"You'll do it now. I'm not having that filth sleeping in one of my beds." She glared at the girl, who was playfully grinning at Hammond. "And you're a little too forward for my liking, young lady. Now off to bed with you, and mind you keep to your room tonight."

Catherine Schmidt obediently headed for the door. The old woman called after her.

"And use one of the rooms at the back of the house. Stay away from the front."

The old woman turned to a still red-faced Hammond. He stood his ground and shook his head. There was no way he was going to undress; not under these circumstances. Hoping to buy some privacy, he offered a compromise.

"When you've gone up to bed; I promise."

She nodded to a single bed pushed up against the wall in the far corner.

"That's my bed, and the kitchen is where I sleep these days. It's warmer in here, and I can't easily make the stairs any more."

Hammond shuffled uncomfortably and tried not to look as embarrassed as he felt. She stood with hands on hips and an expression of exasperation written across wizened features.

"Herr Hammond, in the seventy-eight years I have been on this earth, I have seen many different armies come and go, and led more than my share of conquering heroes up those stairs, but not for the last twenty of those years. And if that doesn't set your mind at rest, perhaps I should add that in that sink I've washed and scrubbed a great-grandson, three other grandsons, two sons, a loving husband, and an invalid father.

"I promise you, I don't embarrass easily, and you're safe. . . from me anyway, I can't speak for others." She glanced pointedly at the ceiling, but then gave a smile as she added, "Twenty years ago I might have offered to bathe you myself, but I'm a little past all that nonsense these days. And now I'll see if I can find something for you to wear."

She shuffled off and he watched her leave, realizing there was more to this elderly lady than the simple peasant he'd assumed. He grinned at his own foolishness and began to undress.

Standing naked at the sink, he began scrubbing away the offending dirt and odour. He could hear her searching through cupboards and drawers, grumbling and complaining about men in general, and him in particular.

He wondered how she had become involved with western intelligence, and why she risked so much in helping them. Whatever the reason, it would have to be better than his had been in helping the girl. He doubted he would discover the answers. The rules of the game and the dictates of common sense favoured ignorance.

By the time the old woman returned, he had finished washing. He stood in front of the sink, feeling foolish and shielding his well-scrubbed nakedness with an inadequate towel. She handed him a nightgown and he saw her smile as she viewed the well-muscled torso.

"Well, maybe not twenty years ago. Now I come to think about it, maybe it was nearer ten."

He accepted her teasing in good grace as he took the nightgown and mumbled his thanks. Then he snatched up his belongings and scurried out and up the stairs. On reaching the girl's door, he paused and listened to the even breathing from within before tiptoeing into the next room. He placed the automatic under his pillow, pulled the nightgown over his head, wrapped the blankets around an exhausted frame and was instantly asleep.

****

When Hammond woke the next morning, it was gone nine. He hurried downstairs to collect his clothes and found them, washed and ironed and piled neatly alongside the girl's, at the foot of the stairs. He took them back to his room, changed quickly, and then headed back downstairs.

When he wandered into the kitchen, he found the old woman sitting at the table eating breakfast and drinking coffee. She saw him and started to rise. He told her to sit and finish her breakfast. She pointed to the pot and said there was plenty of coffee.

He poured a cup, and then sat down opposite her. She asked if the girl was awake. He said she was in the room next to his, but he'd not heard her moving around and assumed she was still sleeping. The old woman nodded, and leaned across the table.

"That's good, because I need to talk to you."

She seemed in earnest.

"About what?"

"Beria."

"Lavrenti Beria?"

"Yes. We have a man in the Soviet offices. He says that Beria has taken a special interest in the girl and issued specific orders that she must be found at all costs. Paslov has more than a thousand troops out looking. They're searching everywhere, and they're not giving up. You were lucky to have made it this far."

Hammond asked the obvious question.

"Did your man say why they want her so badly?"

"No, but if Beria's involved, it must be something more than simple murder."

Hammond heard Catherine Schmidt coming down the stairs. He held up a cautionary finger and then waited until she sauntered into the kitchen. The old woman looked up.

"And how are you this morning, young lady? I trust you slept well?"

"Yes, I did, and I feel much better. Any coffee left?"

Catherine Schmidt studied them for a moment, then moved to the stove and tested the coffee pot. She poured her coffee, came back to the table, and sat down.

"Well?"

Hammond stared blankly back at her.

"Well what?"

"What were you talking about?"

Hammond hesitated, unsure if she should be told about this additional complication. She waited a moment.

"If it concerns me, I have a right to know. . . It's my life at stake here, and I'm not a child."

The old woman answered.

"It is all of our lives at stake here, young lady, and a good many other lives as well."

Hammond relented.

"No, she's right. It is her life, and she does have a right to know." He looked hard at the girl. "Tell me, have you ever heard of a man called Beria? Lavrenti Pavlovich Beria."

"No, why? Is he important?"

"You could say that. How about a man called Paslov, Stanislav Ivanovich Paslov?"

She nodded.

"Oh yes, I know him. He questioned me in Magdeburg. They all seemed frightened of him, but I thought he was sweet; well, for a Bolshevik."

The old woman looked to the heavens.

"Paslov works for Beria. I promise you, he is anything but sweet."

"So, who's Beria?"

Hammond explained, and told her that Beria wanted her for some reason. When she smiled and made a flippant comment about feeling flattered, he shook his head.

"I wouldn't be, if I were you. Among his many other talents, he's a sadistic killer. He's chartered Paslov with getting you back. He's determined, he's angry, and he's dangerous."

"So what does that mean?"

"It means you must be important to them, and it means they won't give up."

She leaned across the table and stroked at his arm.

"Never mind; you're strong and handsome and clever. You saved my life on the train, and you'll protect me now. I know you will."

Embarrassed, Hammond drew back from her touch.

"So why would such a powerful man as Lavrenti Beria be after you?" he asked.

The pout changed to petulance, and then to a look of cold determination.

"It could be because I killed one of his filthy Russian officers in Berlin. A Bolshevik pig, who thought he could rape and kill German women just because they were German and he was Russian. Well, he won't rape any more. I made certain of that."

Hammond carefully framed the next question, shocked by the girl's sudden transformation from flirtatious seductress to cold-eyed killer.

"And there were others, too, weren't there, Catherine? Other men that you killed?"

She glared at him.

"Don't patronize me with your soothing tones and condescension. I saw how easily you did those bastards on the train. Don't speak to me as though you're some all-American hero, and I'm a lunatic bitch. Your country and mine have a common enemy, it's called Bolshevism, and we're both in the middle of a total bloody war. It was in forty-one, and it still is. They were the hated enemy then, and they still are: barbarians, and rapists, and bloodthirsty butchers."

Hammond broached another question, this time without the soothing mannerisms and conciliatory tone she had found so irritating.

"So who was this Russian officer? The one you killed in Berlin?"

"There were many more than one."

"All of them Russian officers?"

"Yes."

"It may be a naive question, but why?"

"The teachings of Kali: cut the head from the demon, and the body dies."

She spoke in monotones and stared into her own private torment. Hammond pressed.

"So who was the first?"

He had raised his voice, intending to interrupt her abstraction. She snapped back at him.

"In Berlin?"

"I suppose so."

"I didn't know his name, but he was the same filthy Bolshevik pig who made me watch while his soldiers gang-raped and then murdered my mother. The same filthy Bolshevik pig who laughed in my face when I begged them not to hurt her. The same filthy Bolshevik pig, who mauled at my breasts and put his hand between my legs while he held me there. The same filthy Bolshevik pig who left his animals to defile and murder my mother, while he took me into the next room and raped me. The same filthy Bolshevik pig whose laughing face I can still see, and whose filthy breath and vile stench I can still smell whenever I close my eyes."

She suddenly directed her anger to the old woman.

"You're German. I shouldn't need to tell you. You must have seen enough of them.

"Well, I swore an oath on the grave of my mother, and I swear it again now. I don't give a damn if you think I'm a murdering lunatic bitch. I won't stop and I won't rest. Not until I'm dead, or until I've wiped every single filthy Bolshevik pig from the face of this earth."

A long uncomfortable ten seconds followed, during which nobody spoke.

Hammond didn't quite know what to say. He just knew that he suddenly felt so sorry for her, and, for a reason he didn't fully understand, he also felt ashamed.

The old woman broke the silence. She placed a comforting arm around the girl's shoulders and led her from the table.

"I understand, my dear. We both understand, and we're sorry. Now you're cold, and shivering. Come and sit by the fire, warm yourself while I make some more coffee."

8

Stanislav Paslov was a worried man; not that he advertised the fact. Publicly advertising such insecurity would have been both foolish and dangerous for a man in Paslov's position, and Stanislav Paslov was no fool.

Paslov was a man to instil terror in friend and enemy alike, and panic in all those who considered themselves somewhere between the two. Obeyed without question and avoided if possible, he held the power of life or death over every captive German between Berlin and the Czechoslovakian border. Stanislav Paslov was also a man who had more reason than most to hate those same captive Germans.

Not that Paslov was, at first sight, a striking or imposing individual; all appearance to the contrary. Stanislav Paslov was short and thin, with greying hair, bad skin, and bad teeth, the product of a desperate childhood spent under the yoke of Romanov indifference.

Twenty-five years of personal sacrifice in the Bolshevik cause, topped off by two years of malnutrition and abuse in a Nazi labour camp, had aggravated that earlier decay. However, and despite his lack of immediate presence or stature, Paslov terrified everyone he met, important official and lowest proletarian alike. This was partly due to him being the regional head of state security, and in part because Stanislav Paslov was known to be a close friend of Lavrenti Beria.

It was gone seven when Paslov walked through the door of his Leipzig apartment. He dropped a stack of folders on to the table, and turned to his wife as she came out from the kitchen with his customary evening glass of schnapps.

To those who knew them both, Anna was everything Stanislav was not. She was round and plump, with homely features and soft brown eyes, a gentle and pleasant woman, with a ready smile and a genuine warmth of spirit.

"You are late," she said, then noticed his downcast demeanour. "What is the matter? What is wrong, Stanislav? Tell me."

She passed him his drink, and then brushed his cheek with her hand. He took her hand in his and softly kissed each fingertip in turn. It was a demonstration of affection and gentleness that anyone who knew Comrade Colonel Paslov, the cold and calculating state policeman and infamous public tyrant, would have found hard to believe. But this was the other side of Paslov, the personal and private side. He forced a smile, and shrugged.

"We lost her."

"Lost who? What happened?"

Paslov didn't want to say too much. There was so much about his work he couldn't tell her; so much that was too secret, or too sensitive, or simply too grisly to relate. So much, too, that made him feel ashamed.

"Just a girl who killed some Red Army officers. We were taking her down to Prague by train. Someone helped her to escape, and now we do not know where she is."

Anna stared pointedly at the folders on the table.

"So you think being late is not bad enough? Now you want to ruin what is left of our evening by going through that lot as well."

"I am sorry, Anna, just for an hour or so. It is important. You see, I have to be missing something about this girl and her escape. It has to be something simple, something obvious; it always is. Whoever rescued her was a professional, an American agent, we think, but I cannot understand why they should want her. Now Beria is involved. He telephoned. He wants her found at all costs, but he would not say why. I do not understand why she is so important to him. There has to be something I have missed, something stupidly obvious."

Anna suddenly looked worried.

"Beria?"

"Yes. After sending her down to Prague, I was supposed to send her to him. It was one of his people who told us where she was hiding. Now she has escaped, and he is not happy."

Stanislav Paslov controlled a large section of Soviet-occupied territory with terror and fear, and the proverbial fist of iron. However, inside this particular Leipzig apartment, his wife maintained a similar measure of control, with warmth, and love, and the occasional manufactured frown. He was watching that frown as she said,

"You have forty-five minutes, until dinner is ready; not a second more."

He nodded gratefully. She returned to the kitchen and closed the door. He sat down at the table, opened the first file, and began scanning the documents.

The first showed sketches of a derelict apartment in Berlin, where a Russian army detachment had discovered the mutilated remains of an officer. It provided a copy and translation of some political graffiti found drawn on the wall, and a sketch of a reverse fylfot cross. An attached forensic report confirmed that the killer had used the victim's blood to draw the symbol. It went on to describe the condition of the corpse, and provide drawings of similar crosses carved into the face and torso. At the bottom of the page, a number of other files were referenced. Paslov searched through the pile until he found them.

Each contained reports of unsolved gruesome murders. The first had been committed in Prague, the remaining five in Berlin. Each of the victims had been officers in the Red Army, and each had died under similarly bizarre circumstances.

They had been found naked, bound hand and foot with a woman's silk stockings, their mouths gagged with a pair of silk knickers. In every case, reverse fylfot crosses had been gouged into the face and torso, and the genitals crudely hacked away. The cause of death given was the same in each case: loss of blood, from stab wounds to the jugular veins. Traces of semen and strands of blonde hair had also been found at each of the scenes.

Paslov downed the schnapps. He shuddered as the harshness hit home, and then read on.

No less than seven 'experts' had documented their opinions on the reverse fylfot crosses. Their conclusions ranged from the sign of a Hindu goddess, to all manner of Nazi insignia and trappings of the occult. They had considered geographic origins as diverse as Scandinavia, Central America and the Indian subcontinent. Some claimed the sign to be Pagan, some said it was Runic, others thought Mayan or Celtic. Someone had even suggested medieval witchcraft.

They had seemingly agreed on only one thing. It wasn't an official Nazi-party symbol.

As Paslov studied the sign, he recalled an earlier conversation on the subject of Thor's hammer. One of the 'experts' had claimed it was that, and said the connection between the hammer and the reverse fylfot dated back to medieval Norse and England before Christianity. Norse mythology claimed that Thor's Hammer could strike anywhere, any time, and he never missed his target. That same expert had insisted it was a message to the authorities: there would be more killings, and the killer would strike without warning.

That was when Paslov had headed for home. He'd had enough of 'experts' for one day.

But it still left him with many questions, and no answers. What was the symbol, and what, if anything, did it mean? Was it the sign of some fanatical neo-Nazi group, targeting Red Army officers, or just a haphazard scrawl from the warped mind of a lunatic girl? When he had interviewed the girl she seemed sane enough, and denied any knowledge of the killings. When he showed her the reverse fylfot cross, she shrugged and looked blankly at it. She said she had no idea what it was, but he hadn't believed her then and he still didn't.

He put the reports aside, and worked his way through the stack until he came to the file on the girl. It contained scant information. The profile had her photograph glued to the top. The Soviet authorities had obviously taken the picture when she was in custody. The result did her less than justice. The information gave her full name as Catherine Louise Schmidt, born in Köpenick, Berlin, on May 29, 1928, to parents Joseph Conrad and Marta Alice Schmidt.

Apart from a transcript of Paslov's interview with her, the arrest report, and two witness statements, there was nothing else. The girl had blonde hair and had been detained coming out of the same derelict apartment block in which they'd found the latest victim. Both witnesses identified her as having been with the victim, in a local bar, on the previous night.

During Paslov's interview with her, he had asked about her parents. She said her father had been assassinated in Prague during the war, and her mother had been raped and murdered by Red Army soldiers in Berlin. That offered an obvious motive, but the reason Paslov and the MGB had been called in was not the cross-border murders of Red Army officers, or the alleged Soviet responsibility for the death of the mother.

It had been an early morning call from Lavrenti Beria, telling Paslov about the girl's arrest. Beria had also talked about the identity of her former guardian and, it was rumoured, lover. The man had been a friend of the family and a close colleague of her late father. Following Schmidt's death, he had taken over all espionage activities for the then Reich Protectorate of Bohemia and Moravia. He was Gestapo Kriminaldirektor Martin Kube.

But Kube was now dead. Paslov had no doubt about that, because he and the Smersh teams had located and identified Kube's body in Berlin. According to a note from the records clerk, Lavrenti Beria now held the file on the ex-Gestapo spymaster. However, Paslov still had the file on the father; there might be something in that. He found it at the bottom of the stack.

Documents within the folder affirmed that Oberführer Josef Conrad Schmidt had been an important Nazi during the early years of the war. He would undoubtedly have gone on to greater rank and infamy, had he not been assassinated in central Prague, at four p.m. on May 27, 1942. Eight hours earlier, in a northern suburb of the same city, a bomb thrown into his car had fatally injured Schmidt's close friend and colleague, SS-Obergruppenführer Reinhard Heydrich. Czech resistance fighters, parachuted in by the British, had assassinated Heydrich in the morning and Schmidt in the afternoon. It had been a disastrous day for the Third Reich.

So, Paslov thought, where was the connection and what was the connection? There had to be one. Was the girl part of some fanatical group, left over from the old Prague SS and Gestapo? If so, what group and why her? Her father had been important, but he hadn't been an iconic figure, or someone whose name could be used to rally support. He had just been another ruthless and fanatical SS colonel, and there had been plenty of those.

Paslov moved on. It had to be something connected with Martin Kube. Kube was dead, so why did Beria suddenly need his file? A thought occurred. Perhaps, before he died, Kube had given the girl some of the old Prague espionage network files to look after? Perhaps she still had them? Was that why the Americans had rescued her? Was that why Beria wanted her? It made sense, but where would she have hidden them, assuming they existed?

He shook his head. There was no proof they did. Yet again, he was going around in circles. His wife saved him from any further guesswork and frustration. She came in with a stack of plates and cutlery and told him to get his junk off her table. He didn't argue.

Two minutes later they were sitting at the table, eating their meals, when he suddenly remembered something. In all the commotion over the girl, he had forgotten about it.

"The other day, you asked about Lavrenti; about why we have not seen him for so long."

"Yes, I remember. I was worried that we might have fallen out of favour. You know how easily such things can happen these days. You laughed. You said he was probably just busy."

He nodded, but on this occasion there was no humour in him.

"Yesterday I heard something else, about the weapons the Americans have: the atom bombs. I am told that Stalin has ordered Lavrenti to build the same. He has set a very tight deadline for the first test, and this is now Lavrenti's absolute priority."

"So you were right then; he is busy, but why the sudden panic?"

Paslov tried not to show his concern and scepticism as he answered.

"Stalin believes that only the atom bomb will halt western imperialism and allow our continued expansion."

"But you obviously do not agree?"

Paslov smiled. She knew him too well. He could never fool her. He recalled an earlier time.

"Do you remember that time we went to Kazan, and you first saw the Volga there? You said it was so big, it had to be an ocean?"

Anna smiled and nodded.

"I do not remember saying that, but I do remember the river was impressive."

He ignored her good-humoured denial and pressed his point.

"However vast that expanse of water might seem, it begins life as a simple stream in the Valdai Hills, joining with other rivers that also began their lives as simple streams. Flowing through the wilderness, and turning the arid land fertile as it travels, growing in strength, until it becomes a mighty torrent that carries everything before it and will stop an army in its tracks.

"That was always the ideal of communism, Anna, nourishing minds as it spreads, nurturing and growing until it, too, becomes an unstoppable force.

"You cannot nourish minds with threats and bombs. You can only do such a thing with knowledge and ideas, by convincing others to believe in those things that you believe in."

"And you think Stalin wants to threaten the Americans?"

"I think that one day he will do more than just threaten."

"Go to war with America, you mean? Why would he do such a stupid thing?"

Anna Paslov sat open-mouthed. He met her incredulity with a shrug of resignation.

"Ioseb Vissarionovich runs with the wolves; he always has. He kills sometimes to survive, but mostly he kills because it is in his nature to kill. Now he has tasted the blood of Europe's sheep and he likes it. He thinks the blood of America will taste even sweeter. For now, he lacks the teeth to attack, but in the space of four days last year he saw two bombs turn America from a country fighting an endless war against Japan into the most powerful nation on earth. He imagines how powerful he might become with a hundred such bombs."

"And when he has his hundred atom bombs, then he will attack America?"

"Sooner or later he will summon the courage. It is in the nature of wild animals to attack that which they are afraid of, and he is frightened, Anna. He is terrified. He cannot see that a similar fear is the last thing we should be creating in such a wealthy and powerful nation as America."

"My God! But, can we stop him? Can anyone stop him? What does Beria say?"

"I have not spoken to him yet. I am not supposed to know about this. It is highly secret, but somehow we must find a way to distract Stalin from this foolishness before he destroys us all."

Paslov saw the concern in her and knew he had said too much. He knew his wife as well as she knew him. Anna was such a worrier. Something like this would nag at her. He smiled an apology, hoping to allay her fear and lighten the moment.

"I am sorry, my love. I am getting carried away again. You know how I get. I am just worried about this girl. This business with Stalin and the bombs will probably come to nothing. Things like that usually do."

He got to his feet, headed for the kitchen, and called to her over his shoulder.

"And now, I think, we should open a bottle of wine and relax."

She called back.

"You are just trying to get me drunk, so you can get back to your papers and files."

"Not true." He popped his head around the door, and delighted in the smile that met his suggestion. "I just thought we might have an early night."

9

Hammond heard the commotion outside and hurried to the bedroom window. He stayed hidden behind the curtains and peered into the garden below. Two bedraggled-looking Red Army soldiers had opened the door to the chicken coop and were stealing that morning's eggs. As he watched them taking the eggs he felt anger, but he also felt impotence. The eggs were important, but they weren't important enough to risk giving away their location, and they certainly weren't important enough to risk three lives.

"Those Bolshevik pigs are stealing our eggs."

He heard Catherine Schmidt cry out from the next bedroom. Apparently, she had also seen the two soldiers. Unlike Hammond, she had greeted the sight with all the recklessness of youth. He followed her as she stormed downstairs and into the kitchen, but wasn't quick enough to stop her as she snatched up a carving knife from the dresser.

"If they take the eggs, we will have nothing," she said, marching towards the door.

The old woman called out from where she had been sitting in the rocking chair.

"Catherine, no! Wait!"

She was also too late. In an instant the girl was out of the door. Hammond pulled the automatic and then watched from the kitchen window as she strode towards the soldiers. When they saw her, one of them laughed, and reached out to take the knife. She feigned a thrust, and then suddenly slashed down. The blade cut through the coarse material of his uniform and bit hard into his forearm. He gave a cry and clutched at the wound.

The second soldier was made of sterner stuff. He parried the lunging blade and punched her in the stomach. She squealed and sank to her knees, dropping the knife as she clutched at the pain. The soldier watched dispassionately for a moment, then put his boot against her shoulder and sent her sprawling to the ground.

A few moments later she made a grab for the knife. He had obviously anticipated that. He stamped down on her hand when she reached out, and smiled a smile of malicious triumph when he heard the resulting shriek. Again he shoved her back to the dirt, but this time held her pinned beneath his boot.

With blood seeping from the cut on his arm, the first soldier bent down and picked up the knife. He stood weighing it in his hand and then looked down on her with murder in his eyes.

"You vicious Nazi bitch!"

The second held out a restraining hand.

"No, Comrade, not that. It is only a scratch. You want to kill her for that? Look at her." The wounded soldier stared blankly at his accomplice, who nodded to the pinioned girl. "Look at her face, and her hair. She is beautiful. Look at those tits. See how round and firm they are. I bet those little nipples are like bullets." He hooked his boot under the hem of her skirt and lifted it high. She scrambled to push it back down, while he leered at the momentary exposure and shoved her back to the dirt. "Did you see that? She's young, too, really juicy and tight. So tell me, Comrade, what would you rather do: cut her throat or fuck her?"

The girl struggled and tried to rise, but he held her pinned beneath the sole of his boot, while she loudly cursed him. The two men stood in silence as they watched her struggling and cursing. Then they turned and looked blankly at each other. Then they smiled.

That was when Hammond knew. He would have to kill them both.

The old woman stood in the doorway to the garden. Hammond watched from behind the curtains. He had the HDM and was now checking the load and waiting for the right moment. The distance from the kitchen to where they had the girl pinned to the dirt in front of the chicken coop was more than thirty paces. The soldiers still had their rifles close at hand. He couldn't risk them getting in a shot. He also had to be careful not to hit the girl.

The HDM was a special weapon, but at thirty-odd yards the benefit of silence came at the cost of power. The manufacturers claimed the silencer improved the weapon's accuracy but he had never found that, and hitting two out of three closely grouped and struggling figures from distance was too risky. He would have to wait until their distraction was complete. Then he could move nearer. Then it would be over.

The old woman called out.

"Please, Comrades! She is my granddaughter. Please let her go. She was only trying to save our food. She meant no harm."

They ignored her. It was clear that neither man spoke German. The first soldier threw the kitchen knife to one side and started unbuttoning his slacks. The second grabbed the girl's wrists.

One was kneeling in the dirt now, with his trousers unfastened, carefully avoiding her kicks as he shoved her skirt to the waist and started dragging her knickers down. The other held her arms pinned above her head with one hand, and began separating the fastenings on her jacket with the other.

With the jacket undone, he fondled and mauled, and bent down to kiss her mouth. She turned her head aside, then turned back and spat into his face. She called him a Bolshevik pig and spat again. He wiped away the spittle, slapped her across the face, and called her a bitch. The force of the blow rocked her head to the side, but she immediately turned back to him and bravely spat for a third time. He made to strike her again, but she didn't flinch. He held back the blow and looked to where his comrade was having problems of his own avoiding lunging feet and separating disobedient thighs.

He watched the struggle for a moment and then sneered.

"For the sake of God, get on with it!" He laughed, loudly and artificially. "I tell you, this is a little wildcat we have here, a real little Nazi wildcat. If you ever manage to get her legs apart, she is going to be a fuck to remember. . . and you wanted to cut her throat."

The girl was clearly tiring, her struggles subsiding, her curses falling into silence, and her previous mask of hatred replaced by a look of hopelessness. As one soldier continued to maul and gloat, the other pushed unresisting limbs apart and moved to take his prize.

Hammond heard her groan of despair and watched them closing in for the kill. Their distraction was complete. It was the moment he'd waited for. He inched towards them and levelled the silenced automatic. They would never know what hit them.

But then a voice called out, from somewhere to the side of the house. It startled the two soldiers, and sent Hammond hurrying back into the kitchen.

"What are you men doing?"

The two men heard the voice of authority and instantly released the girl.

"It's Reznikov."

The old woman had obviously recognized the voice. She whispered to Hammond. The name meant nothing to him.

"Who?"

She whispered again.

"Marat Reznikov; the local commissar."

Hammond stayed behind the curtains and watched. Outside, the two soldiers had scrambled to their feet. They stood, hastily refastening their uniforms, as the commissar came into view.

Marat Reznikov was tall and thin, with sallow skin and sunken features. His prematurely-grey hair had been cropped. His eyes were dark and emotionless. He wore a black leather coat and highly-polished black boots. In his right hand he carried a Walther. The protruding indicator pin showed there was a round in the chamber. The safety catch, in the off position, told Hammond that Reznikov was ready to kill.

Catherine Schmidt scrambled to her feet, pulling her knickers up and tugging her skirt down as she rose. The first soldier answered, with a waver in his voice that betrayed the fear.

"She attacked us, Comrade Commissar. She tried to kill us. We were arresting her."

He held out the wounded arm in mute testament. Marat Reznikov smiled coldly.

"Arresting her? And do you always arrest women with your cocks sticking out?"

"No, Comrade."

"Wait there." He stopped speaking and stood silently watching while she refastened her jacket. He spoke to her in German. "And who are you, young fräulein?"

The old woman called out.

"Her name is Ingrid Riefenstahl. She is my granddaughter, Comrade Commissar. She is staying with me for a few days. She meant no harm."

"If she meant no harm, why did she attack these men?"

"They were stealing our eggs. It is all the food we have. She did not understand. She is just a child. I apologize, Comrade Commissar."

Reznikov stared his obvious admiration at the young woman.

"A child she is certainly not."

Catherine Schmidt played her part to perfection. With jacket rebuttoned, she stood brushing away the dirt and looking back at him with an expression that offered a seductive mixture of gratitude and helplessness.

Reznikov held out a hand, and then theatrically led her back to where the old woman stood waiting. As they reached the kitchen doorway, Catherine Schmidt looked up at him with a timid smile on her lips and her eyes held wide.

Like so many before him, Marat Reznikov was instantly and obviously captivated. He smiled back at her, and then left her at the doorway, while he returned to the two men.

"Why were you looting eggs?"

"We were not, Comrade."

"I find this girl lying pinned to the dirt with her knickers down and her legs spread, and you tell me you were not raping. I find the door to the chicken coop open, with the hens clucking and the eggs scattered, and you tell me you were not looting? Do you think me a fool?"

"No, Comrade Commissar."

"This is our country now, and these people are now our comrades. Do you understand? We do not loot any more, and we do not rape any more. I thought I had made that clear."

"Yes, Comrade Commissar."

The two soldiers hung their heads and said nothing further. Hammond knew something of Russian commissars. They were not known for their forgiving natures. Reznikov spoke again.

"Turn around."

Hammond continued watching from behind the curtains, seeing this most real and terrible of dramas being played out before his eyes. Both men obviously knew what was about to happen, but said nothing and did nothing to avoid their fate: no cowering or pleas for leniency, no arguments or attempt at flight. They merely turned around and waited for death, with their limbs trembling and their eyes closed.

Marat Reznikov showed no qualms as he shot each man. No pity, no shame, no disgust, and not the slightest hesitation. He calmly aimed the pistol at the back of each head in turn, and just as calmly pulled the trigger. He didn't look to see the holes he had made in their skulls, or consider the blood and bone and matter that sprayed across the chicken coop. He didn't look to see where they had slumped, or check to ensure their deaths. He simply took each life with no more emotion than he might have shown when wringing the necks of the chickens beyond.

He shoved the pistol back into his coat pocket and casually gestured for his men to remove the bodies. Then he returned to the doorway and spoke to Catherine Schmidt.

"I apologize, fräulein. I hope you will forgive us?"

The old woman looked stunned, but Catherine Schmidt seemed unfazed by the horror. She lowered her gaze as she spoke.

"Of course, Comrade Commissar. I am sure that not all Russian men are like those."

Reznikov gestured disparagingly to the bodies as his men carried them away.

"They were not Russians. They were Mongol scum who disobeyed my orders and disgraced the cause. They were only ever worthy of a single bullet each. Forget them."

He smiled down on her.

"Perhaps I will return tonight, with some more eggs for you. Perhaps some ham and some cheese, too. Would you like that, fräulein?"

She nodded, and smiled a smile of gratitude and promise.

"Yes, Comrade Commissar. Thank you, Comrade Commissar."

Reznikov turned away and started walking back to his car, but then suddenly stopped. He turned back, and called to her.

"Fräulein, what did you say your name was?"

"The old woman seemed to have recovered.

"Her name is Ingrid Riefenstahl, Comrade Commissar. She is my granddaughter."

Marat Reznikov wandered back to the door.

"Perhaps, while I am here, I had better check her papers."

Catherine Schmidt stuttered her answer.

"I, uh, I do not have them."

Anxious at this turn of events, Hammond prepared to intervene. He didn't know how many soldiers were on hand, but there was no way he was going to allow the girl to be taken. Marat Reznikov looked puzzled. The old woman saved the day.

"They were taken two days ago, Comrade Commissar, by the authorities in Wittenberg. Ingrid was on her way here, but they stopped her. They said she looked like someone they were searching for. The officer told her he wanted to check that her papers were not forgeries. I rather think he liked her and wanted an excuse to see her again, but he has not returned the papers. I expect he is very busy."

"This happened in Wittenberg?"

"Yes, Comrade Commissar. Two days ago."

"And who took these papers?"

"Ingrid could not recall his name. She said he was tall handsome man, an officer she thought, with a blue cap. He told her that he would personally return the papers when he had checked them. I expect he will bring them soon. Someone said they knew him. They said he is very important, a Mladshiy Leytenant with the MVD. I think they said he is called Gromyko."

"About thirty years of age?"

He looked hard at Catherine Schmidt. She gazed back at him and nodded.

"I think so, Comrade Commissar."

He smiled a warm and comforting smile, but his eyes remained cold.

"Do not worry, my beautiful little Ingrid. I will go and see Comrade Gromyko and get your papers back. He will not bother you again. You go inside now, and I will visit you later."

Marat Reznikov marched purposefully away. The old woman ushered Catherine Schmidt back into the kitchen. She closed and bolted the door, and then glared at the girl.

"I told you not to show yourself. What in God's name made you do such a stupid thing? You could have got us all killed. When he comes back from Wittenberg, you still might."

Catherine looked contrite.

"I'm sorry, I didn't think. It was stupid of me.

Hammond turned to the old woman.

Who is Gromyko?"

The old woman explained. She said he was based in Wittenberg, and was an arrogant Mladshiy Leytenant with the MVD. She said Gromyko and the sallow-faced Comrade Commissar Marat Reznikov were fierce rivals, and their rivalry was known throughout the Dessau and Wittenberg area. It was also common knowledge that Reznikov had been waiting for a chance to settle his score with Gromyko for some time.

"Great, but now what do we do?"

Catherine had asked the question. Hammond voiced the only obvious solution.

"We get out of here. . . all of us, and quickly."

The old woman moved to the front window, peered around the curtains, and shook her head.

"That won't be easy. He has left a guard outside. Commissar Reznikov is no fool."

Hammond followed her to the window. He peered around the same curtain and studied the guard. The man looked bored, but entirely more capable than the two luckless soldiers who had tried their hand at pillage and rape. He was traipsing back and forth along the front of the house. Every now and then he would disappear for a few seconds, presumably to check the back. Then he would return, and continue the same routine of traipsing back and forth.

Hammond checked the automatic. Catherine Schmidt offered an alternative.

"Perhaps, when the commissar comes back, I could take him upstairs." That familiar look of insanity and hatred returned to her eyes. "He won't come back down again."

Hammond shook his head.

"You won't get the chance. When he finds that you lied to him, he'll be back here with half the Red Army. No, it is best we. . ."

"There is another possibility."

The old woman had interrupted. Hammond stared at her.

"What?"

"It is Monday morning. Reznikov always has breakfast with the Bonhoeffers on Monday mornings. That was where he was going just now."

"So?"

"When he gets to the cottage he sends his bodyguards back to headquarters. After breakfast he sits and drinks coffee. Then he makes Franz wait outside while he takes Hedda upstairs."

"This Franz and Hedda; they are husband and wife?"

The old woman nodded.

"Franz either does as Reznikov tells him or he goes to a Siberian Gulag, and then what would happen to Hedda and the child? He has no choice, neither does she."

"Charming man, your Comrade Commissar Reznikov."

Hammond had intended the sarcasm as flippant, but there was a fury in the old woman he'd not seen before.

"Reznikov does the same with other women in Dessau and Rosslau. He has a rota. On Monday the baker's shop closes, and so it is poor Hedda's turn. Reznikov thinks, because the women are too afraid to resist, it does not count as rape. He is a pig, and a hypocrite, and a killer, but he is also very powerful."

Hammond was considering a possibility.

"Where do these people live, this Franz and Hedda whatever their name is?"

"Bonhoeffer. They live just a few meters down the road, in the cottage next to the baker's shop. Franz bakes. Hedda works in the shop. She gives me bread in exchange for a few eggs, and sometimes talks to me about it. Poor woman, she has to talk to someone."

"Will Reznikov be there now?"

"I would think so. He likes to take his time. Hedda is an attractive woman, and he enjoys tormenting Franz. Hedda thinks Reznikov enjoys the thought of Franz listening and waiting outside almost as much as he enjoys the disgusting things he does to her. Anyway, you will know if Reznikov is there. He always leaves his car behind the cottage so nobody can see."

For the umpteenth time that morning, Hammond readied the HDM.

"I'll need a distraction; for the guard outside."

"I'll do it."

The girl had volunteered. He shook his head.

"No, I don't want any more incidents. You seem to have an effect on Russian men."

She laughed and pouted, seemingly recovered from her ordeal.

"Not just Russian men."

Hammond didn't smile back.

"You stay here. Keep out of the way." He nodded to the old woman. "Take the guard some coffee. Keep him at the front of the house for a few minutes. I'll slip out back and work my way down to the cottage."

The old woman voiced her concern.

"You mustn't do it there; not inside the cottage. It is too close, and Franz and Hedda are good people. We don't want to get them into trouble."

Hammond nodded. If things went according to plan, he wouldn't need to involve them.

I'll do what I can."

The old woman headed to the front door, carrying a mug of hot coffee for the guard. Hammond smiled a parting reassurance at an uncertain-looking Catherine Schmidt. Then he slipped out of the back door and went to find the Bonhoeffer's cottage.

10

Hammond could see Reznikov's car. He had left it parked in the shade, under a tree at the back of the cottage, but there was no sign of its terrifying driver. Nor was there any sign of the unfortunate Bonhoeffer family.

The Commissar's car was an old and heavily-rusted Fiat 508 Torpedo, one of thousands that had flooded into Germany from the Italian company's pre-war manufacturing plant in Poland. It wasn't the prettiest of cars, but it boasted four seats and that was ideal for Hammond's purpose.

He smiled to himself as he eased open the rear offside door. The all-powerful Comrade Commissar Marat Reznikov obviously didn't expect anyone would be bold enough or foolish enough to steal his prized possession. Hammond squeezed into the foot well, behind the front passenger seat, and carefully pulled the door to. Despite his best efforts to muffle the sound, it closed with an audible click. He sat unmoving, with the automatic ready and the suppressor fitted, waiting to see if anyone in the cottage had heard.

A few heart-thumping moments passed without anyone stirring, and so he made himself comfortable and sat quietly waiting for Reznikov's return.

An hour passed before the door to the cottage opened. A pale and unhappy-looking man came out. Hammond assumed it was Franz Bonhoeffer. Upstairs the bedroom window opened and a gloating Marat Reznikov smiled down. The man didn't look up at the window. He lit a cigarette and hung his head in obvious shame and desolation.

Then a woman appeared and stood framed in the open window, a striking woman, dressed in a crimson negligee. She was trembling and looked pale and drawn. Her eyes stared blankly out, unseeing and unfeeling. Her lips offered only silence. Marat Reznikov stood behind her, looking over her shoulder and stroking at her hair. He smiled down on the man below.

"Comrade Bonhoeffer. Look. Look at your beautiful wife. See what I have bought for her. You see how generous I am. Do you like the colour? It is red, Comrade, the colour of a patriot." He paused, before adding, "Or the colour of a whore." He stopped stroking and grabbed a handful of hair, then dragged her head back until her eyes were directly opposite his. "So tell me. What are you, my beautiful Hedda? Are you a patriot, or are you a whore?"

Hedda Bonhoeffer made no attempt to push him away or protest. She stared straight through the sadistic smile with unseeing eyes and answered his question in a monotone voice.

"I am both, Comrade Commissar."

The sadistic smile didn't waver.

"You know, I think you may well be at that." Reznikov returned his attention to the figure of Franz Bonhoeffer. "Are you pleased with my gift? Does your wife not look wonderful in it? Well, answer me, Comrade. Does she not look wonderful?"

Franz Bonhoeffer looked despairingly up at his wife.

"Yes, Comrade Commissar. She is a beautiful and wonderful woman."

Marat Reznikov clearly wasn't finished with his sadism.

"Perhaps, if she has anything left to give when I have finished, she will wear it for you. I give her my permission. Would you like that, Comrade Bonhoeffer?"

"Yes, Comrade Commissar."

"But now she has other, more pressing, duties to perform."

Hedda Bonhoeffer gave an involuntary cry of shame and shock as Reznikov suddenly dragged her away from the open window, but it was her only utterance.

From within the shadows of the car, Hammond watched Franz Bonhoeffer look up in alarm, then slowly bow his head as the rhythm of the bedsprings and Reznikov's grunts of animal satisfaction flowed through the open window to puncture the morning's stillness.

As he listened to the continuing shame of Hedda Bonhoeffer and saw the tears streaming down her husband's face, Hammond felt acute sorrow. He would enjoy settling their score with Reznikov.

Bonhoeffer remained like that for some time, listening to Reznikov's animal grunts and crude commentary with his head bowed and the tears streaming.

But then the tears stopped.

He hurried to the lean-to shed beside the back door and rummaged through it for a few moments. When he reappeared he was clutching an old and heavy claw hammer.

Hammond watched the agitated Franz Bonhoeffer with hammer in hand. He obviously intended confronting the commissar and avenging the family's shame. He was now standing to the side of the back door, presumably waiting for Reznikov to appear.

Gerald Hammond shook his head in silent condemnation of Bonhoeffer's foolishness. He didn't have a chance. From the little Hammond had seen earlier, Marat Reznikov was an expert killer. He would be prepared for such an obvious attempt at retribution. Franz Bonhoeffer would be no match for an accomplished killer. If Bonhoeffer tried to use that hammer, there could only be one outcome. Reznikov would kill him.

Hammond couldn't let that happen.

Almost forty minutes had passed and the commissar still hadn't appeared in the doorway. On two occasions Bonhoeffer had put the hammer down. On two occasions he had picked it up again. He was putting the hammer down for a third time, when a voice called to him.

"I do hope you intend repairing the fence with that, Comrade Bonhoeffer. If not, I could be forced to shoot you."

The brutal and devious Reznikov had obviously seen Bonhoeffer's indecision from the window above. He must have left the cottage through the front door, and then slipped along the side of the building. He now stood with the Walther in his hand, smiling unpleasantly as he watched the surprise and fear on Franz Bonhoeffer's face.

Marat Reznikov had clearly anticipated Bonhoeffer's feeble attempt at retribution. What he, equally clearly, had not anticipated was the presence of Hammond and a tactical brain that was every bit as devious as his own. On realizing Bonhoeffer's intent, Hammond had left the car and slowly worked his way through the shrubbery. He now stood behind the commissar.

"And I could be forced to shoot you, Comrade Commissar, unless you put the gun down."

Reznikov stayed absolutely still, but kept hold of the Walther.

"And if I choose not to do that?"

"That would be a mistake, Comrade. I have no desire to kill you, but I assure you I will if you do not do exactly as I say."

Reznikov slowly turned his head to see the HDM and assess the man holding it. He shrugged and nodded, and allowed the Walther to fall from his grasp.

"It seems you have the advantage of me."

"And the second gun, Commissar."

"I do not have a second gun."

"Of course you do, Commissar. It is the one that makes an even bigger bulge in your left pocket than the Walther did in your right. Take it out, very carefully and very slowly, and drop it to the ground."

Moments later, the bulkier Tokarev had followed the pocket-sized Walther to the ground. Hammond glanced to where a bewildered Franz Bonhoeffer stood, claw-hammer still in hand.

"Herr Bonhoeffer. Would you mind picking up the commissar's guns for me?"

Franz Bonhoeffer let the hammer slide from his hand. When he shuffled over to collect the automatics, Reznikov sneered at him.

"Comrade Bonhoeffer, if you help this killer in any way, I promise you that when I have dealt with him, as I surely will, I will then deal with you and your wife and child."

Bonhoeffer collected the automatics and then levelled the Tokarev.

"You will not touch my son. Do you hear me, Reznikov? And you will never touch my wife again. If you ever do, I will kill you."

Marat Reznikov studied the levelled automatic and answered disdainfully.

"I think not. You see, you are not a killer, Comrade Bonhoeffer. I know this, because I am a killer, and I can tell the difference." He gestured behind him, to where Hammond stood quietly watching. "Now, he is different. Look at him, Comrade. He is a killer, and he is a good one, but you. . ." Reznikov shook his head slowly and exaggeratedly as he continued to goad. "You are a coward, and a cuckold, and a poor excuse for a man, but you are not a killer." He paused again, before adding, "You are also a fool if you think the beautiful Hedda does not yearn for the feel of my cock throbbing inside her whenever she is required to accommodate yours."

Whatever else Marat Reznikov might be, he was certainly not a coward. He watched the rage build in Franz Bonhoeffer and sneered again.

"The safety catch is still on, Comrade. If you want to shoot me you will have to release it first. But you do not want to shoot me, do you, Comrade? You do not want to shoot me, because you do not have the courage."

Gerald Hammond watched the rage in Franz Bonhoeffer, and saw him scrambling to release the safety. He didn't believe Bonhoeffer would fire, but couldn't take the risk. He stepped forward and brought the HDM down hard on the side of Reznikov's neck. The commissar slumped to the ground and lay unmoving.

Bonhoeffer's shaking hands stopped trying to release the safety and allowed the weapon to slip to the ground. Then he looked back at Hammond and confessed.

"He is right. I do not have the courage. I never did. Even in the war, I would aim high."

Hammond bent down to collect the fallen automatics and smiled benevolently at Franz Bonhoeffer as he picked them up.

"So did most soldiers, Herr Bonhoeffer, but do not tell the generals. It would break their hearts. You are not alone in not wanting to kill. Very few wanted to kill, other than in self-defence, but never think that you do not have courage. Yours is a different kind of courage. It is the courage that raises a family and puts their welfare ahead of selfish pride and revenge. You must be proud of that, Herr Bonhoeffer; it is a more worthy courage. Never be ashamed that you do not want to kill."

****

Gerald Hammond sat quietly in the back of the Fiat while he waited for Marat Reznikov to fully regain consciousness. He had placed the commissar in the driver's seat and left the key in the ignition, then doused him with cold water and slapped him back to semi-consciousness.

Earlier, he had told Bonhoeffer to go inside and comfort his wife, explaining that he would deal with Reznikov, and they shouldn't worry. If anyone asked, Bonhoeffer was to tell them that Reznikov had left that morning. Bonhoeffer had listened intently, then nodded and hurried inside.

Reznikov groaned a little and rubbed at his head as full consciousness returned. A sixth sense must have told him, because he turned around to look at Hammond. From there, his eyes looked down. He studied the HDM and nodded sagely.

"I knew you were a killer. What is it you want?"

"I want you to drive, Commissar, very carefully to the road and then turn left. You will not drive too quickly or too slowly. When you reach the guard outside the old guesthouse at the end of the road, you will stop on the opposite side of the road and call to him. You will tell him the papers belonging to the girl are in order, and she is not the one they are looking for. You will then tell him that you are going to Rosslau, and he must return to headquarters immediately.

"If you do exactly as I tell you, Commissar, I will let you live. If you do anything else, or say anything else, or try to warn the guard in any way, I will kill him, and I will kill you. Do you understand?"

Hammond watched the eyes suddenly widen into understanding.

"Ah, of course, the girl at the guesthouse. I should have known she was the one."

"Time to go, Commissar."

Reznikov shook his head and sat unmoving.

"You think I am a fool. When I have dispatched the guard you will kill me. You have no choice. If you do not, the moment I am free I will deal with the Bonhoeffers and the old woman. You have to realize that?"

It was Hammond's turn to shake his head.

114

"Not if you understand that I will make it known to Comrade Colonel Paslov and Comrade Deputy Premier Beria how your incompetence and lust allowed us to escape. Not only allowed us to escape, but also provided us with this vehicle, safe passage and weapons."

The laughter in his voice fell away.

"And I will tell them, Comrade, if any harm comes to the Bonhoeffers or the old woman." He watched Reznikov frown. "You were wrong when you called me a killer, Comrade. I only kill when it is necessary, when there is no other way. Fortunately, for you, there is another way. Now drive, and if you want to live you will remember what I have said."

Despite his predicament, the familiar sneer had returned to Marat Reznikov's face.

"I will never understand the squeamishness of you Americans. That is what will ultimately defeat you, and all your money, not your decadence, or even your imperialist ambition. You will fail because you value life too highly."

Hammond shrugged.

"I think that is enough of the speeches, Commissar. Now drive."

As they passed the back of the cottage, Hammond looked up at the window. Bonhoeffer had draped a blanket around his wife's shoulders. Both stood at the window looking down. Bonhoeffer nodded his gratitude. Hedda Bonhoeffer showed no emotion of any kind; no joy or relief, no hatred, no fear. She looked back at Hammond with hollow eyes that showed nothing of whatever trauma lay within.

Hammond and Reznikov left the cottage and headed towards the guesthouse, with Hammond holding the HDM, and Reznikov driving. On nearing the guesthouse, Hammond left the seat, crouched low in the foot well, and cautioned him again.

"Do not let the guard approach the car. Tell him there is no further need to stay here. You have checked the girl's papers, and they are in order. Tell him to get back to barracks. Say you are going to Rosslau and will be some time. And remember, Commissar: no signals, no coded messages. Just tell him exactly what I have told you and then drive on."

"And I have your word that if I do that I will live?"

"Yes."

The meeting with the guard proved anticlimactic. Reznikov recited the words. The guard simply nodded and saluted, and then wandered off down the road and back to barracks. Reznikov drove on, heading farther north, toward Rosslau and the main crossing of the river Elbe. As they neared the bridge, Hammond told him to stop.

Reznikov drew the car to a halt on the up-ramp. He turned off the ignition, looked apprehensively down at the steep slope to the river below, and sneered at Hammond.

"The end of our journey together, I presume."

Hammond looked back at him.

"You knew?" Reznikov slowly nodded. Hammond had to ask the question. "If you knew, why did you do as I ordered?"

Marat Reznikov turned to look at him.

"You are undoubtedly a killer, Comrade, no matter how much you might protest the description. You see, as I said to Bonhoeffer, I can tell these things. And, when we meet again in hell, you will know I was right."

"You have not answered my question."

Reznikov gave a cynical smile and then turned back to look at the road ahead as he spoke.

"There was always a chance that you might also be stupid. . . Unfortunately for me, you are obviously not." He placed two hands on the steering wheel and braced himself for the impact. "Well, come along, Comrade. Am I not also worthy of a single bullet?"

Hammond hit him, hard across the back of the neck, and then spoke quietly as Reznikov slumped against the steering wheel.

"No, Comrade Commissar Reznikov. You were worthy of much more."

Hammond replaced the pistols in Reznikov's pockets and then slipped the Fiat's handbrake. He pushed and steered the car over the edge of the ramp, then stood back and watched it rolling towards the water, lurching and creaking and gathering speed as it hurtled down the slope. Seconds later, the rusted Torpedo hit the swollen river with a crash. It floated downstream for a few meters, before slowly disappearing beneath the surface.

He reasoned that, when and if the Soviets found the car, they would assume Reznikov had lost control and drowned, or at least before an autopsy proved otherwise. If they somehow found the car early on, the lack of any obvious foul play would allow Hammond the time he needed. With Soviet troops still combing the countryside, the more time he could buy, the longer they could stay hidden, and the better their chances of reaching the American sector.

He stood watching the river for a while longer, confirming that his lethal skills were still as lethal, and there had been no miraculous last-minute reprieve for Marat Reznikov.

The river remained cold and dark, its terrible secret hidden below the surface.

As Hammond watched the water flowing by, he again found himself thinking about Rouen. He wondered why it was always Rouen that haunted him, more than any other mission. Perhaps it was the obscene number of lives he had taken that night. Perhaps it was the cold-bloodedness and sheer savagery of the taking. Perhaps it was the faces of the victims; so many faces. . . slumbering faces, bewildered faces, disoriented faces, faces with unseeing eyes and minds dulled by sleep, faces of alarm, faces of panic, faces of entreatment, faces of dread.

His mind wandered on, as it so often did, to all the other violent deaths he had occasioned in the name of freedom or patriotism or duty.

Then he thought about Marat Reznikov's words, and knew the truth of them.

When Hammond finally turned away and began making his way back to the guesthouse, he also thought about the man he had just killed.

Comrade Commissar Marat Reznikov had been a bully and a hypocrite, a rapist, a sadist, and a cold-blooded killer, but he had also been one of the bravest men Hammond had ever known.

11

"Mr Carpenter, is it? Mr Davis Carpenter?"

Davis Carpenter had been on his way to work. He was standing at the corner of Massachusetts and 18th Street, about to thread his way through the jostling Washington rush-hour traffic, when the sudden enquiry disturbed his concentration. He stopped and turned in bland anticipation, but made no effort to disguise his disappointment as he surveyed the frail and dishevelled figure of an elderly man.

Dressed in a shabby raincoat, the old man was unshaven and unkempt. Brown corduroy trousers hung heavy on spindly legs, before slumping into further unkemptness over the top of scuffed brown leather brogues. He stared back at Carpenter through blue-grey eyes that offered little relief to nondescript features, and less to a grey complexion. Skeletal fingers suddenly appeared from the raincoat's right-hand pocket. They politely tipped the brim of a spotless black homburg, an item of apparel that appeared entirely incongruous.

"Yes?"

Carpenter had snapped the syllable. The elderly man answered politely.

"I'm sorry, but I've been waiting to see you for over a week now. You're always so busy. I thought I would try to gain a few moments of your time before work. My name is Schulman, Alfred Schulman. I work with a man called Wiesenthal, in Linz. Simon Wiesenthal? Perhaps you have heard of him?"

"No."

"That surprises me, Mr Carpenter, because we are working closely with members of your U.S. Army in Linz, gathering evidence on Nazi war criminals. Are you sure you've not heard of him?"

Davis Carpenter made no effort to disguise his hostility.

"No, I can't say I have, but I do recall my secretary mentioning your name. I also recall telling her to tell you that if you and Mr Wiesenthal are looking for Nazi fugitives in the United States, you should be talking to the FBI. It was my understanding that she subsequently passed that message to you?"

The old man smiled ruefully.

"Oh, she did indeed, but somehow I did not believe her then, any more than I believe you now. Oh no, Mr Carpenter, something tells me I'm talking to the right man."

"I'm sorry?"

"You see, Mr Carpenter, if for some reason I wanted to find communist agents hiding in Washington suburbs, I would go and talk to Mr Hoover's men, but I am not. I am looking for ex-Nazis, hiding right here in the Washington government, and so I have come to you."

"But I can't help you, Mr Schulman. All I can suggest is that you do as I first encouraged you to do, and talk to the FBI."

Davis Carpenter turned and hurried across the busy street. He dodged two cars and a speeding taxi before reaching the other side, then turned back to see Schulman wearing a sardonic smile and watching him from the safety of the opposite sidewalk. The smile faded as the old man said something, but Carpenter couldn't hear what.

****

It was just gone six that same evening. Davis Carpenter had been travelling in the opposite direction, about to negotiate the same crowded thoroughfare, when the old man reappeared.

"Mr Carpenter. I do need to speak to you."

Carpenter turned and glared, and then spoke in a voice heavily laced with exasperation.

"I believe I already told you, Mr Schulman. Talk to the FBI. I'm not the right person. I'm just a minor State Department official."

The same sardonic smile relieved whiskered features.

"Oh, I think you are being modest, Mr Carpenter. I think you are far more important than that.

"You see, I need answers, Mr Carpenter, and so I intend stopping you every morning and every evening until you find time to speak to me. Or perhaps I should be talking to Mr Carlisle or Mr Allum?"

Davis Carpenter listened to the names of his superiors at the Office of Occupied Territories and realised the old man's persistence was a product of knowledge and not chance.

"And if I do find the time to speak to you? Will you then leave me in peace?"

"You have my word."

"Come to my office, tomorrow at ten. Now, if you'll excuse me, I'd like to get home."

"Thank you. I will be there at ten precisely. Have a pleasant evening, Mr Carpenter."

Carpenter nodded, and made his way across the busy street. When he reached the opposite sidewalk he stopped and looked back, but the old man was nowhere to be seen. He continued scanning, while his mind turned over the many possible reasons for the old man's persistence.

Carpenter was still thinking about that as he climbed the stairs to his second-floor apartment in Woodley Park. He opened the door, took off his hat and coat and hung them in the hallway. Then he wandered into the kitchen, mumbled a perfunctory 'hello darling', and dutifully kissed an unsmiling wife on the cheek.

Davis Carpenter wasn't surprised to see his wife looking unhappy. Clara Carpenter had felt and looked that way for almost seven years. He'd always known that she had never truly loved him, but seven years ago she had pretended to and that had been enough. In those days he had bought her affection, with jewellery and expensive vacations, and she pretended it was him and not the money that she loved. But those days were gone.

Carpenter could remember the exact time and day that Clara had stopped pretending. It had been 6.30 p.m. on the 3rd September 1939, when he returned from work and told her that Britain and France had declared war on Germany. That was the day his overseas investments crashed. That was the day the money ran out.

He walked into the lounge, sat down in his favourite armchair and began reading the evening paper, as he always did. This evening, though, a jumble of thoughts disturbed his routine. He allowed the paper to fall to his lap, and stared at the wallpaper in unfocused reminiscence. Newspaper headlines held no interest for Davis Carpenter that evening, because he couldn't get the memory of that frail old man out of his mind. Nor could he clear his mind of all those painful memories the old man's sudden appearance had evoked.

For some minutes after that, he continued to sit and stare blankly into space; recalling the old man's frailty and dogged determination, while so many terrible images of the Holocaust invaded his mind. He remembered the film, so damningly shown at the ongoing Nuremburg tribunals, with graphic evidence of genocide, and pictures of the aftermath's horror that would forever shame a nation.

They were pictures of mass graves, and the tangled remains of countless women and children and old men, all haphazardly piled into sickening mountains of tragic humanity. They were pictures of emaciated human skeletons, still somehow clinging to life and staring back at the cameras insensitivity in bewilderment and gratitude. They were pictures of unspeakable horror, and the monumental suffering of an entire human race, a suffering beyond the belief of those who had not shared in the grief or lived through the abomination. They were pictures so graphically shocking they brought disgust and revulsion to the very soul of humanity.

"Davis, are you listening to me? I said, get that, will you?"

There had been a knock at the door. Carpenter had been so preoccupied it hadn't registered, until his wife hollered at him. Her voice dismissed the images and interrupted his thoughts. For that he was grateful. He strode to the door, grumbling about needing some peace after a long day at the office, then slipped the chain and opened it, only to find the same incongruous homburg and whiskered features that had been uppermost in his thoughts just seconds earlier.

"Mr Schulman, you have to stop this. This is my home. This is not the way we conduct ourselves in America. I thought we had made an appointment for tomorrow morning."

"Oh we did, Mr Carpenter, and that was most kind, but then I thought. Do I really want to talk to a senior State Department official who will give me a brief five minutes of official policy before showing me the door? Would it not be better to get away from shabby politics, meaningless rhetoric, and uncaring government protocols?"

The old man shrugged and smiled.

"That was when I decided to talk to Davis Carpenter, an ordinary decent human being, relaxing at home with his lovely wife. That was when I decided not to talk to an important senior government official at the all-powerful State Department."

Carpenter wearily nodded.

"I can see the reasoning, Mr Schulman, but it has been a long day, and. . ."

"You said that you had not heard of a man named Wiesenthal, Mr Carpenter. I suppose there is no reason why you should, but have you ever heard of Mauthausen?"

Carpenter breathed a heavy sigh of exasperation.

"I believe so, yes. A Nazi labour camp, wasn't it? Look, I don't see what any of this has to do with me or my department. As I said before. . ."

"It was a death camp, Mr Carpenter. In fact it was worse than that. It was the death camp where they sent all those hundreds of thousands of innocent people they had somehow failed to murder in all those other death camps.

"I was there, you see, with Wiesenthal. We were two of the lucky ones, we survived. So many others did not. But now it is time for the guilty to pay for their crimes. Now it is the turn of all those millions of innocents who lie in anonymous graves, faceless and nameless and forgotten by the world. Now it is their time for justice."

Carpenter quipped back, largely to combat an uncharacteristic sense of shame.

"But Mr Schulman, you must believe in justice and retribution through Almighty God, on the final day, on the day of reckoning? Shouldn't you be leaving such vengeance to God, rather than taking justice into your own hands, vengeance is mine and all that?"

The old man shook his head.

"Mr Carpenter, I believe it is only through mankind that we meet God's justice on earth, and yes, of course I pray to him, I pray to him every day. But when you have lived on this earth for as long as I, and when you have seen the many horrors that I have seen, you do not pray to God for justice and retribution. You pray only for his existence."

An overwhelming sense of guilt engulfed Davis Carpenter as he studied the whiskered features and listened to Alfred Schulman speaking with such passion. It was a passion all the more intense for the old man's frailty, using words all the more powerful for the suffering they described. More images of the Holocaust invaded his thoughts. He placed a comforting hand on the old man's shoulder.

"Look, I'm so sorry. I know it must have been terrible. I sympathize with you, but I just don't see what I can do to help you."

"Davis, you do know your dinner's spoiling?"

An angry wife had appeared from the kitchen. Carpenter immediately pulled back his hand. The momentary weakness had passed.

"Look, Mr Schulman, the war's over. America spent hundreds of billions of dollars, and hundreds of thousands of lives, making sure the Nazis didn't succeed, but now it's over and we must all move on. I can understand how you can never forget, but if we cannot forget, then we must all somehow try to forgive. I'm sorry if that seems like a meaningless cliché, but I can't help you. I'm not the right man. I'm sorry."

He backed away and began to close the door, but the old man moved with a speed that belied the frail appearance. He placed his foot against the door and glared as he spoke.

"I'm sorry, too, Mr Carpenter, about your dinner spoiling, but I was wondering if you would like to tell me about Camp King? I know you were there a few days ago. Perhaps you would like to tell me what you were doing, in a place that doesn't officially exist? Perhaps you could also tell me who it was you met when you were there?"

"I'm sorry, I don't know what. . ."

"Was it Heinrich Müeller, Mr Carpenter, or was it one of his vile henchmen? Is Müeller working for you now, Mr Carpenter?"

At the mention of Camp King, Carpenter had listened nervously. Few people in America had ever heard of the place; fewer still understood its purpose. But when the elderly Jew mentioned Heinrich Müeller, Davis Carpenter, hugely relieved, suddenly laughed.

"Heinrich Müeller? I take it you are referring to the former head of Section Four of Reich security, the former head of the Gestapo?"

The old man looked confused. A suddenly more recognizable and supercilious Davis Carpenter theatrically shook his head as he dropped the bombshell.

"I'm sorry to have to tell you this, but you've had a wasted journey, my friend. I don't know who told you that I'd been to Camp King to see Müeller, but I would have strong words with your informant if I were you.

"You see, you've come to the wrong town in the wrong country, Mr Schulman. You should be knocking on the door of a man called Lavrenti Beria. He's the new Russian Deputy Premier, and Joseph Stalin's overall head of espionage and terror. You will find him in Dzerzhinsky Square, not far from Red Square in the centre of Moscow. His office is on the third floor of a large yellow-brick building called the Lubyanka. You see, Mr Schulman, Heinrich Müeller works for Lavrenti Beria, and has done for some months."

12

Stanislav Paslov listened as his wife answered a knock at the door.

"Comrade Deputy Premier Beria, you honour us."

"Anna, Anna, why so formal? Are we not old friends?"

Paslov remained in the lounge of his Leipzig apartment, listening intently as Anna finished greeting their unexpected guest.

"Of course we are old friends, Lavrenti. I apologize, but you are now such an important man, I did not want to appear presumptuous. Tell me, how is Nina? Is she well?"

"Fine, fine. I will tell her you asked."

Stanislav Paslov's thoughts raced as he switched off his music and stood waiting for his guest. For Beria to leave the security of Moscow was unusual. For him to travel to occupied Germany with no more than a few bodyguards was unheard of. As Beria wandered into the room, Paslov saw his eyes flicker left and right, missing nothing in that one brief scrutiny

In many ways, Lavrenti Beria reminded Paslov of the late and unlamented Heinrich Himmler: the shortness of stature and humourless peasant features, the pale complexion and receding hairline. Beria's soft damp handshake, and Himmler's general clamminess. The Mingrelian's bulging-eyed stare, enlarged through round pince-nez eye-glasses, and the Bavarian's cold-eyed stare, magnified by thick round granny-glasses. The Uriah Heep obsequiousness of Beria, and inoffensive facade of Himmler. It all served to further the resemblance and belie the brutality of genuine monsters.

But there was more to the comparison than mere appearance, because each man's infamy lay in the brutal suppression of totalitarian states, and the personal security of paranoid, mass-murdering tyrants. Both held the sanctity of human life in contempt, and permeated an aura of fear that enveloped any who approached or dealt with them.

"Stanislav, it is good to see you again. How are you, my old friend? Was that Berlioz I heard just now?"

"A minor excess, Comrade, 'La Damnation de Faust'. It is an inoffensive piece, and we are after all in Leipzig."

Lavrenti Beria was obviously unaware of the connection. That didn't surprise Paslov. Beria must have seen the record sleeve when he arrived, because he wouldn't know Berlioz from Bach, and he certainly would never have heard of Goethe. Paslov dismissed the music's insignificance with a wave of his hand and smiled as he greeted his old comrade.

"It is good to see you again, Comrade."

Paslov waited until Anna had left and closed the door behind her before asking,

"So why are you here, Lavrenti? Is it to share a glass of wine and talk of the old days? Or is it to tell me you have a new master for me, one I might resent, and to assess my loyalty?"

Beria looked puzzled.

"I do not understand you, Stanislav. Who do you mean?"

Paslov allowed the fury to explode.

"Müller!" he roared. "Heinrich Müller. How could you ever employ such scum?"

The look graduated from puzzlement to perplexity.

"I take it you are referring to the Heinrich Müller, the head of the Nazi Gestapo?"

"You know I am."

"But I thought the Americans recruited Müller: the U.S. Army, they say."

Paslov was too angry to play games. He, nonetheless, chose his words carefully.

"Lavrenti, we have not always agreed, but we have never lied to each other."

Beria held no scruples, and would lie without conscience. Paslov knew that, but he also knew that Beria held their friendship in high regard. The Mingrelian returned his stare for a few seconds, before abandoning the façade and confirming the truth.

"Stanislav, Heinrich Müeller's recruitment is an important state secret. The Americans still believe he is assisting them. I have to know how you discovered this information. I have to know who else is aware of it."

In contrast to Beria's caution, Paslov's answered without hesitation. He said a friend in America had sent him a telegraph. The American army may still believe that Müeller was helping them, but the U.S. State Department knew all about the double-dealings of Beria's new Nazi lapdog. Davis Carpenter had told his friend about Müeller's defection. His friend had asked Paslov to help bring him to justice.

Beria good-humouredly chided him, but there was an undercurrent of anger in his tone that didn't go unnoticed.

"So, you have friends in America now, Stanislav. Are you sure that such liaisons are wise?"

Paslov spoke fondly of Alfred Schulman. He said Schulman was working to expose Nazi war criminals hiding in America. Schulman had nothing to do with the American government. He worked with Wiesenthal in Linz.

"You surprise me, Stanislav. Here I find you listening to decadent music and boasting of Zionist friends in America. I think it at best imprudent, and at worst foolhardy."

Paslov refused to be goaded. He said he and Schulman had been together in the concentration camp at Mauthausen. Schulman had saved his life many times, just as he had saved Schulman's. Schulman was a good man and a good friend, and Paslov was similar to Beria. He did not betray his friends.

It was a crude and obvious compliment. With the notable exception of Stanislav Paslov, Lavrenti Beria had no friends, and both men knew it.

Beria came back at him with the party line. He said the time may come when Paslov would have no choice; it was his duty to denounce those who pollute Russia, irrespective of blood or friendship. He added that many believed the betrayal of family and friends to be a measure of trust, but then made a throwaway gesture, slumped into an armchair, and lit a cigarette.

Paslov refused to let the matter to drop.

"Lavrenti, this man is a Nazi, an enemy of the people, and a mass murderer of Bolsheviks. How could you do this?"

Paslov watched as the dark eyes chilled and the peasant features contorted into aggression.

"Stanislav, the next time you communicate with your Zionist friends in Washington, perhaps you would do something for me. Perhaps you would ask them to tell you the whereabouts of Reinhard Gehlen, and Martin Kube and, for all I know, Josef Mengele and Martin Borman."

Paslov listened to the names and instantly recalled the faces from the hundreds of photographs that had once decorated his office wall. All but a few were dead, assigned to rightful places in hell, or so he'd thought. He spluttered his confusion.

He knew about Reinhard Gehlen, but Kube was dead. He couldn't say what had happened to Borman and Mengele, but he did know about the old

Prague SS and Gestapo hierarchy. They were all dead. He and the Smersh teams had found and then burned their bodies.

Beria shook his head. He said these Nazi criminals had fooled both Paslov and the Smersh teams. Many were now working for the Americans or British, some for both.

Paslov suddenly saw the pieces falling into place. Kube had been Catherine Schmidt's guardian. Many claimed he was her lover. He asked if Kube was behind her escape.

Beria seemed weary. Did he need to answer that? Of course that was the reason. Kube was working for the Americans. Part of the agreement obviously involved them rescuing his murdering teenage whore. Paslov had missed it all. He had allowed Kube to slip through his fingers like rain through a grate. Now he had even let this slip of a girl evade him. Some would not think it wise that a man such as Paslov sat listening to decadent music and communicating with Zionist friends in America, while the Soviet Union's enemies roamed free.

Paslov, defensive, argued back. He spoke of the war's immediate aftermath, and accused Beria of pulling the Smersh teams back to Moscow before they had finished. Perhaps, if Beria had allowed them to finish their investigations, this would not have happened.

"I did nothing of the kind. Stalin demanded their recall. Their incompetence and failure to identify even Hitler's body made us look like fools. I merely passed on his orders."

Beria made a visible effort to compose himself. He said he didn't blame Paslov; it had been a fraught and difficult time, with death and confusion everywhere. For once their normally-reliable Smersh teams had failed. He asked about the search for Catherine Schmidt.

"And so, have you managed to find this girl?"

"No, Comrade, but I have only just realised her importance in this. I thought that. . ."

"You thought I was looking for another petal for my flower game?"

"Well, yes. I am sorry, Lavrenti. I did not mean to. . ."

Paslov had always struggled to disguise his abhorrence of the Mingrelian's insatiable sexual and sadistic appetites. The 'flower game' was one of the most disgusting examples.

Far from the innocuous pastime the name might imply, Beria's 'flower game' held its origins in the early days of his rise to power in the Transcaucasian region. He would sit on the back seat of his Buick limousine, sandwiched between his two infamous henchmen, and cruise the streets of Tbilisi looking for young girls. The men would accost the girls, bundle them into the car, and then take them to Beria's house or one of his hideaways. Once there, they would strip the girls naked but for their shoes, and force them to kneel in a wheel formation with heads touching at the centre.

Beria would then wander around his 'flower', inspecting and violating and rearranging their nakedness, while he chose the most alluring 'petal' of that particular 'flower'. The hapless creature would then be dragged into an adjoining room, usually by her ankles, and brutally raped, while the remaining 'petals' listened to her cries and awaited their own fates in terror.

Since his elevation and transfer to the capital, the chilling sight of Beria's ominous black limousine trawling the streets of Moscow for similarly vulnerable young girls had become almost commonplace.

Paslov asked why Beria had not told him about Kube before now. The Mingrelian snarled.

"Because until Heinrich Müeller gave up that information we had no knowledge of it. Now do you see why I employ such a man?"

"Of course, but now that Müeller has given up what he knows he must pay for his crimes. How could you let this devil live, Lavrenti? How could you protect such an evil?"

"You think I have sold my soul to a devil, Stanislav? You think, perhaps, I would make a credible Faust?"

"No, Lavrenti. Mephistopheles, perhaps. Faust was a fool. You are anything but."

Still Paslov refused to let the matter drop. After all those months in Mauthausen, not knowing if each morning would be his last, this was too important to let go. He said now the Americans knew about Müeller working for Beria he had become all but valueless. He asked Beria to give the German to him. He would deal with him. Beria shook his head.

He said Müeller still had much to tell, and pointed to the fact that the U.S. Army still didn't know of Müeller's defection. He said the western intelligence agencies were more at war with one another than the Soviet Union. He stubbed out his cigarette, and leaned closer.

"Right now America is like a fat and lazy whore, without the protection of a pimp. She is lying on her back with her legs spread, and offering us a fuck for nothing. It is our duty as red-blooded Soviet men to ensure she does not walk straight when we have finished."

"Is that why you are now in such a hurry to build these terrible weapons?"

Beria stopped smirking. Paslov felt the elation rise. He had obviously hit a nerve.

"What do you mean, when you say hurry, Stanislav? What do you know about this?"

"I know Stalin is suddenly in a hurry to build atom bombs, and confront the Americans. I know he has told you to build them, and I know he has given you little time in which to do it."

"We have to defend ourselves, Stanislav. You must see that?"

"Defend, yes; confront, no. The Americans did not attack us when we were at our most vulnerable; they came to our aid. Why should they attack us now? The Washington giant is back in his lair, and he is slumbering again. Leave him there, Lavrenti. All the time he sleeps, we grow stronger: in Europe, in South America, in Asia, in Africa. But, if we build these terrible weapons that will all change. They will see us as a threat, and an enemy."

Beria shrugged his indifference. Paslov hammered home the point.

"A war with America is a war we cannot win, Lavrenti. These Americans are not Bonaparte, or even Hitler. The world has moved on so much, in such a short space of time. Russian winters cannot defeat atom bombs and jet aircraft, and they are so wealthy. Even if we build these weapons, they will simply build bigger and better weapons, and we will always be struggling to keep pace. Tactics may win battles, but finance wins wars. You must see that, Lavrenti. You must see that we have to fight them another way; a more cautious way, a more subtle way."

"I see nothing of the kind."

Beria's anger was rising. Paslov read the signs and knew he would gain little by antagonizing the Mingrelian further. He shrugged a conciliatory shrug, and let the matter drop.

Beria looked pleased. He returned to the search for Hammond and the girl.

"What about the hotels and boarding houses? Have you checked them all?"

"Yes, of course."

"Even in Dessau?"

"We have checked everywhere." Paslov saw the smile of knowledge widen. "What do you know, Lavrenti?"

"I, too, have friends in Washington, Stanislav. I, too, have people who tell me secrets. One, in the American State Department, has told me some interesting things. He tells me there is a house in Dessau. He says it was once a guesthouse. He says the old woman who runs it may have started taking in guests again. Perhaps we should see if she has any vacancies."

"He is the same man? The man who told you about the girl being in Magdeburg?"

The answering nod from Beria left Paslov feeling confused. He hadn't expected a response. Beria had always been paranoid and excessively cautious. The fact that Beria had confirmed his source, and the man's location, surprised and concerned him. He rose from his chair.

"I will get some men."

Beria remained seated and calmly lit another cigarette.

"Not just yet, Stanislav. There is plenty of time. They are after all just sprats to catch a mackerel. We do not want to cast shadows on the water. We might frighten the bigger and cleverer fish away. Let us sit and talk for a while, but not about bombs and wars and spies. Did I hear you mention a glass of wine?"

13

Days at the guesthouse settled into routine. Hammond and the girl played cards and drank coffee. The old woman spent much of the time sleeping in her rocking-chair by the fire. The girl asked why they were still at the guesthouse. Hammond said Beria was in Leipzig, and Paslov's men were still searching the countryside. They would need to remain hidden until the furore died down. The answering stamp of a petulant foot was predictable.

"I'm bored with cards. I want to go out. I want some fresh air. I want some fun."

"Well, you can't. Stop being so selfish and childish and make some coffee."

The old woman had woken and grunted the instruction. Catherine Schmidt pouted her petulance and began firing more questions.

She asked Hammond how he had come to work for the government. He told her that he had joined the marines when he was twenty-four, because he hated office work. He said in the marines he had worked on developing amphibious landing techniques, but his heart wasn't in it. When OSS started in forty-two they asked him to join. He agreed, because he had a facility for languages and an aptitude for close-combat. He had no facility or aptitude whatsoever for amphibious landing techniques.

She asked about the incident on the train and whether he had killed the two MGB agents. He asked which was which. When she described Brusilov, he nodded and confirmed the truth. She seemed happy about that. He said he hadn't killed 'the clever one' because it hadn't been necessary. She seemed similarly pleased about that.

She then asked why he had killed the Red Army guards with a knife, when he had his gun. He said the noise would have alerted the regular passengers. When she mentioned the silencer, he said the suppressor took the weapon's overall length to almost fourteen inches. It made it cumbersome to align at close quarters.

"You are good, aren't you?"

She studied him with admiring eyes. It embarrassed, and left him feeling ashamed. He wasn't proud of his lethal skills, or that he had so often used them to such deadly effect. He said the older he got, the more the guilt and shame preyed on his mind, and added that sometimes he wished he'd never heard of OSS. When she asked why, he told her that as a marine he usually faced his enemy; with OSS that was rarely the case.

He tried to stem the questions, but she persisted. She changed the subject to trivia and asked again about his wife. Hammond spoke of his love for the wayward Emma, and how he missed being with her. When she asked what he missed the most, he didn't answer. The old woman saved him any further embarrassment.

"I told you before. You're a little too forward for my liking, young woman. Now stop asking foolish questions, and make some coffee."

"I'm sick of coffee."

"Then make some for us."

She flounced over to the stove, but not before she had increased his discomfiture.

"I bet you miss her because of the sex. I bet you haven't had sex for ages."

Hammond responded to her teasing with patronizing indifference.

"Oh, do you now? And why would you think that?"

"Because you've been away from her for a long time; you just said so. And because you're a man, and men always want sex." She paused. "And because I've seen the way you look at me when you think I'm not watching."

There had been a childlike simplicity in the observation, in direct contrast to the wilful seductress who now stared an invitation. The old woman opened her mouth to interrupt. Hammond growled his anger.

"Let me explain something to you, young lady. You are just a child, a foolish child, and I'm easily old enough to be your father. You're an assignment, a bad assignment, a dangerous assignment, a rude and spoilt and petulant and irritating assignment, but nothing more than that. Now do as you're told. Make the coffee and stop this nonsense."

She grinned and pouted back at him, seemingly unaffected.

"Or what will you do? Would you like to be my father? Is that what it is? Do you want to put a naughty little girl over your knee? Do you want to pull her knickers down and smack her bare bottom? You can if you like. I promise I won't tell anyone."

"I know I've had just about enough of this crap."

He stormed away and up the stairs to his room, feeling flustered and embarrassed, and not entirely understanding why. Minutes later, she was tapping on the door.

"What is it?"

She peeped demurely around the door and offered him his coffee.

"I'm sorry. I was only playing a silly game. I didn't mean to hurt you. I would never hurt you. I owe you everything: my freedom, my life, everything. Please don't hate me."

Hammond suddenly felt churlish.

"I don't hate you. Why would you think that?"

"Because men either want to have me and use me, or they hate me. They never just like me for who I am. It's always been the same."

She sat down beside him and passed him his coffee, pressing firmly against him, with her eyes downcast. Hammond drew back. Suddenly he knew why he had felt flustered and embarrassed. He steadied his coffee with two hands and mumbled his answer.

"Well I don't hate you, I like you. But now, I think I should drink this downstairs."

"You don't have to go."

"Yes I do."

He bolted from the room and charged downstairs, but on reaching the hallway took a deep breath before strolling nonchalantly into the kitchen.

"She apologized."

"Oh did she?"

The old woman didn't disguise the smile. He maintained the façade of nonchalance.

"Yes. Poor kid, she can't have had much of a life."

"I suppose not."

"Having a father like that, mixed up with all those lunatics; growing up in such a place at such a time. It's a wonder she survived with any sanity at all."

"If you say so."

"Maybe I've been too hard on her. Perhaps I should try to be a bit more understanding."

"Oh, I'm sure she would appreciate that."

He tried and failed to ignore the twinkle in her eyes and the half-smile playing on her lips.

"All right, what's so amusing? Come on, out with it."

The old woman answered from behind the same half-smile.

"You know it's funny, but I'd forgotten how gullible men can be. It's refreshing to see how an attractive young woman can still so easily manipulate the strongest of men."

Hammond bristled.

"What do you mean? She's not manipulating me."

"Oh, isn't she now?"

"Of course not; that's ridiculous. I just think we should be more understanding of everything she's been through. She's still only a child, you know."

"Did you just say, we?"

"Yes, I think we should both make more of an effort. I know she's. . ."

A sudden sound from outside had distracted him: the sound of footsteps, approaching the house. The footsteps stopped. Someone tapped lightly on the door. The old woman rose from her chair. She waved him into the hallway. He grabbed the automatic, headed out of the kitchen and silently closed the door behind him. Then he listened from the hallway.

"What is it? is there somebody. . . ?"

Catherine Schmidt stood at the top of the stairs. He shook his head and put a finger to his lips in a noiseless instruction. For once the reaction was instantaneous. She sat dutifully and quietly on the top step, while he checked the automatic and prepared for the worst.

He could hear the sounds of the old woman talking to someone, a man, he thought. The words were indistinct, and the voices low. The muffled conversation continued for almost five minutes. Then the voices stopped and he heard the back door close.

"It's all right. You can come back now."

He returned to the kitchen, with the girl in tow. They found the old woman sitting in her rocking-chair and looking thoughtful.

"It seems we were asking the wrong questions, about Beria and Paslov and why they wanted young Catherine so badly. All this time, we've been asking the wrong questions."

"What do you mean? What wrong questions? Who was that?"

"We shouldn't be asking why the Russians want her so badly. We should be asking ourselves why the Americans sent you to get her. So why did they send you?"

"Who was at the door?"

"Answer the question. Why did the Americans send you?"

Hammond shrugged. He had no answer that would sound in any way credible. He couldn't tell her that he'd taken the job in desperation, and hadn't cared who he was supposed to rescue, or why. He answered matter-of-factly, feeling more than a little foolish.

"I don't know. They just said who I had to get, and that it was important I got her out and back to Frankfurt."

"And you didn't think to ask these people who she was, or why she was so important to them? You didn't think of asking them for a reason before you risked your life?"

"They felt it was safer for everyone if I didn't know. I decided they were right."

"And chivalrous, gum-chewing Sir Galahad flew straight here on his white charger, to rescue a damsel in distress from the fire-breathing Russian ogre?"

Hammond looked guiltily back at her.

"It wasn't exactly like that. They had me in a wringer."

"I just bet they did."

The old woman sat quietly. Hammond's mind was racing. A clearly impatient Catherine Schmidt looked from one to the other.

"Will somebody tell me what's going on?" she asked.

The old woman smiled without humour.

"That's something we'd all like to know, young lady. Perhaps you'd like to tell me who Martin Kube is?"

Catherine's face suddenly fell. For a few moments she said nothing. When she finally answered, her voice trembled with uncertainty.

"Martin Kube is dead."

The old woman shook her head.

"No, he isn't. He's working for the Americans."

"But that can't be."

"Our man in Paslov's office overheard Beria and Paslov talking about this man Kube, working for the Americans."

Hammond had no idea who Kube was, but Catherine obviously did. Her face had drained of colour and she was shaking. He reached out and took her hand.

"So, who is he?"

She seemed not to hear the question. She looked lost in thought, her eyes glazed and unfocused, but then she nodded quietly and began to talk.

"Martin Kube was a Kriminaldirektor with the Gestapo. He worked for my father, in Berlin. My father sometimes invited him for dinner. My mother hated him. At first she put up with him, because he worked with my father, but then he started coming over to the house all the time, and in the end she said something. I heard my parents arguing about it, one night. My mother said it wasn't enough that he was fat, and short, and bald, and ugly; he also smelled. My father laughed. He said it wasn't Kube's fault, but then she said there was something else about him, something that made her feel uncomfortable. He asked her what, but she wouldn't say."

Hammond cut in.

"Did you know what she meant?"

"Not at that time. At that time I didn't understand any of it. I was only eleven. I thought he was nice, because he always brought presents for me, and took me to the park. I used to love going to the park. We used to play French tennis."

Catherine sat quietly. Hammond could see her fighting back the tears.

"He was the only one who ever took any notice of me. My father used to spend so much time at work, and my mother used to spend a lot of time down at Lake Como. We had a villa there. She never took us. She and my father argued about it; they were arguing a lot at that time. He said she must have a lover there. He never did trust the Italians. She said he couldn't have blamed her if she had. They hardly spoke to each other after that."

"Us?"

Hammond had picked up on something she'd said. It seemed to disrupt her train of thought, because she looked blankly back and said,

"I'm sorry, what?"

"You said: she never took us to Lake Como. Who did you mean?"

"Oh, yes. I have an older brother; I haven't seen him for years. In fact I have two brothers; well, one brother and one half-brother, from my father's first wife. I've never met him."

"Where are they now?"

She shrugged and shook her head.

"My father never talked about his first wife. My mother told me about my half-brother, but my other brother, Thomas, was at university in England. He was very clever. He used to come home sometimes, but when my mother and father started fighting, he stopped coming. Thomas hated the Nazis. He said they would destroy Germany. He never did understand. In the end my father refused to mention his name, but I loved him, and I missed him."

"Do you know where he is now?"

"No. I haven't seen or heard from him in years."

Hammond was working through the detail in his mind. Perhaps one of the brothers had somehow organized her rescue. Perhaps this was the link between a beautiful and disturbed young woman, and the covert intervention of the mighty U.S. State Department. Then she started talking about Kube, and he realised just how naive his thought process had been.

She said it had been on her twelfth birthday. Kube brought her a new dress. She was so happy. She said it was pink, with little blue flowers. When she put it on, Kube said she looked so grown-up. He suggested they go to the park, but said she should leave the racquet and ball; they could play hide-and-seek instead.

"It was my turn to hide, and so I hid in some bushes. Martin found me easily, because I was giggling. At first he laughed, too, and began tickling me. Then he stopped laughing.

"He pinned me to the grass and lifted my dress. He pulled down my knickers, and said he was going to teach me a new game. I didn't understand. I thought he was going to spank me.

"After that he came to the house every weekend, and always took me to the park. We would go in the evening, when it was quiet. He used to give me chocolate and tell me not to say anything. He said if I ever spoke of it we would both get into trouble."

Hammond felt numb. He was thinking back to the time she had spoken about her mother's death. For one so young to have seen so much and suffered so much was shocking. This wasn't the femme fatale who had earlier teased and embarrassed him. This was a frightened child. At that moment he just wanted to put his arms around her and comfort her; hold her, ease her pain, tell her everything was all right now, and help her to forget all those terrible memories.

When he asked why nobody had confronted Kube or tried to stop him, she said nobody knew. When the family moved to Warsaw, Martin Kube was posted there, too. When her father was transferred to Prague, Kube followed. She couldn't get away from him. In Prague, Kube became bolder, and began taking her back to his rooms at Petschek Palace.

She said, as time passed, her mother began to suspect the truth, but she spent most of her time in Berlin or down at Como. On the few occasions her mother did visit she didn't dare say anything to Kube, and Catherine's father had always been too busy to notice.

Hammond asked what happened when her father was killed. She sat for a moment, staring into space as she gathered more memories. When she started to tell the story, he saw her pain, and cursed himself for asking.

"I remember that day so clearly. My father came home at lunchtime. It was unusual; he normally only ever came home late at night. I remember he looked so sad. He said that some cowards had tried to kill Uncle Reinhard."

"Uncle Reinhard?"

"Reinhard Heydrich. He wasn't my real uncle, of course, but I liked him very much. He was always so nice to me. He and my father were good friends. My father didn't believe Uncle Reinhard would die. He said he was indestructible, and that it would take more than a cowardly ambush to kill him. Then my father gave me a kiss and went back to work.

"I only found out that they'd killed him, too, when Martin came to the house that night.

"It was very late. He woke me. He looked upset. I thought he was going to tell me that Uncle Reinhard had died. Then he said the same cowards who had tried to kill Uncle Reinhard had killed my father. I couldn't believe it."

As Catherine recounted those events, the tears finally began to flow. Hammond tried to imagine how she must have felt. So much death and suffering; it was no wonder she had felt the need to strike back.

"That was the worst moment of my life; even worse than that moment in the park. My mother wanted to take me back to Berlin, but Martin said he had promised my father that he would look after me. There was nothing she could do."

"But she was your mother. She had the right to take you with her."

She smiled another weak smile, and shook her head.

"You don't understand. Martin personally knew the Führer, and he was Himmler's favourite. I hated Himmler; he looked so creepy, but he controlled everything. My father and Uncle Reinhard didn't like him either. They always laughed at him. My father once called him a barbarian chicken herder. Uncle Reinhard smiled, but he didn't say anything.

"I didn't think of it at the time, but I always felt so safe when they were with me. Nobody dared disobey them, not Frank, not Martin Kube, even Himmler was wary. But suddenly they were both gone, and I felt so frightened and so alone."

Catherine went on to talk more about Prague. She said, after her father's death, life wasn't too bad. Kube allowed her to run wild, providing she returned to his bed each night, and she began mixing with some of the many unsavoury characters in occupied Prague. She learnt many of their skills in survival and scavenging. They were skills she would come to rely on in those dangerous months following Germany's surrender. She said she learnt something else, too. She learnt about men. She learnt about their lust and their weaknesses. She learnt how to manipulate them by using her body, and then, one day, she learnt about their fears.

"By that time we lived mostly at Petschek Palace. One morning someone came up to the room. He said a patrol had captured one of the people who had helped the cowards kill Uncle Reinhard and my father. Martin went downstairs to see the man. He took me with him. He told me the man was very stubborn, and wouldn't say who else had helped them. He said maybe the man would tell me.

"I went into the room and saw the man. He was naked and strapped to a chair. He was bleeding and he was bruised and in a bad way, but he wouldn't say anything. When Martin told him who I was, he looked at me, but still said nothing. When I asked him about my father, he looked straight through me.

"I have never hated anyone as much in my life as I hated that man. I hit him, in the face. Everyone laughed, and so I hit him again. They kept laughing, and so I kept hitting him. Then one of the SS men, a major, gave me his dagger.

"I remember holding the dagger and looking at it. It was beautiful. It had a silver eagle on the handle. The major said it was very sharp. When I started walking towards the man, he looked terrified. When Martin told him I was going to cut his thing off, he started screaming. Everyone was laughing. I felt proud. I had never known anyone be frightened of me before."

"And did you?"

"No. I would have done, but he started talking. Martin told me to keep the dagger. He said I'd achieved more with it in one minute than the major had done in his lifetime. I don't think the major was very pleased, but he didn't dare say anything, and so I kept it."

Hammond watched as she talked about the dagger, and laughed about the poor devil she had helped to torture. She didn't seem to see anything wrong in it. She went on to talk about the rest of her time in Prague, and how she had learnt so much, but mostly she talked about Kube.

"I hated him. I hated what he did to me when I was a little girl, and I hated him touching me. I hated the sight of him, especially when he was naked. He was so ugly, all those folds of fat, and he always sweated so badly, and he smelled; especially afterwards."

She said, as the Bolsheviks neared Prague, Kube ordered her to stay at Petschek, but she ran away. She hid in the Old Quarter of the city, in a house that had belonged to friends of her mother. The Reich recalled Martin Kube to Berlin for one last desperate stand, but she stayed hidden. Kube knew she was in Prague, but he didn't know where. When he returned to Berlin, he left SS patrols scouring the city. She knew it would only be a matter of time before they found her.

As fortune would have it, just as they began searching the Old Quarter of the city, the people of Prague rose in revolt against the Reich. A few days after that, the Red Army arrived. What remained of Hitler's armies had to get out of the city and the country, while they still could.

"When the Bolsheviks arrived in Prague, I was so happy. I thought I had finally got away from him. I thought I was free. . . But I wasn't. Only the uniforms had changed.

"It started during the Sudeten German expulsions. The mobs were on the streets. They were killing anybody who even looked German. I was very scared. Everywhere there were expulsions to labour camps, and people being tortured and murdered. A Red Army patrol caught me stealing bread from the local bakery. They took me to the platoon commander. He took me back to the house. He said he wanted to speak to my parents.

"When we got there I told him I was lying. He laughed. I laughed with him. I showed him the cupboard, where I kept some schnapps, and then took him upstairs and let him have me."

"Why didn't you just tell him that your parents were dead?"

The casual manner in which she had so matter-of-factly related her shame had astonished Hammond. He watched her shrug, and give an answer that further astonished and shocked.

"He was going to have me anyway. I knew it, and so did he. It's the way in Soviet territory. The younger and prettier women give themselves to the officers. That way they don't get gang-raped by the men. I was just lucky that I was young and pretty."

"Who was he?"

Her eyes blazed as she spoke of the man and his death.

"He was just another fat Bolshevik pig who thought I was a spoil of war. He threatened to give me up to the mobs, and so I stayed with him. I pretended I liked him. He didn't know. He was infatuated with me. He thought I was infatuated with him.

"Then one night I tied him to the bed, with my stockings. He liked that. They all did. . . Well, they did at first. He'd been drinking. He thought I was going to play. I did, but then I took the dagger and cut the drunken pig into pieces.

"I got out of Prague, made my way back to Berlin, and hid with my mother in her apartment, because Martin was still in Berlin. The Führer had committed suicide, and the Bolsheviks had taken control. Martin came to see if I was still alive, and where I was. She didn't tell him.

"Later, someone told me the Bolsheviks had killed him. I didn't hear any more, and so I believed them. But if he survived he'll never stop looking, not if he thinks I'm alive."

"Well, let's not panic just yet. We can't be sure it's him."

The old woman had chipped in with some reasoned argument. Catherine was insistent. She said if Martin Kube was still alive, he would be working for the Americans. It all fitted. Kube had worked for her father, controlling the Reich's espionage networks in Bohemia and Moravia. When her father was assassinated, Kube took over.

It was if a light had suddenly gone on in Hammond's head.

"Of course! That explains why Beria wants you. He wants to use you to get to Kube."

"But I don't know where he is. I didn't even know he was still alive."

"Yes, but Beria doesn't know that. He may see you as his only link."

For a while all three were silent. Hammond sat pondering the facts, and considering the implications. He realized that if the order to get Catherine Schmidt out of Germany and into the States had come from her childhood abuser, it left only one possibility: the power and influence that former Gestapo Kriminaldirektor Martin Kube had once enjoyed with the Third Reich now extended to the highest levels of the U.S. State Department.

14

It was gone midnight when Hammond climbed the stairs to his room. Catherine Schmidt, frightened and emotionally-drained, had retired earlier, and so Hammond had sat talking with the old woman.

They decided to ignore the presence of Kube, at least in the short-term. There was little doubt the former Gestapo chief introduced a new and undesirable complication, but the danger posed by Beria and Paslov formed the more immediate and significant threat.

The only sensible solution was to deliver the girl to the authorities at Camp King. Only after that would Hammond be in a position to address any threat posed by the continuing existence and influence of Kube.

It was one a.m. and Hammond lay awake, turning the facts over in his mind. It was a mess, a complex mess. He dozed for a while, but then a movement on the far side of the room jolted him into consciousness. Slowly and noiselessly he reached for the automatic, silently watching the figure in the shadows as he secured the weapon.

"Good heavens, Mr Hammond, that looks so big. What are you going to do with it?"

She giggled as she spoke, and Hammond felt so many conflicting emotions filling and confusing his mind. His relief at knowing it was not an aggressive intruder struggled with his annoyance at her impudence and childish persistence. His concern for her youth and vulnerability struggled with masculine instinct.

He replaced the automatic and watched the young seductress approach, following the exaggerated motion of her hips as she drew nearer and spoke again.

"I thought you told me anything that long was too unwieldy for close quarters?"

As he listened to the words of seduction dripping from her lips, a desperately unfair struggle became ever more desperate and ever more unfair.

"I'm frightened, and cold. I want you to hold me and protect me, and keep me warm."

Suddenly the child had returned. Hammond stammered a refusal.

"You know I can't do that. Look, it's late. Go back to bed. We'll talk in the morning."

She moved closer, while he lay in the shameful awareness of his own fragile resolve. She eased the nightgown from her shoulders and allowed it to slide to the floor. Flaunting her nakedness, she whispered words that echoed among the shadows and hung on the night air.

"Then take me, and use me, and love me."

"I can't do that either."

"Why? Don't you want me?"

"It has nothing to do with not wanting you."

"Then why?"

He studied the beauty of her face and the splendour of her nakedness, caught in three-dimensional magnificence by obliging shafts of moonlight that bathed every facet. She shivered, and he wavered, but then the moment had passed and his conscience remained.

"Because it would be wrong. You're beautiful, but you're still so young. You should be making love with a young man of your own age. Anyway, it's my job to protect you, not take advantage of you."

He blushed furiously and drew the blanket closer as he stammered the refusal, knowing he had to somehow dissuade her youthful infatuation before lust overwhelmed.

"You take advantage of me?" She giggled at the apparent absurdity. "You're so sweet, but I'm not a child. I'm a woman, and I need a man."

She reached for his fingers, and he meekly allowed her to guide them to her breast. More impudent fingers reached out, and then slipped beneath the blanket to discover his guilt and destroy whatever inhibition remained.

"And I need to feel this inside me."

"Catherine, no."

He had tried one final unconvincing denial. She grinned, and pouted, and eased her nakedness against his.

"You can't say no. It's not allowed. I found it. The law says it belongs to me."

At first he'd only thought of her as a child, stunningly beautiful but nonetheless a child, innocent and enchanting, petulant and precocious, with impressionable values and brittle opinions. But that was before he had listened to her speaking of so much hatred and violence and wickedness. Before he had come to think of her as vicious and cruel, shamelessly debauched and emotionally disturbed.

And then, when she had spoken of her life in Berlin and Prague, he had seen her as the victim, and his heart had gone out to her. A beautiful and vulnerable child, in need of love and care, despoiled and abused by the very people entrusted with her welfare and protection.

Now, though, he came to know her as a woman. The graceful felinity as she moved against him and the whispered intimacy of each breathless persuasion. Her hair's gentle fragrance as she nuzzled at his neck, and the softness of her thighs as she drew him close and wrapped him in her lust. The fullness of her breasts, and the nipple's jutting adamance; the arch of her back, the tenderness of her touch, and the erotic perfection of her form.

He held his breath as she wriggled and writhed and drew him deeper, and then closed his eyes as delirium took hold and a thousand velvet teeth nibbled and grazed at his flesh.

But then, almost before it had begun, a spasm of helpless lust preceded a groan of despair, and all that remained of those fleeting moments of sensual perfection were thoughts of inadequacy and remnants of shame.

"I'm sorry, but it's been so long since. . . I'm so sorry, I. . ."

She held a finger to his lips, and soothed his wounded pride with whispers of praise.

"Shush. It was beautiful, and you're beautiful. The only man who ever cared enough to worry. The most beautiful man I ever knew. The most beautiful lover I ever knew."

Lips that had lied so generously only moments ago, now moved to replenish lust and repair a shattered ego.

"And we have all the time in the world to make it perfect."

****

It was gone eight when Hammond woke with the memory still fresh in his mind. He lay still, listening to footsteps on the stairs and hearing the old woman moving around the kitchen. Then the door opened and she brought him his coffee.

"Shiva, my Lord, you're awake. I thought I'd almost danced you to death."

"I'm sorry?"

"Oh nothing, just some silliness. Look, I've brought you coffee."

She smiled and carried the coffee to the bed. He took the cup.

"Who's Shiva?"

"You are, my lord."

"I don't understand."

"You are Shiva, one of the greatest of the Hindu gods, and I am Kali. . . your wife."

"Wife?"

He must have looked horrified, because she suddenly giggled.

"Don't worry, it's not real. It's just a silly game I play. You don't have to look so worried. I'm not expecting you to marry me."

"Oh good."

The petulant child returned.

"Why good? Don't you want me any more? That's not what you said last night."

He began to protest, but then saw the mischief in her eyes.

"I think you're still playing games with me."

She smiled coyly.

"Perhaps."

"So how do you know so much about Hindu gods?"

She sat on the bed and explained.

"When I was seven, my father sent me to England. He said I should always remember that I am a child of Etzel, and be proud of my country and its language and culture and heritage. But he also said English is the language of nations, and I had to learn to speak it without an accent."

"And who is Etzel?"

"Etzel comes from the *Nibelungenlied*."

"The what?"

"The *Nibelungenlied*. The poem: the three thirteenth-century manuscripts."

He shrugged his ignorance. She explained further.

"Originally there were many more than that, over thirty I think, but only three are really important. They are famous in Germanic literature, and refer to Attila as Etzel."

"You're talking about Attila the Hun?" She nodded and smiled, seeing the look of disbelief and seeming to take a perverse pleasure in shocking him. Hammond held the scepticism. "So your father told you that you were a child of Attila the Hun, the descendant of a warmongering barbarian, a man who slaughtered thousands of innocent people?"

She pouted a contradiction.

"No. He told me that I was a child of Etzel."

"And he was serious?"

"Of course, but Etzel wasn't that. He wasn't what you said. Etzel was a great warrior and a nomad, and we are his children, at least, those of us who continue the fight. We have become nomads, just as Attila was. They have stolen our lands and enslaved our people, just as they did with Attila, just as the Führer predicted. But some of us, the chosen ones, the Children of Etzel, will continue the fight. Like him, we will drive the invaders from our lands and free our people. One day it will happen and the Reich will be great again, you'll see."

"But Attila wasn't German. I thought he was Asian. . . or was he?"

She set her jaw in determined pose.

"In the *Nibelungenlied*, Etzel married the Burgundian princess Kriemhild, the sister of King Gunther; that is enough for me. Anyway, nobody knows who he was, or what he looked like, or exactly where the Hunnish people originally came from, but over the centuries the tribes united and the race became pure. Now we are all of us his children. We feel it. We know it."

"And just how do Hindu gods come into all of this?"

"Oh yes, that's right. I'd forgotten. Drink your coffee before it gets cold."

He dutifully sipped at the coffee. She resumed her story. She talked of her days in England, and how the girls at boarding school had bullied her because of her German nationality and accent. At first she had been so miserable and frightened, but then one of the older girls had helped her to deal with them.

Ashna had been the daughter of a diplomat from Calcutta. She stopped the bullying and introduced Catherine to the truths of the Veda. She spoke of the Hindu gods and goddesses: of Vishnu and Shiva and Durga and Kaushiki and Ganesha, but she especially spoke of Kali.

She gave Catherine a book on the Hindu gods, and told her how understanding their teachings could help to overcome so many problems. Catherine studied the colourful assortment of mythical characters in juvenile fascination.

When Hammond confessed he couldn't see her as a practicing Hindu, she said she only remembered the bits that interested her, the bits she liked, and she had always liked Kali. She added that she had liked the goddess Kaushiki as well, because Kaushiki had been Durga's most beautiful form, but said she preferred the wrathful form of Kali.

From that moment on, she kept a picture of Kali by her bed, and confessed to talking to the picture whenever she felt afraid or needed to fight back. Somehow, having a picture made Kali so much more real than an abstract Christian god she couldn't see or imagine. Kali had been different.

Kali had sat by her bed and taught her to face her fears and walk through them.

"And since then, understanding this goddess has helped you in other ways?"

"Yes, she has. Kali killed demons, you see. She cut off their heads, and drank their blood, and danced on their corpses, and so do I."

"You're talking about the Russian officers?"

"That's right."

"And what about these Children of Etzel people? I'd always thought the Allied troops used the term 'Hun' as a form of insult. So who are these people?"

"Yes, they did. I asked my father about that. He laughed, and said, if they thought it insulting, all the more reason for us to use it."

Appearing to suddenly realize an indiscretion, she waved away the question.

"Anyway, forget it. Let's not talk about that now. We've only just found each other. Can't we do something else: something fun?"

Hammond relaxed the formality as he looked across at the seemingly endless contradictions of Catherine Louise Schmidt. Despite her youth, there was a complexity to the young woman that he was finding both dangerously hypnotic and seriously disturbing.

In the space of a few days he'd seen her play precocious child and compassionate woman, dutiful servant and erotic seductress, articulate protagonist and racist bigot, playful teenager and lunatic fanatic. Hammond's problem wasn't so much that he couldn't keep pace with the personality changes and mood swings. Hammond's problem was that he found each more seductive than the last.

"If you don't want to talk, you don't have to. I didn't mean to pry."

158

"Yes you did. You keep asking questions because it's part of your job, and I understand that. It's all right. I don't mind. You're my lover. You saved my life. You have a right to know. Perhaps one day I'll tell you all about it; we'll have to see."

"All right then, so tell me about this other god, this Shiva, what does he stand for?"

"Shiva is part of Kali, and Kali is part of Shiva. They are one. Shiva is the destroyer and restorer, the Lord of the Dance and the Herdsman of Souls, and he is the Linga."

"The Linga?"

"The symbol of sensuality, the phallus."

That familiar childlike simplicity was there again. It was a trait that Hammond found both delightfully amoral and shockingly wanton. But there was nothing childlike about the tongue that skimmed across her lips. He mumbled a half-hearted protest.

"No, Catherine, this is getting too serious. We have to talk. I'm old enough to be your. . . well, I'm a lot older than you. I have a responsibility to ensure. . ."

"Oh, don't be so silly."

Mischievous fingers slid beneath the covers and he jumped at the contact, but then felt the blood surge and mentally cursed his own weakness. An infatuated middle-aged fool lay submissively back against the pillow. A forceful young seductress slid back the covers and lifted her skirts. Smiling happily, she added a playful observation.

"There, now, that's much better. You know, I do believe my Lord Shiva wants Kali to dance for him again."

15

Hammond dozed until lunchtime, but then woke with a start. He lay still, wondering what had woken him, with the memory of that morning's foolishness tugging at his conscience. The rattle of crockery from the kitchen below interrupted the guilt.

He dressed quickly and hurried downstairs, fully expecting the old woman's acerbic wit to greet his tardiness.

"I'm sorry, I didn't realize how late. . ."

The ominous sight of five ten-inch barrels, pointing directly at his midriff, caused his arms to rise and his words to falter into silence.

On the other side of those same five, pah-pah-shah forty-one sub-machinegun barrels stood five regular Soviet army troops. Standing at the sink and rattling two coffee cups together, stood a smiling individual who addressed him in faultless English.

"Ah, the warrior has risen. Mr Gerald Hammond, I presume. Come along in, Mr Hammond. I trust you are recovered from your earlier exertion? I apologize. I neglected to introduce myself. My name is Stanislav Paslov."

There was no sight of either woman. Hammond held his arms high, while a nervous-looking soldier removed both knife and automatic. The soldier stepped back and nodded to Paslov, who replaced the cups on the draining board and then gestured to Hammond.

"Sit down, please, Mr Hammond."

"Where are they?"

Paslov was clearly enjoying himself.

"Oh, they are safe enough, but let us not concern ourselves with them. Let us talk about you, Mr Hammond, and some of your friends in Washington. So how is my old friend Davis Carpenter, and how is that harridan of a wife of his?"

Hammond could see little point in small talk or denial.

"How do you know my name?"

"You are not the only one with friends in the State Department, Mr Hammond."

Hammond shrugged a nonchalance he didn't feel.

"So, what do you want from me?"

"What makes you think I want something from you?"

"Well, my testicles aren't attached to a generator. I'm not dead, and I'm not in chains and on my way to the Lubyanka. That can only mean you must want something from me."

Paslov gave an enigmatic smile, and then nodded to the troops, who began withdrawing from the room. One of them handed him Hammond's weapons. The emaciated spymaster weighed the automatic in his hand.

"You do realize that by carrying this little technological marvel, you have committed an act of war against the Soviet Union?"

"I don't see how."

"Carrying a weapon across borders is an act of war. Unless of course I am mistaken, and the Hi-Standard Company now produces these in Magdeburg?"

"Whose borders? Russia's a thousand kilometres to the north."

"Soviet borders, Mr Hammond, Soviet borders."

Hammond sniffed his contempt.

"Much as he may wish otherwise, international law and international boundaries aren't determined by Joseph Stalin's IS2 tanks, Comrade Colonel Paslov. . . And I found that."

"Oh, I see. And where did you stumble across it? On a train perhaps?"

Paslov suddenly looked bored. He rested Hammond's automatic alongside the cups on the draining board and then drew a Tokarev from his jacket.

"This is just a precaution, Mr Hammond. I am told that for a man of your age you move quickly, and might not otherwise give me time to explain."

Paslov waited until the last of his troops had left the room and closed the door, before matter-of-factly dropping a bombshell.

"I wish to defect. I and my wife wish to become citizens of your United States. I want a new identity, and a home in Florida, or perhaps California. Precisely where does not concern me, as long as it is somewhere warm, somewhere I can look at the ocean. I want enough money to provide an income for the rest of our lives, and I want you to arrange everything."

Hammond tried a bluff.

"I work in risk assessment, but we pay out on insurance policies, not welfare claims. As for the rest of it, maybe you should contact U.S. Immigration."

He should have saved his breath. Paslov continued issuing orders.

"You are to arrange matters with Alan Carlisle, and nobody else. That is vital. You are not to mention this to anyone else, not to Carpenter or Allum, not to Daniel Chambers. No one but Alan Carlisle. That is critical. Do you understand?"

"And what do we get in return?"

"Your freedom, Mr Hammond."

"You think too much of me, Colonel. That doesn't begin to balance the books."

Again Paslov ignored him.

"I will be in Frankfurt during the first week of July to discuss border controls with your people. I will bring my wife. She could do with a few days holiday, or should I be saying vacation now? Make sure that you have everything ready by then."

Hammond stood his ground and repeated his comment about balancing the books. Paslov studied him closely. At first he seemed unwilling to answer, but then the enigmatic smile reappeared and he dropped the second bombshell.

"Beria has an agent in your State Department, an important one, which is why you must deal only with Carlisle directly."

Hammond suddenly understood how Catherine Schmidt had been captured so easily in Magdeburg. He had initially suspected a leak in one of the German cells, but now it all made sense. He similarly realised how Paslov had found them at the guest house. The Office of Occupied Territories had a mole.

"He's the man who gave me up to you, the man who told you where we were?"

Paslov shook his head.

"You do not really expect me to answer that, do you? How I found you is of no consequence, but I will give you the name of that agent, and. . . "

"And what?"

"I will give you another name, an even more important name."

"Why is it more important? Who is it?"

"Another of Beria's special people; one of his top people."

"Another agent?" Paslov nodded slowly. Hammond pressed for more. "So who is he, and where is he? In Washington?"

"I did not say 'he' but you must tell Carlisle that Beria's agent lives in 'The Poplars'. Carlisle will understand, and I will see you both in July. Oh, and remember, Mr Hammond, you are to speak only to Alan Carlisle about this; not to the old woman, not to the girl, not to anyone but him. Your future, and our lives, may depend on it. Tell Carlisle I will only meet him if both you and he are there, in person, in Frankfurt, in July."

Hammond said he could understand why Paslov wanted to meet Carlisle, but he didn't understand why Paslov wanted him at the meeting. Paslov said he needed a favour, a personal favour. Hammond didn't like the sound of that.

"I can't make promises of that nature."

"Oh, I think your government will happily sanction this, Mr Hammond. They may even give you that medal you never got for your efforts on Jedburgh and in Rouen."

Hammond's eyes widened and the weather-beaten features formed into a frown. Only a handful of people knew any details of his background and trip to Germany; each of them enjoyed a senior position with The State Department. A few pregnant moments passed before the spymaster answered the unasked question.

"I know a great deal more about you than that, Mr Hammond. I would like to stay and chat, but I have work to do. I shall direct my teams to the south-west, nearer to Leipzig. We have reports of two people hiding there, people who fit the descriptions of our fugitives. Have a pleasant journey home, Mr Hammond. I will see you in Frankfurt, in July."

"I don't understand. Why are you doing this? You're a powerful man in Russia. You have friends in high places. Why give all that up?"

The Russian shrugged.

"You will undoubtedly discover, on your rise through The State Department, that power is a transitory commodity, Mr Hammond. Those friends in high places you spoke of are equally fickle, and often the highest placed boast the lowest standards. That is also true in America, is it not?"

"You're saying you've fallen out with Beria?"

"Let us say that Lavrenti Pavlovich and I are not as close as we once were, but now I must go. If you take my advice, you will leave quickly. We brought a vehicle for the prisoners. It is only a Gaz, I am afraid; not as fast and reliable as the Jeeps your president so kindly loaned to us during the war, but it should get you to Frankfurt.

"Oh, and one more thing. Although I shall pull my search teams across to the Leipzig area, I cannot countermand orders already given to the rest of the army. There will be guards and checkpoints, and they will be looking for you. Take care, Mr Hammond, take care."

"What about the girl?"

"You can take her with you, the old woman, too, if you wish, but before you do there is something you may wish to see."

Paslov replaced the Tokarev and fished a stack of photographs from an inside pocket. He moved to the table, and spread them out on its surface.

"Come here, Mr Hammond, come and look."

Hammond wandered over and began studying the photographs. Each showed a man's corpse. If the horror of each death mask hadn't told him, the wounds where the genitals had been cut away and the crosses gouged into each torso left him in no doubt as to the agony suffered by each man at the point of death.

His eyes followed, as the Russian pointed to each victim in turn.

"Major Christiakov, served with distinction with the Fifth Guards Tank Army, received the Order of Lenin for heroics in the battle for Kursk. He left a widow and four children. Captain Grigolyuk, served with the Third Belorussian Front, awarded the Order of Suvorov, second class, for gallantry in the battle for Königsberg. He is survived by a wife and seven children. This was how we found Captain Valerie Lisovskii. He was. . . "

Hammond interrupted.

"I'm sorry, Colonel, but I fail to see. . ."

Paslov abandoned the recital and returned his attention to Hammond.

"They were all officers with the Red Army, Mr Hammond, and they were all intimately acquainted with your young friend. You see, the crosses gave her away."

"The crosses?"

Paslov gave a grim smile and pointed again to each picture in turn.

"You see there, on the chest, and there on the forehead, and again there. They are called reverse fylfot crosses, Mr Hammond. I have to admit they had us puzzled, but then we found her old apartment in Berlin, and there it was."

"There what was?"

"The picture of Kali, the Hindu goddess of destruction and dissolution. The girl kept the picture by her bed. It showed the reverse fylfot cross in the palm of one hand. I have to assume the girl left hurriedly and had no time to gather her belongings. Our finding that picture explained a great deal."

Hammond sniffed a nonchalance he was a long way from feeling.

"In America, we would call that circumstantial."

Paslov grinned.

"Yes, I suppose in America you would. Perhaps such a distinction will act as a source of comfort to you, the next time you climb between her thighs."

"And so what now, for the girl and the old woman?"

"As I said, you can take them with you. I have no further need of them. Until July then."

Hammond nodded mutely. Paslov scooped up the pictures, slipped them back into his pocket, and then left without further explanation. Seconds later, the old woman appeared in the doorway. Catherine stood behind her, looking pale and frightened. The old woman ushered her into the kitchen.

"What was all that about?"

"It seems the Soviets have an agent in the State Department. He gave us up to Beria."

The old woman looked incredulous.

"All of us? The network cells in Magdeburg and Dessau as well?"

"I have to presume so."

"But they aren't spies, with guns and knives. They are decent people with families; people whose only crime was to believe in democracy."

Hammond had nothing he could say, bar the obvious.

"I'm sorry, but they knew the risks."

The old woman was suddenly furious.

"Of course they didn't know the risks. They didn't know that America would betray them. They thought America would protect them. They believed in America, and it has cost them their lives. So, who is this spy?"

Hammond looked blankly back at her.

"I have no idea, but something tells me we had better leave here while we still can."

"What did Paslov say?"

"Nothing much. He just said we could go."

"So why spend all that effort trying to find you, and then just let you go?"

Hammond feigned ignorance and shook his head. The old woman didn't press.

"I think we need a cup of coffee."

****

Hammond and Catherine left the guesthouse late that afternoon. The old woman refused to go with them. The memory of her steadfast refusal brought a smile to his face. He had been about to set out, and again asked her to come with him. He stressed the risk of her staying there, and said Beria and Paslov might not agree on her continuing freedom.

He was unable to sway her. She set the wizened features in a portrait of determination, nodded to the bedroom above their heads, and wagged a finger at his presumption.

She had lived all her life in this house. Her mother had given birth to her in the same bed and in the same room as her mother before her. She had grown up playing along the landing outside that bedroom. She had lost her virginity, and given birth to both of her children in that bedroom.

In all that time she had never allowed the Stalins and Hitlers of this world to frighten or intimidate her. She had never allowed anybody to dictate how she lived her life, or tell her where to live, or what to think or say. She didn't intend changing the habits of a lifetime, not while she still had an opinion left to give and a breath left to draw.

She apologized for her obstinacy, but nobody was driving her away or ordering her from her home, not even him. She had lived all her life in the same house. When she died they would carry her out of it. That was all there was to it.

She told him to stop looking so cross, and get a move on. He allowed the frown to fade as he took her frail fingers in his. He said it had been a privilege to know her. She looked back at him and held his gaze with her own.

"Mr Hammond. . . When you get back to America, you find this spy, this traitor of yours. You explain to him just what his treachery has cost, in terms of so many decent human lives. . . and then you kill him."

"I will."

"You promise me now; you promise me that you will."

"I promise."

She studied his face for some moments, seeming to assess the sincerity behind the promise, before finally nodding. He leaned forward and kissed her on a wizened cheek, and then left her sitting by the fire, nursing the inevitable cup of coffee and rocking gently back and forth.

It was the last time he saw her alive.

****

The hastily conceived plan was to head cross-country to the south-west, and then skirt to the north side of Erfurt and Thuringian Wald. The Gaz was less than ideal for a chase, because the acceleration was poor, but off-road it came into its own. Hammond intended using that feature to the full. The cell in Magdeburg had already provided details of known checkpoints. They would bypass each one, until they were close enough to make a dash for Hessen and the American sector. After that it should be plain sailing all the way down to Frankfurt.

"I think someone's following us."

Hammond had been looking back for the last few kilometres. Catherine shook her head.

"But Paslov let us go. You said he didn't need us."

"I know, but somebody is following us. I can feel it."

That feeling was like an old friend returning. Hammond knew it well. He respected it. It had saved his life on too many occasions not to. As they passed a copse he suddenly swung off the road, reversed into the shadows of the undergrowth, and switched off the engine.

Less than three minutes later they came past: an M72 motorcycle combination, riding point, with a machine-gunner in the sidecar. The men on point were followed by two fully-manned Kübels, fore and aft of a Mercedes 340 saloon. Bringing up the rear of the main cavalcade was a Gorky armoured car. Fifty meters after that, and straining to keep up, was a canvas-backed Opel, packed with troops. Whoever was sitting in the back of the Mercedes was obviously important.

Even then Hammond might have put it down to coincidence, had he not caught a glimpse of the man sandwiched between two bodyguards in the back of the saloon. He remembered the face from newsreel footage. The peasant features and those round pince-nez glasses. Catherine asked the question.

"Who was that?"

"Beria. . . What the hell is he doing here? He's not supposed to know." Catherine didn't answer. Hammond found himself musing. Perhaps Beria had found out. Perhaps, rather than the ocean-front warmth of sunny California, poor old Stanislav Ivanovich Paslov would be defecting to the freezing austerity of a Siberian Gulag.

Catherine didn't understand.

"Not supposed to know what? Found out what?"

Hammond didn't answer immediately, because he didn't have an answer that was in any way credible. He was mulling over all that Paslov had said. Maybe it was just an unlikely coincidence. If not, there had to be more to it than Paslov's defection being blown; more, too, than Beria sitting back and waiting for the girl to lead him to Kube.

"I don't know, but perhaps we should take the scenic route back."

****

Apart from a stuttering and spluttering Polikarpov biplane, which circled for a few minutes but didn't appear to have spotted them, they saw no further sign of a search. Other than the regular checkpoints, they saw nothing of the Red Army, and crossed into the American sector at just after midnight. They reached Camp King two hours after that and drove straight to the debriefing block. The duty officer woke Howard Strecker, who looked less than happy at having his sleep disturbed.

"Couldn't you have chosen a more civilized hour?"

Hammond growled back at him.

"Sorry if we disturbed your beauty sleep. Beria didn't give us a lot of choice."

"Beria? You mean, the man himself?"

"In person. I think he wanted to give us an escort. I declined."

Strecker looked through the window, to where Catherine Schmidt sat waiting in the Gaz.

"Christ! Who the hell is this girl?"

"What makes you think he wasn't chasing me?" Strecker stared impassively back at him. Hammond smiled wryly and stated the obvious. "I'm not that important, huh?"

Strecker didn't answer. He picked up the phone and told the operator to get him the airfield at Wiesbaden.

"The package, for Mr Carlisle. You have an aircraft waiting. The package will be with you within the hour." He put down the phone and nodded to Hammond. "That means you. The car's waiting outside."

"What about the girl?"

"She stays here."

"Who says?"

"Conrad Zalesie, Marcus Allum, Carlisle, Carpenter: take your pick."

Three of the names were well known to Hammond, but not the fourth.

"Conrad who?"

"Zalesie."

"Who the hell's he?"

Strecker shook his head.

"Like you said; you're not that important."

"And the girl? What happens to her?" Hammond held up a lone finger of warning as he saw Strecker mentally rehearse the same perfunctory answer. "And if you tell me I'm not important enough just one more time, you're going to seriously upset me."

"I don't know. When you're gone I have to call one of them, and they'll tell me what to do with her. That's all I know. Don't worry. Nothing bad is going to happen to her."

Hammond studied him closely and decided he was telling the truth. He also decided it was time to address the problem of Kube.

"There is a man called Kube; former Gestapo Kriminaldirektor Martin Kube. Do you know of him?" Strecker shook his head. Hammond didn't believe him, but continued anyway. "He raped her when she was a child. He wants her again. I intend making sure he doesn't get her."

Strecker shrugged.

"So?"

"So, I expect you to help me."

"I have to follow the orders I'm given."

Hammond was on a short fuse, but spoke quietly and evenly.

"While she is here, you are responsible for her. And your Commander-in-Chief sits in The White House, not the State Department."

"Thank you for reminding me. Now, if that's all?"

Strecker's apparent indifference bordered on callousness. It didn't sit well with Hammond in his weary and belligerent mood.

"Colonel Strecker, I don't believe you. I think you know this man Kube, and if I hear that you've handed her over to him, I will find him and deal with him, and then I will find you and deal with you. Do you understand?"

Strecker slowly nodded, and then called for back-up.

"Guards!" The two uniforms standing guard outside burst into the room. Strecker spoke calmly. "Mr Hammond is leaving for Wiesbaden. There is an aircraft waiting. Make sure he gets on it."

One of the guards placed a restraining hand on Hammond's arm. It was a foolish thing to do.

A moment later the guard was on the floor, with the HDM at his head. His face turned ashen. His partner froze. Hammond turned to a stunned-looking Howard Strecker.

"I would keep your guards here, if I were you, Colonel. Your need is obviously greater than mine. Now I've warned you once. I don't give second warnings. Remember that."

He pocketed the HDM and sauntered out of the office without looking back. Catherine left her seat in the Gaz and hurried to meet him.

"What did he say?"

"I have to go to Washington. You'll stay here for a while. Don't worry. You're safe now."

One of the waiting guards stepped forward and tried to usher her away. She ignored him and clung to Hammond. She kissed him on the mouth. She asked why he wasn't staying with her. He repeated his earlier assurance. She was safe now. She shouldn't worry.

It was a guarantee he was far from convinced of.

"You will come to see me, when I get to America? I couldn't bear it if you didn't come to see me, if you didn't look after me any more."

The vulnerable child had returned, uncertain and timid and overwhelmed, clinging to him and pleading for reassurance and constancy. The provocative beauty who had so easily seduced him at the guesthouse had vanished. The cold-eyed and blasphemous incarnation of a Hindu goddess of fear had similarly disappeared. Hammond brushed away her tears and stroked at her hair as he held her close and smiled the necessary words.

"Of course I will. You're not getting rid of me that easily, and Kali will look after you until then. She always has, hasn't she?"

"Promise me. Promise me, when you have finished what you have to do, that you will find me again and protect me."

"I promise."

"No matter what?"

"No matter what. I swear."

Hammond thought back to the old woman at the guest house as he made yet another uncertain promise, but the young woman seemed satisfied. She nodded, sniffed back the tears, smiled her gratitude and then walked away with hips swivelling and head held high.

He saw her hesitate at the entrance to the block, and then turn to watch him leave. He waved at her through the rear window as the car taking him to Wiesbaden sped out of the main gate. After that he flew non-stop to Andrews Field, on the same prototype Stratofreighter that had brought him to Germany almost a lifetime ago.

16

It was the day after her estranged husband's formal induction into the State Department. An unashamedly naked Emma Radcliff-Hammond sat posturing before the dressing-table mirror. She brushed her hair into an auburn sheen, and then turned to admire the firmness of her breasts and the ungoverned flatness of her stomach. Clearly delighted with the result, she turned again and studied the reverse profile, then smiled conceitedly and raised her chin to accentuate the curvaceousness.

Six months had passed since she'd left her husband and moved into the Georgetown apartment. In all that time the helter-skelter of a recklessly promiscuous life had lost none of its excitement or appeal.

She angled one of the dressing-table mirrors and studied her latest beau as he slept. He was strikingly good-looking, and deliciously young; so young that, even to Emma Radcliffe-Hammond's esoteric moral standards, his seduction had seemed almost an act of devilment.

Her mind drifted back to the previous evening and that ostentatious dinner table.

It had been a mind-numbing evening, as Washington dinner parties so often were. Emma had sat in the thick of it, smiling occasionally and politely listening to the mindless small talk on either side. Until that point the only remotely risqué entertainment had been a few wide-eyed stares, responding to glances of vampish promise. Then someone began tapping a crystal goblet with the back of a silver teaspoon.

"Ladies. Excuse me, ladies! I think now would be a suitable time to leave the gentlemen to their brandy and cigars. Gentlemen, if you will excuse us? Ladies, shall we?"

The matriarchal Alicia Travers herded the ladies away to liqueurs in an adjoining room, looking for all the world like a clucking mother hen gathering her brood before waddling back to the hen house, with old and young, fat and thin, seductive and odious, all clucking and tripping along in her considerable wake.

Emma had been the last female to leave; she'd made sure of it. She'd waited for the precise moment to make her provocatively-choreographed exit before rising from her chair. Scarlet-tipped fingers smoothed non-existent creases from the tightest of satin gowns. A sigh of feigned boredom dragged any remaining eyes to the cleavage that spilled from a plunging neckline.

With provocation complete, and masculine breath collectively held, a jubilant temptress strutted from the room. She kept the head high and the breasts proud, and smiled a smile of mischief as she moved, treating masculine imaginations to a glimpse of private feminine thoughts, and mesmerized stares to the erotic promise of sashaying hips and undulating buttocks.

But for the click of stiletto heels on woodblock flooring and the seductive rustle of satin against silk, you could have heard a pin drop.

She reached the hallway and glanced around, looking for the mother hen and her chattering brood. She spied them, clucking and gossiping, in a drawing-room to the side. In the dining-room behind her, a booming masculine voice offered some wonderfully chauvinistic advice.

"Gentlemen, I must caution you. . . That is a coronary just waiting to happen."

A babble of sycophantic laughter and chuckling profanity followed, but then the dining-room doors closed. Reluctantly, Emma made her way to the waiting boredom, selected a glass of yellow chartreuse from a tray of garish-looking liqueurs, and retreated to a corner.

"My dear, he's had them all. Half the women in this room, I shouldn't wonder."

"Two and three at a time, I hear. I just don't understand what they see in him. He's drunk half the time, he's not exactly handsome, and he's anything but discreet."

"Poor Martha Saunders can't leave the house for the stares and the gossip."

Sipping politely and studying a cross-section of Washington's most pampered, Emma privately cursed the dictates of etiquette and listened to the unceasing vitriol.

"Given all the promiscuous little sluts up and down Penn' he's supposed to have bedded, it wouldn't surprise me if she's picked up a contagious disease or something."

"Ugh, poor Martha! Oh no, don't say that."

"Ugh, no! It makes me shudder to think of it."

One of the gossiping women suddenly noticed Emma sitting quietly in the corner.

"And on the subject of promiscuous little sluts, have you seen who's finally deigned to join us?"

The obvious cause of resentment glanced contemptuously and purred a warning.

"What's the matter, Angela? Same old problem with the haemorrhoids, or are we still not getting enough?"

According to Emma, Angela Carlisle's antipathy toward her was due solely to jealousy. Emma claimed the woman had married too young, and bred too young, and now felt deprived at missing out on so much youth and fun. The fact that Emma had slept with Angela Carlisle's husband had nothing to do with it.

Not that Angela Carlisle was unattractive. Still in her mid-thirties, she was tall and curvaceous, with long black hair framing a classic bone-structure and pouting lips that spoke of hidden passion. Sadly, she invariably pinned the hair high to complete a façade of austerity, and rarely relaxed the pout into a smile. She mockingly responded to the barb.

"Don't tell me you've finally run out of husbands to bed. Or are we simply in here looking to convince little miss bored and beautiful to make up the three?"

An unfazed Emma answered matter-of-factly.

"I'll never run out of husbands, Angela; not as long as they have wives like you at home. As for having to talk little miss bored and beautiful into a three, I find if they're that bored they're usually boring, and if they're that beautiful I've probably had them already."

"You're disgusting."

"Oh, and in my experience, which is considerable, I've found it's often those who scream the loudest and protest the most who have the most to hide. . . And who eventually turn out to be the horniest dykes and the biggest hypocrites."

Angela Carlisle considered the inference and fumed.

"And just what are you implying?"

"I was about to say don't knock it until you've tried it, but maybe you already have? I always say, there's a slut and a lesbian in every one of us."

Angela Carlisle was no match for this. She blushed. She swallowed. She looked uncomfortable. Emma moved to press an unexpected advantage, but a timid-looking woman interrupted.

"We were just wondering how well you know Morton Simmonds? You hear such shameful stories."

Emma answered the woman's impertinence with a smile.

"I know him well. He's a friend."

"And we all know what that means."

Angela Carlisle had obviously recovered her composure. Emma snapped back.

"I doubt you do, Angela, but I happen to think Morton Simmonds is a charming man. An excellent friend of your husband's, I understand. Like two peas in a pod, they say. I couldn't, because I never saw them both naked. Well maybe I did, but not at the same time."

"You're a slut."

She ignored the insult and continued goading.

"They say, if you want to tell the difference, Morton's the one with some modicum of technique." She shrugged, and maliciously added, "I guess you chose to bed the wrong buddy."

Somebody sniggered. Angela Carlisle's glare turned to one of open hostility.

"And so whose husband will you be having tonight, or haven't you made up your mind yet? You will let the poor woman know when you finally decide, won't you?"

"All I can tell you, dear, is that it won't be yours."

Emma turned and spoke to a group of women who had been enjoying the confrontation.

"To tell you the truth, I had him last month. It was in a moment of weakness, and I swear I'm not exaggerating when I tell you he was just about the lousiest fuck ever." Amid maidenly gasps of shock and sniggers of feminine delight, she ruthlessly added, "If that's all the poor bitch is getting once a week, it's no wonder she never smiles."

"You promiscuous little slut!"

Suddenly it was open warfare and Emma was angry.

"So who came first, Angela, the frustrated bitch or the lousy lay? Mind you, knowing Alan Carlisle as we unfortunately do, maybe I should be asking if anybody came at all."

"Right, that's it, you bitch!"

"And that's enough from the pair of you."

Moments from the snarling cat-fight that would have sent the chattering ladies who lunch into verbal orgasm, the bustling authority of Alicia Travers made a timely intervention.

"Did you hear me, Angela? I said, that's enough. You're not turning my home into a cathouse. Go and cool down on the terrace. Go on, out you go. Emma, I think you'd better come with me."

The two snarling women reluctantly separated. Emma followed her generously-proportioned hostess across the hallway and into another drawing-room.

"Scotch?"

Alicia Travis smiled knowingly as she held out the tumbler. Emma snatched at it.

"Oh God, yes please. I could do with a sensible drink."

The knowing smile turned to one of benevolence as Alicia Travers ushered Emma on to a settee and sat down alongside her.

"Try to be a little kinder to Angela. She's not having an easy time of it at the moment."

Alicia Travers was a close friend, and a lady in every sense of the word. When Emma began to protest, she shook her head and smiled warmly.

"And don't you dare say that she started into you first. From what I could see, you must have vamped just about every man at that dinner table tonight, including my Benjamin, I might add, and he's got a weak heart. You're just lucky he's too short-sighted to notice."

"Oh come on, Licie, you know I like to flirt. It's fun, and what's the harm?"

Alicia Travers favoured her with an old-fashioned look.

"Emma Radcliff-Hammond, I've known you all your life, and you're a charming girl with a kind heart and the face of an angel. Unfortunately, you also have the mind of a harlot and a body that most men would sell their souls for. If that weren't enough, you have disgracefully catholic tastes and an appetite for sex that I frankly find staggering. So don't play the innocent with me. I know you far too well."

They paused to drink their whiskies. Alicia Travers broached a sensitive issue.

"How's Gerald? Seen much of him recently?"

"No, not much. I think he's still upset."

"Well, you can't blame him for that. He loves you, Emma. He always has. In my book, you don't deserve him."

"I know. He's a kind and decent man. He just picked the wrong woman to fall in love with."

"If I remember rightly, you loved him once."

"I still do, but I'm having fun, and he can be so interminably bloody boring."

"Yes, that's so often the trouble with kind and decent men."

Emma felt the sadness suddenly and briefly overwhelm her as she considered her estranged husband. She dismissed it with a change of subject.

"So what's up with that miserable bitch Carlisle this time?"

"It's Mathew. He's not going back to Princeton, or joining Alan at the State Department. He wants to work his way around Europe. She's beside herself."

"Mathew?" The name was familiar. "Do I know him?"

"Angela's son. He's turned out to be a nice young man. She dotes on him."

"Oh, you mean that Mathew. God! It only seems like yesterday he was still at school."

Alicia Travers nodded knowingly and grinned.

"Careful, dear, or you'll be giving away your age. Well, anyway, he's here tonight. You must have seen him. He was sitting next to her at the dinner table."

"So that's who it was, I did wonder. Mmm, good-looking boy, but maybe on the youngish side of beddable, even for me. I did wonder if she'd finally. . ."

A glare accompanied the interruption.

"Well, I've had her here all day, pouring her heart out. She doesn't want to let go of him."

"She never did know when to let go of anything. I don't know why she doesn't get out of that mausoleum of a house occasionally and get herself laid. Do herself and the rest of the world a favour. She's an attractive woman, or she would be if she ever smiled or made an effort."

Alicia Travers nodded.

"Yes, that's what everyone says, but I'm not sure everything's as it should be in that household, what with her and that boy being so touchy-feely, and

Alan so often away. It's all too intense, almost bordering on, how shall I say it, the intimately unhealthy."

"How wonderfully incestuous! Do tell me more."

Alicia Travers frowned and wagged a matriarchal finger.

"No, Emma. I know what you're thinking, and I'm telling you no. This is all far too sensitive to have you causing your usual mayhem. You're to say nothing and keep away. Now you promise?"

A mischievous smile met the caution, but then she relented.

"All right, Licie, I promise, but hadn't we better be getting back?"

"Oh yes, I'd almost forgotten." Alicia Travers leaned forward to plant a maternal kiss on Emma's cheek and then got to her feet, before matter-of-factly asking, "So was it true; that bit you said earlier, about you and Alan Carlisle?"

Emma put down the glass and got to her feet.

"Yes. I met him at a White House reception. He came straight out with it."

"Came straight out with what?"

"Said he'd always wanted to fuck me."

"Emma, you know I don't care for that word."

"Sorry, Licie. Anyway, I had nothing better to do and he's not bad looking."

Alicia Travers gave her another old-fashioned look.

"Now count to ten, and tell the whole truth."

"Well, maybe I did also think it would be fun to get one over on that miserable bitch."

"Emma Radcliff-Hammond, you are thoroughly disreputable. And. . . ?"

"And what?"

"Stop playing games. You know precisely what."

She saw the earnestness in Alicia Travers and laughed wickedly.

"Licie, you have to be the most incorrigible of all my friends. And I know you don't like the word, but there's no other way to describe it. Alan Carlisle really was the most god-awful fuck."

Alicia Travers seemed intrigued.

"I take it by that you mean he couldn't. . . I don't know how to put this delicately. You mean, he wasn't able to, uh, to perform, as it were?"

"No, he was instant and solid as a rock. That was the problem. Only part of me had any time to get moist were my eyes."

"Bit of a bull at a gate, you mean?"

"Worse, darling. At least a bull paws at the ground a couple of times before he charges. With Alan Carlisle it was all over and done with before anybody got the chance to say Olé."

"Oh, my dear girl. Then perhaps we'd better spare a thought for poor Angela."

"Maybe he's not as frantic and bloody ephemeral with her. After all, you know what they say?"

"No dear, but I'm sure you're about to tell me."

"That there's no such problem for us girls as too damned big, or too damned rough, or even too damned clumsy for that matter. . . just too damned early."

17

Still giggling, the two women made their way back. The gentlemen had completed their cigar-smoking ritual and rejoined their spouses. Emma felt bored with polite conversation and constant double entendre, and mildly offended by the impertinence of so many groping hands. Another clumsy fool loudly admired her dress while discreetly fondling her buttocks. Yet another brushed his hand against her breasts, and grinned moronically at the intentional contact. Somebody pressed a partial erection against her thigh, while aged lungs wheezed a soulless apology into her ear and offered her beauty as his only mitigation.

Suddenly she'd had enough. She studied the hostile glares from so many legitimately-insecure wives, and decided to make her escape.

Offering up the usual round of polite excuses, she ducked away and found her host.

"Licie, I'm going to slip away. I'll give you a call in the week. Thanks for everything."

Alicia Travers smiled politely, but appeared relieved at her going. Emma wandered off to collect her car and head back to Georgetown.

She saw him as she was waiting for the attendant to fetch the car. He was standing by the door, smoking a cigarette and looking bored. He blushed when he noticed her watching.

She began studying him more closely, admiring the artless beauty of youth, and considering the physical athlete beneath the tuxedo. He was tall for his age, his torso firm and strong, his limbs powerful, and yet still possessing the ungainliness that boys only seem to lose on the day they become men. His hair was yellow and curled tight, his eyes brilliant blue, and his features classically formed. She wondered how a besotted mother would react to his seduction. She wondered, too, if she should break her promise to a friend. The resulting consideration lasted fewer than five seconds.

Smiling wickedly, she sidled over to engage his blushing naiveté in whatever passes for polite conversation between a scheming sexual sophisticate and a beautiful tongue-tied youth.

She said hello and asked his name. He blurted that it was Mathew Carlisle. She moved closer, until she'd breached an already-fragile comfort zone, and candidly studied his agitation. She told him her name, and said she knew his parents. He studied his shoes, and mumbled that he already knew her name. She asked him how he knew. He said his mother had told him. He added that his mother didn't like her.

She said she already knew that. She said his father was a friend. He shuffled uncomfortably, and said that was why his mother didn't like her. She put on her most coquettish look and asked him if he liked her. The blush turned an even deeper red. The eyes stayed glued to the shoes. She tried another tack. She'd heard he wanted to travel. He seemed more at ease with that. He said his mother didn't want him to leave. She said she'd heard that, too. Then he asked her what she thought he should do. It threw her for a moment.

She said he should do what he wanted. He was old enough to know his own mind. He suddenly blurted, 'Yes.' She asked what he was referring to.

After a period of silence, he finally muttered his answer. 'Yes, he liked her.' She playfully claimed not to have heard. He looked away and mumbled that he thought her beautiful.

She saw her car pull up and the attendant jump out. More worryingly, she saw Angela Carlisle across the hallway. She had seen them together. Emma would need to hurry.

She told him she liked him, too. She invited him back. He didn't answer and began openly trembling. She repeated the offer, and asked if he thought her scandalously forward.

When he again failed to answer, she spoke of her boredom. She had decided to return to her apartment in Georgetown. Would he like to come with her, for a drink or whatever? Despite the obvious handicap of painful shyness he said 'yes' and nodded furiously.

Angela Carlisle saw and heard. She crossed the hallway in an instant and glared at her son's seductress. She called his name and tugged at his arm. She told him to come back to the party with her. She begged him not to go with Emma.

Mathew Carlisle shook the grasping fingers from his sleeve and scolded his mother for making a scene. He said this couldn't go on. He said it wasn't right. He said he would see her tomorrow. He was leaving the party with Emma. He was sorry, but he had to go.

He turned his back and walked to the car, then stamped out his cigarette on the drive and climbed into the passenger seat. His doting mother silently watched him go and hung her head in the abject humiliation of one who has lost everything. She looked pleadingly at Emma. She was sorry for being rude. She was sorry for everything she had ever said. She begged Emma not to take her son. He was all she had. Emma thought the sudden transformation from aggressive rival to desolate loser almost farcical.

She told Angela that her son was a grown man. He was still young, but not a little boy any more. She should let him be a man, and do what men do. She added another worn cliché. If he loved her he would come back to her, but first she had to let him go. She followed that with a mischievous suggestion. Perhaps Angela should find a man. There were plenty on the lookout in there, and it wasn't as if Alan had ever been faithful.

Angela Carlisle shook her head. She didn't want her husband. She didn't love her husband. She had never loved or wanted him. She didn't want another man either. All she wanted was her son. If Emma took him away she would have nothing. The intensity of her plea stunned Emma into silence, but then she recalled Alicia Travers' recently-aired doubts about the worrying tactility between Angela Carlisle and her son. She similarly recalled the woman's earlier insults and all the bitterness and spite.

She said Angela should look on the bright side. She could reassure the gossiping ladies who lunch that their husbands were safe, for a night at least. Angela needn't worry about her son, either, because Emma would send him back to her. . . eventually.

She turned on her stilettos and flounced to the car, slid into the driver's seat, and looked at him with eyes that openly devoured the innocence. She asked if he still wanted to come back with her. When he nodded, the pout she offered was sheer seduction.

He asked what his mother had said. Emma looked back at the open door. The desolate figure of Angela Carlisle stood silhouetted against the light from the hallway.

"She said she wants you back."

"And what did you say?"

She turned the key in the ignition and then revved the engine unnecessarily, raising her voice so that both he and his distraught mother could hear above the noise.

"I told her she could have you back. . . But only when I've finished with you."

She rammed the gear shift home, and shot away with engine racing and tires squealing.

Back in her apartment, she turned down the lights and taught him a little of what she knew, arousing and cajoling, governing and preparing, punishing and rewarding, until a cry of gratitude and relief announced the shattering conclusion to an enduring lesson.

Now, though, it was the morning, and she was alone with her thoughts. The previous night's excess had long since passed into memory, and only the guilt remained.

But that was as it should be, because Emma had always maintained that nights are for alcohol-fuelled liaisons with passing strangers and the seduction of innocence. Mornings are for strong coffee and weak remembrance, and the guilt and shame that such iniquity always leaves.

She finished brushing her hair and wandered over to where her beau lay sleeping, recalling his blushing naiveté, and the wicked excitement she had felt as she'd taken him. She studied the softness of his hair and the smoothness of his skin, the even tempo of his breathing and the litheness of his body. Mischievous fingers slipped back the covers. Admiring eyes studied the rise and fall of a well-muscled abdomen and the naked beauty of a trusting youth.

She playfully walked her fingertips across his belly and down, feeling the wickedness return and the blood surge, and murmuring in anticipation as his eyes flew wide and his flesh pulsed.

"Shush."

Calmly and deliberately she mounted him, with a long and slender leg that leisurely straddled his body, and a softly-grasping vagina that hungrily claimed his excitement for its own.

Then the telephone rang.

"Damn!"

She glared as she reached for the receiver, but then smiled when she heard the voice of Marcus Allum.

"Did you hear about Gerald?"

The panic suddenly rose.

"What about him? Is he all right?"

"Oh yeah, he's fine."

"Marcus, don't do that to me." The smile returned, but an indignant beau was becoming angry. "Darling, I'd love to hear about it, but can I call you back? You see, I'm kind of in the middle of something right now."

"Emma Radcliff, you're not. . . ?"

"I am."

"You're disgraceful."

"I know."

"Boy or girl? Or are we being greedy?"

"Oh no, a boy, an enchanting boy."

"By that you mean young?"

"Very."

"Obedient?"

"Totally."

"Doing it for you?"

"Almost there."

"I could always pop over and finish things off. That is, if you're still, well, you know?"

"Oh I think he'll manage. Look, I'm sorry, darling, but I'm going to have to call you back."

Mathew Carlisle had finally lost control. She dropped the phone and giggled provocatively, then expertly tutored his youthful ferocity with murmurs of gentle persuasion and limbs of subtle command.

And as each successive lunge drew an answering gasp of approval from her lips, she allowed the primal rhythm to take control and left the groans of pleasure's aftermath lingering in her throat.

18

As the taxi turned into the drive, Alan Carlisle studied the rambling mansion and decided it was too big, particularly with Mathew away. It was too big for a large family, let alone the two of them. But at least it allowed them space, and if there was one thing they needed, it was that.

Then he remembered that Mathew wasn't at Princeton; he was home. He gave a sigh as the tires crackled on the drive and the taxi slid to a halt. Yet another family row was looming.

The driver stood waiting for him to get out. He summoned his courage, gave another heavy sigh of resignation, and climbed out. The driver held out his hand.

"Seven bucks."

Carlisle looked around for his suitcase. It was still in the trunk. He felt slightly offended. A house and grounds of this size and quality in Takoma Park were worth a fortune. Did the man really think that someone who lived in a place like this would stiff him for seven bucks?

He shrugged and handed over the exact amount. If the driver thought he looked like a cheapskate and a crook, he'd act like one.

"No tip?"

"You lost my suitcase."

The driver hurried to the trunk. He dragged out and then held the suitcase high, to display the evidence. Carlisle took it from him without speaking, and then headed for the front door, without tipping. The driver mumbled something derogatory, then climbed into the cab and sped off, leaving tire marks in the gravel. Carlisle smirked; that'd teach him.

He found his keys and opened the door, stepped inside and kicked the door to.

That was when he saw her there, leaning against the doorway to the kitchen, heavily made up and dressed in translucent lingerie, with a matching smile. He stopped for a moment and studied her with appreciative eyes, seeing the fullness of her breasts, the slenderness of her waist, and the smoothness of thighs transforming to silhouette beneath a pastel chemise. He smelt her perfume on the air. He allowed his lust to build. She was still such an incredibly desirable woman. He knew how much he still cared; how much he still wanted. It was all such a waste.

But then he saw the sudden recognition on her face, and watched in sadness and regret as the seductive smile faded to sullenness, and sparkling eyes dulled into their customary loathing. Whoever she might be wearing that for, it obviously wasn't him.

"Oh, it's you. I suppose it's no good asking where you've been or who you've been with."

He snapped an answer as she turned away.

"And I suppose it's no good asking who you're wearing that for; obviously not me." He looked to the heavens. "Mathew, I suppose. What am I saying? It's always Mathew."

A thought suddenly occurred, a dreadful thought, a terrible thought.

He put it to the back of his mind and followed her into the kitchen, admiring her buttocks and noting her unsteadiness. She'd obviously been drinking again, and heavily, but, Christ! She was gorgeous. He recalled a time when he would have reached out and taken. A time long before the current misery of a marriage filled with recrimination and bitterness; a time of tenderness and gentle passion, when love had been so intense and life had been so good. She had lost none of her allure over all those years of sadness. He wished it could be different now.

She returned to her seat and her vodka, and sat in silence. He poured himself a coffee.

"This coffee's cold."

"So make some more. You're not helpless."

"I thought I told you to get some staff? This place looks like a bomb hit it."

"Who were you expecting me to get, Alan, a couple of teenage cheerleaders, flouncing around in French maid's costumes? I told you: Mrs Reid is fine, and I don't like strangers in the house when it's dark or over the weekend. Perhaps I should get a man in, someone to attend to my needs for a change?"

If she'd hoped to upset him, it hadn't worked. He sat down opposite her at the table.

"I wouldn't mind. If there was another man, I'd probably understand it. Given that you haven't spread your legs for me in almost twenty years, I'd probably applaud it." As he studied her indifference, the bitterness and frustration boiled over. "You see, I could cope with another man, a rival. I could handle a rival. Someone to point at and say, what's he got that I haven't?"

"Oh, for Christ's sake, play another record."

He continued to rant.

"I could even cope with more than one. What the hell. If I came home and found an entire regiment of fucking marines, progressively book-ending you on the kitchen floor, I'd cope.

"I wouldn't like it. I'd be jealous as hell. But at least it would show me that you still had physical needs, still had sexual ambition, could still function as a woman. If I knew that I could try to cope, somehow try to compete. But this. . . I can't compete with this. I can't cope with this."

She suddenly started shouting.

"You've got a damn nerve. How about me having to cope, when I stand next to those bitches and listen to them whispering about your disgusting perversions? How about me having to cope when I catch them watching me, and talking about you, and see them sniggering behind their hands? How about me having to cope when that Radcliff-Hammond whore announces to the world that she had you in a moment of weakness? Oh, and by the way, it's now official. You're the lousiest fuck in Washington. Emma Radcliff-Hammond told everybody last night, and if anybody should know it's that little slut.

"Do you ever think about me when you're out there, Alan, screwing your whores? Do you ever consider me at all? Do you ever wonder how I manage to cope?"

He looked blankly back at her for a suspended moment of disbelief.

"She said what? Where was this? When was this?"

She spat back at him.

"It was at the Travers's dinner party last night. She was talking about you and your old boozing and whoring buddy. She told everyone that Morton Simmonds has good technique. She said you were the lousiest fuck ever, her precise words. That was just before she told me she was going to take my son's virginity. Just before she took him away to that overpriced brothel she calls an apartment. Just before she broke my fucking heart."

Alan Carlisle sat open-mouthed as his furious wife poured on the scorn.

"I know you've had hundreds of women, Alan, and I couldn't care less. And I knew you'd had her. It didn't bother me. You see, I don't want you. I can't stand the thought of you ever touching me again. It makes me physically

196

sick to think of it. But I do care about Mathew. I do care that one of your filthy whores is out there laughing at me, while she violates and spoils the only decent thing that ever came out of our godforsaken marriage."

"For Christ's sake, stop it!"

Mathew had arrived unnoticed.

"Mathew, I didn't hear the taxi. Darling, I didn't mean for you to hear. . ."

She stood up and rushed to surround him. He pushed her away and shook his head.

"Mum, you're drunk again, and Emma's not a whore. Don't you dare say that about her. She's beautiful, and she's fun. She loves life, and she loves living. You shouldn't be calling her names. You should be asking yourself why you're not more like her."

He studied his mother's drunken condition and half-naked body with a look of disgust.

"Mum, I don't want to see you looking like this, dressing like this. Not for me, it's not right. You're my mother, for God's sake. Don't you understand what that means? You're my mother and I love you, but I don't want this. It's just not right."

He looked down at the floor, as though ashamed to look at either of his warring parents.

"And I don't want you touching me any more. Not that way. It's disgusting, and it's wrong. I'm not a little boy, I'm a man. And I'm sorry, but if anybody looks like a whore, it's you."

Angela Carlisle slapped him hard across the face, and then burst into tears. She babbled an apology and clutched at his arm, and then watched with a look of panic and despair on her face as he took the stairs two at a time. He reached his room and wrenched open the door, and then slammed it shut behind him.

She called after him, declaring her love, begging forgiveness. When he didn't answer, she sank to her knees in the centre of the hallway.

"Mathew, I love you. I didn't ever want you to. . . I'm sorry, I didn't mean. . . . I wouldn't. . . I just wanted everything to be like it used to be. Darling, you must believe me."

Alan Carlisle had watched the drama unfold in numb disbelief. But now, as his wife knelt on the hall floor, sobbing hysterically and denying the truth of a sickening ambition that was all so shockingly obvious, he felt ashamed. Ashamed of so seldom being there for them. Ashamed of long suspecting but never voicing his suspicions. Ashamed for not asking any of those nagging questions, for fear of hearing the answers. Ashamed for not hammering that final nail into the coffin of a lifeless marriage.

He no longer remembered the girl who had stolen his heart and inflamed his passion all those years ago. He no longer recalled the voluptuous siren he'd found waiting at the door only moments before. All he could see was the face of a lonely and desperate woman in the throes of moral torment, a pitiful, shameful, and deluded woman, refusing to accept the shattering reality of her own disgusting desires.

Suddenly repulsed, he stepped around the ungainly sprawl of naked limbs and crude exposure, walked into the lounge and poured himself a glass of bourbon. He threw it to the back of his throat, then poured another, and another after that. Then he studied the empty glass, listened to her sobs of anguish, and knew what he must do.

He returned to the hallway, scooped her into his arms, and carried her up the stairs to her bedroom. As he laid her on the bed she stopped sobbing and looked up at him.

"Please don't. I'm too tired and too drunk to fight you, but please don't."

Alan Carlisle smiled grimly down at her.

"After all those insults, and all those spiteful refusals I've had to suffer over all those years of misery, what makes you think I could possibly want that ever again?"

He walked to the bathroom and turned on the shower, then returned and lifted her from the bed. He ignored the kicks and struggles as he carried her to the bathroom and stepped into the shower, holding her prisoner beneath the icy cascade until the voice of drunken outrage stilled. He ignored her sobs of anguish and the stream of vitriol that spewed from her lips, waiting until her body hung limp in his arms and her rage subsided into despair.

"Now stand up, and sober up, and wash that muck off your face. Then get some sleep."

She stood under the shower in chastened obedience, her hair hanging in lank saturation, her eyes downcast, her mascara running. For a moment of masculine weakness he studied the sodden lingerie that clung to her flesh, in betrayal of every magnificent contour.

Then he reached out.

"No!"

He snapped each flimsy strap in turn and then ripped and tore the chemise from her body. Angela Carlisle staggered and almost fell. She gave a shriek and frantically scrambled to cover her nakedness. He snarled his disgust.

"Don't kid yourself. You're not that enticing, and I'm not that desperate."

Alan Carlisle stepped away from the shower and held up the torn chemise, then spoke in words of barely-controlled fury.

"Now this goes into the trash, where it belongs, and all the sordid memories go with it, you understand? Later I'll talk, and you'll listen. I'll tell you what to do, and you'll do it. Then we'll either go our separate ways or start over, but this disgusting sickness stops, right here and right now. . . Now get some sleep."

For the first time in a long while, Alan Carlisle felt a genuine sense of pride as he strode away from her puzzled stare and mute obedience. He reached his own room and closed the door, then dried his hair and changed out of his ruined suit and waterlogged clothing. After that, he walked across the landing to Mathew's room and tapped on the door.

"May I come in?"

"It's your house."

He found his son packing a suitcase.

"You're leaving?"

Mathew Carlisle stared sullenly at the carpet.

"I'd have thought that was obvious. Don't try talking me out of it."

"I didn't intend to."

Carlisle sat on the edge of the bed and tried to repair the damage.

"Matt, your mother didn't mean that. She didn't realize what you were thinking. She didn't understand that it made you feel uncomfortable."

Mathew Carlisle scoffed.

"Dad, don't be naïve. She was always touching me. She used to come into the bathroom, when I was in the bath. She used to touch me while I lay there. She even got into bed with me."

Alan Carlisle smiled gently and offered a possibility he didn't believe.

"Matt, it was just maternal instinct. Sometimes mothers don't know when to stop being mothers. Sometimes they feel so much love for their children, they don't realize they're growing up. Sometimes they don't realize the children they love so much aren't children any more. It's only natural."

"Dad. . . She used to make me come."

19

Alan Carlisle stopped smiling, and stopped pretending.

"I'm sure she didn't mean to. It must have been an accident."

"Dad, it wasn't just the once. She did it all the time. She. . ."

"She must have said something. She can't have meant it. Why didn't you say something? Why didn't you stop her?"

Mathew Carlisle hung his head. He was obviously suffering. His words confirmed it.

"It was on that morning you telephoned from Frankfurt. After we talked, I decided to take a bath. She came home. She said she'd been staying with friends. She knelt down by the bath and started washing me. She used to do that. I didn't think anything of it, but then she touched me."

"What, you mean, she touched your genitals?"

Carlisle couldn't believe what he was hearing. Mathew nodded.

"Yeah, I think it was an accident, but I started to get. . . well, you know."

"You started to get an erection?"

"Yeah, I tried to cover up, but she pushed my hands away and told me not to be silly. She said I always got like that in the bath; you know, when I was young. She said it was natural."

Carlisle nodded. Years ago, he could remember Angela telling him about it. At the time they'd laughed together and he'd felt quite proud of his son. Mathew went on with his confession. He seemed relieved to have someone to talk to.

"For a while she just soaped and sponged, but then she dropped the soap and took hold of me; you know, properly got hold of me. . . I told her not to. I told her to stop, but she didn't. She started massaging me, you know, up and down. I couldn't help it. I just came."

Mathew looked down at the floor.Carlisle felt numb, but he could sense there was more, and he had to know it all.

"Go on."

"I felt dreadful, but she looked so happy. She asked if it felt good. When I didn't answer, she said she'd enjoyed doing it. She said it made her feel good to make me feel good. She said I shouldn't worry about girls. She said they were cruel and they'd hurt me. She said she'd look after me, until I was older and more experienced. . . I'm sorry, Dad. I didn't know what to say.

"After that she never said anything much, and I never knew what to say. She used to stop me and say I looked tense, or upset, and then she'd just do it to me."

"But you must have said something, or tried to stop her. Mathew, you're a young man. You're so much stronger than her. You could have stopped her."

Alan Carlisle was becoming angry, but then he saw the shame and hurt in his son's eyes.

"I'm sorry, go on. I didn't mean to get angry."

Mathew nodded and continued.

"I tried staying up here until she'd gone out, but a few days ago she came into the bedroom. I was still in bed. She started talking about nothing in particular, but all the time I knew what she was thinking. All the time I knew what she wanted.

"She said I looked really tense. Then she took off her dress. I said I was fine, but she took no notice. She got into bed. She said she wanted to teach me about girls. She said she'd show me what they liked. I said I already knew. She said I only thought I knew.

"She put her legs around me and started pushing against me, and saying things like how sexy I was, and how hard I was, and how I was making her excited. Then she told me to take off her panties. She said it was time I learned about women."

Carlisle had tried not to show his disbelief and anger, but the emotion suddenly overwhelmed him. "Mathew, I can't believe you. . . you didn't have sex with your mother?" He watched Mathew shake his head and felt the resulting relief flood through him. "Oh, thank God."

Mathew spoke in earnest. He looked distraught.

"I nearly did. She wanted me to. She said it to me. She said, 'Fuck me'. She said it out loud. She was tugging at me, and pushing up against me. Then she pulled me on top of her. She wrapped her legs around. She had hold of me. She was pulling me closer, and I nearly did."

"But you stopped?"

"Yes. Something made me stop. I pushed her away. I told her I couldn't."

"What did she say?"

"At first she didn't say anything. She had her eyes closed, and she was breathing heavily, but then she sort of groaned and asked me why.

"I said it wasn't right. She didn't say anything for a while. Then she told me not to worry about it, and went back to her room.

"For a few days after that I stayed with friends. I knew, if I didn't get away. . . Well, I wasn't sure I could stop her again. I was going back to Princeton, but I knew she'd find an excuse to visit. I decided to get as far away as possible. That was when I decided on Europe."

Alan Carlisle had listened in horror. He began defending the indefensible.

"Look, Mathew, I know your mother was wrong, and so does she now. I'm sure she didn't realize she was taking it too far. She just didn't realize. Not until it was too late."

"It doesn't matter. I'm leaving anyway."

"What about Princeton?"

"I don't want it. I never wanted it. It was only ever your idea. It was never mine."

"You could always defer. Someone could have a word. I'm sure they'd agree."

He was clutching at straws. Mathew looked scathingly back at him.

"One of your old boy network, you mean? Dad, I don't want it."

Carlisle tried to convince him, but Mathew refused. When he talked of a career in the State Department, Mathew shook his head and said he wanted to make his own way. He said he'd never had any influence in the decisions that affected his life. He didn't want to become like his father, sleeping with strangers in hotel rooms, married to someone like his mother. He vowed that everything in his life would change.

When Carlisle asked if he had discussed this with Emma, Mathew shook his head.

He said he was going to Europe, to forget and start a new life. He would find work and somewhere to live. He wanted to do something useful for a change. Maybe he'd even find a proper girlfriend. He'd already checked with airline reservations. There was a Boeing Constellation taking off for Paris at six. He would be on it.

****

It was gone eleven that night when Alan Carlisle returned to the house. He found her sitting up in the bed and reading. She turned to look at him, her eyes still red from crying. She appeared calm, but spoke in a voice that betrayed the presence of disturbed emotions.

"You locked the door. Why did you do that? Am I a prisoner in my own home now?"

He smiled weakly as he slotted the key back.

"Of course not. I just thought you were a bit overwrought."

"Is that why you took my sleeping tablets from the dressing table?"

"Sorry. I didn't want you waking up and doing anything stupid."

She shook her head.

"I wouldn't have done. I'm upset, and sad, and ashamed. I've been stupid and foolish, and you probably think I'm a terrible pervert. Maybe you'd be right, but suicidal is one of the few emotions I'm not feeling. Where's Mathew?"

"Halfway to Paris. I wired ahead and asked them to look after him. He'll be all right."

He steeled his nerve and then asked the question he had to ask.

"Why, Angela? I need you to tell me why."

She put down the book and looked at him with a tenderness he hadn't seen for years. She said it was because Mathew had always been so gentle and vulnerable. She loved him so much. He would close his eyes, put his arms around her, hold her hand, kiss her cheek. He would do whatever she asked, without condition or question, and always with such gentleness and love.

Alan Carlisle spoke of his own confusion. He asked what physical pleasure she got from the affair. He couldn't understand. He needed to know. He tried not to be bitter or defensive, but it must have shown, because she asked him to try to understand.

She admitted that being with Mathew heightened her arousal, and said that afterwards she would go to her bedroom and lock the door. She would recall a confused young man's gentleness, and imagine herself making love with someone just like him. She would lie on the bed and touch herself until a climax arrived and released her from the torment.

Alan Carlisle felt the tears welling up as he watched the guilt and sadness in her. He said he could have done that for her. He could have been gentle and caring, tender and loving, if only she had asked.

She shook her head.

"You always used to hurt me whenever we had sex. I was afraid of you. I couldn't take the pain. That was why I stopped sleeping with you. That was why I started sleeping in here."

He looked at her in astonishment. So many years of misunderstanding, clarified with one simple announcement.

"And for all these years you never explained. You just let me go on thinking you were. . . that you didn't have feelings, and didn't want love; that you didn't care?"

"What could I have said? I was afraid of penetration and I still am. It's as sad and as simple as that. When you get aroused you lose control. . . It used to hurt.

"I'm not blaming you. It's just the way you're made. It's not my fault either. I can't stand pain. That's why Mathew was caesarean. I thought you understood that. Maybe it's different for other women. Maybe they're built larger, or aroused easier. Maybe they're able to take the pain. But I can't. I can't stand any form of pain."

He sat on the edge of the bed, frightened to ask but knowing that he must.

"So why did you want Mathew? I mean, if it hurts; if you're frightened of. . ."

"Mathew wasn't like that. He wasn't aggressive and uncaring. He was gentle, and I was in control. Even if I hadn't been, Mathew would never hurt me, no matter what."

He asked her about other men. She laughed.

"There were plenty who tried, in the beginning, when we were arguing so publicly. Some of your so-called-friends were the first to offer their sympathy."

When he asked about Morton Simmonds, the contempt returned to her eyes. Was that all that worried him? He said he had to know. Did Morton Simmonds try to sleep with her?

"No, Morton didn't even try, unlike some. Anyway, I couldn't do something like that."

"I don't see why. If another man could excite you, arouse you. I would. . ."

"Alan, stop it. When I said I was afraid of penetration, I meant petrified."

He hung his head. He hadn't realised. He felt so foolish.

"I'm sorry. I'm so sorry. I didn't understand."

She said it didn't matter; they'd had eighteen years to deal with it. She paused for a moment and the colour rose in her cheeks.

"I did try it with a woman once."

"What?"

"Remember Sarah, Sarah Pearson, from about six or seven years ago?"

"Of course. She used to be your best friend. You mean that you and she. . . ?"

He spluttered his shock and saw her smile. Suddenly the tension dissolved.

She said it had happened when they lived in Georgetown. Sarah Pearson lived in the apartment downstairs. She often popped up for coffee. They would talk for hours. Angela would talk of her problems with Alan. Sarah would talk of her problems with husband, Archie. The conversations would often include details. The details would always be intimate.

"Mathew was away on summer camp, and I was feeling miserable. I met Sarah for coffee that morning and told her how I was feeling. That afternoon she came up to the apartment and brought a bottle of wine with her. I think it was French. Sarah said it was expensive. She said Archie had been up to his old tricks again and she was punishing him. I assumed she meant that she was punishing him by drinking his wine. God! I was so naïve.

"Anyway, we drank the wine, and I got a bottle of cheap Riesling from the cupboard. We drank that, too. Then, for some reason, I started to cry.

"She was comforting me. She put her arms around me and held me, and suddenly we were kissing. I don't know how it happened. It just did.

"I always thought that kissing a woman would repulse me, but it felt beautiful; soft, and gentle, and wonderfully erotic. I closed my eyes and pretended she was a man. I let her touch me, too, in fact I think I even encouraged her, but then she spoke, and that was that."

Alan Carlisle had found the story disturbingly erotic. He tried to look nonchalant, but wanted to know more.

"What did she say?"

"Oh, Sarah was so sure of herself, so domineering. She said she'd been waiting to ream me since the first time she saw me. I'd never heard that expression before."

"It put you off?"

"No. You see, it wasn't the coarseness. It was the voice. It told me I was with another woman. I had to stop pretending. I had to open my eyes, and return to reality."

"So, what did you say?"

"I just wanted to curl up and die. I called her a filthy dyke and told her to get out. She turned and fled. It was the last time I saw her."

"And do you still wonder? About other women? Do you think, maybe. . . ?"

"Of course not. It's disgusting and perverted; it's just plain wrong."

Her interruption had been a little too fervent. He noticed, but was too tired to press. He changed the subject. He'd had enough of confessions. He asked what they should do now. Angela said she'd expected a lecture; she'd expected divorce. He scoffed. He did want her to take more interest in his work, though.

"I thought you couldn't discuss your work?"

"Maybe I'm just sick of all these meaningless secrets. Maybe I don't see the point in all of this cloak-and-dagger crap, not when the nation's really important secrets are leaking through a sieve. Maybe I just need someone who tells me the truth. Then there are the receptions and social events and that; they're difficult when your wife's never there.

"I don't want to lose you, Angela. I love you. You're beautiful. I like people to see how proud of you I am. They don't have to know we don't. . . but that still leaves Mathew."

She gave a weak smile and nodded.

"I'll write and tell him I'm sorry, promise it will never happen again, tell him we'll always be there for him. . .

"And then I guess we're going to carry on. You'll continue sleeping with every promiscuous little tramp in Washington, and I'll try to be kinder and more supportive, and pretend not to notice. I still care for you, whatever I said earlier. I don't want to make love. Not with you, not with anyone, and I know that must seem unfair. But I do still care."

He felt a little guilty at that. Much of the problem had been his fault.

"I think that lets me off rather lightly."

She looked sadly back at him.

"Do you think so? Somehow, I don't think it lets either of us off all that lightly."

20

Hammond was feeling a complexity of emotions as he sat waiting outside Davis Carpenter's office. On the upside he had secured a position with the State Department, and a relatively-senior one at that. He'd escaped from Soviet-occupied Germany physically, if not mentally intact. He still had the congratulations of a call from a relieved Marcus Allum ringing in his ears and now when he walked down the street, people didn't turn away or nip into coffee shops the moment they saw him. In the space of a few weeks, he had become persona grata again.

So why was he feeling depressed?

The answer, of course, was the girl; he couldn't get her out of his head. When he'd broached the subject with Allum, his new State Department boss had simply hung up the phone. He didn't expect to get much more from Carpenter or Carlisle, but he had given the girl his word, and that meant a great deal to him. And then there were his feelings for her.

In Dessau, he had convinced himself that he was falling in love with her, but back in the hustle of Washington he wasn't so sure of his feelings. She was so young, and he was in love with Emma, or was he? Perhaps his feelings for the girl had been a product of the danger and the tension and her obvious vulnerability; and she was beautiful. One thing he was certain of. He had to protect her from Kube. The only question was how?

"You can go in now."

He found Carpenter sitting at his desk, puffing on an oversized cigar. The pompous bureaucrat smiled and offered his congratulations. Bleary-eyed and single-minded, Hammond ignored that. He asked about the girl. Carpenter said it was none of his concern. Hammond shook his head. He had given the girl his word. He always kept his word. He asked again.

Carpenter said he didn't know. When Hammond asked where they had taken her, Carpenter said he didn't know that either. Even if he had known he couldn't tell Hammond.

Hammond decided that, for once in his life, Davis Carpenter was telling the truth. In that case, he needed to speak to Carlisle.

Carpenter doubted that Alan Carlisle would know. It seemed the State Department's proverbial rough diamond wasn't his favourite person. He said Carlisle was merely a functionary, and not an especially bright one. When Hammond insisted on speaking to Carlisle, pomposity became belligerence. He said Hammond must make his report first.

Hammond, equally belligerent, refused. He had rescued the girl as ordered, but Carpenter clearly didn't know what was going on. He would make his report to Carlisle.

Carpenter wanted to know more. Hammond explained angrily.

Carpenter had sent him to Magdeburg to find a girl and get her to Frankfurt. He hadn't said that she also happened to be the Soviet Union's public enemy number one. He hadn't said that he'd be going head-to-head with Beria and Paslov. He hadn't said that he'd be taking on the Red Army. He hadn't said that she was the daughter of one of Reinhard Heydrich's closest friends. He hadn't said that she had been the sexual chattel of another Nazi war criminal, a man officially listed as dead, but in truth still alive. He hadn't said that this same Nazi war criminal had an unhealthy amount of pull around the State Department.

Carpenter looked stunned. He tried to deflect Hammond's anger with a familiar lie. He said it was better for Hammond that he didn't know too much.

Hammond didn't buy that for a second. Carpenter hadn't said, because Carpenter hadn't known. Now he intended talking directly to Carlisle. A sullen-looking Carpenter mumbled that Carlisle wasn't there. He was up in New York, meeting with Marcus Allum and Conrad Zalesie. Carpenter said he had no idea when he was due back. Hammond would have to wait.

****

Carlisle returned later that week. After explaining all that had happened, Hammond told him of Paslov's offer to defect. Carlisle seemed less than enthused, but, when Hammond told him of Paslov's offer to name Beria's agents in the State Department and The Poplars, his attitude changed.

"Are you certain he said The Poplars? Could he have said something similar?"

"No, it was The Poplars. He was clear on that. Why, is that important?"

"Of course it's bloody important. Where the hell have you been for the last three years?"

Despite his dislike of Carlisle, Hammond had kept his self-control. Now that was gone and he was furious.

"I was in Europe for most of it; fighting a war, preserving our freedom and our way of life, and all that crap. I was out there with the others, risking our lives, while cowardly bastards like you stayed here in Washington screwing the wives we left behind."

Carlisle didn't flinch. He apologized.

"I'm sorry, Hammond. It was nothing personal."

Hammond let the anger go, but couldn't resist twisting the knife.

"From what I'm told it didn't even qualify for an apology. You weren't the first, and I doubt you'll be the last. Now you were telling me about The Poplars?"

"If it's any comfort, my wife hasn't slept in my bed for a hell of a lot longer than your wife hasn't slept in yours."

Carlisle seemed to need absolution. Hammond was in no mood to provide it.

"It's not. So tell me about The Poplars: what is it, and where is it?"

"Think Spanish."

"I speak German, Russian and a little French, but no Spanish, so tell me?"

"That's a shame, because then you would have known the Spanish translation for The Poplars is Los Alamos."

"You mean Manhattan?"

"I mean Manhattan."

Hammond, taken by surprise, asked if Carlisle believed that Beria had an agent at Los Alamos. Carlisle nodded. He said, according to the latest official estimates, the Soviets should be fifteen years from developing nuclear weapons, but he thought they were a lot closer than that. He had heard that Beria's priority was an order from Stalin to build and successfully test a nuclear bomb within three years.

When Hammond questioned the Soviet ability to achieve that, Carlisle said Beria had no choice. He knew the Americans were building a super-bomb. He also knew that if the Soviets didn't catch up soon, it was unlikely they ever would. More to the point, if the Mingrelian failed to do his master's bidding, Stalin would either shoot him for treason or force him to take a long-term vacation in his own Gulag.

Many of Russia's nuclear physicists were either dead or on a one-way trip to the Gulag, ironically because of another of Beria's purges. Many others had either defected or were hoping to do so. Lavrenti Beria had only one way he could make up the ground in the time available. Hammond voiced the only logical conclusion.

"Steal it from us."

"Exactly."

"But how the hell do you go about stealing an atom bomb?"

Carlisle was coming alive. It was obviously a pet subject. He said it was a lot easier than Hammond might think. First take a report full of holes, a report designed to justify spending on nuclear programs, for example, and use it as a flawed model. Then bring in somebody capable, like Igor Kurchatov, to identify where all the holes are. Then begin patching the holes with information your agents have stolen. After that you send out teams to collect the materials, the uranium and so forth. Suddenly you have a nuclear programme back on track.

"This Igor Kurchatov. . . he's good?"

"Yes, he is."

"And this report you mentioned. Does it exist?"

"Oh, yes. They hawked it around the media not long ago. They called it the Smyth report. It was the full technical history of The Manhattan Project.

"They published the Smyth report to make everyone look good and keep the funding rolling in. To that end they succeeded. But to Beria it was so much more. It was manna from heaven. It gave him the one thing he couldn't steal: a full project organization, and tried and tested model, for the entire Soviet nuclear programme."

Carlisle said there were people in Washington who didn't agree with him. They thought him a zealot, but he believed the collation and publication of the Smyth report was one of the most foolish and damaging security blunders America ever made.

Hammond was suddenly nervous. If Beria did have an agent at Los Alamos, and if that agent was working at a senior level, with the necessary authorization, Russia could be almost there. America could be in trouble. Carlisle nodded furiously, but then contradicted him.

He said there had to be more than one agent. He said Beria was like Stalin; he was thorough, cautious, and paranoid. Lavrenti Beria believed that successful espionage was the product of concerted effort rather than individual craft. That was the way he had always worked: multiple teams competing for information, with none having any knowledge of the others. It was classic espionage, and it was classic Beria: infiltration by a series of independent cells, all autonomous and all reporting directly to him.

When Hammond asked why the FBI hadn't gone through Los Alamos with a fine-tooth comb, Carlisle said it wasn't as easy as he might think. The FBI didn't believe these spies existed, and Hoover was still on a crusade to clean up the White House. He said Hoover didn't care if somebody stole a few technical documents from somewhere way out in the desert. His only interest was finding Washington moles, and proving a point to Harry Truman.

Carlisle said he'd been working on this since Igor Gouzenko's defection in forty-five had first alerted him to the possibility of spies in the Manhattan Project. Since then he had been working with Morton Simmonds and the people at Los Alamos. Carlisle seemed genuinely fond of the FBI's notorious son. He said he'd first met Simmonds at Princeton. They were still friends today. One day they would go public with their findings, but that was long term.

"And in the short term?"

"There is no short term. Hoover wouldn't give me the time of day without concrete proof."

"But when you hand over Paslov they'll have no choice. They'll have to believe you."

Carlisle shook his head.

"That's not gonna happen. The last thing anybody wants is Paslov talking to The Bureau. He knows too much. . . Why do you think I wasn't keen on taking him?"

Hammond couldn't believe what he was hearing.

"So you're saying that a Russian spymaster knows more about the steps we're taking to protect this country than our own federal government?"

"That's about the gist of it."

"So what are you going to do with Paslov?"

"If he tells us everything we need to know, that's fine. Maybe we can deal."

"And if he doesn't?"

"I'll give him to Conrad Zalesie."

Until his argument with Howard Strecker, the name had been unknown to Hammond. Now it seemed to be on everyone's lips. Carlisle provided some background.

Conrad Zalesie was an exiled Lithuanian count, and one of the wealthiest men in America. He ran the ATLI Corporation, and was one of the key players in the drive to build European networks. Zalesie owned property all over the world, but currently lived up in Connecticut, according to Carlisle, on an estate the size of Rhode Island. As for what he would do with Paslov? If Carlisle knew anything about Conrad Zalesie he would probably pull Paslov's fingernails out one by one, and enjoy doing it.

"And this man Kube, this ex-Gestapo chief. Where does he fit?"

"Kube will work with us, integrating our new networks in Poland and Czechoslovakia."

"What do you mean, work with us? The man's a war criminal."

"For god's sake, don't be so naïve."

Carlisle glared. Hammond changed tack.

"And rescuing the girl was part of his price?"

Carlisle looked hard at him.

"No, whatever makes you think that?"

"Because he's infatuated with her?"

"Seems he's not the only one. No fools like old fools, huh?"

"Did you know that he raped her when she was twelve?"

"Now that I didn't know, but it makes no difference. I can assure you, Hammond, Martin Kube had nothing to do with your trip to Germany."

"Then who did?"

"I can't tell you that. Anyway, the girl's a serial killer. She's mentally unstable."

Hammond wasn't letting him get away with that.

"She needs help. So would anybody who'd been through what she's been through, but she doesn't see it that way and neither do I. She sees herself fighting a war against the Bolsheviks. It happens to be the same war that we're fighting."

"You have become infatuated with her, haven't you?" Hammond had been about to protest. Carlisle didn't give him the chance. "I'm telling you to let it go, Hammond. This is all way above your head, so let it go."

"And if I refuse?"

"In case the simple fact has escaped you, I've just given you a direct order."

"A direct order from a Washington rake who sleeps with other men's wives behind their backs, because his own wife doesn't want anything to do with him?"

"If you're expecting to survive in this job I suggest you do as you're damn well told. Take a few days off. Give your wife a call. Perhaps you could try banging someone a little nearer your own age: maybe someone who doesn't still wear pigtails and fit into her school uniform."

Hammond leaned across the desk and hit him, hard across the jaw. The force of the blow rocked Carlisle back in his chair, but he recovered quickly. He wiped a smear of blood from his lip and smiled a rueful smile.

"I probably deserved that, but you ever do it again and I'll have you back in that insurance company so fast your head will spin. Now if you want to keep your job you'll do as I told you to do and take some time-out."

Direct order or not, Hammond had no intention of abandoning Catherine. He wondered why, and tried to analyse his feelings.

He should have been angry about Carlisle sleeping with Emma. He should have been angry at being duped into risking his life in Germany. He should have been angry about being called an old fool. Strangely, he wasn't especially angry about any of that, but he was angry about Carlisle's obvious lack of concern for Catherine.

Carlisle made a belated effort to curb the antagonism.

"Look, man, forget what I said. I spoke in anger, and I apologize. If you take my advice, you'll talk to Emma. At least talk to someone who's not involved in all this mayhem, someone you can trust. It makes a difference when there's someone there, even if they only nod their head and listen."

Hammond held the glare. Carlisle shrugged.

"All right, have it your way. I'll let you know when we're ready to talk to Paslov. Now get the fuck out of here."

21

Mathew Carlisle had been in Paris for almost a month when he first saw the girl. Thanks to his father's contacts in the American Embassy, Mathew had found both accommodation and work of sorts, and settled in well. He worked for ten hours a day, and six days a week as a general dogsbody in a luxury hotel just off the Avenue George V, on the north end of The Place de la Concorde. In its time the hotel had boasted the patronage of European royalty and American presidents. More latterly, and less proudly, it had housed members of the German high command. But royalty and dignitaries held no interest for Mathew, not when compared to the beautiful young woman he had briefly met in room 307.

Mathew's own room was little more than a cupboard in the basement. His below-stairs work consisted of fetching and cleaning, and polishing anything and everything. However, the concierge would occasionally call on him to carry guests' luggage during busy periods, and it was during one such period that he met the young woman in room 307.

Her name was Lara Therese Scholde, and she was the most perfect creature Mathew had ever seen. She smiled at him when he carried her bags to the room. When he refused a gratuity, and said her smile was more than enough compensation, her face lit up and the smile widened into radiance.

The following day he bumped into her when taking a stroll in the Tuileries. She was by the fountain, feeding the birds. He wandered over to bid her a badly-pronounced *bonjour*. He couldn't believe his luck when she invited him to join her for coffee. When he told her the hotel didn't allow such liaisons, she winked and told him she wouldn't breathe a word.

They walked along the Champs Élysée for a while, and then stopped at a pavement café. He wanted to know everything about her, and began by asking where she lived. When she told him she was Austrian, he asked her why she was in Paris. She said her father had died in the war and her mother now ran the family fashion and accessories business in Vienna. She giggled and told him that she was in Paris looking for new ideas to steal. He thought she was wonderful.

Two hours and a long lunch later they crept their way back to room 307 and made love all that afternoon and into the evening. Lonely and vulnerable, Mathew Carlisle was instantly smitten. She ordered room service. He hid in the bathroom when it arrived. They ate and drank, and then made love again.

The following morning Mathew crept from her room at five a.m. and ran straight into the night concierge, who reported him to the day concierge, who took him to the duty manager. The duty manager was a pompous individual, who hated Americans almost as much as he hated Nazis. He gave Mathew a long lecture on morality and hotel standards, and then told him that he no longer enjoyed a position at the hotel. Two porters escorted him to his basement cupboard, to pack his bags. The same two men escorted him from the building.

When the girl complained about his treatment, they evicted her. The duty manager tore up the bill in front of her. He said the days when his hotel had to take Nazi whores as guests were long gone. Mathew stood waiting for her outside the hotel. He said he wanted to hit the pompous little man. Lara said he wasn't worth it. She smiled and suggested the pompous little man was obviously jealous of Mathew's good looks. Mathew positively beamed with pride. She said her eviction was the hotel's loss and Mathew's gain. When she hailed a taxi and asked him to come with her, Mathew was into the taxi and beside her in an instant.

They found another, cheaper, hotel, farther up the Champs Élysée, on the Rue de Beri, and settled into an idyllic five days of making love and drinking champagne. She talked of her home in Vienna, and he talked of how much he hated Washington. She told him about her father and said how much she missed him. She said she loved her mother dearly, but had loved her father more.

She asked him about his parents, and he blurted out all that had happened. He said his father was an important State Department official. He added that Alan Carlisle was also a rake. He told her of his reason for leaving the United States, and described his mother's shocking behaviour and incestuous ambition in vivid detail. He said his parents sickened him. He said they needed help. He hadn't known why he needed to share all those details of his shame and trauma with the young Austrian woman. He just knew that he had, and it had helped.

Towards the end of the week, when his money was getting low, he swallowed his pride and telephoned his father. He asked for some money and said he needed a vacation. He'd met a girl. They wanted to go skiing. He said she was special. He said he was in love with her. He said when he came back from his vacation he would need to find a new apartment and a new job. Alan Carlisle, conscience-ridden, wired him five-thousand dollars the same day.

But when Mathew returned from the bank, he found her looking miserable.

"What's wrong?"

Her eyes were red; she had obviously been crying.

"I just spoke to my mother on the telephone. I have to go back to Vienna. I'm sorry, darling. I'm going to miss you so much."

Mathew felt a surge of panic at the thought of losing her.

"What do you mean? Don't worry, I've got plenty of cash." He held out a hefty wad of American dollars. "Look, we're rich; you don't need to go."

She smiled a weak smile and shook her head.

"I can't stay, darling. I've already stayed longer than I should. I have a job to do, and my mother needs me. When I'm not there she has to manage the business and do my job as well. It's not fair on her and I have to go back some time."

He stuttered more objections.

"But I need you, too. I love you. I thought we were going skiing; you were going to teach me. You said. You promised. I can't let you go. Stay here with me. I'll get another job. We'll be fine. We'll get married. I'll look after you."

She clung to him, and they made love again. Later she told him how much she loved him and didn't want to lose him. Then she suddenly sat up in bed.

"Come with me. To Vienna. Come with me. Why not? There's plenty of work, and plenty of room. Say you'll come? We can go skiing. We can make love all the time. We can be together. Please say you'll come?"

Mathew voiced a concern.

"What about the Russians? I thought they controlled it all?"

She shook her head.

"Not in Vienna. They control the surrounding areas and some sections of the city, but the British control the airport and my family lives in Neubau. That's the seventh district; it's controlled by the Americans. It wouldn't be a problem. Darling, please say you'll come."

"You know I will."

****

The following morning they took flights on an Air France Dakota, and touched down at Schwechat just after lunch. The British official hardly looked at Mathew's passport as he waved them through. It was all so easy. They caught a bus outside the terminal, and settled down to the forty-minute journey to the city centre. Then they hit the first roadblock.

A couple of bedraggled-looking Red Army soldiers standing outside the Soviet headquarters in Favoriten flagged them down at gunpoint. Two more stood waiting to board the bus. The bus driver looked nervous. He turned to Lara and said something in German. She turned to Mathew and translated the driver's concern.

"He said this is unusual. This is District Ten. It's Favoriten; it's Russian-controlled. He said the Russians don't usually stop the bus until we get to District Four. That's Wieden; it's much closer to the city centre. He thinks something must be wrong."

The first soldier went straight to Mathew. He held out his hand and asked for Mathew's papers. Mathew showed him the passport. The soldier shook his head and asked again for his papers. Mathew shrugged. He didn't have any papers. Not for Austria. He hadn't thought it necessary. He was after all an American. They had won the war, hadn't they?

The soldier immediately arrested both Mathew and Lara. He took them from the bus and marched them into the local headquarters. Mathew protested. He understood that he should have obtained the correct papers. He hadn't realised he needed them, but the girl had done nothing wrong. She was an Austrian; it was her country. She had the right papers. They had no cause to detain her. They should let her go.

The soldiers ignored him. One marched Mathew along the left-hand corridor, to a cell at the far end. The second marched Lara along a similar-looking corridor to the right. Mathew called out to her. He told her not to worry. He said his father was important. As soon as his father found out about this, the Russians would release them. Lara Scholde didn't answer.

****

The guard shepherded Lara up the stairs, along the corridor, and into an office at the far end. A thickset man in civilian clothing sat behind a desk. The man ignored her and continued writing. Only when the guard had retreated and closed the door did he acknowledge her presence.

"Ah, the lovely Lara Scholde." He looked up at her and smiled a smile of sorts. "Well done, my dear. Now, tell me everything you did and everything he told you. Miss nothing out."

Lara Scholde studied Sachino Metreveli, in disgust. Metreveli was an old-school chekist, a thug and a bully who took delight in abusing and tormenting his victims. Post-war Vienna offered Metreveli and his MGB cohorts an ample supply of those.

Lara spoke of Mathew Carlisle in glowing terms. She said he was a decent young man. She said he was naive. She said she had felt so ashamed to have used and tricked him in such a way. She spoke of their time in the hotel on the Rue de Beri, and how sweet he had been. Metreveli showed no interest in that, but when Lara spoke of the problems Mathew had experienced with his mother, his brutish features broke into a smirk.

Lara Scholde finished her report, and then asked the most important question.

"And will you now release my father?"

Metreveli assumed a pained expression.

"That will be difficult. He is a subversive. His crimes are more serious than I realised."

She spoke evenly and deliberately.

"You gave me your word. I have kept to my side of the agreement. Now you keep to yours." She paused before adding, "Or is the word of a Russian man not worth the breath it takes to give? Is it not worth as much as the word of an American boy?"

Metreveli glared at her, but the barbs had clearly found their mark.

"I am Georgian. We always keep our word." She held the determined posture. He relented. "Very well, my dear. I will have your father released."

She nodded.

"Good. Can I go now?"

"Not just yet."

Metreveli stood up and rounded the table. Lara Scholde prepared herself.

He grabbed her by the arm and spun her around, then kissed her hard on the mouth, while his hands dragged her skirt to the waist and his tongue forced its way between her lips. He shoved her back on to the desk, and then held her pinioned with one shovel-like hand. The other hand reached up and tore open her blouse. It mauled at her breasts, and then moved lower to drag down her knickers. Sachino Metreveli gave a snarl of triumph as she lay spread-eagled before him. He scrambled to open his fly, pushed her thighs wider, and then fell on her.

Lara Scholde said nothing and did nothing to prevent the rape. She murmured no protest, and offered no resistance. She gave no cry of anguish, no whimper of fear, as he lunged and groped and ravaged, no sign of unwillingness or shame. She merely lay crushed beneath him and allowed him his moment of brutish triumph and vile dominion.

But when it was over she allowed a tear to fall. Metreveli saw and snarled an order.

"Now you may go, but I may decide to visit you tonight. Make sure you are at home."

Lara nodded as she got to her feet and collected her strewn clothing. She dressed, self-consciously, and then looked back at him as she sought one final reassurance.

"My father. You will release him soon?"

"Yes."

"And the American boy? What will you do with him?"

"Not that it is any of your concern, but no harm will come to him. You have my word. There is a jeep waiting outside. Go home, Lara Therese Scholde. You have done well today."

He picked up the telephone. As she left the room, she heard him say, "Comrade Metreveli, for Comrade Deputy Premier Beria." Then the door slammed behind her.

Adjusting her skirt, she walked back along the corridor and down the stairs. She gathered her tattered blouse in trembling fingers, and then hung her head in shame as she left the building. She didn't dare look at the group of Red Army soldiers, who grinned at her dishevelment, for fear of further abuse. She shuffled past the leering faces, and then hurried to where the jeep and its driver waited to take her back to the Scholde family's patrician house in the Russian zone of Wieden.

22

It had been over six weeks since Hammond had recklessly punched Alan Carlisle on the jaw, and the tension between the two men had, if anything, heightened. This was largely because Hammond had tried and failed to discover where they had taken Catherine. He had met with similar failure when trying to unearth details of the sinister and mysterious Martin Kube. Hammond disobeying his orders had angered the dictatorial Alan Carlisle. Failing to discover anything of value had equally enraged Hammond.

"How do we contact Paslov?"

Much to Hammond's surprise, Carlisle had asked the question on the journey to Frankfurt. He had previously assumed Carlisle to be familiar with such matters.

"He'll know where we are. We just have to make it easy for him to contact us."

"And what does that mean?"

"It means we take in the sights."

Hammond had no interest in spending any more time with Carlisle than necessary, but Paslov saved any further friction by appearing on the first evening. Hammond spotted him from the foyer as they were about to leave the hotel. He was sitting outside a café, on the opposite side of the road, calmly reading an out-of-date Soviet newspaper and nursing a beer. When they left the hotel, he called to them. He asked them to join him for a drink and stood up to shake hands when they wandered over.

Hammond was watching Carlisle. He seemed ill-at-ease as he scanned the surrounding area.

"Isn't this all a little too public?" he asked.

Paslov smiled. He seemed relaxed; too relaxed.

"What would you have us do, Mr Carlisle? Meet in your hotel room so the MGB can listen in on their wireless receivers, or meet in mine so the CIG can listen in on theirs? Look around you: there is not a car parked for fifty meters, and not a bush or a tree to hide behind for over a hundred. None of the other customers are foolish enough to sit out here in the cold. Look, even the waiter seems intent on ignoring us."

Carlisle still looked nervous. Paslov still looked too relaxed. He stood up and walked to the entrance, put his head around the door and ordered two more beers. A taciturn waiter delivered them to the table. The Russian spymaster eyed him disparagingly and shook his head, then shrugged an acceptance and raised his glass.

"In my jurisdiction he would be dispensing water in the Gulag. . . *Za vashe zdorovye.*"

The two Americans nodded politely and waited. Paslov seemed intent on pleasantry.

"There, now, what could be more natural than this? Celebrating the new spirit of co-operation between wartime allies, with a glass of excellent German beer? So let us sit, enjoy our drinks, and take in the evening air."

"You said you wanted to defect?"

Carlisle was clearly impatient. Paslov seemed in no hurry.

"All in good time, Mr Carlisle; all in good-time. First there is something I would like Gerald here to do for me." He leaned across the table. "I take it I may call you Gerald?"

Hammond shrugged his indifference. Carlisle leaned closer.

"What is it you want?"

Paslov stopped smiling.

"Heinrich Müeller. I want him found, and I want him dead."

Offended, Hammond cut in.

"I'm nobody's assassin."

Paslov condescendingly patted his arm.

"I understand that, Gerald, but you do have to admit you are good at it."

"Only as part of my job; when necessary. I'm nobody's hired killer."

Carlisle asked the obvious.

"What's the matter, Paslov? Doesn't Abakumov run Smersh teams any more?"

"Not for this."

To Hammond's fury, Carlisle considered the request before shaking his head.

"Müeller doesn't work for us. He works for the U.S. Army. It's all top secret. Even if we wanted to, we probably couldn't get any closer than you."

Paslov looked hard at him before answering.

"Müeller now works for Beria. I assumed you knew?"

Carlisle looked surprised.

"He defected, again?"

The Russian shrugged.

"This month for us; next month, who knows?"

"Well, it's the first I've heard of it, but then it's not my province."

"Yes, I did hear that your departments have problems communicating."

"At least we're not here asking for asylum in Moscow. Where is Müeller now?"

"In Berlin, I understand. Probably still manipulating both sides as we speak."

"And if we did manage to find a way of helping you? What do we get in return?"

"You would get a name."

"From The Poplars?"

Paslov shook his head.

"No, not there, not yet. But if you perform this service for me, I will give you the name of Beria's man in the State Department. Perhaps we can talk about The Poplars after that."

Carlisle's was clearly only interested in The Manhattan Project.

"No, Hammond's right, we're not murderers. We leave that to people like Beria."

"Very well, Mr Carlisle; if that is your final word."

The Russian obviously had no intention of negotiating.

"You're not here to defect, are you, Paslov? You never intended defecting." An apologetic shrug of the shoulders met the accusation. Carlisle scowled. "So, why waste my time?"

Paslov again shook his head.

"I am not wasting your time, Mr Carlisle. I had to make sure that you came in person, and I know how passionate you are about that particular subject. We must talk, in private. I am sorry, Gerald. I do not wish to be rude, but. . ."

Carlisle nodded his agreement. Hammond reluctantly stood up.

"I'll wait over at the hotel."

Hammond ignored Paslov's outstretched hand. He turned and crossed the street, then stopped and looked back when he reached the hotel entrance. He felt angry, incensed that Carlisle would consider using him as an assassin, but curious to know why Paslov wanted to talk in private. He wondered, too, if he should ready himself for a rescue.

He needn't have worried. The two men sat engrossed in conversation, but then Paslov reached into his jacket and passed something across the table.

Whatever it was, Carlisle clearly found it distressing. He sat studying it in obvious disbelief, with his mouth wide and his shoulders hunched.

An agitated Paslov leaned closer, talking quickly and scanning the surrounding area as he spoke. Carlisle stared blankly back, but then suddenly slammed his fist on the table and stood up.

Paslov seemed unfazed. He leaned forward and spoke with a finger raised. Carlisle returned to his seat. He picked up the item and studied it again. Hammond could see more clearly now. It was a photograph. Carlisle took out his wallet and placed it between the billfolds.

More discussion followed, during which Paslov ordered schnapps from the taciturn waiter. Finally the man from the MGB raised his glass in a parting toast, left the table, and climbed into the back of a chauffeur-driven Mercedes that had appeared from nowhere. The Mercedes disappeared into the evening gloom, leaving Carlisle sitting slumped at the table.

Hammond waited in the foyer until the car dipped out of sight. Then he walked back across the road, studied the ashen features of Carlisle, and barked a question.

"What the hell was all that about?"

"Nothing that concerns you."

"You look pale. Are you o.k.? Is there anything I can do?"

With colour slowly returning, Carlisle growled an order.

"I said it doesn't concern you. Now, for once in your life, do as you're damn well told."

Alan Carlisle stormed back to the hotel. Hammond sat at the table. With Paslov and Carlisle gone, and the bill unpaid, the taciturn waiter had left the warmth of the bar. He stood hovering at a nearby table. Hammond called him over, ordered another beer, and picked up the tab.

23

Angela Carlisle sat at the kitchen table. The clock read twenty-to-six, and that meant another twenty long and arbitrary minutes of abstinence before she could take a drink. She thought about her husband, due home at any minute. She tried to assess her feelings for him, and felt a degree of ambivalence. They had been together for almost twenty years, more than half her lifetime. He was the only man she had ever really known. She thought about that and smiled to herself. Apart from a nervous and fumbling young man called Harry, whom she'd met at a college dance, he was the only man who had ever known her.

Alan was entirely unfaithful, and always had been. Angela knew that. She had thought of leaving him on more than one occasion. Her parents were wealthy. She could afford to move out and not suffer in any financial sense. But part of his infidelity was undoubtedly her fault, and twenty years of marriage had institutionalized her. She thought about that, too. Was that the truth, or just a convenient excuse? Wasn't the real reason her abject fear of being alone?

She again looked up at the clock, only fifteen minutes to go, but then she heard the sound of a car on the gravel. It had to be him.

Now she really needed that drink, just to face him, just to look at him, and listen to him, and pretend she was interested in him. To hell with the time. She reached for the vodka, poured a generous measure into a tumbler, took

234

an unhealthy swig and felt much better. Then she topped up the glass and stood waiting for him to appear.

Alan Carlisle opened the front door, threw his suitcase into the hallway, and slammed the door shut with his foot; much the same as always. However, this time when she made the effort to greet him there was no answering smile. He looked tired and drawn, and something else, something she couldn't quite place. Was it disgust, or fury? Maybe it was both.

In the six weeks since their son had flown to Paris she had tried to repair some of the damage caused by her confused emotions and incestuous intent. If she hadn't already known it, the look on his face told her there was still some way to go.

"You want coffee?"

He nodded wearily and followed her to the kitchen. She poured a fresh cup and set it down on the kitchen table. He searched her features as he asked,

"So who was she?"

"I don't understand. Who are you talking about?"

"The young blonde. The one in the photograph, with you and that other dyke bitch."

Angela suddenly felt cold. It was the one thing she had dreaded him discovering. She felt her legs go weak. She sat down heavily on the nearest chair. Now she knew what that look had meant. She had been right; it had been both.

"Oh God, no. I thought I'd. . ."

"So who was she?"

She looked at the fury in him and struggled to find the words.

"I didn't know her name. Well, not her real name."

He spat back at her.

"You didn't know? You're telling me that you let some filthy little dyke stick her tongue between your legs while they photographed you, and you didn't even know who she was? Well, you'd better get hold of the other one and find out, hadn't you? You do remember the other one, don't you, Angela? Sarah fucking Pearson, the dyke slobbering all over your breasts, while that little blonde bitch went down on you."

She continued staring at the floor, unable to meet his glare of accusation and thinking back to that terrible, shameful, and utterly wonderful night.

"What does it matter who she was? It happened, and I couldn't be more ashamed."

Contempt dripped from every answering syllable.

"What does it matter? Let me see. I guess it matters when the head of Russian Intelligence in southern Germany shows me a picture of a couple of lesbians gang-banging my wife. I guess it matters when he demands I hand over top-secret details of U.S. Intelligence, or else."

She buried her head in her hands. It was worse than she'd expected, much worse.

"Oh, Alan, I'm so sorry. I thought I'd dealt with it."

"And I thought you told me you'd given that Pearson bitch her marching orders. I'm a married woman. Fuck off, you dyke. That was the gist of the conversation, wasn't it?"

He was right, of course. She had said that. She had been lying then, and just now, when she said she couldn't be more ashamed, she had lied again. Yes, at the time, she had been ashamed, but she had also been elated.

She couldn't have told him that, though. He would never have understood.

"Yes, but then I met her again, a few months ago."

"Tell me."

"Tell you what?"

"Everything. And this time, Angela, I do mean everything. Not some pathetic tale you've invented to save yourself from the shame of your own degeneracy."

"I didn't keep it from you for that reason. I did it for us."

"Well, I would have to say that 'us' is the least of our worries right now, so tell me."

She finished her vodka and reached again for the bottle. He snatched it away. She glared.

"You want me to tell the story or not?"

He nodded. She stared her obstinacy and pursed her lips. He shook his head in obvious contempt, but then handed over the bottle. She took it, refilled the glass, and began her story.

She had bumped into Sarah Pearson while grocery shopping at the local market. At first she had felt awkward, because she hadn't spoken to the woman since that moment of drunken foolishness on the sofa. Sarah Pearson seemed so different. She said she had missed her former neighbour. When Angela responded with an old-fashioned look, Sarah said she hadn't meant it like that. Angela had stupidly believed her.

Sarah Pearson spoke proudly of her new life. She had separated from husband Archie, and fallen in love with a young woman. She apologized for the circumstances of their parting. She hadn't meant to upset Angela. She'd had too much to drink that day; they both had. Sarah swore she had changed. She seemed sincere. She invited Angela to meet the new woman in her life. The offer seemed innocent. Angela agreed to drop into Shelley's bar later that day.

When Angela arrived at the bar, Sarah Pearson led her to a table in the corner. Sarah introduced the young woman as Cat. When Angela queried the name, the girl laughed, and meowed, and pretended to claw Sarah with her nails. Angela thought she seemed fun.

Alan Carlisle interrupted.

"And she was American?"

"No. Sarah said she was Danish. I didn't think anything of it, because she was blonde, you know, Scandinavian-looking. She had that same-sounding European accent."

"But later you found out that she wasn't Danish?"

Angela nodded. She said the girl was slim and attractive, fresh-faced and outgoing, with blue eyes and short blonde hair. No, that was a lie; the girl was more than attractive. She was stunning, but she was also in love with Sarah, or so Angela believed at the time.

Alan Carlisle sneered. He was surprised to hear she was still an admirer.

Angela shrugged. She said everyone in the bar had admired the young blonde, or at first, but then the girl grabbed Sarah and kissed her on the mouth. That was when the mood in the bar changed. The two women seemed oblivious of the disapproving stares from so many previously-admiring faces. They sat holding hands and told her they had rented an apartment in Alexandria with views of the river. They seemed so happy. Even when they asked her to come with them to see the apartment and the views, she hadn't suspected.

The apartment was on the third floor of an old block, the decor bland, but the views lovely. It boasted a balcony overlooking the river, and so they sat outside drinking wine. Dusk was falling, and behind a blackened and eerily-motionless river the city lights were coming on.

The blonde went to the lounge and put a record on the turntable, some mellow jazz, with a slow and haunting saxophone that perfectly described the mood. Then she came back to the balcony, but didn't return to her seat. Instead she began swaying to and fro, sipping at her wine, and allowing the music to take control.

Whether it had been the view, or the wine, or the music, or the girl's intoxicating presence, she didn't know, but Angela found herself disturbingly aroused and imagining all manner of shameful scenarios.

When they went back into the lounge, Angela made a show of leaving. She said she had to go. The girl looked deep into her eyes and asked her to stay. The girl said they should all have supper together. The invitation had been innocuous, but her eyes had spoken of so much more.

That was when Angela finally accepted the truth of all those thoughts she'd kept hidden for so long. Her heart was thumping and her body tingling. She felt dizzy and light-headed, like a schoolgirl with a teenage crush. She felt confused and embarrassed and nervous, and was thinking thoughts and experiencing emotions she didn't think she would ever think or feel.

She didn't know what to do, or what to say, or what to think. She wanted to leave, to get out and run away, but she couldn't stop trembling, or tear her eyes away from the girl.

So Angela stood transfixed, watching the girl and waiting for her to make a move, knowing the girl would have her that night, knowing, too, that there was nothing she could do about it.

Alan Carlisle shifted on his chair. He said he didn't want to hear any more, not all the sordid details. He'd seen enough of that in the photograph.

"You did before."

"Before was different, a sexy game. This is just plain sordid, sad and desperate little women, poking their fingers into each other."

Angela stared her hurt back at him. It hadn't been like that. It hadn't been sordid. Maybe it became sordid, but at the time it was erotic and thrilling.

She said she wanted him to know how she felt, and why it had happened. She said maybe she got a kick out of telling him and arousing him, or maybe she just wanted him to know that she could still function as a woman, even if it was only with teenage boys and other women.

He nodded and said he understood. His tone patronized. His remarks annoyed. Suddenly she was furious. How could he possibly understand any of the emotions she had felt? For the first time in almost twenty years, her knickers had been wet. For the first time, in so very, very long, she had wanted another warm, soft, beautiful human being to hold her and touch her and kiss her, and yes, she had wanted the girl to fuck her. . . Was that so terrible?

"What with? A couple of fingers, or six inches from the neck of an empty wine bottle?"

She saw the jealousy and anger in his face, and, for the first time in twenty years, she saw something else: she saw cruelty. She said he had a right to be angry, but he had never been cruel. They'd had their differences and problems over the years, but he had never been that.

She tried to make him understand as she listed the misery of almost two decades without love and tenderness and physical release. Eighteen years of holding back the tears and hiding her feelings. Eighteen years of pretending to the world and lying to herself. Eighteen years of refusing offers she secretly wanted to accept. Eighteen years of going home alone, and sleeping alone, and having imaginary lovers climb into her bed at night. Eighteen years of touching herself when nobody else was there, and imagining what it would be like. Eighteen depressed and frustrated and bitter and empty and desperately lonely years.

The tears began to stream. She couldn't stop them. He looked contrite

"I'm sorry. I didn't mean to be. . . So, what happened?"

"You said you didn't want to know."

"I shouldn't have said that. It was wrong of me. Of course I want to know."

She sniffed, wiped away the tears, and returned to the story.

She didn't understand why, but the girl reminded her of Mathew. Both had such beautiful symmetry to their bodies. They were almost Adonis-like, delicately formed and precisely proportioned, with beautiful features, clear blue eyes and soft blonde hair.

He asked if that had been when the problems began with Mathew. She wasn't sure. It had been about then. She said God only knew what a psychiatrist would make of it. She wondered if she had been trying to prove she wasn't a lesbian, to herself if nobody else. Maybe Mathew reminded her of the girl. She didn't know. She wasn't sure what she had been thinking at the time. She was less sure now. She shrugged her confusion and returned to the story.

Sarah and the blonde began dancing together in the lounge, but as the dancing became more intimate Angela, flustered, returned to the balcony. Behind her, she heard the sounds of passion. The girl was dominant; that excited her. Sarah was obviously in ecstasy; that brought back the trembling. When Angela heard the girl boast of having her next, the trembling became uncontrollable.

He asked if the thought of making love to a woman had excited her more than the act. She scoffed. It hadn't been love, or even the pretence of love. It had been sex: raw, uninhibited sex. That was why she had been so helpless to resist. She said she had never felt such a surge of sexual adrenaline before, but when the two women came out to the balcony, she saw them smile and realized what a fool she had been. They had obviously planned this from the start.

She felt angry and cheap and ashamed. She got to her feet. She told them they were scheming bitches. She pushed them away. She picked up her handbag. She started to walk.

But refusal hadn't been an option. Strong hands pulled her back into the apartment and dragged her to the floor. They held her still, while more hands stripped away her clothing. She blushed as she recalled her embarrassment and trepidation and excitement. The bitches had made such a meal of it.

She tried to get up, but their hands were everywhere, restraining and caressing, grasping and fondling. A tongue forced her lips apart and began exploring her mouth. More lips nuzzled at her ears and neck, and then moved to kiss her breasts, delivering her to that gentle world of delirium and pleasure she had always craved. She looked up and saw the blonde smile down in gloating triumph, while mischievous fingernails traced erogenous patterns across her belly and down. She gasped and jolted in response to each deliciously sadistic twist and turn, and then whimpered in shame and anticipation as commanding fingers gripped and lifted her buttocks.

Angela Carlisle couldn't help herself and she couldn't stop them. She closed her eyes, and spread her legs, and let them have her. It was as shameful and vulgar and disgusting as that, but it was also the most electrifying sexual experience she had ever known.

They took turns with her for most of that night, and she took turns with them, because she had never before felt so brazen and irresponsible and marvellous, and truly, truly, liberated.

Then, around a week later, Sarah came to see her. Apparently, someone else had been there.

She shuddered as she recalled the first time she saw the photographs. Sarah told her that she and the blonde were through. She said the girl wanted two thousand dollars for the negatives. She said Cat wasn't a Danish name; she worked at the Russian Embassy.

Alan Carlisle stated the obvious.

"And that was when a little Danish dyke called Cat turned out to be a Katya, or Katinka, or Katerinka, or something equally unfeline and bloody Soviet, and equally bloody dangerous."

Angela nodded. When Sarah claimed not to have the money, the girl said Angela was rich. She would have to pay, because Alan was an important man at the State Department.

Sadder and wiser, Angela Carlisle met the blonde in the park. She couldn't believe the unfeeling woman who took her money was the same girl.

The blonde handed over the prints and negatives and walked away. Angela burned them when she got home. She put it down to experience. She thought that would be the end of it.

"For Christ's sake, Angela, talk about naïve! Why the hell didn't you tell me?"

"I hadn't seen you for days. We weren't even speaking."

"God! What a mess."

"You look tired."

"Exhausted. I haven't slept for three days."

She nodded and said he should get some sleep, but when she asked to see the photograph he shook his head. He said a girl had bumped into him in the hotel. She took his wallet. The photograph was inside. He said the wallet was returned, minus the photograph. He assumed the girl worked for Paslov. Paslov wanted to see if he would make a fuss. If he called the police, it would mean he didn't care about people seeing the photograph and wouldn't bow to blackmail. When he'd said nothing, it told Paslov that he had a new informant in the State Department.

"In many ways you have to admire him. He's a clever man."

"He's an evil bastard."

"For anyone to survive around people like Stalin and Beria, I guess they'd have to be."

He looked guilty. She asked why. He said Paslov had said something about Mathew.

Angela felt her heart suddenly stop.

"What about Mathew?"

Alan Carlisle moved to the coffee machine, poured another cup, and began to explain.

He said Mathew had called and told him that he had met a girl in Paris, someone special. They wanted to go skiing. They needed money. He had wired the money, because he assumed Mathew had meant skiing in the French Alps: Meribel or Val D'Isere or somewhere sensible.

When he didn't receive any further contact from Mathew, he called a colleague, who checked into it. Mathew and the girl had taken a flight to Austria, but disappeared after arriving in Vienna. He assumed they'd gone skiing in the Tyrol.

Angela didn't understand. How could they just disappear? Surely Vienna was one of the safest and most civilized cities in Europe? He said it used to be, but the occupying forces had sectionalized it, much the same as Berlin. The city was in a state of flux. Worse still, although the British ran the airport, the Soviets controlled the surrounding area. When Paslov showed him the photograph, Carlisle said he wouldn't betray his country for anything, least of all blackmail. However, when he started to walk away Paslov said something else. He said Angela having lesbian sex must have made a refreshing change from incest.

Angela blurted an explanation she didn't believe.

"He was bluffing, he had to be. He couldn't possibly have known about that. Somebody obviously saw how tactile I was with Mathew. They can't have any proof."

"What if Mathew had told him, or, more likely, told the girl?"

"Mathew would never do that. He'd never tell a soul."

A rare smile softened Alan Carlisle's tired and anxious features. He said he had thought that, too, but then he remembered when they first met. He said he had been so in love with her, he'd told her secrets he wouldn't tell another living person. He said that was the way love gets to you sometimes; especially when you're still young and naive.

Angela's mind was cluttered and racing. Why hadn't he told her about Mathew as soon as he got home? Hadn't Mathew been important enough?

Was some stupid photograph more important to him than the life of their son? How could he be so selfish?

She could feel what little affection she held for her husband receding by the second. She assessed the sequence of events and broached another question.

"Why are they targeting us like this, Alan? They are targeting us, aren't they? First me, and then you, and now Mathew. Why are they doing this to us?"

Carlisle said ex-Nazis were working for the West. Paslov wanted details of their identities and locations. He assumed they intended assassinating them.

Angela came to an instant decision. He had to give Paslov what he wanted. Carlisle shook his head and said he didn't have that information. He knew the people. He spoke to them often enough, but always in secure environments. He didn't know where they lived, when they were away from those environments, or the security measures in place. It wasn't his responsibility.

Angela was panic-stricken. He had to find out. He had to give Paslov what he wanted. He said it would make him a traitor and result in murder. She scoffed. He wasn't a traitor. Nobody cared more about America than him, but this was their son. Who cared if the lousy Russians killed a few more murdering Nazis?

He relented. He said, if they hadn't heard from Mathew in a few days, he would visit Conrad Zalesie and try to get the information from him. Angela remembered the name.

"Conrad Zalesie? That name's familiar."

"He's the head of the ATLI Corporation. He's also been the linchpin and conduit for every important defection from Europe since we entered the war."

"And he'll have this information, the information you need?"

"He's bound to have it. Whether I can get it from him is another matter."

"Alan, we have no choice. Whatever it takes, we have to do it."

24

Hammond smiled happily when she answered the phone. It was good to hear her voice again. It seemed ages since they'd last spoken.

"Gerald, it's good to hear from you."

"How are you keeping, Emma?"

"Fine, fine. You?"

Most of the ensuing conversation was small talk. He made a couple of tongue-in-cheek remarks about her social calendar. She congratulated him on his new job. Then he invited her for a drink. She asked why he was calling her, after so many months of not speaking, and reminded him of the last time they'd spoken. He had been less than polite and they'd parted acrimoniously. He refused to apologize. He said, after the way she had behaved, if anyone should apologize, it was her. She snorted, but she didn't hang up.

He said he wanted to see her. He said he needed to ask her something, something important. He didn't tell her what. When she asked, he said it was nothing to do with their relationship, but it was important. She sounded intrigued and asked again: why did he want to see her?

"I can't talk on the phone. Meet you in the cocktail bar at the Washington, about an hour."

He got to the Washington Hotel fifteen minutes early, ordered himself a large scotch, and her a martini with two olives. Then he sat and watched the people toing and froing, seeing them strut and posture, and remembering when he had been young enough and stupid enough to be impressed by such things.

She arrived on the dot, faultlessly made-up and dressed to the nines in a tight black skirt and dangerously high-heeled shoes. He watched her glide into the room and saw everything he had fallen in love with. The archetypal head-turning Washington socialite beauty, stylish and stunning, with that delicate arrogance which seemed to tower over would-be suitors and less fortunate rivals alike. He still loved her, he always would, but now something had changed.

He suddenly realized. It was the pain; the physical pain he had felt since returning from Europe to find her gone. That gnawing ache in his heart and his stomach that had hurt him so much whenever he saw her or thought about her; it was no longer there.

He stood up and waved to her and smiled a weak smile when she crossed the room to his table. The kiss on her cheek was dutiful.

"I got you a martini. Two olives. I assumed that was ok?"

"Yes, thanks."

She eyed him suspiciously.

"That was all a little perfunctory."

He grinned.

"Maybe I've come to terms with things. That was what you said you wanted, wasn't it?"

"I suppose so."

"Well, good. . . Come and sit."

She sat down, but continued to eye him with that same suspicious look on her face.

"You've met someone, haven't you, Gerald? I can tell. So, have you brought me here to tell me about her, or ask for a divorce, or both?"

"Neither. I wanted information, and I need your help."

"Invitation or introduction?"

He didn't smile.

"I want you to talk to Marcus Allum for me."

"Is that all? I thought he was your friend. And didn't someone tell me that you work for him nowadays?"

"Yeah, but we don't talk much. I think he likes to keep me at arm's length; channels and all that. Look, before I say anything else, I want your word that none of this will go any further."

"Sure."

"I mean it, Emma. This is serious. . . It could be dangerous."

She stopped smiling.

"All right, Gerald. If it's important, you have my word."

"I want you to tell me if you know these people."

He produced the photograph that Paslov had given to Carlisle. She studied it for a few seconds; her mouth open, her eyes shocked wide.

"Good God! I don't know who the other two are but. . . No, wait a minute, yes I do. The one with the long hair is Sarah, Sarah Pearson: screaming lesbian, and a real aggressive bitch. I guess you already got that from the picture. She married some bible-thumping rake from Utah, or Pennsylvania, or somewhere out in bible-thumping land. He divorced her when he found out she'd tried it on with just about every good-looking player in Washington." She gave a wicked laugh. "People used to say it wasn't his

249

wife's flagrant infidelity annoyed the bible-thumping rake so much, it was because so many of his mistresses claimed she was better in bed than him.

"I haven't seen her around for a while, but no surprise there; she did burn a few bridges. I have no idea who the blonde is, but the one getting all the attention is Angela Carlisle."

"You mean Alan Carlisle's wife?"

"If you'd ever gone to a single social function when we were together, you'd have known that. But yes; real miserable cow, and the last person you'd imagine as being up for this."

Emma talked a little about Angela Carlisle, all of it defamatory, most of it unrepeatable. She asked about the photograph. He said he'd stolen it from Carlisle's wallet. She grinned and called him a thief. He said he sent back the wallet and contents, minus the photograph, of course. When she asked why Carlisle had the picture, he spoke of the meeting with Paslov, and his belief that Paslov had used it to blackmail Carlisle.

"And does Carlisle know you've got it?"

"No, or I hope not. He thinks a girl stole it in the hotel lobby."

"Why would he think that?"

"Because I nudged her into him, after I'd lifted the wallet."

She eyed him again and he knew why.

This was a side of him he'd never shown her before. He had always treated her as a fragile ornament, wrapped in cotton-wool and protected from anything to do with the more violent or clandestine aspects of his work. All he had ever allowed her to see was a doting fool of a husband, and she had wanted so much more. He could see that now.

"Are you becoming ever so slightly devious in your old age, Gerald?"

"Maybe ever so slightly."

"So why did you want me to talk to Marcus?"

Hammond talked a little about Catherine Schmidt and said he needed to find her again. He said Marcus Allum should know where she was.

When Emma asked if Catherine was the blonde in the photograph, Hammond smiled, suddenly enjoying her obvious jealousy and the unfamiliar reversal of roles.

"Oh no. . . Catherine's younger, and much prettier."

She met his smile with her own. She pretended not to care, but he could see that his enthusiastic description of Catherine Schmidt had temporarily thrown her.

"Then she must be something special. So what makes you think Marcus would know anything about her? And what makes you think he'd tell me if he did?"

"Because there's not a great deal that goes on in the State Department that he doesn't know about. And because the two of you have always been as thick as thieves."

She laughed at that and warned him to be careful. Alan Carlisle was a powerful man, with powerful friends.

She said there had to be a payphone somewhere in the lobby. Assuming she could find him, she'd talk to Marcus Allum. Hammond explained that he needed to talk privately with Allum, without the usual secretaries and department gossips listening at the door.

"What about, or don't I need to know?"

"The photograph. Thought I'd let him deal with it. Either that or burn it."

Emma went to make the call. She returned a few minutes later with a broad smile on her face. Allum had claimed not to know anything at first, but she'd pressed him into talking.

She said Allum thought the girl was somewhere in New York City, but he didn't know where. He said there was a man who might know, but if he ever found out that Hammond had told anyone, it would be the last favour Allum would ever do for either of them.

Emma passed him a scrap of paper torn from her diary. Hammond read the name.

"Conrad Zalesie. Now I wonder why I keep hearing that name."

"Marcus said you should phone first. He said Zalesie's not a man to welcome uninvited guests. He said you'd know what that meant. What does that mean, Gerald?"

"It means he's dangerous."

Hammond asked about the meeting with Allum. She said Allum would be up in New York all week. They could meet in Daniel Chambers' 'special room'. She asked where that was.

"I've never been there, but I'm told it's at the Council on Foreign Relations."

"Marcus said you should get there tomorrow, around three. Now, tell me about the girl. Tell me why you're so determined to find her."

Hammond shrugged.

"I gave her my word."

"Come on, Hammond, quid pro quo. How old is she? Did you sleep with her? Are you in love with her?"

Hammond stared moodily into his glass as he recalled the beautiful and capricious Catherine Schmidt.

"I'm not sure how old she is. She's claims to be almost twenty, but I think she's more likely around eighteen, maybe even younger. And yes, we slept together, but I'm not in love with her, or I don't think so. I just feel responsible."

"Why?"

Hammond shrugged. It was a question he had recently asked himself.

"I don't know. After all, I did save her. Trouble is she's not much more than a child, and I'm not sure if the people I saved her from are any worse than the people I delivered her to."

"And then there's the added complication that you screwed her." She instantly apologized. "I'm sorry, Gerald, I shouldn't have said that. I've been getting very bitchy lately."

Hammond viewed the novelty of his estranged wife's obvious jealousy, before relaxing the frown into a smile and confessing.

"Actually, she screwed me. More than once, if I'm boasting. Does that bother you?"

"Of course not. Well, maybe it does, but I have no right to let it, not after everything I've put you through. You deserve some happiness, too."

Hammond was more philosophical.

"Maybe. . . All I do know is that I have to keep my word to her, for my own self-respect as much as anything. As for the rest? Perhaps when I've found her I'll know. I'll have to see."

She leaned closer and was suddenly serious.

"Apart from the little you've just told me, I don't know anything about this girl, Gerald, but I do know she's young, and that will always be the problem."

"I don't follow."

"A word from the wise, my love. Youth may have more than its share of beauty and sensuality, but all that fades in weeks at best and hours at worst. When that early rush fades, we rarely find anything to take its place: no wisdom, no compassion, no understanding, and none of the patience to enjoy all those silences we sometimes need to share."

"Is that what all those silences were? I just thought you weren't speaking to me." She didn't smile back at him. He abandoned the flippancy. "That's all a little deep for you, isn't it?"

"Perhaps there's more depth to me than you realized, Mr Hammond."

"And so what are you saying, about the girl?"

"I'm saying that is the way it has to be, my love. Youth was always intended to be adored by youth. The rest of us must use their bodies and move on. Anything else is simply too cruel to contemplate."

"Philosophy and melancholy from you. . . Am I hearing this?"

"Philosophy and melancholy, no. Bitter experience, perhaps, and the tiniest hint of jealousy."

She suddenly looked sad, and he felt so sorry for her. He wondered why. When he had found out about her infidelity, it had broken his heart. He thought he would never recover, never love again, and yet he had somehow survived, perhaps even become stronger for it.

He glanced around the bar and saw so many jealous faces looking back, envying her, wanting her, envying him, wanting to be him. He thought to himself that life was such a strange and complex experience. So many times, the people who seemed to have everything in their lives were the very people who actually had nothing of any value. Here she was, Emma Radcliffe-Hammond, darling of Washington's socialite world, rich and beautiful and sexy and vivacious. And yet, underneath it all, she was just sad and lonely and empty.

The obeisance of others was her only energy source. Without it she was unable to function, and, for some inexplicable reason, he was no longer able to provide it.

Hammond hadn't realised that about her, or himself; not until now.

"Gerald. I'm still here, you know."

She had interrupted his abstraction. He cleared his thoughts and took her hand in his as they shared an unexpected moment of intimacy.

"You know, Emma, you'll always have a home wherever my home is."

"You're the sweetest man, Gerald, and I love you dearly. Maybe one day. . ."

She pulled her hand away, and the moment was gone.

"Now let's think of somewhere outrageously expensive for you to take me to dinner."

25

Set on a corner of fashionable Park Avenue, the innocuous limestone-fronted mansion known as Harold Pratt House had many a tale it could have told since its construction in 1919. None was more interesting than its anointing as the headquarters for the Council on Foreign Relations.

Within the limestone confines of Number Fifty-Eight, East Sixty-Eighth Street, Daniel Chambers' 'special room' was one of the best-kept secrets in America. Superbly appointed, with soft leather furniture, deep-pile carpet, and ornate panelling, the room exuded luxury. However, the room had also been soundproofed, a feature of far greater comfort to certain clandestine individuals than the luxurious furnishings upon which they rested deceitful frames.

Hammond saw Marcus Allum waiting at the door. Allum ushered him into the room, closed both doors, and sat him down at a long polished mahogany table. A man sat at the far end. As Allum began to speak, the man held out a hand to stem the introduction.

"I remember, Marcus. This is the man who pulled that idiot Carpenter out of Rouen. Welcome, Mr Hammond. My name is Daniel Chambers. Would you care for coffee?"

He gestured to a silver coffee pot set out on a table at the side. Hammond shook his head.

"Thank you, no."

"And so, what can we do for you today?"

Despite the affable façade, it was clear that Daniel Chambers was not a man to suffer fools. Hammond began tentatively.

"It's about Alan Carlisle and a meeting he had in Frankfurt with a man called Paslov."

"Go on."

"I think Paslov tried to blackmail him, but I don't know why."

"And what makes you think that?"

Hammond passed the photograph to Allum, who studied it before passing it to Chambers.

"The woman in the centre is Carlisle's wife Angela. I don't know the blonde, but the other woman's name is Pearson, Sarah Pearson. Paslov gave that photograph to Carlisle when they met in Frankfurt last week."

Chambers considered the photograph with obvious distaste, and then framed another question.

"Why was Carlisle meeting Paslov?"

A nervous-looking Marcus Allum interrupted.

"I sanctioned it, Daniel. Paslov said he wanted to defect. He offered to name names on the Manhattan Project. I'm sorry, but we didn't tell anybody, not even senior department members. You know how Beria works, and how disinformation can spiral out of control. I didn't believe it, but you know what Alan's like on that subject. Of course, it came to nothing."

Hammond knew exactly why Allum was so worried, and so dismissive. If the possibility of one of his most senior staff being compromised wasn't enough, it appeared he also had a Soviet mole somewhere among his staff.

"Paslov offered to give up two names. One in The Poplars, the other in the State Department."

"And did he give these names to you; either of them?"

Hammond pretended not to see the glare from Allum.

"Not to me. He may have given them to Carlisle, but not when I was there."

Marcus Allum continued to ridicule the possibility.

"It was all just smoke and mirrors, Daniel. Beria and Paslov up to their old tricks again: sowing seeds of disinformation, getting us chasing our own tails. They were using Alan's preoccupation with the Manhattan Project to do it. I'm certain of it."

Chambers frowned and returned his attention to Hammond.

"Did you believe him?"

"Paslov?" Chambers nodded. Hammond thought carefully before answering. "Yes, I did. Paslov knew my name and a lot more. He said I wasn't the only one with friends in the State Department."

"What did you take that to mean?"

"That he had a contact in the State Department, supplying him with confidential details."

Marcus Allum restored the glare. Chambers nodded quietly.

"And how did you happen to come by this particular item?"

Chambers held the photograph aloft, gingerly pinching a corner extremity between forefinger and thumb as though afraid that any securer hold would somehow incriminate or taint him by association. Hammond answered truthfully.

"I stole it from Carlisle's wallet, on the same evening that Paslov handed it to him. I saw the effect it had on Carlisle. I needed to know what it was all about."

"How dickensianly artful of you. And what do you expect me to do with it?"

"I don't know. Discover the truth, I suppose."

Chambers gazed up at the ceiling.

"The only truth I can see, Mr Hammond, is that I am now holding a pornographic photograph; a dirty picture is, I believe, the modern idiom. However, the picture you paint is a far more pornographic one, is it not?"

Hammond kept his self-control. Recent revelations had concerned the sombre and pretentious Daniel Chambers more than he was willing to admit. Hammond could sense it.

"I'm not painting any picture for you, Mr Chambers. I handed you an unsavoury photograph and explained how I came by it. You paint your own dirty pictures."

Chambers allowed the merest flicker of a smile.

"Bravo, Mr Hammond. Was there anything else?"

"The girl. I need to find her. I want you to tell me where she is."

"Why?"

"Because I promised her that I would keep her safe from a man called Kube."

"And whatever possessed you to make such a promise?"

"Human decency."

Hammond had finally allowed the anger to show. Chambers seemed unimpressed.

"Now that is a pity. For a moment there, I thought I had miraculously found someone in the State Department with some small degree of intellect. How disappointing." He noticed the anger on Allum's face, and begrudgingly added, "Present company excepted, Marcus."

Chambers returned his attention to Hammond, without studying Allum's reaction. Had he done so, he would have seen the look of resentment graduate to outright hostility.

"The answer is no. You may not find her, or even look for her, not under any circumstance. Why the hell do you think we separated the two of you?

"You have made a not inauspicious start to your State Department career, Mr Hammond, but the watchword from here on in is cooperation not confrontation. For goodness sake, don't ruin a promising career at such an early stage, not for something as trivial as this."

Chambers stood up, and rounded the table, the meeting apparently over.

"I advise you to forget about all of this and go back to Washington. Put your feet up, take a well-earned rest and leave this with us. I assure you, we do appreciate your efforts."

Arrogant dismissal didn't sit well with Hammond, but he held the anger in check. He briefly clasped the outstretched hand and casually asked,

"And what if I choose not to do that, Mr Chambers? What if I choose to keep looking?"

Daniel Chambers ignored the question and gestured expansively.

"What do you think of our little building? A trifle bland, perhaps? I assure you that is not necessarily a disadvantage. However, what do you think of this room? Is it not exquisite?"

"This room's pleasant enough; just a shame about the name."

Chambers frowned. Then understanding dawned with a humourless smile.

"Oh, you mean the name of the building: Harold Pratt House. Yes, I suppose that may seem unfortunate to the uninitiated, but take a look around, Mr Hammond. . . study the décor and the furnishings, feel the luxury. Look at that panelling, look at the craftsmanship, see how detailed it is? One would have to be a philistine not to appreciate such beauty."

"It's impressive, but so what?"

"If I were not previously aware, I would find it hard to believe that we are now standing in a soundproof room, one of the most private and secure environments in the country.

"When someone in this room speaks, you cannot hear from the adjoining room. Yet those words will shortly echo in places as far apart as Pennsylvania Avenue and Downing Street."

"And so, what are you telling me: that you control democratically-elected governments?"

"Influence, Mr Hammond, influence."

Chambers was now being overtly supercilious. Hammond's anger was rising.

"With all due respect, I don't remember anyone voting for you, Mr Chambers, or even voting for anyone who sponsors you. You have no jurisdiction over me. I work for the State Department, and we answer directly to the President of The United States."

The smile evaporated. Chambers suddenly looked bored.

"You'll find that this organization is part of the State Department, and has been for several years. The answer to your question is no. Do have a good trip back to Washington."

Chambers turned his back in a clear gesture of dismissal. Furious, Hammond moved to where Marcus Allum stood waiting to open the inner door.

"Thanks for taking the time, Marcus. It's been an education."

26

Wealth beyond the dreams of avarice was how many described the aristocratic Conrad Zalesie, but that was only part of the story. The exiled Lithuanian count was also a man of great influence and connection in immediate post-war America. Zalesie was an entrepreneur without equal, who owned property and corporations all over the world. It was, however, his New York based business ATLI that was the mainstay of a huge and rapidly expanding commercial empire, and similarly increasing measure of political clout.

Beginning life during the war as the American Trading and Lithuanian Investment company, ATLI had rapidly become one of the world's leading armament suppliers. Although happy to court the wholesale private market, the corporation focused on government supply, and this was where the already wealthy Zalesie substantially increased his fortune.

Whether the need was Italian pistols, Swiss mechanisms, British combustion engines, or American carbines, Conrad Zalesie and ATLI would guarantee both delivery and support. Many claimed, if anyone on either American continent became involved in a firefight, there was a good chance that ATLI and the wily Zalesie would have sourced and sanctioned the weapons and equipment used by both sides.

This well-documented success story was not without its critics, though. A Lithuanian exile profiting in the great American way of liberty and opportunity was acceptable to most and applauded by many, but a Lithuanian corporation was a different matter. Even the most insular of politicians knew that Lithuania lay behind the recently-drawn Iron Curtain, and that begged a question. Why was the American government investing its defence budget in a puppet state of the Soviet Union?

Fortunately for thousands of worldwide ATLI employees, the wily Conrad Zalesie was primarily a businessman and only secondly a proud Lithuanian descendent. He recognized the political xenophobia and commercial shenanigans as just that, and immediately changed the corporation's registered title from Lithuanian to Libertarian. With essential cosmetic change effected, Zalesie watched the government contracts come rolling back in and all those sycophantic politicians return with caps held firmly between forefingers and thumbs.

But there was another more disturbing reason for Zalesie's business success that bothered some and intrigued many. How had he ingratiated himself with so many politicians and bureaucrats in so short a period? And how had a newly-arrived Lithuanian exile secured so many confidential and profitable armaments contracts?

The answer lay partly in the weakness of those same politicians and bureaucrats, and partly in the deviousness of Zalesie.

Conrad Zalesie knew human nature. He understood political expedience, and knew how to manipulate the political animal. He believed that greed and ambition were both the driving force and Achilles' heel of politicians. He also believed that a body acted on by a steady force suffers constant acceleration, and that this paradigm applied as much to human nature as the second law of Newton.

Zalesie held scandalous parties at his estate in Connecticut, to which he invited only the most beautiful, wealthy, and powerful. Behind locked doors, and protected by sophisticated security and heavily-armed guards, beautiful people encouraged the wealthy and powerful to relax and indulge. Nothing was too decadent, too depraved, or too expensive for Zalesie's honoured guests. No individual beyond seduction, be they wife or whore, husband or gigolo. No substance frowned on, no demand refused, and no practice too offensive or degenerate.

It was Zalesie's wife, Theresa, who hosted these 'occasions', as she called them. Theresa was a woman of striking looks and deviant inclination, with a voluptuous body that she made available to many, and a mind as dissolute as the most depraved of her party guests.

Once in the magnetic field of Conrad and Theresa Zalesie's curious brand of immoral gravity, the impact and resulting damage to political careers were as bruising and unavoidable as unyielding ground to falling apple. The higher the branch, the greater the impact. The higher placed the individual, the greater the potential damage of disclosure. Unless of course, at some point before impact, a helping hand reached out to save either falling apple or plummeting career. Since their arrival in the United States, the voluptuous Theresa had shaken many a lofty branch, and the wily Conrad held out many a helping hand to catch many a falling apple.

Angela Carlisle studied the welcoming smile and wondered what it was about Conrad Zalesie that made him so successful. Why was he so revered by the clandestine power-brokers of Washington, and so resilient to the vagaries of Capitol Hill policy? Why was he so hypnotically attractive to so many beautiful and celebrated women? How did he come to be so enormously wealthy, and why was he so feared by so many of the people around him?

She studied the man behind the reputation. He wasn't especially tall, standing around five feet nine in his stockinged feet, and neither was he especially imposing. The features were handsome and distinguished, the bearing poised to the point of elegance. The body was slim and well proportioned, but lacking muscular definition. The hands were slender, and the fingers long, but lacking the essential grace and descriptive movement that more usually accompanies an artistic bent or sensitive touch.

If she were to be even more pernickety critical, and Angela Carlisle often was, then perhaps the nose was a little too hooked and the mouth a little too thin. Whenever Zalesie contrived a laugh, he studied others' reactions with eyes that didn't share in the humour. Whenever he spoke, his voice was a little too weak and a little too shrill to be overtly seductive.

Nonetheless, and despite the negatives, there was a presence to Conrad Zalesie. The innate authority was clear to see, as was the self-confidence that came with wealth and power. The blue-grey eyes were clear enough and bright enough, and his short brown hair, prematurely greying at the temples, served to further the aristocratic distinction. Most striking of all, though, was Zalesie's charisma, a charisma so powerful and so compelling it was almost tangible.

"Alan, you didn't tell me you had such a beautiful wife! Shame on you! All these months and years we've worked together, and you never mentioned how stunningly beautiful she was. Well, you come with me, my dear. We'll see if we can't make up for all that wasted time."

She allowed him to take her arm and guide her into the crowded ballroom, through the throng and toward a vacant settee. She sat down, feeling shocked and flustered as she saw his eyes blatantly scanning her body. She felt herself blush.

"Allow me to fetch you a drink, my dear. What will you have?"

He waved away a hovering waiter. She gathered her wits and remembered her breeding.

"A dry sherry would be fine, thank you."

"He leaned forward to briefly pat and fondle her thigh. She gave an involuntary start. A gasp of shock escaped her lips. Zalesie merely smiled.

"I shall return immediately. Now you just sit there and look beautiful."

Angela swallowed hard and sat open-mouthed. Zalesie strode to the bar. She watched him order the drinks and speak to a woman. When he returned, the woman followed.

"Angela, you must meet my wife. Since Alan told us you'd be accompanying him, she's been so looking forward to meeting you."

Angela smiled politely, and again found herself mesmerized as his eyes resumed their domination. Then a woman's voice broke the spell.

"Well now, and who do we have here?"

Zalesie began the introduction.

"This is my wife, Theresa. Theresa, my dear, this is Alan's wife, Angela. I do believe he's been hiding her away from us."

"I can see why."

Theresa Zalesie was a good twenty years the junior of her charismatic husband, but the seductive syllables that oozed from her lips were just as suggestive, and the eyes that collected Angela's own were even more intense. Angela Carlisle sat transfixed.

Theresa Zalesie was undeniably attractive: the complexion clear, the eyes hazel, the hair long and auburn, and pinned high. Red high-heeled shoes, supporting long slender legs, ensured she towered some way above her husband. A bright red velvet skirt, scandalously split to the stocking tops, matched the shoes. Ample breasts spilled beyond an outrageously-transparent blouse, flirting with both the laws of obscenity and every pair of eyes in the room.

She summoned the nearest waiter without diverting the gaze, addressed him by his first name and told him to fetch a bourbon and ice. The waiter hurried away. Angela broke the stare and looked despairingly around the room for her errant husband. Conrad Zalesie smiled.

"And now, as much as I would rather stay here and talk to you, I have to go and talk to that boring husband of yours." He again leaned forward to pat and fondle her thigh. Angela saw his eyes flash as she gave another involuntary start and locked her knees together. He glanced at his wife. "Never mind, I'm sure Theresa will keep you entertained."

He had delivered the apology with a smile, but the instruction to his wife had been unambiguous. She nodded, and studied the allotted task with appreciative eyes.

"Of course I will, Conrad. Nothing could please me more."

Zalesie turned and walked away. Angela sipped politely at her sherry, and feigned a self-assurance that denied her current pulse rate.

****

Zalesie's study was a large, luxuriously-appointed, room. It sat at the back of the main house, overlooking the grounds and the lake beyond. Zalesie ushered Carlisle in, then took his seat behind a large expanse of mahogany and leather.

"So what are you doing here, Alan? Not that you and your lovely wife aren't welcome, of course, but it is only ten days since we last met. Nothing happened to concern us, I hope?"

Carlisle casually glanced around the study, and then lied.

"No, nothing special. It was something Marcus asked me to check. Said he'd heard rumours about you running for office; wanted to know if it was true."

"What office?"

"Is there more than one?"

"And you flew all the way up from Washington to ask me that? Are there no working telephones at the State Department?"

"Well, it is confidential, but it wasn't just that. Angela seemed in need of a little excitement. Thought I'd let her loose on Manhattan."

Carlisle listened to his own words and found them hollow and implausible. Whatever Zalesie might have thought, he gave nothing away.

"I'm sure she'll enjoy that, but as for me and the highest office? Doesn't the Constitution have something to say about that?"

Carlisle shrugged.

"We farmed in your citizenship for the CFR, and we've amended the Constitution before. America always has been a nation of converging nationality. This wouldn't be without precedent. You have the necessary connections, and you clearly have the wherewithal."

His eyes flickered around the study's opulence in an unnecessary effort to amplify the point. Zalesie frowned.

"Shackled, and placed under a microscope? Why would I ever allow such a thing?"

Carlisle was momentarily thrown.

"I don't understand. Shackled? Shackled how?"

The Lithuanian pointed to a picture on the far wall. It was a signed photograph of a boxer, hanging among many other similarly-framed portraits of boxers, but positioned slightly higher.

"Do you know who that is?"

Carlisle squinted at the picture, unable to identify either face or signature from where he sat.

"No, not a boxing fan, I'm afraid."

"That's Max Schmeling, one of the great heavyweight champions."

Carlisle sneered.

"You mean the guy Joe Louis almost killed?"

Zalesie smiled. He said Americans always talked about the second fight, when Louis won. In Europe they preferred to talk about the first, when Schmeling won.

When Carlisle said the second fight had been a walk-over, Zalesie's smile didn't waver.

"Some say Louis had weights in his gloves. Some say it was a freak punch that broke a bone in Schmeling's vertebrae. I don't believe that. I think Schmeling lost that fight before he stepped into the ring."

Carlisle knew this was no idle chatter. He asked what that should tell him. Zalesie said the real difference between the fights had been a little Jewish trainer called Joe Jacobs. He laughed, loudly and artificially, and said he couldn't recall another time in history when a Jew has held so much power without abusing it, then added that maybe there had been one.

He pointed to the figure of Joe Jacobs standing in the background, and explained that Jacobs had been in Schmeling's corner for the first fight. Joe Jacobs took his work seriously. He noticed that, after throwing a series of jabs, Louis dropped his left. The little Jewish trainer's keen-eyed assessment of the flaw in Louis' defence gave Schmeling the edge he needed. Until then, all the experts had claimed that Joe Louis was unbeatable.

When a jingoistic Carlisle asked about the second fight, the Lithuanian said Joe Jacobs hadn't been in the corner for the second fight. He died before it took place. They brought in an inexperienced man, who didn't find a weakness in Louis' guard, or check the gloves as closely as Joe Jacobs always did. The world knows what happened after that.

Carlisle sat trying to fathom the message.

"I don't follow."

"You were talking about running for president. I was talking about power, real power."

"More powerful than the President of The United States?"

Zalesie nodded. He said many in Washington thought politics was power, but he believed political power was merely an illusion. Incensed, Carlisle took issue.

"But he makes decisions that affect the entire world; decisions that change the wealth of nations, that start and end wars. As the sign on Harry Truman's desk says. . . The buck stops here."

"So what does that make him? A president or a patsy?"

Carlisle frowned as he listened to the insult. Zalesie smiled briefly.

"I, too, have a sign. If you look at the back it says, I'm from everywhere but Missouri."

"He's a great man, Conrad, and you're a cynic."

"No, Alan, I am a realist. If I were a cynic I would say that what that sign tells you, and what you see sitting on the other side of that sign, isn't power or even a pretence of power. It is just another politician with more vanity than sense."

Just as he had brow-beaten the sycophantic Howard Strecker in Frankfurt, Carlisle was now taking a spoonful of that same medicine. He had no choice but to defer to the Lithuanian. Zalesie was powerful, and clever. Carlisle desperately needed the information on Kube and Gehlen. He frowned, but said nothing as Zalesie clarified the point.

"No matter how senior or powerful a politician may seem, advisers control his actions and public opinion decides his thinking. He may appear as a giant, a colossus, a champion of the world, but if he doesn't listen to advice and public opinion that illusion will quickly disappear."

"And what would happen if the President didn't follow your advice, if he refused to listen? He'd still be the President, and you'd be out of the advice business."

"We call them rogue democrats, Alan. They're like rogue State Department officials. . . They seldom achieve and they seldom last."

The glare warned Carlisle to change the subject, but he was too angry.

"What you're telling me is that you hold more power than the President of the United States? You're telling me they do as you tell them, or else?"

Zalesie waved away both indignation and question.

"Whether I hold that power or not is an irrelevance, but I will say this: whatever power I do hold will last a good deal longer than the eight-year cycle of a punch-drunk president, with a cupboard full of skeletons and a season ticket to The White House."

"They haven't proposed that two-term limit yet."

"I assure you they will. Roosevelt was a warning shot. We would all do well to heed it. And now, if you will excuse me, Alan, I do have guests to attend to."

Carlisle stood up, and then pretended to remember.

"Yes, of course. Oh, just before you go, there was something. The European networks. We're setting out plans to tie them into Occupied Territories when the time's right. I need details of the key players; in confidence, of course."

His unease had been obvious. He cursed himself. The Lithuanian appeared not to notice.

"Details?"

"Yes, the usual stuff: names, personnel and contact details, security measures in effect. It's all red tape, but if something happened to you or any of the key players it could be disastrous. We'd look damn silly if we weren't able to pick up the threads, especially after all this effort and expense. Perhaps you could let me have whatever you've got?"

"You do realize they're running Reinhard Gehlen directly out of Camp King?"

"If you sanction it, I'll contact them directly, but that still leaves the Czech connection."

"I'll think it over and get back to you. Now I must return to my guests."

27

"Where the hell have you been?"

Angela Carlisle hissed at her husband while smiling across the room at Zalesie. Zalesie nodded and returned the smile. Theresa had excused herself earlier, saying she needed to organize something. She left Angela alone and squirming with embarrassment.

Carlisle turned to her.

"I've been talking to Zalesie," he whispered. I think he'll give us what we want."

"I should hope so. This place is like a scene from ancient Rome. I've literally had to fight people off. I tried to move into another room and found a women having sex with three men. A crowd of people were watching. I think they were waiting in line. . . It was disgusting."

"Well, as long as you didn't join the queue."

"Don't be crude. They've treated me like a sex object since we arrived. It's not only that. I know some of these people. I've seen them in Washington. Look, can't we get out of here?"

"Of course not. It'll look as though we only came so I could talk to Zalesie. You should have sat at the bar. It's less obvious if you're alone. Come on, we'll wander over."

"You're not leaving me again?"

"No choice, I'm afraid. Theresa wants to introduce me to someone."

She glanced across to where Theresa Zalesie stood talking to two women.

"Pimping for you now, is she?"

"Don't be petulant. Look, we daren't upset them. Zalesie's already suspicious, and it's essential we get these details. I don't want to give him an excuse to say no, so be friendly."

"What do you mean, when you say 'friendly'?"

"You know what I mean."

"Alan, I'm not a whore."

"Do you want Mathew safe?"

"Of course."

"Well then."

"You bastard! I can't believe you're doing this to me. I'm your wife, for Christ's sake."

Still bickering, they made their way to the bar. She perched on a stool in the corner and glared at him as he turned to leave.

"It's that Zalesie woman, isn't it? She's getting you out of the way, so. . . and you're allowing it to happen. For all I know, you suggested it."

There was no trace of apology in his answer.

"Well, it's not as if you haven't done it before."

"I can't believe you're using me like this."

Carlisle hissed back at her.

"You were happy for me to be a party to murder, but this is too sensitive for you, is it? Look, I've got to go, she's waving at me. We'll talk later."

"Alan, please don't leave me here, not so. . . Christ! Don't I mean anything to you?"

She watched him saunter over to where Theresa Zalesie stood chatting with two dusky and attractive young women. She saw the girls smile obvious invitations, and heard Theresa say.

"Alan, I'd like you to meet Marisa and Christina. Don't ask me which is which. They've come all the way up from Panama and insist on doing everything together."

"Do they now?"

"Perhaps you wouldn't mind showing them to their room, settle them in, pour them a drink; give them whatever they need? I've put them in the lake-view suite, in the north annex."

Angela sat fuming, but then saw Theresa Zalesie look straight at her and heard her say,

"Don't worry about that wife of yours. I'm sure we'll find something to do."

Angela Carlisle swallowed hard and looked away. She ordered a cognac and downed it in a single swallow. Then curiosity bettered poise and caused her to steal a second glance.

The knowing look was still there, imagining and suggesting, undressing and anticipating. She realised how vulnerable she now was and felt her stomach churn and her heart begin to thump. Moistened palms wiped anxious perspiration against the tautness of her skirt. Frantic fingers tugged at a hemline's sudden inadequacy.

She ordered another cognac as her confidence continued to drain, shockingly aware that she was once again thoroughly aroused by thoughts of lesbianism and lust.

Suddenly the woman was beside her, determined to press an unscrupulous advantage, heightening arousal and confounding resolve as her eyes flashed and her fingers idly stroked.

"Are you feeling all right? For a second there you seemed a little faint."

"No I'm fine; just warm. There's no need for. . . I'll be all right. Thanks anyway."

"Well, I think we'd better get you some air. Come with me."

"My purse and my bag. I have to. . ."

"I've got them. Now let's get you that air."

Insistent fingers tugged her from the stool. An assertive arm looped its authority around her waist. She tripped and staggered as her fashionably-heeled shoes reached the ground, but recovered and reluctantly made her way across the floor.

"Look, I'm fine. I just had too much to drink, but I'm fine now. I ought to get back."

"Well, let's get you some air first. Perhaps the balcony would be best."

A commanding hand slipped from waist to buttocks. Governing and fondling, it guided her up and toward the balcony, but on reaching the galleried landing suddenly altered direction. Instead of the balcony's revitalizing air and the cool of the night, it gripped a little tighter and shepherded her toward a room at the corridor's end.

Once inside the room, she leaned against the nearest wall and watched in tacit compliance, seeing the untidiness of an oversized bedroom, with shoes and clothes strewn across the floor, and an ornate dressing-table covered in perfumes and cosmetics. Half-a-dozen glasses and some bottles of spirit sat on a trolley at the far end of the dressing-table. Her eyes wandered from there to where an unmade bed of ivory satin further increased her pulse rate.

Theresa Zalesie slouched to the trolley, picked up two glasses and reached for the bourbon.

"Not for me, thanks. I think I might already be a little tipsy."

The fingers briefly hesitated before opening the bottle. They poured out two full measures, and then returned the bottle to the trolley without replacing the cap. Angela watched as dainty feet with painted toenails kicked off a pair of high-heeled shoes and then padded their way towards her. A jubilant predator moved closer and whispered into her ear.

"We both know why I brought you up here, and we both know you're no more drunk than I am."

Propped against the wall in fixated readiness, Angela spluttered a hollow denial, and allowed the gloating seductress to press the glass into her hand.

"I think you must have the wrong idea. I'm not like that. I have to get back to my husband. I'm sorry. I didn't mean to give you the wrong. . ."

She realised the obvious transparency of her lies and faltered into silence. Theresa Zalesie unpinned her hair and allowed the sheen to cascade, then leaned forward and whispered,

"Liar!"

"No, I'm not like that, I. . ."

"But that's not true, is it, Mrs Carlisle?"

As she heard Zalesie's voice, Angela's imagination raced. She stuttered a refusal and shrank against the wall, her eyes flickering between the menace of Zalesie and the promise of his wife. He put a finger to his lips.

"Hush."

To Angela, trapped and confused, that single syllable held more menace than a thousand threats. It sent waves of panic through her frame, and left her shaking with fear. She watched him pour a drink and raise the glass, then pause again.

"So, tell me, Angela, why are you here tonight? And why does Alan suddenly want so many security details? And what did he and my old friend Stanislav Paslov talk about in Frankfurt?"

She spluttered her answers.

"I don't understand. I'm here, because Alan said it would be fun. I don't know anything about security details, and I've never heard of Stanislav whatever his name is."

Zalesie put down his glass and crossed the room. He took her by the arm and led her to the bed. She whimpered a refusal and shrank from him.

"No, please; please don't."

"Whatever do you think I'm going to do to you?"

She must have looked as terrified as she felt, because he gave an artificial laugh and offered a reassurance. "You are a highly attractive woman, Mrs Carlisle, but I have never yet felt the need to force myself on houseguests."

She breathed a silent sigh. He smiled a comforting smile and returned to his drink, leaving her sitting on the bed, and trying to steady her nerves. When she risked another glance, she saw the smile had gone.

"I have seen the photograph, Angela; of you and those women, but I don't think that's the whole story. So why else did you come here tonight? What was so important?"

She found herself unable to summon an answer. He asked again.

"I can help you, you know. I can protect you from whatever it is you're so terrified of, but you have to trust me and you have to tell me everything. Now, please, tell me."

As she sat watching Zalesie watching her, Angela felt isolated and afraid and confused. She didn't know what she should do, or how much she should say. She thought of Mathew in danger and felt the panic rise. Her son was in trouble. It was her fault, her responsibility. Suddenly the whole sordid story came gushing out.

She talked of Sarah Pearson and the Russian girl. She spoke of how the women had tricked and seduced her. She spoke of the photographs, how much she had paid, and how ashamed she had been. She spoke of Paslov's meeting with Alan, and his demand for details of the Nazi spymasters. She spoke of her love and fear for Mathew, and how she had abused and alienated him. She said he had disappeared in Vienna, that Alan suspected Paslov and Beria. She blamed herself. The emotion overwhelmed her. She began to sob. Then, through the misery, she heard him say,

"Don't worry. I'll see what I can do; see if we can't find that son of yours and get him home."

She wiped the tears and then looked at him with a mixture of gratitude and uncertainty.

"Thank you; thank you so much. How can I ever. . . ? I mean. . ."

He listened to her stuttered words and viewed her trepidation, then smiled and shook his head.

"One day, perhaps, but now I rather think my wife wants to finish what she started."

As Angela watched him stride from the room, comforting fingers arrived. They brushed the hair from her eyes. They reached for a tissue and dabbed at the tears. They stroked at her cheeks and neck. They calmed, and caressed, and prepared.

They brought to mind a similar occasion from some months before, and she recalled the mixture of excitement and disgrace she had felt when Sarah and the Russian girl had plied her with wine, and then forcibly seduced her on that apartment floor.

This time, though, when Angela closed her eyes and allowed another woman to explore and arouse, there was no fantasy or delusion, no anger or feigned disgust, no screams of outrage to cover her shame, and no guilt of any description.

All she allowed herself to imagine was a world of gentle deviance and illicit pleasure. All she allowed herself to feel was a desire she no longer had any need or reason to deny.

28

Following his discussion with Chambers and Allum, Hammond spent most of the afternoon and evening walking off his anger. On return to his hotel, he found an unlikely visitor waiting.

The concierge told him as he collected his key. An agitated Marcus Allum sat waiting in the bar, with frown fixed and soda water untouched. Hammond sat down opposite his one-time friend and patently furious boss. Allum spat an accusation.

"What is it with you, Gerald?" Hammond shrugged and stared blankly back. Allum went on. "Carlisle told you, I told you, and now Chambers has told you. Stop chasing this girl. Why the hell aren't you doing that?"

"I gave her my word."

"You gave her your word? Jesus! I stuck my neck out for you. This is how you repay me?"

"How do you mean?"

"What the hell were you playing at, talking to Chambers like that?"

"I was doing the job you should have done."

Allum's fury was obvious, but the counter accusation had obviously caught him off balance. He looked confused. Hammond explained. Just where the hell did these people get off, ordering government officials around?

Allum raised his eyes to the heavens. He said he couldn't believe it. Hammond was as bad as Carlisle. He glanced around the room. Not only were these people officially part of the government, but in many ways they ran the country. They were some of the most powerful men in the country, and Daniel Chambers was one of them. Hadn't Hammond understood anything Chambers had told him?

Hammond glowered. He said the president and the people's representatives ran this country, or they would, if someone smacked down people like Chambers once in a while.

Allum swore. Did Hammond honestly believe that politicians had a divine understanding of people's opinions? Most people didn't know what their opinions were until the press told them.

"Are you telling me these people run the media?"

"Of course." Allum corrected himself. "Well, apart from the Times-Herald. That is. That's Hoover's personal attack dog. Don't you understand, Gerald, these people run everything: politics, Wall Street, the Federal Reserve, the police, the judges, the church, the academic communities, and not just here in the U.S."

"And the people who make the rules meet in that house on Sixty-Eighth and Park?"

"Some of them do, yes."

"Then maybe we should pull it down. . . preferably with them inside."

"And who would replace them? Without these people, the west would fall into anarchy."

"Did you say anarchy or democracy?"

Hammond considered he'd made a valid point. Allum disagreed. He said these weren't bad people they were talking about. Hammond shouldn't listen to the lunatic fringe. There was no big lie involved, no conspiracy to subvert democracy. On the contrary, there was a concerted effort to keep it on track. America was a capitalist country, the finest and most prosperous in the world. It was largely due to these people that it was.

When Hammond asked if he got that from the newspaper, the answer staggered him. Allum claimed the good of the country was too important to leave in the hands of people so easily manipulated. When Hammond spoke of democracy and elections, Allum scoffed.

He said elections were like going up to Yankee Stadium. People could shout and cheer and applaud, if they happened to like what they saw, or hiss and boo and whistle if they didn't. But ordinary people didn't get to play, and they didn't get to pick the teams or decide the tactics. All they could do was decide which team to support, pay their entrance fee at the gate, make some noise, eat their hot dogs and watch the game.

"And what if I stop going to the game? What if I stop paying my entrance fee?"

Hammond set the features in determined pose. Allum was equally intransigent.

"You mean go back to the Little League and sit in the bleachers? Buttonhole the coach on his way out of the ballpark?" He looked exasperated. "Take a good look around. This is the only serious game in town. For every disenfranchised Joe who walks past the stadium, there are sixty-thousand waving greenbacks at the turnstiles. You turn those around and maybe you'll make a difference, but how are you gonna do that? You don't run the media. You can try stopping them in the street, but I doubt they'll listen. Why should they, as long as they're happy and their team wins one every now and then?"

Hammond found it difficult to disagree. Allum threw a further question.

"When was the last time you saw a change from Democrat to Republican or vice versa result in a true change in policy? I'm not talking about a few cosmetic changes. I'm talking about real sea change. Think about it, and you'll find the answer's never, because as soon as they get to run the team there's somebody else telling them the rules they have to play by. That's just the way it is. You might as well accept it."

When Hammond asked how many people were members of the Council on Foreign Relations, Allum spoke of hundreds. Then he asked about the inner circle. At first Allum denied the existence of such a group, but then confirmed the truth. Hammond finally felt he was getting somewhere, but when he mentioned Conrad Zalesie, Allum spat a warning.

"Zalesie's one of the most powerful of all. And a word of advice. . . You might get away with upsetting Chambers, but don't ever upset Zalesie."

"Why does everybody keep telling me that?"

"Because it's good advice."

"What about the girl?"

"Forget her."

"I can't do that."

Allum shrugged in resignation.

"That's what I thought you'd say."

"So where is she?"

"More than my life is worth, even if I did know, which I don't. But I will do something for you." He nodded to the newspaper on the table. "There's a number written inside, the number of a man who might help. His name's Gabriel. He's the best detective in New York. I've used him before. Assuming the girl's still in New York, if anybody can find her, it's Gabriel."

Hammond looked closely at his old friend. He seemed worried.

"They've got you scared, too, haven't they?"

Allum shook his head.

"No, just cautious. After your little chat with Chambers, they now know that Beria has a man in the State Department. If that's true, there's only a handful of people it could be; only a handful who knew about your trip to Germany."

"So who did know about it?"

"Apart from the two of us? There's Carlisle and Carpenter. Other people in the office knew some of it, but never all of it."

"Nobody else?"

"Not in the Department, not that I'm aware of."

"And outside the Department?"

"Zalesie, Chambers, and one or two people in Zalesie's organization, whose names I don't intend sharing."

"What sort of people?"

"I can't tell you that."

"What about Martin Kube?"

"We didn't get to him until you'd left. He didn't know anything about it."

"So that's what, six, eight, including us? What about the team in Germany?"

Hammond was desperately searching for alternatives. Allum shook his head.

"You said Paslov knew all about you. The German cell didn't have that information."

"So what happens now? What will these people do?"

"They'll find him, and they'll kill him."

Allum stood ready to leave. For a few seconds he seemed undecided, but then posed another question, seemingly more in hope than expectation.

"You're still hell-bent on chasing after this girl?"

"I have no choice. I gave her my word."

"Then call the number I gave you. . . Gabriel's the best there is."

"Gabriel? You mean like the angel?"

Allum's previously worried and angry features broke into a smile.

"No, not even close." The smile broadened. "I think you're probably gonna like him. For some reason I've never been able to understand, people do. But he's not like any angel I ever heard of, and especially not that one." Allum was still chuckling as he turned to leave. "In fact, Dawid Gabriel's just about as far from angelic as it gets." The chuckle faded. "But remember what I've said, Gerald. Find this girl, if you must, but after that you let it drop. You're not equipped to take these people on. Nobody is."

"So why are you helping me?"

"Because you were right. We may not be able to stop them, but sometimes people like Daniel Chambers need a quiet reminder that they're not God, and they're not infallible."

"Seems like he got to you, too, huh?"

"He always gets to me."

Allum nodded a curt goodbye before walking out of the bar and away. Hammond watched him go and then sat quietly assessing the many disturbing revelations about the clandestine group of power-brokers from Harold Pratt House. He similarly pondered Allum's true motivation in offering support. Nothing came to mind.

He wandered over to the bar, ordered a large scotch and water, and then headed for his room. When he got there he found a note pushed under the door. It was from Davis Carpenter, and unusually succinct for the pompous bureaucrat. It ordered him to return to Washington. Hammond mouthed an obscenity, screwed it into a ball and threw it into the bin.

He ran through the list of suspects, turning over what he knew of each, and assessing their potential as Soviet agents.

He thought of his pompous boss Carpenter, the fat bureaucrat and State Department makeweight. Hammond thought back to late April of forty-four. He recalled the look of terror on Carpenter's face when his team had first hit the Gestapo outpost in Rouen. He compared it to the bloated superciliousness that had greeted him in his office that day.

Carpenter was everything the Soviets looked for in an agent: weak and arrogant, self-indulgent and opinionated, lazy and cowardly. The State Department had passed him over for promotion and appointed Carlisle. They'd passed him over and appointed Marcus Allum before that. Carpenter would have to be a little bitter, a little vengeful. He'd be the ideal candidate.

Well, perhaps not ideal. Davis Carpenter wasn't high enough up the State Department food chain to be of significant value to Beria, but he could be useful in minor ways.

Then he thought of another flaw in his logic. Beria didn't do usual. Lavrenti Beria did anything but usual. He moved on. Alan Carlisle was a possibility, but why blackmail an agent already turned? It didn't make sense. That left Allum.

Marcus Allum was devious enough, and vicious enough. He would turn, if it suited him, but how could the Soviets offer him more than he already enjoyed, and the risk was significant.

That left blackmail, but if the Soviets had already blackmailed Allum, why would they need to blackmail Carlisle? Anyway, he had known Allum since Princeton. Allum hated communists and he wasn't the type. But if Allum wasn't the type, who was?

Hammond drained his glass. Thirsty work, this spy catching. He left his room and wandered downstairs for a refill, then returned to his room and his contemplations.

He thought about the other candidates Allum had mentioned. He assumed they were defectors too, spymasters of some description, SS usually, but in Kube's case, Gestapo. What if it was one of them, or both? Wouldn't that be a coup for the Soviets? Two Nazi triple-agents, betraying the capitalist west to the Bolshevik east; it was the stuff of Lavrenti Beria's dreams. Two Nazi war criminals, absolved for some of the most heinous crimes in history by unelected factions in the democratic self-righteous west. Two war criminals hidden from the tribunals and paid enormous sums of public money for providing a fledgling western intelligence service with lies and disinformation. The only man who would like that more than Beria was Hoover.

He recalled the pretentious Daniel Chambers. How would he explain that, when it echoed around the walls of 10 Downing Street and 1600 Pennsylvania Avenue? Hammond didn't know Lavrenti Beria, but he'd met Stanislav Paslov on two occasions. He imagined that such an embarrassment for western intelligence would hugely amuse the emaciated spymaster. But that was too fanciful, or was it? Wasn't that a perfect example of the unexpected tactic with multiple strikes that had made Lavrenti Beria so revered by western spymasters in the past?

His mind moved on, to the hugely wealthy and powerful Conrad Zalesie. He knew about Hammond's trip to Germany. He could be the one. Hammond hoped to meet him soon. Maybe after that he could better assess his potential as a Soviet agent. Now, though, it was late, and Hammond had finished another glass of scotch and water. It was time to sleep.

29

Carl Strieder got the call at seven that evening. By ten he had briefed the team and reached the outskirts of Salzburg. By eleven they had slipped through the airfield perimeter fence and were in the air and on their way. He listened to the familiar drone of the three Pratt and Whitney Hornets and looked around the corrugated interior of the old JU52, remembering so many previous occasions and studying the faces that looked back at him.

They were fourteen faithful comrades from a hundred previous drops, and more scrapes and battles than he cared to recall. They had been together since Leningrad in '43. Some had been with him since long before that; the old Seventh Flieger, the first of the Fallschirmjäger. They were men he trusted with his life. They wouldn't let him down; they never had. Carl Strieder didn't believe they ever would.

He checked the MP40, and smiled again when he saw the others nudge one another and grin. Before any action he always checked it every ten minutes, and they always grinned at his caution. Peter Lischka had once called it compulsiveness, but then Peter knew all about that sort of thing. The rest just grinned and shrugged, and called it plain old-fashioned craziness. Carl didn't know why he checked the weapon so often. After all, there wasn't all that much in the MP40 to check. He just knew he felt better doing it.

After the carnage of Monte Cassino the rest of the Fallschirmjäger had retreated north, up through the Italian peninsula, towards the Gothic Line.

Many gave up at Imola, but not Carl and his men. They had gone north and crossed the Apennines with the rest, but instead of surrendering, had kept going north and west across the Po Valley. After that, they threaded their way through the Dolomites to the west of Carinthia, and from there they crossed the Austrian spine to Salzburg.

Some mistakenly believed they were part of Otto Skorzeny's old 500th SS parachute division, the men who had so daringly rescued Mussolini from his prison on Gran Sasso. Some called them the last of the Blitzkriegers. Others said they were The Führer's final tears that would one day fall again like rain from the sky.

Most people simply called them the Werwolf. Not the acne-studded Hitler Youth of Heinrich Himmler's final command and Hans-Adolf Prützmann's lunatic crusade, but the Fourth Reich's mythical Übermenschen, the bloodied but unbowed warriors of a thousand battles past.

At the final reckoning Grand Admiral Dönitz ordered the Werwolf to disband, although why Dönitz ever thought that men like Carl would listen to someone like him Carl Strieder had no idea. And while Prützmann's Werwolf adolescents threw down their arms and lifted their hands in surrender, the Grand Admiral sat in his Nuremberg prison cell, twiddling his thumbs and awaiting a token sentence.

Dönitz, to his amazement and fury, would spend ten years in Spandau. A wiser Carl Strieder and his men would remain hidden in their mountain retreat, recalling the Goumier's barbarism in Cassino's aftermath, and awaiting a time when they could take their revenge.

The Russians didn't believe the Werwolf existed. The French had finer tales of partisan resistance to tell. The Americans and British thought the stories exaggerated, and any potential threat a meaningless one. The Austrians and Italians didn't all that much care if they existed or not.

Whenever pressed, former Wehrmacht and SS soldiers would say the idea of German partisans and guerrillas was anathema to the national characteristic of order and respect for law. They would argue that for partisans and guerrillas to fight on, there had to be some chance of victory, or at least some measure of hope. Then they would shake their heads in despair, and sadly reflect that their once-glorious Reich had neither.

Only the wives of a defeated nation kept the dream of the Übermenschen Werwolf alive. They told tales to their children, of a hope that still lived and of men who still fought, but it was only the children who truly believed.

But they had all reckoned without Carl Strieder and his men's loyalty and resilience. And none had any knowledge of the weapons and supplies that magically dropped from the skies to the east of Salzburg on the third day of the third week of every third month.

At the end of the war they had replaced the old JU52 Luftwaffe insignia and camouflage with commercial advertising and lurid colours. An overstretched western alliance had commandeered, and repaired, and repainted it yet again. They now used it for ferrying overnight mail and cargo to and from Salzburg and Vienna. But the pilot wasn't British, or American, or French. He was an old night fighter and wartime comrade of Carl Strieder, a Dornier 17 pilot from those nights when the Luftwaffe had carried rather more than just mail.

Carl had contacted him two days before, when they knew the young man was somewhere in Vienna, but didn't know exactly where. Then someone spoke to the bus driver on the route from Schwechat Airport to Innere Stadt. He told his tale of an unusual roadblock outside the Favoriten headquarters, and the arrests of a beautiful young woman and a young man with an American passport. That was when Carl Strieder and his men hitched a ride.

Around twenty minutes after midnight they saw the lights of Vienna in the distance. Ten minutes after that they dropped, using static lines attached to a temporary anchor cable, six hundred feet above fields to the west of Kledering.

Carl Strieder smiled proudly as they buried the chutes and then gathered on him; a night drop onto unknown terrain, with minimal dispersal, and not so much as a twisted ankle between them.

Five kilometres north, and an hour after that, they met their contact and studied the building's blueprints by torchlight. Then they took up a position to the front of the local Soviet headquarters at Favoriten and finalized their plan of assault.

Two men would position themselves a hundred meters farther on, to watch the road to Wieden and hold off any reinforcement from the north. Two more would position themselves a hundred meters south, and prevent the same from there. Two men would work their way around and cover the rear exit; one would remain where they crouched and cover the front. The last man would wait for the firing to begin, and then rustle up some transport from the vehicle compound at the side of the building. Five minutes for the cover to settle into their allotted positions, and then Carl Strieder and six more would go in through the front.

After that, Carl estimated ten minutes to get the job done, and ten to get out and on their way. Then a final ten after that for good measure and any unseen problems, before half the Red Army arrived from their various barracks and blew the last of the Werwolf to hell.

With the orders complete, and cover dispatched to the four points of the compass, Carl Strieder cleared imaginary dirt from the MP40's cocking handle and slot for one last time. He grinned across at Peter Lischka. It was time to go.

Then he was up and running, across the road and on to the first sentry post, with six following and only the building ahead. A guard called out and reached for his rifle. Carl shot him three times in the chest. Another ran for his life, and got three more nine-millimetre slugs in his back. Someone came around the corner of the building with a pah-pah-shah raised. Peter Lischka shot him twice. Someone else ran from the vehicle compound and raised his rifle. Two of those running in Carl Strieder's wake took him out at the same instant. Now they were at the door and the lights were coming on. Suddenly they were inside.

To the north, a returning Soviet patrol picked the wrong time and the wrong place. The two men posted at the side of the north road hit the canvas-backed Gaz with everything they had. It burst into flames and crashed into a disused concrete pillbox. One man screamed in agony, and instantly drew more fire, but nobody else in the burning vehicle stirred. To the south, it was still eerily quiet.

Those inside the building shot everyone they saw not already locked in the cells, male and female, uniformed or not. From the far side of the building they heard the sound of more gunfire. It came from those covering the rear door. Carl Strieder heard the small arms chatter and smiled in grim determination. Not one bloody Bolshevik would escape the wrath of the Werwolf that night.

He found the keys and started down the left-hand corridor, calling out Mathew Carlisle's name through the smoke, and unlocking each cell door as he moved. A voice at the far end called back. Carl Strieder hurried to unlock the door and get the young man to safety. Upstairs, they could hear the sounds of grenades as they cleared the accommodation section one room at a time. At the back of the building the gunfire had stopped and the men were returning.

He threw open the cell door and barked a question.

"You are Mathew Carlisle?"

The terrified youth nodded his head.

"We are here to get you out. Come with us."

Mathew Carlisle began to follow, but then shouted,

"Lara! I have to find Lara. They have her here somewhere."

"There is no time."

"I have to find her."

Mathew Carlisle shook his head in defiance and headed along the right-hand corridor. Carl Strieder swore loudly and followed him. All they saw were empty rooms. All they found were the bodies of luckless Soviet soldiers. They climbed the stairs and ran along the first floor, checking each room in turn. Carl saw the bullet-scarred body of Sachino Metreveli, naked and still sprawled across his bed. The body of a naked young woman lay alongside him. He pointed to the woman. Mathew Carlisle shook his head. He said it wasn't Lara Scholde.

Two of Carl's men came down from the floor above. He asked them about the girl. They said nobody was alive up there. They also said they were positive there hadn't been a girl.

Clearly frantic, Mathew Carlisle said he had to check for himself. Carl Strieder stepped in front of him. He shook his head. He said there wasn't time; they had to leave now. The young man stood his ground, and again shook his head in defiance. Carl Strieder punched him hard across the jaw, and then draped the inert frame across his shoulder and headed downstairs.

Outside, another patrol had returned at the wrong time. Caught in a deadly crossfire, the Gaz sat skewed across the road, with the occupants dead and the canvas back ablaze. A truck waited beyond that with the engine running. It was a two-and-a-half ton Studebaker, decked out in Red Army logos, its belly packed with men anxious to be on their way. Carl Strieder dumped the still-unconscious Mathew Carlisle into willing hands. They lifted him up and dumped him into the back. Carl grinned up at Peter Lischka.

"If he wakes up, punch him again. How many in there?"

"Including me and the boy, there are twelve. Two more to pick up from the south perimeter, and that is it; we are clear."

Carl nodded and then headed for the passenger seat. He hauled himself up and into the cab, and told the driver to hit the accelerator. The driver stopped to pick up the final two on the south perimeter, and then they were on their way.

The entire assault and rescue at the Favoriten headquarters had taken a fraction over eleven minutes. During the raid they had freed eight bemused prisoners of the MGB from their various calls, and left twenty-three dead bodies in their wake. Seven of the eight bemused prisoners had stolen away into the night. One lay unconscious in the back of the Studebaker. Not one of Carl Strieder's men had suffered so much as a scratch.

They headed south from Favoriten, and then turned east toward Rannersdorf, then north-east up to Schwechat, before turning south-east on the road towards Schwadorf. They stopped after six kilometres and drove into a field, then headed east again on foot across the fields until they reached the south-eastern end of the runway. A sullen Mathew Carlisle had finally come around. He shook his head to clear the fog and then glared at Carl Strieder.

"What about Lara Scholde?"

"She was not there. We checked."

"You're certain?"

"I swear."

Mathew Carlisle nodded.

"What now?"

"Now we wait here until three."

And true enough, at seven minutes past three, the returning overnight mail and cargo run from Vienna to Salzburg paused for a few minutes at the south-eastern end of the runway. The pilot called air traffic control on the radio, and said he needed to check a misfiring Pratt & Whitney Hornet. He added that it wouldn't take long.

At precisely ten minutes after three, the old JU52 took off from Schwechat on time. Nobody noticed that it stayed on the runway a little longer than usual before lifting off. Nobody noticed it straining to get airborne. When it touched down at Salzburg, nobody noticed it pause for two minutes on the far side of that airfield either; or if anybody did, they never felt it important enough to mention.

And while the old aircraft they once called 'Tante Ju' took its time in taxiing back to the terminal at Salzburg, sixteen men slipped out of the rear left-hand door and back through the same hole in the fence that fifteen of them had come through around five and a half hours earlier.

Nobody had any idea that it was Carl Strieder and his men who had rescued the young man from Lavrenti Beria's clutches that night. Nobody knew for certain who it was or where they had come from. But from that night onward the Soviets always claimed open-mindedness on the possible existence of the Übermenschen Werwolf.

30

They called the grand old building Gründerzeit, and the ornate façade neo-Gothic. Both had survived countless battles for historic Leipzig's favours over the years. More recently they had survived the threat of post-war demolition. They now stood haughtily surveying less pretentious neighbours, under the gaze of Leipzig University, not far from where Luther once preached.

Beyond the fourth floor balcony and double-doors, a large spartan room had recently been converted into a large spartan office. Standing against two of the four cream-plastered walls, banks of grey-metal filing cabinets housed a thousand buff-coloured folders, and a thousand terrifying secrets. In the centre of the room the surface of a large oak desk lay littered with photographs of soldiers and spies, and papers containing many more terrifying secrets.

In the Old Town streets the people of Leipzig hurried about their business, unaware of the secrets hidden above or the grand old building's clandestine purpose. Three floors higher than the street, and sitting motionless at his desk, Stanislav Paslov sat pondering the actions of those around him, and in particular those of his Machiavellian friend and paranoid boss, Lavrenti Pavlovich Beria.

Stanislav Paslov kept his private office well away from the more celebrated and intimidating government buildings and the notorious departments that did his bidding and ruled the Soviet-occupied territories.

Paslov liked it that way. It reduced the possibility of interruption, it allowed him to think, and thinking was what Stanislav Paslov did best.

Beria was up to something. Paslov knew it. He could sense it; he could almost touch it, but he had no idea what. The capture of Hammond and the girl had taken so much manpower and so much effort, and yet Beria had simply let them go. 'A sprat to catch a mackerel,' he had said, but who was the sprat, and who was the mackerel? Was the girl the sprat? The obvious answer was yes, but maybe it was Hammond, or maybe even Paslov himself? And who was the mackerel? Was it the Nazi turncoat Gehlen, or even fat Martin Kube? Paslov thought not.

It had to be Carlisle. That was the obvious answer, but maybe the obvious was too obvious. It usually was whenever Beria was involved. But if the mackerel was Carlisle, the sprat couldn't be the girl; or could it?

The mackerel could even be Marcus Allum or Daniel Chambers, or any one of a dozen more, but if Carlisle was the mackerel, which seemed more likely, then why Frankfurt, and why him?

To Paslov's knowledge, Beria had three separate Smersh teams working in Washington. In New York City he had three more. If he'd wanted Carlisle removed, a speeding car on Dupont Circle could have done that on any night of the week. Why use Paslov's promise of defection to entice Carlisle all the way back to Frankfurt? Why take so much trouble to ensure Hammond and the girl reached Camp King? Why invite Hammond as a spectator, just to witness such a tawdry and unimaginative blackmail plot? Why risk the cover of Beria's most important agent in the State Department? Beria had to realize that once the Americans became aware of a mole's existence it would only be a matter of months before they dug him out, maybe less. Why sacrifice him so needlessly?

Stanislav Paslov knew Lavrenti Beria as well as anybody could. Beria was a master at directing watching eyes to the wrong place at the wrong time; the supreme illusionist, performing a sleight-of-hand conjuring trick while everyone looked the wrong way. He was paranoid and clever, but most of all Beria was a consummate magician who knew his audience and exploited their gullibility.

Paslov knew it had to be a diversion of some kind, that was obvious, but a diversion from what? Where should he look, and what should he look for?

Was it all simply about Nazi turncoats, or was it something else? It had to be something else, or why make such a fuss about milk already spilt, and why use Paslov to try to mop it up?

A knock at the door interrupted his thoughts. An attractive young woman dressed in a plain grey skirt and white blouse stood waiting.

"What is it?"

"Comrade Colonel, I have Comrade Demidov on the telephone. He says he has to speak to you, in person. He says it is important he comes to see you."

Paslov knew the name and person well. Vladimir Demidov was one of Beria's former bodyguards, a senior sergeant plucked from his job as an infantry sniper. He was now one of the MGB's most gifted assassins. When Demidov spoke it was in sullen monotones. On those odd occasions he listened, unless the subject was to do with mindless brutality and slaughter, the information usually went in one ear and out the other.

"Does he want to meet me here?"

"Yes, Colonel."

Paslov nodded his consent. The girl hurried back to the telephone. She returned moments later and told him that Demidov would be with him in ten minutes. Paslov's mind began racing.

Demidov made the journey from local Soviet offices to Paslov's hideaway in less than eight. He stood framed in the doorway to Paslov's office, dressed in a crumpled blue serge suit, grey open-neck shirt and scuffed brown leather shoes. Demidov had a surprisingly small head for such a large man, but the legs were hugely powerful as were the arms. The clothes were threadbare and dirty, and his barrel chest strained the buttons on the tattered shirt to such an extent that one was hanging at the end of a thin thread of cotton. Another was missing altogether.

"Comrade Colonel."

He waited until Paslov turned to acknowledge his presence, before snapping to attention and saluting, catching his hand on the door frame on the way up. Saluting a superior officer out of uniform was unheard of, particularly in occupied territory, and especially when the soldier doing the saluting was an ex-sniper who should have known the danger of directing watching eyes to a high-ranking officer. Paslov ignored the salute. Demidov introduced himself in a high-pitched voice that elevated his bizarre appearance and behaviour to the brink of farce.

But, as Paslov was only too aware, Vladimir Demidov was anything but that.

"Come in, Comrade. What can I do for you?"

"The files on the Nazi girl and Carlisle, I need to see them. They tell me you have them here."

Paslov nodded to the files, clearly marked among a number of similar-looking files on the cluttered desktop, but as Demidov made a move toward the desk the Russian spymaster snatched them up.

"Why do you need them?"

"It is confidential, Colonel."

Paslov wasn't about to let him get away with that.

"The files are here because I am responsible for them and the information they contain. Now I asked you a question, Comrade. I expect an answer."

Demidov cautiously eyed Paslov and then puffed his barrel chest.

"Comrade Deputy Premier Beria has approved my. . ."

Paslov had expected as much. He angrily interrupted.

"Comrade Beria is not here, and he is not responsible for the files. I am. Now you either answer the question, or get out of my sight and have Comrade Beria call me."

Demidov hesitated.

"I have a plane to catch. The flight leaves in two hours."

Paslov smiled coldly.

"Then you had better hurry, Comrade."

Paslov remained unmoved. Demidov relented.

"Very well. Carlisle had a woman at Camp King, a lover. I need information on her."

"He had many lovers at Camp King. Which one especially interests you?"

"This one was special, and recent. The affair lasted for many visits. It may still be going on."

Paslov nodded and passed him the file on Carlisle. He explained as Demidov grabbed at it.

"Her name is Melody Strand. He recently arranged her transfer to Fort Hunt in Virginia, where her husband works for the army as an interrogator. I believe Carlisle still sees her there. They continue to be lovers. The husband knows nothing of the affair."

Demidov nodded and scanned the file as he spoke.

"She is black, this woman called Strand. He likes to fuck the blacks?"

"Part African slave, from the mother, and Cajun from the father." Demidov was obviously unaware of the term. He looked puzzled. Paslov elaborated. "This one is more brown than black."

"He likes them, the girls with brown skins? He has a weakness for them?"

"That is what it says in his file. So why do you want the file on Catherine Schmidt?"

Again, Demidov hesitated. Paslov remained unwavering. Again, the assassin relented.

"Her father, the Nazi colonel. Comrade Beria wants to know who in the Prague Headquarters signed the death certificate and report." Paslov handed over the relevant file. Demidov scanned the pages. This time, the assassin failed to discover the necessary documents. He looked questioningly at Paslov. "The documents are not here. Is there a file on the father?"

Paslov shrugged.

"He died some years ago. There was, but we may have destroyed it. I will check, if you like, but it will take some time. If the documents still exist and we have them, I will call Comrade Beria personally and give him the information."

Demidov looked anxious.

"I am sorry, Comrade Colonel, but if Comrade Beria finds out that I have told you anything about this. . . well, he will. . ."

Paslov smiled a comforting smile.

"Not a problem, Comrade. I can call you when I have the information, and you can tell him. I will call you tomorrow. Where will you be?" Demidov still looked nervous and failed to answer. Paslov offered a reassurance. "Do not concern yourself with Comrade Beria. I will not mention our little chat."

Demidov didn't seem any happier with that. Paslov knew he had little choice. He stood quietly waiting until the assassin answered.

"You can contact me at our embassy in New York: from tomorrow at noon."

Paslov nodded, wondering why Beria would send his top assassin to New York with information on Carlisle. They'd only just turned Carlisle, or maybe they hadn't. Paslov wanted to ask, but knew that Demidov would lie, and so he said,

"It is not a problem, Comrade. I will call you at the embassy."

Demidov returned the folders to an outstretched hand, and then walked to the door. He reached the doorway and turned to face Paslov, then dramatically snapped to attention and saluted, taking care to avoid the door frame. Paslov tried not to smile.

"Thank you, Comrade Colonel. You have been very helpful."

The most awkward of assassins turned and marched away. Paslov finally allowed the smile to escape as he called after him,

"Have a good flight, Comrade. I will call you tomorrow."

Paslov waited on the balcony until he saw Demidov crossing the street below. Once the assassin had disappeared into the crowd, Paslov returned to his desk and reached under a pile of photographs. The hand reappeared clutching a file marked 'Prague: Non-Wehrmacht personnel 17/42'. Underneath the location and reference number was a white label. Typed on the label were the words, Josef Conrad Schmidt, Waffen SS-Oberführer.

Paslov quickly flipped through the file, but then paused when he came to the death certificate and studied the information. Army doctors always signed German army officer's death certificates in times of war. Platoon leaders or junior administrators usually witnessed the signature. The doctor's name was Oberleutnant Hermann Spengler, and that seemed genuine enough, but the witness was nothing to do with administration and anything but junior.

Paslov smiled as he compared the signature to the same signature on the incident report below and realised why he'd missed it before. Both signatures were the same partially-legible scrawl and difficult to decipher without the aid of negative entropy. However, when compared side-by-side, redundancy compensated and the name became obvious.

It was Gestapo Kriminaldirektor Martin Kube.

31

Three fruitless and frustrating days after his chat with Marcus Allum in his New York hotel, Hammond gave up chasing people who were never in and leaving his number for people who didn't return his calls. At seven a.m., as agreed on the telephone the previous night, he found Gabriel kicking his heels on the corner of Madison and East 39th Street. Hammond drew the car alongside the curb, then climbed out and spoke to the waiting detective. He explained who he was looking for, and why a recalcitrant Marcus Allum had suggested Gabriel.

Dawid Gabriel turned out to be every bit as colourful as Allum's intimation: modestly overweight with a receding hairline, and dressed in a crumpled brown suit and plain white shirt. He would have appeared unremarkable, were it not for the huge bull neck that sprouted from the unbuttoned collar of his shirt, and a bright red face that grew ever redder with each successive and constantly-recurring expletive.

"You're telling me you wanna find Nazis, fucking Nazis, right here in the middle of New York fucking City? You're fucking with me, right?"

Hammond, slightly taken-aback, gathered himself before answering.

"No I'm serious, I couldn't be more serious. Why, what's the problem, Mr Gabriel?"

"Dave, for fuck's sake; can't be doing with all this mister fucking shit."

"Sure. So, uh, what's the problem, Dave?"

"What's the problem, he says? I'll tell you what the fucking problem is, my friend. You take a good look around Times Square or Forty-Second Street on any night of the week, or kick open any other stall door in this fucking toilet. . . I promise, you're gonna find more cock-sucking Nazis out there than you could shake your dick at."

He continued to rant, crimson-faced.

"You think intolerance in this country's all about a bunch of red-necked fucking hillbillies down in Alabama, fucking over the cotton-pickers? Maybe you think it's about all those whooping and hollering fucking redskins, refusing to forgive the Seventh fucking Cavalry for sticking sabres up their asses? Well, listen up, my friend, and listen good, because when people first get to this city and wanna take a bite, I guarantee it ain't gonna be out of no worm-ridden fucking Big Apple. It's out of any bastard who looks, or lives, or talks, or prays, or eats, or sleeps, or shits, or fucks, different to them."

"It's that bad here?"

"Is it that bad, he says. Let me tell you something. In this city you find the Micks hate the fucking Limeys, and that's o.k. cos that little tête-à-têtes been going on since the battle of the fucking Boyne. But don't get into feeling sorry for the Limeys, because they still hate the fucking Frogs, and have done since way before fucking Agincourt. And don't get into feeling sorry for the Frogs either, cos they hate the shit outta the fucking Krauts.

"And if you're still partially compos-fucking-mentis, it goes on. Cos then you find the Krauts hate the Ruskis, the Ruskis hate the Czechs, the Czechs hate the Polacks, and the Polacks hate the fucking lot, especially the fucking Wops. The Wops hate the Niggers, the Niggers hate the Spics, and the Spics hate any mother who ain't another fucking Spic."

Hammond stood open-mouthed. Gabriel took a well-earned breath.

"Wait up, I ain't finished. You don't need the colour or nationality. You pull any address in this city, my friend, and I'll tell you who the asshole living there detests the fuck out of."

"How's that?"

"Real fucking easy. . . You live in Manhattan, you hate any fucker who uses a fucking bridge or tunnel to get to you. You live up in the Bronx, you hate every mother who lives down in Harlem. You're born in Black Harlem, you hate any fucker who ever got their bare ass slapped in Spic Harlem. You live on the Upper West Side, you hate all those even-richer fuckers on the Upper East Side. It goes on for fucking ever."

Hammond smiled.

"What about all those even richer people from the Upper East Side? Who do they hate?"

"Any mother who drives a better fucking car than them."

"And there's nothing they all agree on?"

"Sure there is. Every last one of them still hates the fucking Japs."

Gabriel paused for breath and then began again.

"Take yourself three blocks north, and four blocks west. Place you're looking for is a humongous twenty-five storey fucking building on Forty-Second and Broadway."

Hammond stopped smiling.

"Why am I looking for that?"

"They call it Times Tower. You can't miss the fucking place. It's where they print the New York fucking Times. Drop in on Anne O'Hare McCormick and Meyer Berger. Make their fucking week. Tell em you've just discovered a bunch of assholes who think they're the fucking master race."

As predicted by Marcus Allum, Hammond found himself instantly liking the highly colourful, slightly unwholesome, shockingly bigoted and outrageously profane detective. Gabriel was still some way from finishing.

"Looking for Nazis in this town's like pulling a loose thread on a fucking sweater. You got any common fucking sense at all you'll tuck the fucker back in and forget about it, cos you keep on pulling and you're gonna end up with no fucking sweater."

"You got a thing about this, huh?"

"I've been wading through this sewer for over forty fucking years. Yeah, I've got a thing about it. You wanna grab a coffee?"

They crossed the street to a diner. Gabriel clearly knew the elderly waiter, because he nodded and grinned when the old man called out to him. They ordered coffee and sat by the window. Hammond decided to further the introductions.

"So, where are you from originally, your family, I mean?"

"Me? I'm New York City born and fucking raised; grew up in a slum just off Delancey Street. That's on the Lower East Side, case you ever wanna take a stroll and get the shit beaten out of you."

"Thanks, I'll bear that in mind. What about your family?"

"You wanna find a bunch of Nazis, or research my family fucking tree?"

"I just think it helps if you know a little about the people you work with."

"Where'd you learn that, Washington Institute of psychological fucking bollocks?"

Hammond smiled. Gabriel shrugged his indifference.

"Well, I guess we're on your fucking dime. What can I tell you? My mother was everything my old man and the neighbourhood weren't. She was beautiful, genteel, dainty, a real lady. One part Irish and three parts Polack, so I guess that's where I get my naturally relaxed attitude and good nature from. Worked herself into an early grave looking after me and my old man during the day, and working as a cleaner down at the local precinct six nights a fucking week."

The coffees arrived. Gabriel drained the scalding liquid in one oversized gulp. Hammond gingerly sipped at his and persevered with his questions.

"How do you manage to drink it so hot?"

"You've obviously never been a fucking beat cop."

"No, that's true."

Gabriel didn't embellish. Hammond returned to the subject.

"What about your father?"

"We still wringing the fucking entrails out of that? Well, like I said, it's your fucking dime. My old man was what you'd call a self-made fucking bastard. Used to come home soused every night, and kick seven fucking bells out of whichever one of us he managed to focus on first. Disappeared with some sorry-assed punch-bag he'd managed to stick his dick in less than three weeks after we buried my mother; when he ran out of clean fucking shirts, I guess."

"Sorry to hear that."

"Don't be. He wasn't Polack or Irish, and he sure as hell wasn't fucking genteel. Son-of-a-bitch was one-hundred-per cent belligerent Wop fucking cop. And if you're wondering about the name, it's Dawid with a W, and that's pure fucking Polack.

"So you feeling properly fucking bonded now, J. Edgar? We done with the Washington psychological mumbo-fucking-jumbo, family-history shit? Or did you wanna hear how a troop of gypsies banged my granny on a long weekend down on Coney fucking Island?"

Gabriel snarled. Hammond grinned good-naturedly and persisted.

"You said your mother was three parts Polish, and your father pure Italian?"

"Pleased to see you were paying fucking attention."

"But you also said the Poles hate the Italians?"

"They didn't use to. . . I guess she must have started it."

Hammond studied the deadpan features and grinned again.

"So you'll help me to find these people then?"

"To do what?"

"First to find the girl. After that, to gather evidence and bring them to justice."

"Fuck 'em over, you mean?"

"Well, only metaphorically. The authorities will deal with them if we get the evidence."

Gabriel raised his eyes to the heavens.

"Jesus Christ! That's all I fucking need. So, you wanna prosecute 'em, do you, bring em all to justice? Well hoo-fucking-ray for you. So tell me something, J. fucking Edgar. Do you have any fucking idea how many crimes they solve in this godforsaken fucking city, and how many of those result in a custodial fucking sentence for the shit-heel involved?"

Hammond shrugged his ignorance.

"Around a half of one fucking per cent, my friend, which eventually pans out around four-fifths of fuck all. Current rate is around three per cent of reported crimes that finally result in banging up some asshole, and the reported rate gets worse every fucking year."

Hammond sipped at his coffee and said nothing. Gabriel went on. "And why is that, my good and true detective, I hear you ask?"

Hammond smiled. Gabriel answered his own question.

"Because every Jack shit knows that those dick-heads, down at the fucking precinct, will more than likely screw up the fucking prosecution. Or some feeble-minded 'Judge middle-fucking-America' will throw it out, rather than risk any flak. Thanks to a bunch of ass-wipe lawyers, rolling around

Manhattan in their Lincoln's and Caddys and Rolls Royce fucking imports, Joe Public doesn't even fucking bother to report most of it."

"That's lawyers the world over, I guess."

Hammond had felt he should say something. Gabriel was ranting again.

"Fuckers! They're the main reason I quit the force. When the fucking revenue finally yanks its dick out of your ass, you get around two thousand bucks a year for enforcing the fucking law, and a hundred thousand for screwing it over. And all those city council assholes still can't figure out why we've got so much fucking crime in this city.

"It's gotten so bad that most of the flatfeet expect to get a fucking commendation for writing up a traffic violation that actually fucking sticks."

"If it's as bad as you say it is, then why don't you get out; move to the country, or maybe another city or something?"

"Cos like I just told you, J. Edgar, I'm born and raised New York, it's all I fucking know. Anyway I wouldn't give 'em the fucking satisfaction. And apart from all that crap, where the fuck else would someone like me fit in? That's the trouble with these fuckin. . ."

"Some of the people I'm looking for are lawyers."

The sudden announcement halted Gabriel in mid-expletive. He looked uneasy as he posed the next question.

"Not Wall Street lawyers?"

"Some are."

"Whoa! Hold on there, J. Edgar. This wouldn't have anything to do with a limestone-fronted fucking mansion, on the corner of East Sixty-Eighth and Park?"

"It's possible."

The mood instantly changed.

"Then do us both a fucking favour, my friend. Climb right back into that shit-box Pontiac and start heading south-west. If you've got any fucking brains, you'll keep on through Philadelphia and fucking Baltimore. If you're seriously fucking smart, and that shit-box holds up long enough, which I seriously fucking doubt, you won't take your foot off the gas until you reach the banks of the fucking Potomac."

"I don't understand."

"Listen up, and listen good. Forgetting fucking turf issues, there are two sets of people in this town you don't fuck with. . . that's the mob, and anyone connected with the mob."

"I can see that."

"Yeah, but what you can't fucking see is there's one set of people that even they don't fuck with. . . That's The Folks at Fifty-Eight."

"The Folks at Fifty-Eight?"

"That's what we call 'em here. It's like a collective fucking noun for every rich asshole who ever took a dump on Joe Public and wiped his ass with green."

"I'm sorry, I don't. . ."

"Nobody fucks with 'em, J. Edgar, and I mean nobody. The City Council don't fuck with 'em. New York's finest don't fuck with 'em. The F.B.I. don't fuck with 'em. Even fucking O' Dwyer and the Mob don't fuck with 'em. . . and for a very good fucking reason."

"William O'Dwyer? You mean the Mayor's in with the Mob?"

"They ain't proved that yet, but so word has it. You knew where you were with LaGuardia, but with this fucker. . . Well, like I said, that's what so much of the fucking Apple's all about: worm ridden and rotten to the fucking core."

Gabriel looked adamant. Hammond tried to placate.

"Look, I understand these people are powerful and it's going to be tough."

"Tough? Fucking tough, he says. You got any fucking idea who we're talking about here? These people aren't just powerful. These people are fucking unbeatable. A grain of sand's got more chance of ending up strung round Joan Crawford's fucking neck than you've got going up against that fucking lot."

"You're saying you won't help me?"

"Fucking right I am."

Gabriel stood up and walked out of the diner, without paying for the coffee. Hammond dropped a dollar bill onto the table and nodded a self-conscious thanks to the old man, before following him out to the street. He caught up within a few yards.

"Hold on a minute. Look, I'm not trying to cause you any trouble, or bring any of these people or the establishment down on top of you. I'm part of the establishment, for god's sake. Look, forget about the rest of them. I'm not interested in going up against people like that. I just want you to help me to find the girl. That's all, I swear."

Gabriel remained intransigent.

"You still don't get it, do you, J. Edgar? Well, forget Meyer Berger. Here's a New York fucking newsflash for you, hot off the fucking press. . . I couldn't give a flying fuck."

Gabriel stood on the sidewalk, shuffling awkwardly. Hammond changed the subject.

"You got any kids?"

"Can you see me with fucking kids?"

Hammond studied him carefully for all of a moment.

"Yeah, I think you'd be a good father, well, apart from the profanity. I think you care about people, Dawid Gabriel, all sorts of people. Despite what you'd have me believe."

Gabriel grinned and shook his head.

"This ain't gonna fucking work, my friend. I've been snowed by the best in the fucking business; you sure as fuck ain't that."

"O.K. So, let's say you've got a friend, someone you care for, a girl, a beautiful young girl. She's in a strange city in a foreign country, and she's in serious trouble, the sort that might even get her killed."

Gabriel shrugged.

"Like I told you, it ain't fucking working."

"So how would you feel about it if the one person in that city who could help her, maybe even save her life, told you he couldn't give a flying fuck?"

Gabriel stood for a few moments and then shook his head.

"Nope, still ain't working. Moving fucking speech, though."

He started to walk away again. Hammond called after him.

"Just to find her. Anybody needs dealing with, I'll deal with them. You walk away."

Gabriel stood quietly for a few further moments of indecision before saying,

"I am walking away. Take a look at the way my fucking feet are pointing."

"Please, Mr Gabriel. I honestly can't find her without you."

The answering expression fell somewhere between annoyance and resignation.

"Like I told you before, it's either Dave or Dawid. The rate's a hundred dollars flat for the hire, and fifty dollars a fucking day."

"That's not cheap."

"You want cheap, go beat down some other asshole gumshoe's fucking door in Wop City, or the fucking Bronx. You want me holding your fucking hand, it's gonna cost. Call it a crazy fucking price for a crazy fucking assignment. Now you wanna walk away?"

"No, that's fine."

"I should fucking hope so. And I swear on all that's holy, J. Edgar, you get me fucking killed and I'll come back and fucking haunt you. So, let's see if we can get this shit-box Blackout into gear."

"Where we going?"

"First to Queens. There's a badge over there, might be able to wave an arm in the right direction, just so long as we stick the other one halfway up his fucking back."

"Queens. Which way is that?"

"North, and then east over the island. Fuck it. Give me the keys, I'll drive."

The Pontiac shot away from the curb with the suspension lunging, the tires screeching, and a suddenly demonic Gabriel cursing at every second individual they passed. After a few incident-ridden blocks, he turned the snarl on Hammond.

"I hope to fuck nobody sees me driving this pile of crap."

"At the speed we're going? I'd have said that was unlikely."

"You wanna fucking drive?"

"No, I'm good. It's just a little fast for my blood."

"You don't feel safe? Well, now you know how I feel, chasing after these fucking bastards."

"You seem to have a fascination with cars."

"Whad'yer mean?"

"The Rolls Royce imports, the Lincolns and Cadillacs, the people from the Upper East Side hating anyone with a better car. . . Now you've got a problem with General Motors?"

"Not all of G.M., just most of it. And yeah, I've got a fascination with fucking cars."

"And you always drive like this?"

"Yeah, I got a fucking fascination with that, too."

"So I noticed. I get the feeling you've also got a fascination for the F-word?"

"You give me a single-syllable fucking word with as much fucking impact, that doesn't have connotations of sewage, or sodomy, or else degrade every fucking woman, and I swear I'll use the fucker. If you can't, then maybe you'd just better just shut the fuck up and let me drive."

Hammond smiled good-naturedly as he offered a contradiction.

"Fucking's got two syllables."

Gabriel shot a sideways glance at him, but didn't answer.

32

It was early on the morning following Hamilton's initial, and somewhat bizarre, meeting with the colourful Dawid Gabriel.

The previous twenty-four hours had seen little or no progress in the search for Catherine. The desk sergeant over in Queens had been unable to help. Other than swilling copious quantities of beer at the local 'cop bar', and telling tall stories about Gabriel and his time on the force, the elderly sergeant had simply repeated much of Gabriel's earlier tirade.

He had suggested they visit an active neo-Nazi group operating up in White Plains, but the group turned out to be the same bunch of black-suited half-wits and straight-arm-saluting Neanderthals forecast by Gabriel.

As Hammond drove down to Gabriel's office in Brooklyn, he felt more depressed than at any time since he'd begun the search. If a man of Gabriel's ability and experience couldn't find so much as a sniff of an intellectual Nazi anywhere in New York, what chance did he have?

Gabriel was already at his desk, in a rented office on the second floor of a house on 6th Street.

"So, where do we go from here?"

Gabriel shrugged.

"There's another twenty thousand of those fucking assholes in this city. You gotta turn your collar up to avoid 'em. They're all pretty much of a fucking muchness, but we could check a few, I suppose."

Hammond couldn't see the point.

"No. There's a disconnect, and we have to find it."

"I don't follow."

"Well there has to be a link somewhere, between the people who wear swastikas and jackboots and think owning a copy of *Mein Kampf* gives them a license to hate, and the people who fan and manipulate that ignorance for their own purposes."

"All very fucking highfalutin, J. Edgar, but how do you suggest we go about finding it?"

"I don't know. You got any ideas?"

"Not really. We could check out that alleyway on East One-Twenty-Third."

"Why? Where's that?"

"Spic Harlem. Came in on the radio, just before you got here. Cops found the body of a male Caucasian: naked, castrated, and covered in fucking swastikas. Might be worth a look?"

Hammond felt the adrenaline surge.

"Let's go."

Gabriel eyed him uncertainly, but didn't say anything as they drove up to Harlem. They arrived just as a crowd had started to gather. An aged lieutenant had apparently arrived a few minutes earlier and was now taking charge. Gabriel appeared to know him, but stood back as the lieutenant spoke to one of the young policemen who had evidently found the body.

"You OK, son?"

"Yes, sir."

"Then wipe your face and straighten your uniform. Then see if you can get the sightseers and rubber-neckers back around fifty yards or so."

The aged lieutenant smiled generously.

"And the next time that sidekick of yours flags down a car to call in a body, tell him to use the correct procedure and codes. Half this city doesn't need to hear graphic details of dead bodies when they're enjoying their breakfast."

"Yes, sir, I'll tell him. I'm sorry, sir."

"And if you look behind me, you'll see another reason we like to keep details like that off the airwaves."

He nodded to where Gabriel and Hammond stood listening. Gabriel grinned.

"Morning, Jimmy."

"Morning, Dave. Thought I told you to hand that radio in last year?"

"Radio, what fucking radio? I told you before, I ain't got your fucking radio. I handed it in with the car when I quit. We were down the street when we heard about a badly-mutilated body, covered in fucking swastikas. Thought we might be able to help out."

"And just how were you expecting to do that?"

Gabriel nodded towards Hammond.

"This is Mr Gerald Hammond. He's up from the State Department in Washington. He's looking for fucking Nazis."

Hammond shook hands with the Lieutenant, who glanced incredulously at Gabriel.

"Nazis, huh? Well, they shouldn't be too tough to find, not in this city."

Gabriel gave a short laugh.

"Yeah, that's roughly what I fucking told him. Mind if we take a look?"

"Be my guest. It's not for the squeamish."

Hammond had either caused or been around violent death for much of his adult life, but the sight that greeted him as Gabriel pulled back the sheet caused the nausea to rise from even his experience-hardened stomach. He studied the lower torso and swallowed back the bile. Then returned his gaze to further study the mutilated remains of Alan James Carlisle, unable to disguise the start of recognition as his eyes travelled to the face.

"Jesus!"

"You know him?"

Hammond saw no reason to lie.

"Alan Carlisle. . . One of my bosses at The State Department, or used to be."

"'Used to be' is about right. You're due a fucking promotion. As for your boss here, I'd have to say this is a real fucking piece of work. Whatever didn't get carved off, got fucking swastikas gouged all over. You think some fucker's trying to tell you something, J. Edgar?"

"I don't know about any intended message, but they're not swastikas."

"They're not?"

"No."

"So what the fuck are they?"

Hammond explained.

"The swastika has the feet pointing clockwise. These point anticlockwise. You see here, and here, and again here? It's what they call a reverse fylfot; similar, but not the same."

"I can see it's fucking similar. My extensive experience and all that sophisticated police fucking training told me that. What I wanna know is what the fuck's it all mean, J. Edgar?"

Hammond's answer was purposely vague, his speech slow and deliberate, but his mind racing as he tried to assimilate the horrific sight and the implications of Alan Carlisle's death.

"No idea. Could be pagan, I suppose, or something to do with the occult or Voodoo. To be truthful, I can't say I know that much about either. Could be some religious symbol: Muslim, or even Hindu."

Gabriel studied the poorly-disguised evasiveness and shook his head.

"It ain't pagan, or not by any fucking pagans I ever met, and the occultists may be a little on the weird side of fucked-up, but as far as I know they ain't total fucking lunatics. As for all that fucking Voodoo shit? Well, if you're looking for Maman Brigitte and Baron fucking Samedi, you're standing on the wrong set of crossroads on the wrong side of fucking Harlem. As for the rest, I ain't never heard of no thuggees carving off the fucking genitals."

Hammond regarded the red-faced detective with fresh eyes.

"So cars aren't the only subject you know? You're an educated man, Dawid Gabriel."

"Only when it comes to homicide. I'm a fucking world expert when it comes to that. Well that, and smelling total fucking bullshit."

Hammond asked a question, hoping to deflect the glare of accusation.

"So what can you tell me about the time and cause of death?"

Gabriel returned his attention to the corpse.

319

"I usually leave that to forensic, but I'd say twelve hours ago, maybe. Cause of death sure as hell wasn't strangulation, though, well, not with any knotted fucking handkerchief or rope."

"Go on."

"My guess would be those puncture wounds to the neck. In case you're wondering, I ain't suggesting fucking vampires, although that would explain the absence of fucking blood. I'd say they did the carving-up somewhere else, then brought him here and dumped him."

"They?"

"Someone would have to drive whatever brought him here. And someone would have to lift him up and dump him, or what's left of him. One person could do it, but it'd take more time and be messy. Hopefully they cut the poor bastard's balls off after he was dead. The rest of it looks like a fucking afterthought. Or, like I said before, maybe a message for someone?"

Gabriel peered hopefully at Hammond, who tried not to look guilty and said nothing further. Gabriel carefully re-covered the remains, before walking back to the waiting lieutenant, who had been quietly monitoring their conversation.

"Our friend from the State Department has some information for you, Jimmy, if you can believe a fucking word of it. You want me, I'll be in the car."

The lieutenant shook his head.

"What the hell have you got yourself into this time, Dave?"

"Fuck knows."

"Well stay close on this one. We can't have lunacy like this, not in this town. If they wanna carve each other up, let 'em do it in Washington. Oh, and, Dave. . ."

"What?"

320

"Don't forget to bring that radio back."

"I told you: I handed the fucker in a year ago. I'll call if I come up with anything."

Hammond spent some time with the lieutenant, providing details and addresses and answering routine questions. When he returned to the car, Gabriel held out his hand.

"You owe me two hundred bucks. That's as agreed: a hundred up front, and fifty a day. I normally load the fucking expenses, but as we've been on your fucking gas, I'll let it go."

"I don't understand."

Gabriel nodded across the street to where the lieutenant had returned to the alleyway.

"What did you tell him?"

"Not a lot. There wasn't a lot to tell. I'm not sure he believed me, though."

"Yeah, that's what I thought you'd say."

"How's that?"

Gabriel replaced the open palm with a single finger of rebuke.

"When you've been asking fucking questions for as long as he has, and for as long as I have, you get to spot a lie before it's even rolled off the fucking tongue. And when someone tells you they're being truthful without even being fucking asked, it usually means they ain't. Now I can put up with the helpless act and all the psychological Washington fucking bullshit. I can even put up with some suicidal asshole who wants to take on the Folks at Fifty-fucking-Eight. But I don't work for liars, and I don't work with liars, not if I've got any fucking say in it. That's another reason I quit the force."

Hammond glared back at him.

"I wasn't lying."

"Maybe you were and maybe you fucking weren't, J. Edgar, but you sure as hell weren't telling the whole fucking truth."

Hammond sat weighing the risk of giving further information, before concluding that he had no choice.

"The body back there."

"Your friend?"

"No, not my friend, but I knew him reasonably well."

"What about it?"

"The marks, and the rest of it. . . I've seen it before."

"When was this?"

"A few weeks ago."

"In New York?"

"No."

"So, that's it then. This is serial killing, cross fucking state, and that's the fucking FBI's jurisdiction. New York's finest is gonna have to back the fuck off. If you've got any fucking sense, you will, too."

"No, it wasn't in another state. It was in central Europe."

"And I'm not even gonna fucking ask what you were doing over there."

"That's probably wise."

"So what else d'yer know?"

"Not a whole lot."

"But you think you know who did it, don't you?"

"Yes." Hammond took a deep breath. "I think it might have been the girl."

Gabriel looked all but lost for words.

"The what, did you say? The girl; the fucking. . . What the fuck's going on?"

"It's a bit complicated."

"Complicated, he says! Fucking complicated! What were those fucking words you used? A young girl, you said, beautiful, helpless; a young friend in trouble." He roared his anger. "Did you see that fucking cadaver back there? Did you see what she fucking did to it? If she's a fucking friend of yours, I sure as fuck don't wanna meet any of your fucking enemies."

"You don't understand. She's a sweet kid, but she's been through a terrible ordeal. She needs help."

By this time the spluttering Gabriel was beyond anger.

"Sweet? Is that what you just fucking said to me? A sweet fucking kid? It may have escaped your fucking attention, J. Edgar, but that sweet fucking kid of yours just sliced-up your boss like a slab of fucking salami and left him out with the fucking trash."

"Now you're beginning to sound like a typical New York detective."

Gabriel bristled.

"I am a typical New York fucking detective. They call us fucking gumshoes, or ain't you never heard that fucking expression before? Now answer the fucking question."

"It may not have been her."

"But you think it could have been?"

"It's possible."

"Then that's it. I'm fucking outta here, J. Edgar. Getting my balls thinly sliced on to a fucking bagel for fifty bucks a fucking day ain't exactly my idea of gainful fucking employment."

Hammond studied the outstretched hand and shook his head.

"No you're not. You want to see this through as much as I do. And what else are you going to do? Go back to taking compromising photographs, or peering through motel keyholes looking for grubby people having grubby affairs and doing grubby deals? Hoping to dump more evidence of deceit and misery and infidelity on to someone else's already miserable life?

"You'd miss all this. I could see it in your eyes just now. I could almost hear what you were thinking."

"So you think you know what I was fucking thinking, do you? Let me tell you something, J. Edgar. You're not even halfway fucking there. All I was thinking about was living fucking long enough to start drawing my fucking pension."

Hammond shrugged and held out four fifty-dollar bills. Gabriel waved them away.

"Fuck it! I probably want my fucking head examined, but what now?"

"You know those people in Harold Pratt House, The Folks at Fifty-Eight, the ones you're so scared of? The ones you say are unbeatable? I think maybe it's time I took a trip up to Connecticut and talked to one of them."

"Which one?"

"A man called Conrad Zalesie, he's. . ."

"I know who he is. Everybody knows who Zalesie is; at least those of us who ain't been in a fucking coma for the last few. . ." He suddenly stopped in mid-sentence. "Hey, wait just a fucking minute. Here, give me one of those fifties."

"Why?"

"I just saw someone who could use it. Wait here."

Gabriel snatched the bill away, then climbed out of the car and crossed the street. He made for the back of the crowd where a man stood watching the comings and goings.

The man was a young Hispanic, dressed in dirty and threadbare clothing. He turned and started moving away when he saw Gabriel. The detective grabbed him by the arm, blocked any further retreat and held out the fifty-dollar bill.

With ownership of the bill transferred, a conversation ensued before the young Hispanic walked away and disappeared into the crowd. Gabriel wandered back to the car, slid into the passenger seat and grinned at Hammond's wry observation.

"I take it that's the last I'll see of my fifty bucks?"

"It's a fucking expensive town. Somebody should've warned you."

"Do I get a receipt?"

"You want information about a homicide, or you want help with the fucking IRS?"

Hammond held up his hands in mock surrender.

"All right. So who was that? More importantly, does he know what happened?"

"You still don't get this fucking city, do you, J. Edgar? Every Spic in the neighbourhood knows exactly what fucking happened. It's just that my man Julio there's the only fucker willing to talk about it to someone from outside the fucking neighbourhood."

"What did he tell you?"

Much to Hammond's rising annoyance, Gabriel began to muse.

"Strange how so many people make mistakes in this fucking game. They think 'cos it's the middle of the fucking night, and the streets are quiet, nobody's watching 'em. But if there's one lesson I've learnt over the last thirty years, in this fucking business and this fucking city, someone is always watching. No matter how late the hour, or how quiet the fucking streets, there's always someone. When you're a cop it ain't worth the fucking trouble chasing 'em down, cos the odds are you're gonna get fuck-all from 'em. But when you're a no-account fucking gumshoe, with a fifty-dollar fucking bill. . . That's a different fucking matter."

"So, what did you learn?"

"New Cadillac, or he reckoned it looked new; shiny black and classy-looking, anyway. It got here in the early hours, carrying four passengers. Stopped just over there. All four occupants got out, two men from the front, two women from the back. The women looked like hookers, expensive Spic hookers: short coats and long evening gowns, tight little asses and sticking-out tits, real classy-looking Manhattan fucking meat. Men were heavy whites, clean-shaven fucking hoodlums in monkey suits. Hookers walked off along the street and then cut south down Lexington in a major fucking hurry. Men watched 'em go, then went to the trunk and took out your friend over there. Hauled him down the alley and dumped him behind the cans. They got back in the Caddy, headed along the street for a while, and then turned north."

"That was fifty bucks worth? Is that all you got? Didn't they even get the license plate?"

"Not the numbers. He said the old woman who saw it was too far away, but she did reckon they were Connecticut fucking plates."

"So will either of them tell that to the police?"

"Not unless the fucking flatfoot asking the question's a little over six fucking inches by two-and-a-half, coloured green, stamped with the number fifty, and a dead fucking ringer for Ulysses S. Grant. Now where did you say this fucker Zalesie lives?"

"Manhattan sometimes, but mostly he's based in Connecticut."

326

"Yeah, that's what I thought you said."

He sat looking straight ahead. Hammond finally broke the silence.

"Coincidence probably. There must be hundreds of Cadillacs in Connecticut."

"Probably fucking thousands."

"Yeah."

"Yeah, just a fucking coincidence."

"He may not even own one."

"Rich fucker like that, probably only buys Rolls Royce and fucking Bentley."

"And if he did have a fleet of Cadillacs, he wouldn't be dumb enough to use one for this."

"Not unless he reckoned himself fucking fireproof."

"You mean, like some of those Folks at Fifty-Eight?"

"So what are we doing here, J. Edgar, looking for a girl, or solving a fucking homicide?"

"We're looking for the girl, and that's it. That was the deal. Anyway, like you said, a grain of sand's got more chance."

"Glad to hear you were paying fucking attention. So what do you want to do now? We've still got the rest of the day, or do you Washington fly-boys only work mornings?"

Hammond smiled briefly, but was then serious.

"I need to go to the office and deal with the fallout. I'll get back as soon as I can."

"Meantime, what do I do?"

"Find out what you can about Zalesie. Check his background. Find out why they kicked him out of Lithuania. See if you can discover where he got his money from, and how he got it out of Europe, but don't press. We don't want the wrong people getting upset. Just find out what you can. I'll take the trip up to Connecticut when I get back, and touch base after that."

"Sure. You know how to get up there?"

"I know it's north."

"Thought you went to Princeton and grew up in fucking Hartford?"

"I did, but I haven't been anywhere near either in over fifteen years."

"Lot of changes in that time. . . Highway One, through Pelham. Get a fucking map."

"I did manage to find my way around before I met you."

"Yeah, but you weren't finding your way around in New York fucking City."

33

Four days had passed since the discovery of Alan Carlisle's body, and Hammond was back in the same room in the same New York hotel. Behind him in Washington, he had left stunned members of the Office of Occupied Territories going through the motions and coming to terms with the news.

He had fallen asleep while reading lurid newspaper stories of Carlisle's debauched lifestyle. Someone had leaked the gruesome details, and the fact that Carlisle had held responsibility for understanding European cultures and traditions. One creative journalist had found a brothel madam, who claimed that Carlisle often paid for sado-masochistic sex. *The New York Enquirer* came up with a clever play on European royalty and the Marquis de Sade, and the entire press corps had a field day.

Nobody took any notice of fact or truth. Nobody took all that much notice of the hunt for the killer. Their only interest was in sordid tales of Carlisle's depravity, whether real or imagined, related by any New York or Washington cutie with a pose to hold and a story to sell.

It was 3 a.m. and Hammond was reliving his most recent nightmare: greeting the faces that so often visited him in the small hours, and hazily recalling their deaths. Once again he'd woken to discover they were no longer here to torment him. Once again he was alone in the darkness, with only his memories and his conscience.

This night, though, the dream had moved on, from guilt-laden reunions to that of his own death in a place of style and soundproof opulence, a place he remembered well.

The hazy backdrop of abstract wasteland, with only gravestones and ghouls to relieve the blandness, had faded. With it had gone all those nameless faces that so often moved in and out of his nightmares with terror-stricken cries on their lips and accusing glares in their eyes. This night the people who haunted his sleep had come from the present, but the nightmare had held more than its share of terror.

Hammond climbed out of bed and switched on the light, as he always did whenever faces from the past came calling in the night. He expected the sudden illumination to hurt his eyes and clear the remembrance, but the graphic horror of his imaginings had remained.

He remembered standing in an ornately-panelled room with a long polished table. Chambers and Allum were there, sitting alongside Carpenter, with the quietly devious Stanislav Paslov sitting on the opposite side. They had been talking in whispers, but stopped to study his arrival.

Someone was sitting where Chambers had sat during the meeting. Hammond couldn't see who. Several other faces were there, too, some murmuring and some listening, but they all stopped and stared accusingly across at him as he entered the room.

It was then that he became aware of another figure, standing by his side.

He turned to see who it was, but other than a mouth that screamed at him, the face had held no features. He looked down, from where the face should have been to see the blood and gore, and immediately knew it was Alan Carlisle. He remembered the mouth, repeating the same words again and again, but he couldn't remember those words.

He walked on into the room, leaving the featureless Carlisle at the door. It was then that he saw the figure at the head of the table: the long blonde hair and porcelain skin, the erotic form and seductive smile.

Bathed in a shaft of light, the extravagantly-costumed Catherine Schmidt sat cross-legged at the head of the table. Suddenly, her arms reached out; numerous long and sinuous arms that snaked toward him, with grasping hands that clutched at his limbs and carried him to the table.

He struggled to break free, but she held him fast and called to him through his cries of panic. She told him not to be afraid. She would protect him. He should walk through his fears.

But then she licked her lips with a flickering tongue, and giggled insanely as she tore the clothes from his body.

He remembered gazing around the room from his position of helplessness to study the faces of Allum and Carpenter and Chambers and Paslov. They showed no emotion as they silently watched his public defilement and nodded a collective approval. Then he looked back, to where the featureless Carlisle continued screaming those same forgotten words.

Then had come the nightmare's moment of greatest horror, when her cries of arousal had penetrated the stillness of death's approach, and the beautiful features had dissolved into a mask of lust and cruelty. The moment he first saw the silver blade glinting in the light, and heard her chanting the ritual words of slaughter. The moment before that split-second of suspended horror, when he watched it suddenly descend, when he perceived the agony, and listened to his own voice scream.

It was as he watched the lifeblood pumping from him that Hammond woke. Released from the terror, he calmed his breathing, looked across to the luminous hands on the clock, and then smiled grimly into the blackness as he realised the extent of his own foolish imaginings.

He climbed out of bed and went to the bathroom to sluice his face and rinse away the sweat, then poured a glass of water and returned to the bedroom. He began pacing and recalling a combination of people and events, marrying the chastening experiences of the day to the fearful images of the night. He downed the water and began again, sifting through the memory of his own subconscious terror.

Still nothing of the words that Carlisle had screamed came to mind, and so he abandoned the nightmare and thought back to previous conversations.

He recalled Carlisle's regret at that brief and unfulfilling affair with Emma and his declared sadness at the failings of his own marriage. He recalled the meeting with Paslov in Frankfurt and the compromising photograph that Paslov had used for blackmail.

Hammond's mind drifted further back to revive earlier conversations. He recalled Carlisle's comments on the danger of handing Paslov to the FBI, and of how much the Russian spymaster knew about all those secrets that were being so carefully hidden from Hoover's people.

He went on to recall why Carlisle hadn't wanted to take up Paslov's offer to defect, and why he intended handing Paslov to Zalesie at the first sign of obstinacy. He also remembered why Carlisle had been willing to take such a foolish and uncalculated risk.

That was when Hammond suddenly remembered what it was that Carlisle had been screaming.

"Manhattan! It's all about Manhattan."

They were the words Carlisle had screamed, he was certain, but what about Manhattan?

With the panic calmed and his mind racing, Hammond more rationally assessed the nightmare. Was the warning significant, or was his subconscious merely feeding his fear and playing tricks with his imagination? Was it all just subconscious nonsense and far-fetched imaginings? Or was it simply another helping of the same guilt-ridden terror that had haunted his sleep for so many years, his nightly penance for so many deadly sins committed?

Was it all that conveniently simple, or had the subconscious been guiding the conscious? Was it steering him to answers that needed questions, and questions he had yet to consider? More worryingly, had it been a warning of approaching doom?

He dressed quickly, headed downstairs, and found the elderly night porter snoozing in an armchair by the remains of the fire. Hammond woke him and asked for a large scotch and water. After much muttering and grumbling and chinking of glass, his drink finally arrived.

"There you go, young sir. Couldn't sleep, huh?"

"No, too much on my mind, I guess. Sorry to have disturbed you."

The old man collected the poker from alongside the grate and began prodding and stirring the embers back to life. Hammond slumped into an armchair and sipped at his scotch.

"Long night for you, I suppose."

The old man stopped prodding and proudly announced,

"I'm used to it, or I should be. Been doing it for nearly forty years now."

"Forty years, huh? Now that's a life's work."

The old man scoffed at the foolishness of an absent management.

"They tried to get me to retire, said I was too old for it. I said to 'em, you start getting complaints and I'll start walking. That was three years ago and I'm still here."

"Doesn't it ever get lonely?"

"Naw, I've always been happy with my own company, and there's always something to do around here."

The old man returned the poker and began tidying the furniture in an intentional show of industry. Hammond sipped at his scotch and persevered with the pleasantries.

"Yeah, I suppose so. Bet you've seen some sights during that time, huh?"

"You could say that. I must've. . ." The old man paused for a moment. "Don't often see that though. That's strange. I wonder. . . ?"

He was peering between the vertical blinds that ran the width of the hotel, studying a lone car in the shadows on the opposite side of the street. Hammond wandered over to join him.

"Cadillac, huh? Nice car; expensive."

"Keep looking."

Hammond studied the Cadillac for some moments, with a picture of Dawid Gabriel waving a fifty-dollar bill in his mind's eye and the alarm bells ringing.

"I still don't see anything unusual about. . ."

Then he saw them, illuminated by a flashing neon sign farther down the street: two men, sitting in the front seats.

"You see that?"

"Yeah, I saw."

"Cops, you think?"

"No, couldn't be, or I wouldn't have thought so, not in a car like that."

"Feds then?"

"They drive around in Caddys these days?"

"Unlikely, but they might do, I suppose."

"Could be the Mob. This is New York, after all."

"You reckon?"

"Don't know. I wonder what they're looking for?"

"Or who?"

"Don't know that either. To tell you the truth, I don't think I wanna know."

Hammond thought back to Dawid Gabriel's comment, about his unsought testament to truthfulness. Gabriel had been right; it was a dead giveaway.

"Either way, I'm going back to bed."

He downed the remains of his drink and headed back to his room. Once there, he dropped the catch, linked the chain, and then moved to the window to again study the car. After that, he collected his suitcase from the top of the wardrobe and removed the Beretta from where he'd left it wrapped in a towel. He returned the suitcase, propped a chair beneath the door handle, and slipped the automatic under his pillow. Then he undressed, switched off the lights, and returned to the many enigmas of his nightmares.

34

The following morning Hammond rose early. Finding the Cadillac gone, he shaved, dressed and then headed downstairs to the restaurant. After breakfast he wandered out of the main entrance and around the corner to collect the Pontiac. He drove west, hoping to see a sign for Highway One, but lost confidence after a few blocks and turned north anyway. He wished he'd heeded Gabriel's advice about the map, and looked for something or someone to tell him where he was and how to get to Connecticut. That was when the Cadillac suddenly appeared in his rear-view mirror.

He pulled the Pontiac to the side of the road, climbed out, and walked back the sixty or so yards to where the Cadillac sat waiting with the engine running. When he leaned forward and tapped on the passenger window, it lowered by no more than three inches.

"You guys ought to be getting more sleep than this."

A thickset individual stared back at him in bleary-eyed apathy. The man was unshaven, but otherwise smartly dressed in a dark-grey suit with a white shirt and red tie.

"You want something?"

"I need to get to Conrad Zalesie's place in Connecticut. I hear it's up along Highway One. I was wondering if you wanted to save some time, and maybe lead for a change."

The man scowled briefly and restored the window without further comment. It left Hammond standing alone on the sidewalk, feeling slightly foolish and none the wiser. He wandered back to the Pontiac and then saw what he was looking for: two of New York's finest, strolling towards him.

He stopped them and asked how he could get to the elusive Highway One. They obliged with the necessary directions. He thanked them, produced his State Department identification, and then pointed to the Cadillac.

"They've been following me. I wonder if you'd check them out?"

"Excuse me?"

"The men in that car. . . I know they're following me, but I don't know why. Perhaps you could check. They might be dangerous."

The two cops eyed each other uncertainly, then nodded and wandered down the street to the Cadillac. One stepped forward and tapped on the window. The other stood back with his hand resting menacingly on the thirty-eight's chequered-walnut grip.

Once again the window lowered, this time by six inches more than the previous three. The thickset individual briefly spoke. Moments later, the two uniforms continued on down the street. They didn't look back.

Hammond grinned and shrugged at the two men in the Cadillac, feigning self-confidence and privately cursing the absence of the streetwise Gabriel.

It was two hours later when he drew the Pontiac to a halt in front of the heavy wrought-iron gates, marking the main entrance to the Zalesie estate. The Cadillac had followed at sixty yards distance, every inch of the way.

Two clean-shaven but otherwise similarly-dressed and belligerent-looking characters opened the gates. Hammond wound down the window, intending to produce his identification, and explain the purpose of his visit. The guard said nothing and waved him on down the drive. Half a mile later he reached a second set of equally sturdy gates. A second set of equally belligerent-looking characters stood waiting.

"You carrying?"

The guard held out his hand. Hammond took out the Beretta and passed it over.

"Look after that. It's got sentimental value."

The guard nodded appreciatively as he weighed the automatic in his hand.

"Mmm, Beretta nineteen-thirty-four. Shade on the lightweight side for me, but a good-looking piece. I hear these are worth a few bucks these days. Old war souvenir?" Hammond nodded. The guard pointed to the glove compartment. "That all?" Hammond nodded again. "OK. Head on down to the house, there'll be someone there."

"You just gonna take my word? You're not gonna search?"

"We're naturally-trusting people, Mr Hammond."

"You know my name."

The expression didn't flicker.

"I wouldn't be letting you in if we didn't."

Hammond grinned good-naturedly.

"Well, it's good to meet naturally-trusting people. You don't see so many these days."

The guard grunted and returned his attention to the ball game on the radio. Hammond headed down the drive. More scenes reminiscent of Hollywood gangster movies greeted his arrival at the sprawling Zalesie mansion, with more Cagneyesque characters sporting ever more belligerent faces. He pulled in under the porte cochère, then climbed out of the Pontiac and looked around.

"Mr Hammond, I presume. Allow me to welcome you to Connecticut."

The accent and tone were English and pretentious, the manner effeminate, the complexion pale, but the eyes that scrutinized his were both black and cold. Beneath the faultlessly-tailored suit, the frame was stocky. The hand that shook Hammond's was firm and strong.

"Count Zalesie?"

"Good lord no, Mr Hammond." The man smiled briefly and condescendingly. "My name is Cowdray, Simon Cowdray. I am Mr Zalesie's private secretary. I also look after his local security arrangements."

Hammond gazed pointedly at the multitude of armed bodyguards.

"You take your work seriously."

The condescending smile returned.

"Mr Zalesie is a busy and important man, Mr Hammond. When he does take the odd moment or two to relax he prefers to do so in peace."

"Does that mean I don't get to see him?"

"Not at all. . . Mr Zalesie is looking forward to meeting you. Do come in."

Hammond followed him in through the door and along the corridor, talking as he walked.

"You keep saying Mr Zalesie. I understood he was some sort of Count?"

"That is not a title Mr Zalesie cares to use. I'm sure he will tell you about it when you meet him. Perhaps you'd like to wait in here. You should be comfortable. I'm sure you're tired after your long journey. I'll send someone over with some coffee."

"I only came up from New York."

The smile was back.

"Yes, but the long way around, I understand."

Hammond grinned ruefully, then eyed the Englishman.

"So they were your men, the two in the Cadillac?"

Simon Cowdray nodded. The smile evaporated.

"After what happened to poor Mr Carlisle, Mr Zalesie felt you might benefit from some, shall we say, additional security?"

"Directions might have been of more use, but thank him for me. That was thoughtful."

"Mr Zalesie is a thoughtful man. Now, if you will excuse me, I shall tell him that you have arrived."

Hammond wandered on into a large and luxuriously appointed suite. To the left, a single door led to a large marble-tiled bathroom. Double doors farther along led to a cavernous bedroom with an enormous four-poster.

French windows on the right-hand side led to a patio. Stone steps stretched the patio's width, and led to a vast expanse of manicured lawn. Beyond that, an extensive lake added to the general air of calm and tranquillity, while, on the slopes in the distance, a leafy Connecticut offered its own spectacular charm.

He gave a low whistle as he assessed the scope and grandeur, and then sat down in one of the patio chairs to take in the view. A knock at the door called him back to the room. A waiter, with silver tray and promised coffee, stood waiting.

"Where would you care to take your coffee, sir?"

"The patio, I think."

"Yes, sir. Would you like me to pour it for you?"

"I'm sure I'll manage."

The waiter carried the tray to the patio. He set it down on one of the tables before returning to the lounge, where he bowed politely and thanked Hammond for nothing in particular. Hammond wandered back to the patio. He poured himself a cup of coffee and sat down again.

"Not bad; not bad at all."

He idly gazed around the grounds wondering how much a place like this would cost to buy, and equally important, how much it would cost to run. It was then he saw her: a solemn-looking woman, wearing a red headscarf and dressed in dark slacks and a white blouse, with a tweed jacket slung across her shoulders. She appeared from the right-hand side of the house, and then wandered past the patio on her way to the lake. She nodded an acknowledgement. He nodded politely back and then called out to her. The last time he'd seen that face it hadn't looked solemn. The last time he'd seen that body was in a photograph.

"Mrs Carlisle. It is Mrs Carlisle, isn't it?" he said. "I knew your husband. We worked together at The State Department. I'm so sorry. . . Please accept my condolences."

She stopped and turned to face him.

"You're Gerald Hammond, aren't you?"

"Yes, I believe you know my wife."

There was no humour in her answer.

"I think, in one way or another, most of my family know or have known your wife."

"Yes, so I understand. . . I'm sorry."

For a moment, as he recalled the wilful Emma and her litany of transgressions, he wondered why he had found it necessary to apologize on her behalf. Then Angela Carlisle climbed the steps and he saw the pain in her eyes.

"Would you like some coffee? There's plenty here. I'll get another cup."

"Thank you, no, but I will sit for a moment. . . That is, if you don't mind?"

Hammond remembered his manners. He stood up and collected a chair.

"Of course not. I'm sorry, please. . ."

She sat down at the table and smiled weakly back at him.

"You were with Alan in Frankfurt, weren't you?"

"Yes."

"The two of you didn't get on, I understand?"

"No, that's true."

"Is that why you stole the photograph and showed it to Marcus?"

Hammond's jaw dropped. He hadn't realised she'd known. He wondered how much she knew of the meeting with Allum and Chambers. He presumed she knew it all.

He studied her face, but saw no hostility or criticism, just a hollow look that spoke of unhappiness.

He apologized, and told her that he'd had no choice. He apologized again, and said he didn't mean to embarrass or distress her in any way. He followed that with yet another apology.

She said she didn't blame him. She should apologize to him. Her question had been impolite. She understood he was only doing his job.

There was a long uncomfortable pause before she spoke again. She told him that Zalesie thought the meeting in Frankfurt had something to do with the murder. She asked what he thought. He said he didn't know. He supposed it was possible. When he asked her if the Russians had blackmailed her husband, she relaxed the formality. He should call her Angela. He found himself remembering the photograph and thinking mildly disgraceful thoughts.

Finally she answered. Yes, the Russians had been blackmailing her husband, and not just with the photograph. They had also used her son, Mathew. He had been in Europe. They used a girl to trap him. She blushed wildly and added that they often did that.

Knowing something of the chaos and confusion in Europe, he asked why Mathew had been there. He said post-war Europe wasn't the ideal destination for a vacation.

She said he hadn't been on vacation, just getting away from a silly family squabble. That had been her fault, too. Thankfully, some of Conrad Zalesie's friends in Austria had managed to get Mathew away from them. She recalled her son and smiled through the grief. She hoped he would join her in a few days. Maybe they could put the past behind them.

Hammond asked how long she was staying at the estate. She said just a few days. She wished she could stay longer. It was so beautiful and peaceful; not like all the hustle and bustle of Washington. The Zalesies had made her feel so welcome. Theresa had been such a comfort, and Conrad had dealt with the police and the FBI and taken care of everything.

"Did you say the FBI?"

"Yes, Morton Simmonds sent some people. He and Alan were friends."

"Your husband did tell me something about that. But Morton Simmonds didn't come in person? I thought he and your late husband were close?"

"They were, but Morton wasn't able to get away from Washington. He's on assignment at the moment. Conrad's been marvellous, though. I only wish Alan had confided in him from the beginning; maybe none of this would have happened."

"No, perhaps not. So, how are you bearing up?"

She smiled a rueful smile.

"We were never that close, Gerald, but then I'm sure you already knew that. Just as I am equally sure you knew that my late husband was corrupt and weak and debauched, what fashionable Washington people euphemistically describe as flawed. I suppose in many ways we were both that. Sadly, in poor Alan's case, the flaws turned out to be fatal."

"I'm so sorry."

She smiled again. She said there was no need for him to keep apologizing. Her husband had been strong in so many ways, ambitious and single-minded, almost fearless. Yet in other ways he had been just about the most debauched and spineless man she had ever known. Living the Washington high-life and suffering an unhappy marriage, served to feed the debauchery and encourage the weakness in them both.

"And it was both of us, Gerald, as you saw from that wretched photograph."

"I wish I'd never set eyes on it."

"Just a lonely woman's moment of foolishness and truth. . . The frailty of the flesh and an excess of wine can be a heady combination."

She shrugged despondently and held that same pathetic smile.

"There's a slut and a lesbian in every woman, Gerald. Most of us try to hide it. Strangely enough, it was your wife who told me that." She saw his cheeks redden. "And now I've upset and embarrassed you. I'm sorry. I didn't mean to make you uncomfortable or open old wounds, but after so many years of keeping feelings and emotions bottled up. . ."

The look demanded reassurance. He offered the necessary words.

"I'm not upset or embarrassed. I guess we sometimes need to talk about problems with strangers, for the same reason we could never discuss them with family and friends, and I've always been a good listener."

He had lied about his embarrassment. She added a further observation.

"Who'd have thought it, huh? Prim and proper me? That wife of yours would have a fit if she knew. Plain, prissy, boring-old Angela Carlisle, a middle-aged hedonist, in middle-class Connecticut. You must tell her when you see her."

This time she was clearly fishing for a compliment.

"You're not plain, or boring, and you're hardly middle-aged." He looked pointedly at the sprawling mansion and manicured grounds. "And this is hardly middle-class." Compliment delivered, it was time to change the subject. "So, how did you come to be here?"

"We were at a party and stayed over. Alan went off with a couple of Puerto Rican girls. Theresa said they were Panamanian, but they looked Puerto Rican to me. Hispanic, anyway."

"You're saying he just left you, to. . . ?"

"Yes, Gerald: to have sex with them."

Astonished as much by the unemotional relating as the tale itself, he spluttered more questions.

"But didn't he. . . ? I mean, didn't you. . . ?"

"Complain about it, Gerald? Try to stop him leaving for the sake of our marriage, play the wounded spouse?" She gave an artificial laugh, seeming to find dark humour in the apparent absurdity. "Of course not, that would have been sheer and utter hypocrisy. You see, Theresa was about to bed me at the time." She looked wistfully at the sky. "Thank God. Oh, I'm sorry, does that shock you?"

"Perhaps a little, I suppose."

"My husband left me there, for Theresa and Conrad, and presumably anybody else who wanted me. That was the sorry stage our marriage had reached. Not exactly a match made in heaven, you might say."

She giggled, and for a moment the sorrow fell away.

"And now I can see that I have shocked you. Why is it that people who are happy to discuss graphic acts of hatred and violence baulk at discussing acts of love and tenderness and physical pleasure? I was just the same, not so long ago. It all seems such puritanical foolishness and hypocrisy now."

Hammond shook his head.

"That's not what I was thinking. I was thinking that if your husband left you for someone else he was a fool."

She stood up to leave.

"How gallant and sweet of you to say so, Gerald. Thank you for that. But now I need time to remember some of Alan's finer qualities. There were some, you know. I also need time to think everything through."

"Do the police have any idea what happened, or who did this?"

She shrugged.

"I don't think so. Alan said he had meetings in Manhattan. I assumed he had a liaison planned. I told the police. I thought it might have involved those Hispanic girls, but they couldn't find any trace of them. I decided to stay here. I think we both knew then that it was over. But now I really must go."

Hammond put down his coffee and began to rise. She stopped him with a hand that reached out to pat his arm, and fingertips that lingered for an unnecessary moment.

"No, please don't get up. It's a lovely day. Sit and drink your coffee. I have no doubt we'll be seeing more of each other, Gerald Hammond, but until then it was lovely to meet you."

She headed off to the lake, while he sat and watched her trip daintily down the steps and across the lawn. He was wondering about all she had said. He was also wondering just how much power the influential, altruistic, sexually degenerate and inordinately wealthy Conrad Zalesie held.

35

Thirty minutes passed before Cowdray returned, during which time a waiter delivered Hammond's suitcase from the hotel. The man asked if he wanted the case unpacked. Hammond growled a refusal. When Cowdray finally appeared, Hammond angrily pointed to the case.

"What the hell's all this about?"

"Mr Zalesie suggested we take the liberty. He decided that, under current circumstances, you'd be safer and more comfortable staying here for a few days."

"He decided? What circumstances?"

"I'm sure Mr Zalesie will explain."

"And what if I decide I don't want Mr Zalesie's protection?"

"That is your privilege, but given the nature of your business, and the uncertain climate. . . I'm sure, when Mr Zalesie explains, you'll come to accept his offer of hospitality."

"We'll see about that."

Cowdray seemed untroubled by Hammond's anger. He walked to the french doors and stood quietly for a moment. Hammond followed the

Englishman's gaze, to where the forlorn figure of Angela Carlisle stood looking out across the water.

"I noticed you chatting to Mrs Carlisle."

"Oh did you? Does that mean you're watching me?"

Hammond turned to see Cowdray shake his head.

"Good Lord no, Mr Hammond. It's just that Mrs Carlisle has suffered a great deal recently. We're keeping a weather eye on her. I'm sure you understand?"

"Yes, uh, yes, of course. I'm sorry."

He'd suddenly felt churlish at the blurting of his own paranoia. The secretary's supercilious features continued to smile a reassurance as Cowdray relayed the invitation he'd been waiting for.

"Oh, and Mr Zalesie asked if you would care to join him in his study."

Hammond followed the Englishman through the main body of the house and up a secondary staircase, to where Conrad Zalesie sat waiting.

"Mr Hammond. It's good to meet you at last. I've heard a great deal about you."

Zalesie smiled as he came out from behind his desk. Hammond took the offered hand and warily studied his host.

"Mr Zalesie. I've heard about you, too."

"Not all bad, I hope?"

"No. . . Well, not all."

The smile on Zalesie's face broadened.

"They did tell me you were forthright. I rather like that. Please, take a seat."

Hammond sat down. Zalesie returned to his chair on the other side of the desk. Hammond gazed around the study and voiced his admiration.

"You have a beautiful home, Mr Zalesie. I understand you prefer to be called Mister?"

"Yes, the Russians gave the title and some land to one of my more disreputable ancestors: payment for betraying their fellow Lithuanians during the third partitioning. As you might imagine, it is not an ancestry that I or my family are especially proud of. Anyway, enough of that. So you're our new man in the State Department?"

"I'm nobody's man."

A frown and note of rancour replaced Zalesie's previous condescension.

"Everybody is somebody's man, Mr Hammond, even you."

Moments later a disarming smile replaced the frown as Zalesie defused the tension.

"Other than admiration for your work in Magdeburg, I have no preformed opinion of you, Mr Hammond, if that is what worries you. I hope you will extend me the same courtesy?"

Hammond was still feeling distinctly prickly.

"Of course, Mr Zalesie. So let me ask you. Did you have Alan Carlisle killed?"

"No, I did not."

"Did Catherine Schmidt kill Alan Carlisle?"

"No, she did not."

Hammond's questions had been naïve to the point of absurdity and candid to the point of rudeness. Zalesie's answers had been predictable to the point of banal.

"Then who did?"

The Lithuanian seemed unconcerned and somehow distant. He didn't answer directly.

"I can recall sitting here with Alan Carlisle. He was sitting where you are now. I was talking about Max Schmeling. You can see his picture on the wall there. I told Alan about the first fight with Louis, and mentioned how Schmeling's trainer spotted the flaw in Louis' defence."

"How he dropped his guard after an attack?"

Zalesie beamed his approval.

"I see you're an aficionado?" Hammond shrugged. Zalesie continued. "Beria has the same flaw. He doesn't drop his guard after an attack, but he will sometimes drop his agents. It depends on their continuing worth, or the risk they may be compromised. You see, Beria is like Stalin; he's paranoid. If he is at all concerned that he can no longer trust them, and more importantly their information, he'll drop them like a stone."

"You're talking about Beria's agent in the State Department?"

"Precisely."

"So who killed Alan Carlisle?"

"I couldn't tell you who performed the deed, Mr Hammond. However, given the condition of the body, I would assume the instruction came from someone familiar with our mutual young friend and some of her, shall we say, more alarming idiosyncrasies."

"And what does all that mean?"

"It means the order undoubtedly originated from inside the Lubyanka, Mr Hammond. Is that plain enough for you?"

"But Carlisle was already working for Beria. Why would Beria want him killed?"

Hammond's unthinking strategy had been to provoke an indiscretion through candour and confrontation. Zalesie seemed little more than mildly irritated.

"Partly because of you." Hammond looked puzzled. Zalesie explained. "By showing that photograph to Daniel, you took away one of Beria's levers. Then, of course, by rescuing young Mathew Carlisle from the Austrian MGB, we took away the other. Beria had no other way of shutting Carlisle up." Hammond still looked puzzled. Zalesie elaborated. "That was why Beria sent Paslov to blackmail Carlisle, to shut him up."

"Not to get to Martin Kube?"

Hammond was still hoping to pry an indiscretion. The reaction was less than he'd hoped.

"Why would they need Carlisle to do that for them? They have you."

"Me?"

"Yes. Following the trail with all the tenacity of a bloodhound, and effectively doing the work of Beria and Paslov as you snuffle your way along."

"I don't understand."

"No, Mr Hammond, you don't, do you?"

"Are you going to explain?"

"No. I've given you more than enough answers to digest. The rest will have to wait."

Casual dismissal didn't sit well with Hammond.

"Why am I getting the impression that you have something to hide, Mr Zalesie?"

Far from provoking annoyance or indiscretion, the question seemed to amuse the Lithuanian.

"I have never met a man who didn't have something to hide, Mr Hammond. Should the day ever dawn, I doubt I will find myself able to trust him. But now I must suspend our little chat for a few hours. I have an appointment in Baltimore. You really should have telephoned. Anyway, I'm sure your questions will keep until I return."

Hammond remembered the nightmare and tried a bluff.

"It's all about Manhattan, isn't it?"

Hammond saw the look of surprise and felt elated. He counted it as his only success so far, but any joy faded when Zalesie posed a question of his own.

"How remarkably perceptive of you. And what precisely is it about Manhattan?"

"I don't know."

Conrad Zalesie chuckled good-naturedly.

"Remind me never to play pin the tail on the donkey with you."

"Pin the what?"

"It is a children's game. Blindfolded children take turns pinning a paper tail onto the outline of a donkey. Whichever child pins their tail closest to the hindquarters wins the game. Children love it. I must admit I am rather fond of it myself."

"I'm not a child."

Hammond had bristled. Zalesie smiled benevolently.

"We are all of us children, Mr Hammond. The games merely become more complex as we grow."

Zalesie was clearly enjoying the banter. Disconcerted, Hammond posed another question, more in hope than expectation.

"But I succeeded just now, didn't I, Mr Zalesie? The tail is on the donkey?"

"You will only know that when you remove the blindfold. But I have an aircraft waiting. Perhaps we can continue this conversation over dinner."

"Which reminds me: my suitcase, from the hotel?"

"Merely a precaution. Losing two State Department officials could be seen as negligence."

"You think I'm in danger?"

Zalesie looked thoughtful for a moment and then shook his head.

"Not as long as you keep that blindfold in place. You are going to have to take it off at some point, though, and then you could be."

"One last question. Why are you bothering with me? I'm not with the police or FBI. You're a busy and important man. You don't have to answer my questions. All you have to do is call Marcus Allum and complain about my pestering you. I'd be on my way back to Washington within the hour. Why haven't you done that?"

This time the smile was warm as Zalesie came out from behind the desk to shake hands.

"Partly because I find myself in your debt."

"The girl, you mean?"

"Yes. So why did you ignore Daniel Chambers' instructions and continue looking?"

Hammond shrugged.

"I promised I would look after her. I gave her my word. And, that apart, I don't like people who address me as though my thoughts and opinions don't matter."

Zalesie's smile broadened.

"Yes, poor old Daniel does have a tendency to infuriate."

"So where is the girl?"

"I'm not entirely convinced that you are ready for that information, not just yet, but I can assure you that she is safe."

That wasn't enough for Hammond.

"Safe from people like Martin Kube?"

It was the second time Hammond had mentioned the name. Zalesie stared impassively back.

"She is completely safe. . . You have my word."

Hammond could see it was all he was likely to get. He returned to an earlier subject.

"So, what was the rest of the reason?"

"I'm sorry?"

"You said you found yourself in my debt, but you also said that was only part of the reason. What was the rest of the reason?"

"I find your honesty refreshing. So what did you think of Harold Pratt House?"

Hammond cast his mind back to the building and to two of the 'folks' he'd met there.

"I thought the building was bland and boring, but what goes on inside that building isn't bland or boring. I believe that what goes on inside that building is an outrage to democracy."

"How wonderfully public-spirited of you, but now I really must go. It was a pleasure to meet you, Gerald Hammond. I look forward to continuing our conversation over dinner. In the meantime, I'm sure Cowdray here will look after you. Do make yourself at home."

36

Hammond returned to his room, his mind cluttered as he sifted and evaluated all that Zalesie had said. It was clear the Lithuanian knew the whereabouts of Catherine Schmidt; clear, too, that he knew of Martin Kube. That combination of circumstance failed to reassure.

A late lunch of sandwiches and fruit was brought to his room on a tray. Hammond spent the afternoon wandering the grounds, but saw no further sign of the widow Carlisle. With the exceptions of groups of industrious gardeners, and the ever-intrusive army of dark-suited vigilance, he saw no one of interest.

He returned to his room around six and found a note from Cowdray. A dinner suit, dress shirt, and black tie hung on the wardrobe door. The note gave directions to the lounge. Dinner would begin at seven, with drinks. Formal dress wasn't compulsory, but. . .

Formally-dressed and fashionably-late, Hammond wandered into the main lounge at ten minutes after seven. The room was already crowded with guests. Cigar smoke hung thick in the air, penetrated by chattering small talk and the occasional shriek of feigned outrage or sycophantic laughter. Four or five groups of formally-attired men stood at the bar with drinks in hand and extravagantly-dressed wives or curvaceous significant others hanging on to their every word.

In the far corner, Marcus Allum stood talking with two men. One, Hammond knew vaguely as Carmine Orsini, a short, stocky, and intensely disagreeable individual of Italian-American descent and homosexual persuasion, with a thick moustache and an unashamed reputation for political machination and highly public trysts.

Hammond didn't know the third man. He was squat and bald, seriously overweight, perspiring profusely, and possibly even uglier than Orsini. Towering above them, the rangy Marcus Allum appeared incongruous. He glanced across as Hammond wandered into the room, but made no effort to acknowledge him.

Hammond headed to the bar and ordered a single malt straight-up. The waiter poured a large measure. Hammond thanked him and began studying the other guests. One in particular caught his eye.

She was strikingly attractive: tall, curvaceous, and oozing sensuality. The dress, in gold lamé, was tight, flimsy and expensive, with the skirt split to the thigh, and the décolleté neckline sculpted to enhance. Shimmering auburn hair was pinned high to accentuate a graceful neck. Matching stiletto-heeled shoes, with gold-painted toenails peeking, performed a similar function for long shapely legs and delightfully rounded buttocks. The gold necklace she wore was simple, to add that essential touch of understated elegance without distracting from her more obvious and licentious charms.

She smiled conceitedly when she saw him watching, and then sashayed over to where he stood. Hammond found one sense breathing in the headiness of her perfume, while another involuntarily gawped. She brushed against him as she leaned forward to order a refill at the bar, and then purred as she turned to more closely study him.

"And you, I presume, must be the immovable object?"

Hammond refocused and regrouped.

"I'm sorry?"

"They tell me you're incorruptible, Gerald Hammond."

"I don't understand. Do I. . . ?"

She looked deep into his eyes.

"It's the age-old question, Gerald. Which will prevail?"

"I still don't. . . I'm sorry. . . Uh, do I know you?"

"I'm Theresa Zalesie. I'm the irresistible force."

Hammond couldn't argue with that. He smiled politely and babbled an answer.

"How do you do, uh, Mrs Zalesie. . . uh, your husband? Will he be joining us?"

"Theresa, please; and no, Gerald, he's still tied up in Baltimore. He sends his apologies and asked me to entertain you." He must have looked disappointed, because she smiled quietly and then said, "I'm sure he'll catch up with you tomorrow. And so, are you?"

"Am I what?"

"Incorruptible, Gerald, an immovable object?"

Hammond shook his head and smiled.

"I used to like to think so, but these days I seem to be anything but."

"I think you're just being modest. Either way, I guess we'll find out soon."

"We will?"

"Oh, I can guarantee it." Her gaze briefly scanned the room. "So, who don't you know?"

His eyes similarly swept the room.

"It would be easier to tell you who I do know."

"Well you know Marcus, of course, and I presume you know Carmine Orsini?"

Hammond shook his head.

"Not well. I have heard that he works for Daniel Chambers."

"Daniel put Carmine Orsini into Occupied Territories to be indispensable to Marcus Allum and keep an eye on him; well, you know what a manic-depressive Marcus can be. He's Daniel's factotum, and the worst kind of sycophant. He'll smile to your face, but don't ever turn around, because you'll either get a dick in your ass or a knife in your back."

Hammond grinned.

"Are you speaking from experience?"

"Good heavens no, darling. God didn't see fit to give me an Adam's apple, and apart from that, just look at him. It's no wonder he has to take them from behind."

"What about the man next to him?"

"Oh, that's Martin Linz. Looks exactly as he is: pig of a man. German, obnoxious, and pugnacious to a fault, but also powerful and dangerous. He's another one to watch out for."

As Hammond studied the German, Catherine Schmidt's description of her former abuser came to mind.

"Did you say Martin Linz? Don't you mean Martin Kube?"

"If you already knew, darling, why bother asking?"

"I didn't know. It was an educated guess."

She studied him with flashing eyes. She seemed impressed.

"I see, devious and manipulative. I think you're going to fit in nicely around here."

She then went on to discuss the rest of the gathering, taking care to point out those in positions of particular power or influence before cataloguing individual strengths and weaknesses. She saved the most interesting two for last.

"The man in the cream dinner jacket, with the pretty little dark-haired wife who can't keep her eyes off you, is Jonathan Hudson. When he's not snorting cocaine or chasing muscular young men around Washington, Jonathan is one of Forrestal's key advisors. Wife's name is Wendy. He stays with her because she has the money. She stays with him because he has the contacts. She's supposed to be good in bed. He's supposed to be brilliant out of it. I always found them complete bores: in and out of bed."

"Forrestal? You mean, Secretary of the Navy, James Forrestal?"

"Conrad likes to ensure he gets the right advice. The heavy-set guy with the beard standing next to him is Peter, Peter Martel; sharp as a whip and just as flexible. He's an advisor to Patterson. The woman with him is Stella. I don't know her second name. I don't think Peter does." Hammond stood, quietly admiring the woman. Theresa Zalesie offered him some advice. "Forget it, sweetie. She negotiates the price going in and you couldn't afford her on your salary."

Hammond grinned broadly. He was warming to Theresa Zalesie, and not solely because of her more obvious charms.

"Presumably there's someone around here who advises Byrnes?"

She paused, and then turned to study him with that same admiring look.

"Clever boy. . . He's currently down in Baltimore, with Conrad. His name's Theodore Hibbard. Conrad calls the three of them his great triumvirate."

Hammond nodded a grudging admiration for Zalesie's deviousness. James Byrnes and Robert Patterson were respectively the U.S. Secretaries of State and War. They, together with James Forrestal and Truman's own advisor, made up the National Intelligence Authority, the overseers of America's new Central Intelligence Group. With trusted advisors to three in his pocket, and himself advising the fourth, Conrad Zalesie had manoeuvred himself into a position where he could significantly influence both the fledgling U.S. intelligence service and U.S. foreign policy.

"So why are you telling me all this? Did your husband tell you to tell me?"

"Of course. He wanted to see how quickly you'd work it out. He'll be impressed. Conrad likes you. He trusts you, and he doesn't trust many. I think he sees the two of you working together."

"And why would I be interested in doing that?"

She wiggled and giggled in an obvious and coquettish way.

"Oh, you'd be amazed at the fringe benefits. But now I have to mingle. We'll catch up later, I promise." She gave a mischievous laugh, and then called across to where the notorious Wendy Hudson stood overtly admiring Hammond. "Wendy, come and meet Gerald Hammond. He's a very good friend and he's dying to meet you." She turned back and whispered, "You will save some energy for later, won't you, darling?"

Hammond took almost half-an-hour to extricate himself from the cloying attentions of Wendy Hudson. The conversation had centered on her, and been interspersed with juvenile double-entendres and crude references to a history of infidelity. She clearly intended adding him to a shamelessly long list. He found himself feeling sorry for her. She was an attractive and vivacious woman, infected with all the pretence of socialite Washington and trapped in a loveless marriage.

Whenever he had managed to steer the conversation away from social tittle-tattle and crude innuendo, she had proved herself intelligent and articulate. She could do so much better, and be so much happier; it was a shame.

When she had bluntly asked him to take her back to his room, he hadn't bluntly declined. Hammond had recent and bitter experience of cruel rejection and held too much regard for feelings. He apologized and said he needed to discuss some important matters with Marcus Allum before Allum left for Washington. He saw her disappointment and added that he hoped to catch her later.

As Wendy Hudson wandered back to her husband with pride intact and sexual antennae on scan, he moved over to where a pained-looking Angela

Carlisle stood sandwiched between Martin Kube's lumbering boorishness and the pretentious effeminacy of Simon Cowdray.

She looked hugely relieved at his arrival. She introduced him to Kube, who grunted a greeting of sorts, then turned his back to summon a waiter and order a refill.

Hammond took the opportunity to study the man more closely. He seemed slightly the worse for drink, and intent on furthering that condition. If Kube did know the whereabouts of Catherine Schmidt, this could be an ideal opportunity to find out.

Simon Cowdray was also watching the boorish Kube, and apparently realizing the potential for careless indiscretion.

"Uh, Mr Linz. I wonder if I might have a word, in private?"

Kube was, equally clearly, in no mood to reason.

"No, you may not. Go away, I am busy."

"Sir, I really do think that we should. . ."

"Did you hear me? I said go away. You are hired help around here. You do as you are told. You are a servant, a lackey. Is that not what the English call people like you? I am one of the original five, one of the original five Children of Etzel. Never forget it."

Fury briefly flitted across the Englishman's face, fury and something else. It was a coldness to go with the fury, the cold, unfeeling and controlled anger of a professional killer. Hammond saw it and read it for what it was. However, by the time Cowdray gave his answer, that look had been replaced by the more usual and servile façade.

"Actually, sir, I believe the term was originally French."

Kube may or may not have seen that look. Either way, he didn't seem to care.

"I could not give a shit. Get out."

Cowdray turned away and then spoke to Hammond and Angela Carlisle.

"Mrs Carlisle, Mr Hammond. Please excuse me. I have duties to attend to."

Cowdray walked away, but stopped at the door and whispered to one of the waiters. The man listened and nodded. Cowdray seemed satisfied. He stepped out of the room and closed the door behind him. Kube sniffed his disdain.

"Faggot!" He turned to Hammond. "Is that not what you call them here?"

Hammond ignored him and began making small talk with Angela Carlisle. She moved closer and gazed up at him with eyelashes fluttering. Hammond took another scotch and asked what she wanted to drink. She stopped fluttering the eyelashes and openly vamped him with eyes held wide. She said that she would have whatever he was having. Hammond glanced to where the predatory Theresa was mingling. He smiled an impish smile and then ordered Angela Carlisle a scotch.

He thought of relaxing, taking a few drinks and seeing where the evening took him, but he needed information. Kube's boast of being one of the original five Children of Etzel had set the alarm bells ringing. From the look of things, the German could soon be in a sufficiently drunken condition to provide more information. That possibility meant staying alert.

Kube didn't disappoint. Half-an-hour later they had moved to an adjacent room and were sitting around the table, tucking into lobster thermidor and sipping chilled white Burgundy.

Only a dozen or so had joined them at the table. Allum and Orsini had taken their whispered conversation back to Washington, Allum, without acknowledging Hammond. Wendy Hudson had latched on to an ostentatious senator from somewhere south of Mason-Dixon. According to Theresa, the senator was a key figure on the Senate Appropriations Committee. Wendy Hudson obviously had something else in mind for him to appropriate. Much to Hammond's annoyance, the senator's exaggerated drawl and her feigned laughter could be heard all around the room.

At the other end of the table, Angela Carlisle sat on Hammond's left, Theresa Zalesie on his right. An isolated Kube sat to the other side of Angela Carlisle. The German drank copious amounts of brandy, sneered his contempt, and ate very little. He peered up from his glass and focused on Theresa Zalesie, who was shamelessly tracing erogenous patterns along Hammond's inner thigh.

"So tell me, Theresa, is there anything on two legs that you would not fuck?"

She sneered back at him.

"Yes, Martin, you."

Everyone laughed, albeit a trifle nervously. The insult failed to disrupt the contempt.

"I don't know why he puts up with a whore like you. . . I would break your neck."

"No, you wouldn't, Martin. You'd have someone else do it for you."

A drunken Kube was no match for the lightning wit. He turned the glare on Hammond.

"And you, Mr State Department lackey. What are you here for, apart from the whores?"

Sensing the sudden menace in the air, everyone in the room stopped and stared. Hammond sat studying him before answering, purposely building the tension and waiting to ensure the hushed audience heard every word.

"I'm looking for Catherine Schmidt. You remember her? You raped her when she was a child. You do remember, don't you, in Berlin that time? How old was she then, Martin? It was her twelfth birthday, wasn't it? You bought her a new dress and took her to the park, where you raped her. And then you continued using her as your personal whore when you were in Prague, even though she was still just a child. I'm here to find her and to ensure that you never abuse or touch her, ever again."

By this time everyone at the table had stopped talking and all eyes were focused on Kube. Even in his condition, the German could sense their combined hostility. He growled back.

"That is not true. She made that up. She is just a whore, like all the others around here."

"Are you saying that she's here?"

"I do not know where she is. And it is not true, what you said about me raping her. She was not a helpless little girl. She knew what she wanted, and she wanted me. She made it clear. If she said anything else, she is a damn liar."

Kube lurched from his seat and then stormed from the room, leaving the remaining diners sitting in stunned silence. Slowly the group at the far end resumed their conversation, but without the ostentatious drawl and coquettish shrieks that had been such a feature of their previous behaviour. Theresa Zalesie withdrew her fingers from where they had graduated to unbuttoning Hammond's fly. She looked disbelievingly at him and asked if it was true. When he nodded, she seemed genuinely distressed.

"Oh, my God!"

Hammond didn't know Theresa Zalesie, but a post-war Washington, still basking in the euphoria of victory, was full of similar people, with similarly 'open' marriages and similarly relaxed attitudes to sex. Their esoteric standards of behaviour and morality never ceased to amaze him.

Just as the prison population has its own fixed lines, whereby certain crimes are seen as morally defensible, even celebrated, and others are frowned upon as being beneath contempt, so the morally avant-garde had theirs. All around the table the mood was suddenly sombre, the previous high-spirits and raucous flirtations forgotten. It was largely Hammond's doing, and that demanded he make his excuses.

"I'm sorry. I think it's probably best I leave. I apologize if I've upset anyone."

Angela Carlisle placed a hand on his arm.

"Don't be silly. It's not your fault. It's that disgusting man. You don't have to go. Please don't. I thought we could. . . It's just that you seem so kind, you. . ."

He smiled a comforting smile.

"I'm sorry, but I seem too have put a dampener on things. It's best I leave."

She looked deep into his eyes.

"Next week I'm going back to my house, in Takoma Park. Please say you'll call me?"

Hammond could see the fear and loneliness in her. He knew both emotions well. He wasn't at all sure he should be getting into any sort of relationship with someone of her confused orientation and emotional instability. He was even less certain of her expectations. But Angela Carlisle was now alone and vulnerable, possibly for the first time in her life. Whatever else she might or might not expect from him, she clearly needed a friend.

"Of course. Perhaps we could have dinner one evening?"

"I'd like that, Gerald. I'd like that very much."

To his right, Theresa Zalesie had a more basic and obvious agenda.

"And we still haven't answered that question. I promise you, we will."

Life for Gerald Hammond seemed to be feast or famine. After so many months of boredom at the insurance company, he had been plunged into a world of unceasing intrigue and violent death. And now, after so many months of loneliness and isolation, beautiful women were suddenly throwing themselves at him. He smiled an enigmatic smile and made his escape.

Back in the room's seclusion, he changed his clothes, hurriedly packed the suitcase and then told one of the guards to fetch the Pontiac. Once behind the wheel, he drove to the first security gate and collected the Beretta. He checked the load, slipped it under the dashboard, and then drove back up to Highway One. From there, he headed on down towards the city.

37

"And I am telling you that I want that bastard dead."

A furious Martin Kube sat in the kitchen. Simon Cowdray, privately unsympathetic, sought to calm the rage.

"But you can't do that, not without authorization, Mr Linz. You know that."

"Cannot do what? I can do what the hell I like. I am one of the original five. Do you understand what that means? I am one of the original five Children of Etzel."

"I understand that, sir, but please keep your voice down. Some of the staff are not. . ."

"Then do as I say, damn you!"

Cowdray studied the ferocity and began to waver.

"Mr Zalesie doesn't want him harmed. He made it clear before he left."

"Mr Zalesie, Mr Linz? What is all this shit?"

"You know the rules, sir. I'm only following orders."

"Follow orders, do you? Well here is another one for you. I want that bastard dead, and I want it done now. No arguments."

"Mr Zalesie isn't going to like it."

"I will deal with him. You do as I say."

Cowdray moved to the telephone and dialled. A man answered.

"Yes."

"Do you know who this is? That's right. Do you have any patrols on Highway One, between here and Pelham? Good. There's a Blackout Pontiac, heading toward the city. Single white male driver, fortyish, name of Hammond, Gerald Hammond. . . I don't know, and I don't have time to check, but I do know it's a rental. He probably picked it up at Municipal. You can get the plate from them. I want it pulled over and the driver detained. What? No, there's no need for that. I just want him detained. We'll do the necessary. I'm sending some people now. Tell your men to get clear when they arrive."

Cowdray replaced the handset, and left it cradled for a couple of seconds, while his mind ran through the choices available. Then he picked it up again and dialled the inner gatehouse.

"The man who just left, in the Blackout. Yes that's right. Get after him. I don't want him reaching the city. . . No, don't bother. Leave everything once the job's done. . . Yes, that's right, shotgun would be best. I've got police patrols looking for him now. They'll hold him until you get there. Make sure they get clear first. What's that? No, take him with you. You'll need an extra gun. I'll send someone to cover. Now get a move on, while we've still got the light. Oh, and don't take any stupid chances. This man's supposed to be good."

Cowdray replaced the receiver and then turned to face a smiling Kube.

"Just like that, huh?"

There was no answering smile from the Englishman.

"That's right, Mr Linz. Just like that."

368

****

Hammond had been driving for almost fifteen minutes when he saw the two motorcycle cops. They kept their distance for half-a-mile or so, obviously checking the car and his identity. A hundred yards behind them, the Cadillac stayed fixed in the centre of his mirror. Then it suddenly pulled across the central reservation and headed back to the north.

With the Cadillac out of sight, the first cop drew alongside the Pontiac and waved him down. The second pulled in behind. Hammond dutifully pulled over, stopped at the side of the road and then sat quietly with the window down and his hands in plain sight. He was studying the famous red motorcycles with interest as he affably asked,

"You boys still using those Red Indians?"

He had no idea why they had pulled him over, but had decided to lighten the moment. The cop nodded back at him but didn't smile.

"That's right, sir. May I see your license?"

Hammond handed him the license and sat patiently waiting while he scanned the details.

"Would you mind waiting for a moment, sir?"

"Sure."

The cop walked to the rear of the car and began whispering to his partner. Both men looked uncertain. That was when Hammond saw the Cadillac speeding towards them. The driver must have seen them, because he slowed and pulled to the side of the road.

Hammond studied the occupants in his mirror as they climbed out of the Cadillac and spoke to the cops. One of the cops handed over his license. The man slipped it into his pocket and then wandered toward the Pontiac. As he approached, Hammond saw the snub-nosed Smith & Wesson a moment too late.

"I'll take the Beretta."

Hammond first studied the barrel of the thirty-eight and then the look of grim determination. He recognized the man as the guard who had relieved him of the Beretta when he'd first arrived. He nodded, then took out the automatic and handed it over.

"You said you liked it. . . Make sure you look after it."

"And the keys, if you don't mind."

He handed over the ignition fob and then sat quietly as the cops kicked over their machines before heading off towards the city. As the two motorcycles disappeared over the horizon, he asked the question, already knowing the answer.

"So, now what?"

"Now you get out."

The second gunman walked up to the car and stood facing the driver's door. He carried a Model Twelve Winchester pump-action shotgun. Hammond studied the twelve-gauge barrel's obvious menace and knew their orders were to do more than simply detain.

"Looks like you get to keep the Beretta permanently, huh? Look after it."

The first gunman glanced appreciatively down at the Beretta. Hammond opened the car door. As the shotgun wielder stepped back from the door's anticipated radius, he briefly lowered the Winchester. It was his last conscious movement.

A point-four-five calibre bullet from the Nineteen-Eleven automatic in Hammond's hidden left hand arrived through an open mouth. It drove up and on through the brain, before exiting via the cranium. As his accomplice slumped to the ground, the first gunman dropped the Beretta and scrambled to realign the thirty-eight.

Less than a second later, two forty-five rounds thumped hard into his chest.

Hammond studied them dispassionately, knowing they had intended killing him and feeling no remorse. The man with the Winchester had died instantly, but the other was still breathing. He lay at the side of the carriageway, staring blankly back at Hammond and the still-levelled automatic. Hammond smiled grimly down as he recalled their first meeting at the gatehouse.

"Told you, you shouldn't have just taken my word for it. That's the trouble with naturally-trusting people, my friend: they're a dying breed. In your business you should have known better."

The smile dissolved as he kicked the thirty-eight away from twitching fingers, then bent down and retrieved his license from the man's jacket pocket. After that he picked up the key fob and Beretta, brushed and blew away the dust, and then climbed back into the Pontiac. He slammed the door, started the ignition, and leisurely drove away, leaving the Cadillac with the engine running and the doors open, and the two failed assassins lying dead and dying at the roadside.

****

"Do you have any fucking idea what time it is?"

Dawid Gabriel roared down from the top of the stairs. Hammond stood in the stairwell and grinned up at him.

"Sorry about this. It is something of an emergency."

"It fucking well better be. You'd better come on up."

Hammond climbed the stairs and wandered into the apartment. Gabriel closed and bolted the door behind him.

"You wanna beer?"

Hammond took the bottle and nodded his thanks.

"So what's it all about?"

Hammond talked of his meetings with Angela Carlisle, and Zalesie. Then he spoke of the altercation with Kube, and the failed assassination attempt. Gabriel looked to the heavens.

"Didn't I tell you? Didn't I fucking tell you? You don't fuck with The Folks at Fifty-fucking-Eight. Christ! How many fucking times did I tell you? The government don't fuck with 'em, I said. Even the Mob don't fuck with 'em, I said, so don't you fuck with 'em. I couldn't have been clearer if I'd slapped it on a fucking billboard in ten-foot-high fucking letters."

"Yeah, I vaguely remember you telling me."

"So what time was this?"

"I don't know. Around eight-thirty, I guess, maybe a little after."

"So where the fuck have you been since then?"

"Looking for this place."

"Jesus Christ! Well you got yourself into this fucking mess, J. Edgar. You're just gonna have to get your fucking self out of it."

"Fine."

Hammond felt a good deal less certain than he sounded. Gabriel asked the obvious.

"So what the fuck are you gonna do?"

"Thought I'd ask you to check out the official reports, find out if I'm on somebody's wanted list. The cops looked like the genuine article to me: Red Indian motorcycles, the lot."

"I'll check in the morning. For now you'd better sleep on the couch, and while you're at it you'd better work out a fucking plan for dealing with all this shit. Either that, or we're both gonna be as dead as your fucking friend up in Spic Harlem."

Hammond's weary nod confirmed the truth of that.

"So, what did you come up with on Zalesie?"

Gabriel shrugged.

"Nothing special. According to police and immigration records, he's exactly who and what he says he is. Seriously wealthy arms dealer, exiled Lithuanian fucking count, friends in high fucking places, one of the inside folks at fifty-eight, and not a man to fuck around with. . . I guess you just fucking well figured that one out, huh?"

"And you're sure about his background?"

"Abso-fucking-lutely. I checked the records, all the way back. He's clean."

"So why would he send people after me?"

"Maybe he didn't. Maybe this fucking Nazi you had the bust-up with jumped the gun."

"Yeah, maybe."

"Anyway, we're not gonna figure anything out this time of night, and I need my fucking beauty sleep. You get the couch. There's a blanket in the cupboard outside the bathroom. I'll see you in the morning."

"Thanks. Just one more question. How did an exiled Lithuanian arms dealer get to be so friendly with the Folks at Fifty-Eight? I mean these are serious businessmen, of long-term financial standing and impeccable social credentials. Zalesie may be hugely wealthy, but he's not one of them. He's just another wealthy immigrant."

Gabriel looked knowingly back.

"How the fuck do you think he got to be so fucking friendly with them? And how do you suppose he got all of that money out of Lithuania or wherever in the first fucking place?"

"I don't know. I never had that problem, I'm sorry to say."

"You ever hear of a Wall Street law firm called Cartwright, Chambers and Kent?"

"Should I have?"

"They specialize in international law. More importantly, they specialize in handling government trade agreements with foreign fucking governments: places like Austria and Germany and Italy. Least they did before the U.S. entered the war and the Trading with the Enemy Act started showing some fucking teeth. Since that screwed 'em, they've spent most of their time trying to get their fucking money out of wherever they fucking made it."

"You mean money laundering?"

"Who the fuck do you think shipped Zalesie's money into the States?"

"Cartwright, Chambers, and whoever you said?"

"Kent. . . And yeah, that's precisely fucking who."

The penny suddenly dropped.

"Chambers! You don't mean. . . ?"

"I mean Daniel fucking Chambers. For a second there I thought you'd fallen a-fucking-sleep on me, J. Edgar."

"It seems you've been busy while I've been away."

"That's what you're paying me for, isn't it? And that reminds me."

Gabriel held out his hand. Hammond grinned.

"How much?"

"If I'm checking out all of this latest shit tomorrow, and with all the expenses so far, we'll call it a flat five hundred. I'll let the night's board and lodging go."

Hammond grinned wryly as he handed over ten pristine fifty-dollar bills.

"You're all heart."

****

The following morning, Gabriel sauntered down to his old precinct. He broke the news when he returned. He had found no mention of the incident, no sign of any dead bodies or abandoned Cadillacs on Highway One, and no reports filed.

"As far as New York's finest go, you're in the fucking clear, J. Edgar. There's no record of any of it, and I mean not fucking anywhere. Looks like someone somewhere cleared everything up in a major fucking hurry."

"In that case I'd better check back into my hotel, call Zalesie and arrange a meeting."

"You gotta be fucking kidding me?"

"No, I'm not spending my life looking over my shoulder, wondering if the man behind me is going to stick a knife in my kidneys. If Zalesie ordered the hit he'll send someone. If he turns up in person, maybe we can talk. Either way, at the end of it I'll know."

"Sounds like a high-risk fucking strategy to me, J. Edgar?"

"Maybe so, but it's not just me involved. You see, there's Emma to think of, and my parents down in Marco Island, and even foul-mouthed irascible you. In fact, anybody I'm related to, or close to, or work with. When you spend your life looking over your shoulder, it doesn't just affect you, it affects everybody around you. I've seen it before in other people, and I'm not living the rest of my life like that."

38

"I gave specific instructions."

Some distance to the north of where Hammond and Gabriel sat pondering his motives, Conrad Zalesie had returned to the Connecticut estate, where he was dealing with those who had disobeyed his orders. Cowed and apologetic, Simon Cowdray offered his mitigation.

"I'm sorry, sir, but Mr Linz gave me no choice. He said he was one of the original five Children of Etzel and that he'd deal with you."

Zalesie stopped ranting and looked hard at the Englishman.

"He said he was one of the original five, and he'd deal with me?"

"Yes, sir."

"And he specifically mentioned the Children of Etzel?"

"Yes, sir. They were his actual words."

Despite his anger, Zalesie remained outwardly calm.

"Were they now? What else did he say?" Cowdray looked uneasy. Zalesie immediately picked up on it. "Well, what is it?"

"It wasn't so much what Mr Linz said, sir. It was something else, something Mr Hammond said."

"Well?"

"I wasn't there, sir. One of the staff told me."

"Told you what?"

"About Catherine, sir. Mr Hammond accused Mr Linz of raping her when she was twelve, and systematically abusing her when they were in Berlin and Prague. . . I don't know the truth of it. I'm sorry, sir."

Zalesie sat in silence. He was recalling bygone days, remembering his late wife's unease over Kube's frequent visits and the Gestapo man's trips to the park with Catherine. It had been so out of character for the boorish Kube, but at the time he had been too preoccupied to listen to his wife, or notice his daughter, or care about anything but the war. Zalesie was also recalling Hammond's warning on protecting Catherine and realizing the reason for it. He felt the guilt and rage welling up, but maintained the calm exterior.

"I think you had better send Mr Linz in. Oh, and unless otherwise instructed, the moment he leaves this room you are to deal with him. Do you understand?"

Simon Cowdray nodded.

"Yes, sir. I'm sorry, sir. I know you were friends."

Moments later, a significantly less subservient Kube took the Englishman's place.

"So what did that little worm have to say for himself? Christ! I could not believe it when they said Hammond had escaped."

Zalesie gestured to a chair.

"Sit down, Martin, and tell me why you gave the order to have Hammond killed when Cowdray told you that I had specifically forbidden it."

Kube had obviously decided that attack was his only defence.

"You had forbidden it? You forget, I am one of the original five. I am the same as you. I do as I damn well please."

Zalesie preserved the façade of self-control.

"Martin, in nineteen thirty-nine the Reich had over one hundred infantry divisions, six armoured divisions and two thousand war planes at its disposal. A year later there were even more. We needed many commanders, and yet had only one Führer. Do you understand what I am saying when I tell you that?"

"You are trying to tell me you see yourself as the new Führer?"

Despite the provocation, Zalesie remained unruffled.

"Of course not, Martin. There was only ever one Führer. We loved him at the time, but now he is dead. I, on the other hand, am alive and the sole appointed leader of the Children, appointed by the Reichsführer, with approval from the Führer himself. I swore an oath when they appointed me, Martin. I swore the Children would endure. The Children of Etzel will endure. It is the same oath that you yourself took. Do you remember that, Martin?"

Kube shrugged his shoulders.

"I remember it well enough, but now I have things to attend to."

Kube got to his feet and turned to walk away. Zalesie's self-control finally snapped. He roared his anger and produced an artillery-model nine-millimetre Luger from a side drawer of the desk. In one practiced movement he pulled back and released the protruding cylindrical grips, and then directed the most famous of World War Two side-arms at Martin Kube's head.

"Sit down, Martin, or I swear on all I hold sacred that I will kill you where you stand."

Kube hurriedly sat down. The bravado dissolved. His eyes scanned the room, as if searching for some avenue of escape, while familiar beads of sweat slid over flabby cheeks and ran down to his neck. He began to speak in a babble of mitigation and contrition, but a second roar from Zalesie stopped him in mid-utterance.

"You are a fool, and you are a coward. Now be quiet."

The wild-eyed stare of apprehension focused on the barrel's menace. Thick and arid lips snapped closed. Zalesie noted the show of submission and calmed his anger. With the Luger still levelled at Kube's head he continued.

"I never liked the Gestapo, Martin; few true soldiers did. No stomach for a fight, you see, no guts and no discipline, but the Reichsführer appointed you and we had to accept it."

He lowered the pistol. Kube visibly relaxed.

"However, my patience is not inexhaustible and I have my limits. If you ever revoke my orders, or threaten The Children's endurance in any way ever again, I swear I will kill you without a moment's hesitation."

"Yes, Josef. I apologize."

"No, Martin. It is yes, Conrad. I have told you many times. You are never to use those names. Is that finally understood?"

"Yes, Conrad."

"And if you ever again refer to my wife as a whore, I will take it as a personal insult. She has her work to do, and she does it well. You are to treat her with respect. Now tell me about these things that Hammond claimed about your relationship with Catherine, in Berlin and Prague."

Kube looked even more nervous. Zalesie smiled a comforting smile.

"Martin, we have known each other for many years. Sometimes we have our quarrels, but I have always trusted you. It was wartime, and I know just how provocative my daughter was. I can only think she must have inherited it from her mother." He smiled again, and idly reminisced. "Her mother was just the same, when she was young. My God! She used to drive me to distraction. She was so beautiful, and teased me mercilessly."

He stood up and rounded the table, then placed a comforting arm around Kube's shoulders. "Don't worry, my old friend. It is of no great importance. The Children will endure, Martin. That was our oath then, and it is our oath now. Nothing will change that."

Kube looked hugely relieved.

"I am so sorry, Joseph. I mean, Conrad. You are right: she used to tease me all the time. She knew exactly what she was doing to me. I couldn't help myself. But I would never hurt her. I loved her. You must believe that. I still do."

Conrad Zalesie nodded quietly and guided him to the door.

"Do not worry about it, Martin. Catherine always has been wilful. She probably always will be. But now I have to try and sort out this problem with Hammond. We will talk later."

"Thank you, Conrad. Thank you so much."

****

"Ah, at last, Herr Linz."

When a smiling Marin Kube opened Zalesie's study door and stepped into the corridor outside, he paid no attention to Cowdray, or to the assassin's smile. Neither could he have seen the nod of affirmation from Zalesie.

Had he done so, he might have heeded the rattlesnake's clatter. He might have detected the serpent's warning and offered a defence, avoided the peril, or evaded the strike. But he did none of those. He merely grunted at Cowdray and began to walk away.

For his part, Simon Cowdray had his own score to settle with Martin Kube. Weeks of insult and humiliation may not have disrupted the Englishman's calm exterior and subservient façade, but beneath that forced servility

Cowdray had seethed. Each time Kube disdainfully summoned him and insulted him and humiliated him, and then arrogantly dismissed him, Simon Cowdray hid his fury, said nothing, and bided his time.

But now that time was at hand.

As he slipped the wire around Kube's bulbous neck and drew it tight, Simon Cowdray didn't consider the man who begged and pleaded for his life in strangled gasps. He didn't feel the fingernails that desperately clawed at his hands, or see the eyes that bulged from their sockets in horror. He didn't feel the weight of the lumbering torso, or notice the legs that thrashed and kicked, and finally buckled.

He didn't even feel the wire that bit into his hands as he increased the pressure, or acknowledge the look of hatred and loathing on the watching face of Conrad Zalesie. But as he choked the last strangled breath from the child rapist and mindless thug who had once been Martin Kube, Simon Cowdray felt strangely elated and somehow cleansed.

Zalesie dispassionately studied the corpse.

"Thank you, Simon. Perhaps you could dispose of that."

Cowdray had never heard Zalesie call him that before. It completed his joy. He slipped the wire back into his pocket and massaged his hands.

"Yes, sir." He suddenly remembered. "I'm sorry, sir, but there was a telephone call, from Mr Hammond. I didn't think that I should disturb you, sir. Should I call him back?"

Zalesie's scowling features suddenly broke into the briefest of smiles.

"I knew that man had character. Yes, call him back, would you?"

****

It was nine on that same evening. Gerald Hammond sat in the corner of the hotel bar. He sipped at a ginger ale as he waited, his eyes fixed on the door to the main lobby.

He had purposely chosen the corner table. It stood in a poorly-lit area and allowed him an uninterrupted view of both lobby and emergency exits. As well as offering a good field of fire, the corner table also offered the chance of escape through the staff exit to the side of the bar. Walls on two sides and behind prevented any possibility of a flanking attack. Intervening tables and chairs provided additional cover. Hammond had chosen his ground well, and the allotted time would see the largely unpopular bar at its busiest.

He felt the comforting bulk of the Beretta in his right-hand pocket, and had the Colt lightly taped beneath the table. He held a license for the Beretta and hadn't fired it in months. If uniformed authority arrived, he'd show them the Beretta. Should Zalesie's hoods arrive and he need the extra firepower, the ballistically-incriminating Colt lay hidden and available.

However, and for all his meticulous preparation, Hammond knew if it came to using either, it would undoubtedly signal the end of a promising State Department career.

He studied Zalesie's arrival through the vertical blinds and saw he was alone. The hotel concierge directed the Lithuanian to the bar.

Zalesie gazed idly around before greeting Hammond with a knowing smile.

"You're a tactician, Mr Hammond."

"And you're a strategist, Mr Zalesie."

"You understand something of strategy?"

"I've read something of Clausewitz. Is war a continuation of politics, or are politics only the result of wars that fail?"

"That's good. I must remember that. Clausewitz was a Prussian, you know? We're related by blood, Prussians and Lithuanians, or at least some of us are."

"Now that I didn't know."

"Oh yes, it's quite true. Did you want to search me before I sit down?"

Hammond shook his head and nodded to the tell-tale bulge in Zalesie's jacket.

"There's no need. I can pull the Beretta a hell of a lot quicker than you could get to whatever that is. And if anybody comes through either of those doors with a gun in their hand, you'll be dead in the same second."

The smile didn't waver as Zalesie gently mocked the wary Hammond.

"I would appear I am in the company of a genuine western gunslinger. Good heavens, Mr Hammond, is there no end to your talents?" The smile faded as he offered a guarantee. "I do assure you that nobody of my acquaintance is joining us, Mr Hammond. As for the jacket. . ." He opened the coat for Hammond to see the cause of the bulkiness, which appeared to be a large silver cigar case.

Zalesie took out the case and flipped open the lid. "I have no weapons, Mr Hammond, I never carry them. I have merely come here to talk, and to apologize for the outrageous and unauthorized behaviour of members of my staff. I had this made for me by a backstreet silversmith in Havana. It is the bane of my tailor's life. Would you care for a cigar?"

Hammond grinned and indicated the seat. Zalesie nodded and sat down. Hammond declined the cigar and offered him a drink.

"Thank you, no. And so, how do we put this unfortunate incident behind us?"

Hammond carefully studied the expression that studied him, before coming to the only possible and rational conclusion.

"You give me your word that you had nothing to do with the attempt on my life? You punish the people responsible, and you promise there will be no further problems of that nature?"

"I have punished the man responsible, and not merely for that."

"Kube?"

Zalesie nodded.

"Yes, Mr Hammond. Martin Kube won't rape any more little girls."

Hammond suddenly realised what must have happened. He asked the question, not sure if the answer would leave him feeling elated or guilty.

"He's dead?"

Zalesie nodded again.

"Catherine, she means that much to you?"

"Yes, she does. As for the rest, you have my word."

"As a Lithuanian Count?"

"No, Mr Hammond. As a gentleman."

Hammond nodded an acceptance.

"Might have been interesting. your total warfare against my guerrilla tactics."

"Let us not talk any more of Clausewitz and warfare. Let us talk of alliance." Zalesie leaned closer. "Stanislav Paslov told you there was a man in the State Department working for Beria. Using simple elimination, we can presumably discount you and me, and poor Alan Carlisle is past such underhandedness. That leaves a great many people, but not too many suspects.

"Beria has thrown his punch and his guard is down. I want you to find his agent in the State Department, and then I want you to give me his name."

Hammond recalled his meetings with Stanislav Paslov and Alan Carlisle.

"Paslov also told me that Beria had another man, in the Manhattan Project. Alan Carlisle believed there were more than one."

"I am aware of that, but let us put our own house in order first. Find Beria's mole in the State Department and I will make life a good deal easier for you."

Hammond bristled.

"I'm not available for bribery. I thought I had made that clear."

"You did. That is precisely why you are the obvious choice. You have ability and integrity, and you're nobody's man. What worthier combination could I or the State Department ask?"

"You once told me that everyone is somebody's man."

"Look upon this as an opportunity to disprove my theory."

"And if I do find him, why would I give him to you? Why wouldn't I just hand him over to the FBI?"

"Because Mr John Edgar Hoover and his FBI people would undoubtedly use whoever this individual is as a stick to beat us with. I will simply deal with the problem."

Hammond could see the logic, but was nonetheless suspicious.

"So just whose side are you on, Mr Zalesie?"

The smile reappeared.

"Why, yours, of course."

"I wish I could be sure of that."

"I am not an American by birth, Mr Hammond, but I believe in capitalism and democracy and the American way. I believe in them as passionately as anyone."

"And what about the rule of law?"

"Sometimes that needs a little help."

39

Hammond had been back in Washington for almost a week when Emma called and suggested he take her to dinner. Since Carlisle's death, Davis Carpenter had stepped into the breach as temporary acting unpaid. Hammond had similarly filled the post vacated by Carpenter. Neither promotion had met with universal approval.

They met at their usual table in the cocktail bar of the Washington Hotel. Emma raised her martini high and congratulated him on one of the fastest promotions in State Department history. Hammond told her it was only acting unpaid. The lack of a formal appointment hadn't bothered Carpenter, though. Since the memo arrived, he had been like a dog with two tails. Hammond was happy for him. Davis Carpenter had waited a long time for promotion. It was a shame about the circumstance, but an ill wind and all that.

Emma seemed more buoyed than Hammond, but said the news had also confused her. She said she could understand Carpenter's promotion, but asked why they had promoted Hammond so quickly, adding that he had only been there five minutes and there had to be some seriously jealous people in the department.

Hammond admitted the atmosphere in the department hadn't been great, but nobody had spoken directly to him. He thought Conrad Zalesie had something to do with it.

She asked about Zalesie. Hammond agreed with Marcus Allum. Zalesie was dangerous. He changed the subject and asked what she had been doing. Her answer surprised him.

"I've hardly been out of the apartment since I saw you last, most unlike me. Perhaps I'm coming down with something, or maybe I've run out of steam. Maybe you've become the interesting one in the marriage. Did you ever think of that?"

"What marriage?"

She looked into his eyes and spoke softly.

"It took me a long time to discover that love isn't about beautiful bodies and perfect smiles and shattering orgasms. It's about comfort and security, and a warm feeling in the pit of your stomach. It's about caring more for the happiness of others than your own. It's about all the gentleness I get from you."

"You want me back?"

She didn't answer, and changed the subject. She mentioned bumping into Morton Simmonds a few days earlier. When Hammond asked if the collision had been pelvis first, she laughed and said he shouldn't be bitter about the past. Morton Simmonds was a decent man and a friend, but not her type. She said Alan Carlisle's death had upset him, and, rumour had it, he was drinking heavily. She said from what she had seen the rumours were right, but added that she had always liked Morton Simmonds and felt saddened by his decline into alcoholism.

When Hammond spoke of Simmonds' reputation for alcohol and women she agreed, but said he had shown a marked degeneration since Alan Carlisle's death. She said, when she saw him, it was only late afternoon and he was already three-parts gone. She had been on her way home. Simmonds had been heading back to the bar. She took him for a coffee instead.

"So why are you telling me this?"

"Because he said he knew why they killed Alan Carlisle. He wouldn't say more. He seemed a bit uncomfortable and told me to forget he'd said anything. Then he scuttled off to the bar."

Hammond was suddenly worried.

"And you make damn sure you do as he said, Emma. You're not to mention he said anything; not to anyone, do you hear me?"

"All right, I know, I'm not stupid. I only told you in confidence."

"Not even in confidence, not to anyone. I mean it. So where is this bar?"

"Remember when we used to go to Sammy's Bar?"

"In Georgetown?"

"Yeah, It's just up from there. They say it's seedy, so I didn't offer to join him. They also say he's there night after night, drinking himself into a stupor. Oh no, Gerald, this is our evening."

"I'll get a cab. I won't be long. I'll see you at the restaurant. I'm sorry. It's important."

"The table's booked for eight-thirty, no later."

"I'll be there, I promise. I can't be late tonight. I've got a report to write for Carpenter; flexing his newly-promoted muscles, I guess. He wants to discuss it in the morning."

"God almighty! Reports? You're not becoming boring again, are you, darling?"

"This isn't boring. It's about the meeting in Frankfurt. He wants to know if we should target Paslov as a defector. . . Idiot! Perhaps I shouldn't be telling you that."

She gave a mischievous grin.

"I wouldn't have thought so. You're just lucky I'm so discreet these days. Mind you, if I do ever meet a tall, dark, handsome Russian, who knows what I might say?"

"Don't even joke about it. I'll be there at eight-thirty."

"You'd better be. I'm not waiting."

"You'll wait."

"Oh will I? And why are you suddenly so sure of yourself?"

He thought back to the dinner at Zalesie's and smiled enigmatically. She didn't realize how much he was in demand these days. She looked quizzically at him, but he didn't elaborate and promised that he'd be back at eight-thirty.

****

"Morton Simmonds, I presume. Mind if I sit?"

When Hammond finally found the bar, Morton Simmonds was already halfway down the label on his first bottle of Tennessee whiskey. A bleary-eyed Simmonds grunted an unintelligible response. He refused the offer of a handshake, and the scowl, rebuffing this clearly-unwelcome intrusion, was similarly less than encouraging.

"Who says I'm Simmonds?"

A Zippo lighter rested alongside a pack of cigarettes on the counter. Hammond pointed to the initials M.S. clearly engraved in orange on the metal casing, alongside another engraving of a drunk leaning against a lamp-post.

"Somebody's got a sense of humour."

"For all you know that could stand for Max Steiner."

"Yeah, but you don't strike me as the musical type. From the look of you, I'd say the chinking of bottle against glass is as musical as you get. Could be Max Schmeling, I suppose, but then I'd have seen your picture on Conrad Zalesie's study wall."

Simmonds stared pointedly at the bar.

"All right, so you know certain people. . . Whad'yer want?"

Hammond studied the emaciated features and bleary-eyed stare with some concern, seeing the drunk personified, and not sure he hadn't wasted the trip. Then he grinned affably and went for the jugular.

"They tell me you're finished, Morton. Too many high-profile affairs, too few success stories, and too much of that." He nodded to the bottle behind the counter. "They also do tell that Jack Daniels lived to be sixty-five. Right now, I can't see you doing the same."

"And just who the hell might you be?"

"My name is Hammond. I work for Marcus Allum at the State Department. I need your help."

"You work for that conniving bastard Allum, and you're looking for help from me? Well, you're an optimist, I'll give you that."

The look of jaded indifference had changed to one of hostility. Hammond sought to reassure. He said his seeking out Simmonds had nothing to do with Allum. If Allum ever discovered that he and Simmonds had spoken, he would probably fire him.

Simmonds carefully studied him, as if trying to assess the truth behind the claim. With study complete, he shrugged his shoulders and drained the glass, then called along the bar for a refill. Finally, he returned his attention to Hammond.

"All right; so I've heard of you, and it's not all bad. What is it you want?"

"I want you to tell me about Alan Carlisle."

Simmonds didn't reply immediately, but reached instead for the pack of cigarettes. He took one and lit it with an ostentatious flick of the lighter's flywheel. A long intake of breath dragged the toxic product deep, before he slowly exhaled, casually tossed both cigarette pack and lighter on to the counter and growled,

"He's dead. What about him?"

"I want you to tell me why he died, and I want you to tell me who killed him?"

"I'm the FBI. You work for The State Department. I should be asking you."

"So why aren't you?"

"Because I've still got some sense; not much, but a little. What's your excuse?"

"I don't like liars. I don't like people trying to kill me, and I don't like people who treat me as a fool."

"You work for Marcus Allum. . . get used to it."

"Who killed Alan Carlisle?"

"I don't know."

"But you do know why he died?"

"Nope, no idea."

Simmonds beckoned the listening barman, seeming to find difficulty in focusing on the approaching figure, before slurring his demand for a refill. Hammond looked closer. He seemed nervous.

"What are you frightened of, Morton?"

"Who says I'm frightened?"

"Jack Daniels for one. Me for another."

"You're placing yourself in exalted company, my friend, but this is not fear you see before you. This is boredom, or maybe it's habit; then again, maybe it's both."

"So who killed Alan Carlisle?" Hammond regarded the answering shrug of bored indifference. "I thought he was a friend of yours. Some friend. I hear you didn't even bother visiting the grieving widow, just sent some men."

Despite the previous façade of indifference, Hammond's criticism stung a response. Simmonds glowered through the drifting smoke and then scoffed at the portrayal of Angela Carlisle as a grieving widow. Yes, he said, Alan Carlisle had been a friend, a good friend, but he had been ordered to stay clear. The newspaper reports on Carlisle's death had been lurid enough, without adding the already discredited factor of Morton Simmonds. He said J. Edgar Hoover had enough problems without creating more.

Simmonds seemed thoughtful. He said, even if he had disobeyed the order, his getting killed wouldn't help Carlisle's widow, grieving or not, and it sure as hell wouldn't bring back Alan Carlisle.

When Hammond suggested Simmonds could help in the arrest and prosecution of the guilty, a drunken smile relieved the anger. The clearly disaffected senior FBI agent began rambling.

Did he say arrest and prosecute? Hammond obviously didn't realize he was talking to the FBI. Simmonds drunkenly repeated the initials and said they didn't stand for Fidelity Bravery and Integrity any more. Nowadays they stood for Fornicators, Boozers, and Incompetents; or was that Incontinents? He muttered something about not remembering, and added that he must have been looking through the bottom of a glass when he'd read it. All he could tell Hammond was that it sure as hell didn't stand for anything to do with investigation and prosecution; not according to the newspapers.

It appeared that Morton Simmonds had issues with the media. He took a swig of whiskey and continued drunkenly reflecting on his unhappy lot in life.

"Did you read what the bastards wrote the other day?" Hammond shook his head and Simmonds rambled on. "When it looked like they fried the wrong man for the Lindberg baby, we said they're new in town, give 'em a chance. When they shot John Dillinger in the back, we said maybe he turned around too fast. We even let it go when they could only nail Capone on tax fraud, instead of multiple homicide, but this has to be an all-time low for the Federal Bureau of Ineptitude."

Simmonds stubbed out his half-smoked cigarette and immediately lit another with the same ostentatious flick of the Zippo's wheel.

"Newspapers, huh, they're like easy women: makes no difference if you lie or tell 'em the truth 'cos they'll screw you either way."

Another strong pull on the whiskey briefly interrupted Simmonds' flow of rambling self-pity.

"What was that other line they wrote? Oh yeah, nearly forgot. They say Morton Simmonds drinks to forget; we say he never knew anything worth remembering."

He suddenly laughed, bitterly and sarcastically. Harsh. perhaps, but he kinda liked that one. How about, 'We haven't seen the Fed's hoovering this amount of booze since Elliot Ness hit Chicago'. He hadn't liked that one, apparently, but he had enjoyed the play on names between William Henry and J. Edgar.

Simmonds took yet another strong pull on the whiskey, and then stared vacantly at the wall for a further moment's contemplation before asking,

"What's the matter? Didn't you like the joke? Didn't you get the hoovering bit? William Henry, vacuum cleaner tycoon; J. Edgar, Head of the FBI? Thought that was neat myself."

"Yeah, I got it."

"Maybe you just don't read the papers. They don't think we're any good at what we do. Bootleggers and bank robbers, that's all we're good for. According to *The Post*, we ain't any great shakes at that."

Hammond had suffered enough of the drunken ramblings and paranoia.

"Good at feeling sorry for yourself, though."

Simmonds shook his head.

"I don't feel sorry, well, not for myself. I feel sorry for Alan, because he meant well and he wanted to do something right for once. And I feel sorry for you. And I feel sorry for all those other poor bastards out there, who think they can make any difference. You wanna drink?"

Hammond thought of walking away and leaving Simmonds to wallow in his own self-pity. A sixth sense told him to persevere.

"Yeah, I'll take a beer."

Simmonds nodded to the far side of the drab and deserted bar.

"Let's grab a booth before this place starts seriously buzzing. Hey, Charlie! Give this man a beer, and give me the rest of that bottle."

The bartender looked warily back as he passed Hammond his beer.

"You know I can't do that, Mr Simmonds."

Simmonds glared at him.

"What's the matter, Charlie? Ddon't you want your license renewed any more? Now give me the fucking bottle."

The barman stood for a moment, weighing up the pros and cons of refusal, before grudgingly handing over what remained of the bottle.

"Here, take it, for Christ's sake. And the name's not Charlie."

"Course it is; every bartender's called Charlie. It's the law."

Simmonds sat blankly gazing at the counter for some moments, then picked up his cigarette pack and lighter and pocketed them. After that he took the bottle and lighted cigarette in one hand, and his glass in the other, before extravagantly weaving his way to the far side of the bar. He slumped into a booth, signalled Hammond to sit and then said in a loud voice,

"Sit down, Hammond. Drink your beer. We'll talk about my old friend Jack Daniels, and toasted Luckies, and good-looking women with firm tits and tight asses, and great baseball players of our time. Now those are subjects I do know something about."

Hammond shook his head and said he wanted to talk about Manhattan. Simmonds grinned affably and slurred what he obviously imagined to be an amusing answer.

"Two parts Jack to one of vermouth would be my preference, then add some bitters. Just a splash, mind you. That's always been the difference between a great Manhattan and a bad one."

"I'm serious."

"I'd have to say you do look kinda serious."

He peered drunkenly across the floor to where the barman sat engrossed in a newspaper, and then refocused his attention on Hammond. With his voice low, and his diction precise, a suddenly sober Morton Simmonds explained the transformation.

"But you have to pick the right time to talk about it, and you have to pick the right place to talk about it. Announcing the fact in front of one of the most garrulous bartenders in the history of drunken gossip and Washington grapevines fails on both counts."

Hammond looked at Simmonds in unconcealed amazement.

"They told me you were a drunk and a womanizer. You play the part well."

"And they were right. I love women and I love booze. I ain't taken a break from either for twenty years, but half a bottle of Jack ain't gonna suddenly turn me into W.C. Fields."

"Emma said she saw you the other afternoon. She said you were three parts gone?"

"Yeah, I remember. I'd had a bad morning."

"So why all this?"

"Why am I a drinking man and a womanizer, you mean? Because I happen to enjoy it. Why do I play the drunken asshole in public? Because people don't feel threatened by drunken assholes. They feel superior, and when people feel superior, they feel safe."

"It doesn't worry you that people don't take you seriously?"

"Why should they? Why should I want them to? It's not as if I'm doing a serious job."

There had been no hint of self-pity. Hammond asked why searching for communists in the White House wasn't a serious job. Simmonds laughed.

"Why don't you sit back and relax? Drink your beer, and let me tell you a story."

"What do you mean, story?"

"A story, the interesting kind, you know how they begin. Well, once upon a time. . ."

40

Hammond sat quietly listening as Morton Simmonds settled into his story. Simmonds said in the fall of nineteen forty-five J. Edgar Hoover sent him to interview a female courier for a Soviet spy-ring. Elizabeth Bentley was the Soviet courier, and what she told Morton Simmonds that day would reverberate around the corridors of power for years to come. Bentley gave him details of her cell, but then took even the experienced Simmonds by surprise. She offered to list another cell of Soviet agents, agitators and sympathizers. The list proved exhaustive.

More alarming was that among the list were names belonging to people employed by the U.S. government. Even more alarming still, was that many of them worked in sensitive areas.

Simmonds took the list to his boss and suggested they begin a full-scale surveillance on the people named. Hoover agreed, but then a further revelation: among the names were ex-members of the disbanded OSS, and being OSS made them William Donovan's people.

Simmonds waited expectantly. Hammond answered the unasked question.

"And it's common knowledge that 'Wild Bill' Donovan and J. Edgar Hoover don't get on."

"That's putting it mildly. Hoover hates Donovan with a passion. Worse still, they're in the middle of a power struggle to run Central Intelligence."

"Yeah, I heard that as well."

"So what does that prick Hoover do next? Well J. Edgar being J. Edgar, he figures this is gold dust. He figures that with this information he'll be able to bury 'Wild Bill' Donovan in Russian fertilizer, right up to the two little stars on his epaulettes. He figures that if he takes this to the President straight away, the President's gonna pat him on the back and slap Donovan around until his head spins. He also figures that Truman will then have no choice but to pass the whole foreign intelligence kit-and-caboodle over to good old dependable master-spy-catcher J. Edgar Hoover."

"But Truman didn't see it that way?"

"No, but he might have done if we'd had any evidence, which of course we didn't, and still don't. All we had then, and all we've got now, is a flaky confession and a list of high-profile names from a not-so-reliable Sov courier. A woman who's now even less reliable 'cos, thanks to Hoover's way with women, she's scared of her own shadow."

"So Hoover dropped you in it?"

"Way beyond the epaulettes. As a direct result of him using our only edge to play power politics, we're trying to trap a bunch of suspects who know we're coming for them."

"So they circle the wagons?"

"I like the metaphor, but they do more than that. They start fighting back; laying down a serious barrage of media and political flak. Well, them and a certain group of power-brokers in New York City, who shall remain nameless."

Hammond, puzzled, interrupted.

"If we're talking about the same people, up in New York, they want these infiltrators flushed out as much as you. I mean, these people are more anti-communist than Hoover."

"True, but they hate Hoover almost as bad as they hate commies, and anyway, what happens if we get all those commie infiltrators arrested and convicted? What happens once we've sat them down and strapped them in, taken their pictures for FBI posterity and the *Washington Post* archives, and then flipped the switch?"

"The problem goes away."

Morton Simmonds shook his head and smiled grimly.

"Not true. The problem doesn't go away. The threat goes away, and the threat is what keeps our New York friends in business. Public apathy is their problem, and fear is their weapon. These people know that as long as the public's scared shitless of communist infiltrators, they're not gonna be asking questions about the methods people are using to combat the problem. They want ordinary people out there searching under their beds every night. They want them scared to death and screaming for a rope. We take out the White House infiltrators, all in one go, and some of that fear goes away."

To Hammond this all seemed too far-fetched.

"So why aren't you fighting back? Why are you happy playing the drunken fool?"

"Ever hear the story of two explorers in the jungle who come face-to-face with a man-eating lion? The first explorer drops his pack and starts putting on his sneakers, so the other explorer looks at him and says 'Don't be stupid, you can't outrun a lion'. . . Remember what the first explorer says?"

Hammond grinned and finished the story.

"He said I don't have to. All I have to do is outrun you."

"That's right. Let 'em bring down someone else. I'm no threat, and I run like hell."

"So these White House communists, these infiltrators, they get away clear?"

"Long-term, probably not. Our New York friends will smoke them out, when it suits them. But it'll only happen over months, maybe years. And every time they nail another commie bastard the press will have a field day, and another million ordinary Americans will grab their lighted torches and join the lynch mob."

"So how does this all tie in with the Manhattan Project?"

"Let's get you another beer. Hey, Charlie, get my friend here another beer."

Simmonds had restored the drunken façade. Hammond turned to see the barman watching.

The barman put down his paper and delivered the beer. As he turned to go, Simmonds looked up at him in bleary-eyed inebriation.

"There you go. Now what did you say your name was again?"

The barman looked to the heavens.

"Charlie."

Simmonds grinned drunkenly across at Hammond.

"See, told yer; they're all called Charlie."

The barman shook his head and returned to his newspaper. Hammond asked about Manhattan. He knew Simmonds had helped Carlisle dig into it.

Simmonds nodded. Yes, and he wished he hadn't, because that was why they killed Alan Carlisle. He drained the glass and poured another. He said Alan Carlisle had been a great orator, because he believed in what he was doing and what he was saying. As a result, several high-profile people in Washington had begun taking him seriously.

Hammond was suddenly confused. Why was that a problem?

The FBI man didn't answer. Instead he related a story. He said for people like Chambers and Zalesie, it had been one of the most damaging tales of the Second World War. It had been during Barbarossa, Hitler's invasion of Russia, when Russian officers forced thousands of Russian soldiers to charge German machine-guns with only a few rifles between them. Whenever the Germans shot a rifle carrier, the next man picked up the rifle and used it. When they shot him, somebody else did the same, and so on, until they either overran the machine-gun nest or ran out of men. The Russians lost thousands of men doing that, for next to no territorial gain.

Hammond remembered reading about it, but why was that so damaging?

"Because any army with only half-a-dozen rifles between every thousand troops hardly represents a threat to the U.S. military. Establishing the threat is what all of this is about."

"So you're saying the Russians aren't seen as a serious threat?"

"Not with the current public opinion and post-war euphoria. Not since the Bolsheviks flooded into Berlin. A bunch of ignorant peasants, the papers said; a disorganized rabble of pillagers and rapists, with holes in their boots and patches in their pants. We could see them off with one airborne division. That's how the average American voter sees the so-called Red Army menace today, because at the time it suited certain people to portray them that way."

Hammond still didn't understand. Simmonds took another drink and leaned closer. He said, politically speaking, the war in Europe hadn't been like the war in the Pacific, which most Americans had seen as a legitimate retaliation for Pearl Harbour. In Europe, America had lost over three hundred thousand men fighting a war that many Americans didn't support. The U.S. administration needed something to show for the sacrifices made. They needed to stop the spread of communism into Western Europe, and show the public they hadn't lost all those lives just to replace one lunatic dictator with another. They needed to take a chunk of Berlin and block Stalin's advance, but didn't want it to seem as though they were risking another war.

Hammond nodded his understanding.

"So we portrayed the Russians as little or no threat to us doing that. Does that matter?"

"Of course it matters."

"Why?"

"Well, how about this for a speech? 'It is essential to our interests, the Soviet Union remains strong. We can only defeat the evils of communism if the public continues to view it as a threat to our lives and our liberty. If it is only ever seen as a distinct and separate philosophy, babbling Marxist gibberish and managed by bellicose impotence, it might well confound us and flourish.' Do you know who said that?"

Hammond shook his head. Simmonds answered his own question.

"I was there at the time. I remembered it word for word. I even wrote it down. It was Conrad Zalesie, speaking at a treasury dinner in nineteen forty-three, when some ragtag bunch of republican senators suggested prematurely pulling lend-lease aid to the Sovs."

Hammond was feeling distinctly dull-witted. Simmonds explained further.

"Don't you see? Zalesie wants Stalin and the Bolsheviks to remain a threat, because that's the only way he can eventually destroy them. Thanks to Hiroshima and Nagasaki, right now the average American feels like his homeland and the American way are all but fireproof. Add in our recently claimed successes in blocking Sov expansionism in Europe, and suddenly Stalin isn't a serious threat any more."

Hammond's eyes widened. Now he understood.

"But a hostile Stalin with an atomic bomb will be a serious threat. Suddenly America's in real danger. Suddenly it's game on again. That's it. They're letting Beria steal the atom bomb, because that's guaranteed to increase the communist threat in the eyes of the American public."

"Way beyond paranoia. The Sovs think it's Christmas. I'm told they send anything coming into the Sov embassy marked 'Enormoz' directly to Beria. No deviation, no delay, on pain of death. Everybody knows, but nobody does anything about it."

"The Soviet project to steal the bomb: it's code-named Enormoz?"

Hammond couldn't believe what he was hearing. Simmonds seemed to have come alive.

"I hear certain people who meet in a certain limestone-fronted building in New York City have known about it for months. But I wouldn't want to try proving that."

Hammond spotted the obvious flaw. If Simmonds' theory was right, wasn't the risk too great? What would happen if it got to confrontation? What would happen if it got to dropping atom bombs on each other? Surely the risk of nuclear war would be unacceptable.

Simmonds said as long as America stayed ahead in the race and the Soviets were trying to catch up, the risk was acceptable. The Soviets didn't have the financial muscle to keep pace with America, and with their economic capacity being hamstrung by the same political philosophy America wanted to destroy, they never would. That was the theory and that was the paradox.

"Some paradox. . . You mean, we hope they don't?"

"Right. And guess who America's gonna turn to, to make sure everything stays that way?"

"Conrad Zalesie."

"He's the man with his finger on the button, and I use that term advisedly."

"But it's still a hell of a risk."

"No more of a risk than a certain jumped-up little Austrian corporal and the German Nazi Party were willing to take not so long ago."

"What German Nazi Party? Conrad Zalesie's a Lithuanian."

"You bought into that Lithuanian count horse-shit?"

"No, not at first, but I had a man check into it. Conrad Zalesie's genuine."

Simmonds asked who did the checking. Hammond talked of the colourful Dawid Gabriel. Gabriel was straight. Hammond said he'd bet on it. When a clearly sceptical Simmonds asked how he came to use Gabriel, Hammond suddenly remembered. . . Marcus Allum had recommended him.

Simmonds nodded. He said the FBI had tried to look into Zalesie, but every time they got to the interesting sections the shutters came down. He asked how a burnt-out ex-cop managed to get to places the FBI couldn't. To a red-faced Gerald Hammond, the question was painfully rhetorical.

He asked if Simmonds thought that Conrad Zalesie had killed Alan Carlisle. Morton Simmonds shook his head.

He said three days before Alan Carlisle's death a new cultural attaché arrived at the Soviet Embassy in New York. His passport claimed he was Sasha Gromyko from Chelyabinsk, but Simmonds knew him from way back, when the only thing cultured about him was the fungus on his feet. In reality, Sasha Gromyko was an old adversary of the FBI called Vladimir Demidov. In his time Demidov had been both infantry sniper and bodyguard to Lavrenti Beria. Nowadays he was the finest assassin in the MGB. At four a.m. on the morning they discovered Alan Carlisle's body, Vladimir Demidov flew back to Moscow on an Aeroflot charter.

"If you knew all about him, why didn't you refuse entry?"

"Oh we did, but someone overruled us. The word came down to let him in."

"But a sniper didn't kill Alan Carlisle."

"Don't let the sniper handle fool you. Demidov's a true artist. You wouldn't pay good money to hear him recite Shakespeare, but if you want a body to die just right and look just right, he's the best there is. You should know about him. I'll let you have a copy of his sheet. You never know when paths might cross."

"Thanks. So you think it was Beria?"

"Had to be. That's not to say there weren't others waiting in line. Alan constantly screaming about Manhattan spies was getting everyone edgy. Beria just got to him first."

Hammond had one last question. What happened to the evidence that Carlisle had gathered?

Simmonds said he had no idea, but guaranteed if Hammond went through Carlisle's office and effects, he wouldn't find a shred of it. He said someone would already have destroyed it and suggested Beria's man in the State Department as the obvious suspect.

"How the hell did you know about that?"

"Most of the time we're good at what we do. Don't believe everything you read in the newspapers."

When Hammond suggested starting the investigation again, Simmonds shook his head.

"This ain't Hollywood, my friend. The good guys don't always win, and the bad guys don't always die. It took Alan over a year to gather enough evidence to make him a threat, and he knew people. You're the new kid on the block. How are you going to do the same? Even if you did somehow manage it, in months rather than years, you'd already be too late. Beria already has most of what he and Kurchatov need. It's only a matter of time before the first test."

"How long?"

"My guess would be a couple of years. . . three, tops."

"So what do we do now?"

"Well, now it's dick-measuring time. Now we make damn sure our atom bomb's a hell of a lot bigger than their atom bomb."

41

"Mr Hammond, is it? Mr Gerald Hammond?"

It was on a familiar Washington sidewalk. Hammond had been on his way home when the voice disturbed his concentration.

"Yes? What can I do for you?"

"My name is Schulman, Mr Hammond, Alfred Schulman. I work with a man called Wiesenthal in Linz, Simon Wiesenthal. Perhaps you have heard of him?"

"Of course I've heard of him. What can I do for you, Mr Schulman?"

They stepped back from the busy sidewalk and into a doorway.

"I was talking to your Mr Carpenter, but nowadays he has become such an important man. I don't think he has the time to spend on me any more."

Hammond studied the grey unshaven features beneath the spotless black homburg, and then took in the shabby raincoat and ill-fitting corduroy slacks slumping over scuffed shoes. He suddenly felt guilty and smiled kindly into the whiskered features.

"Well, I've got a few minutes to spare. Fancy a coffee?"

"Yes, that would be fine."

They wandered farther along the street to a coffee shop, found a table in the corner and sat down. Hammond ordered the coffees.

"Can I get you anything else?' he asked. "A sandwich or something?"

The old man shook his head and smiled.

"No, thank you, Mr Hammond." He waited until the waitress had hurried away to fetch the coffee. "I am not a pauper, Mr Hammond; not especially wealthy, I admit, but not in need of your charity either. I happen to dress this way because I have discovered there are more important things in life than personal appearance."

The waitress returned with two coffees. Hammond grinned his embarrassment.

"I apologize, Mr Schulman. I didn't mean to patronize or insult you, or suggest that you're in any way. . . Sorry, I'm getting myself in deeper here. So, what can I do for you?"

The old man took a sip of his coffee. His mood was suddenly more serious.

"Mr Carpenter told me that Heinrich Müeller now works for a man called Beria. It was good of him to save me so much time and trouble, but he didn't talk about all the others."

"The others?"

"Yes, Mr Hammond. . . People like Martin Borman, Josef Mengele, Adolf Eichmann, Alois Brunner, Martin Kube, Klaus Barbie, Josef Conrad Schmidt and Josef Schwammberger. There are so many others, it is difficult to know where to begin. I think your Mr Carpenter knows a good many of these people, Mr Hammond, as do you. Or do you not?"

Hammond looked straight into the blue-grey eyes and lied without flinching.

"No, Mr Schulman, I don't. I've heard of them, of course, but I have no special knowledge of them, or their whereabouts. You think they're hiding in America?"

Hammond had surprised himself with how easily the lie had come to him, and how convincingly he had delivered it. His question clearly amused the elderly Jew.

"Good heavens no, Mr Hammond. I would have to believe that they are in hiding all over the world. I also believe that your Mr Carpenter tricked me the last time I spoke to him."

"He tricked you?"

"Yes. Because I only mentioned the name of Heinrich Müeller he cleverly only talked about Heinrich Müeller, and not about the others your government undoubtedly shelters and protects. I rather think he outfoxed me. He is a clever man, your Mr Carpenter."

Hammond could only agree.

"Yes, I'm beginning to think so, too. When did Davis Carpenter tell you about all of this?"

"It was months ago, but he has not spoken to me since, and so I decided to talk to you."

"I see, and how did you get my name?"

The blue-grey eyes twinkled.

"From an old friend of mine, and yours, too, I understand. . . Stanislav Paslov."

"You know Paslov?"

"We were in Mauthausen together. We became good friends. Adversity sometimes forges the strangest of alliances, between the most unlikely of people. Do you not agree?"

"Yes, I suppose so. So, why didn't Paslov tell you about Heinrich Müeller's whereabouts?"

"Because at that time he did not know about Müeller, or I do not believe he knew about him. You see, Mr Hammond, I do not believe that Stanislav Paslov would lie to me, at least not knowingly, but I rather think his Comrade Beria is as tricky as your Mr Carpenter."

Hammond smiled.

"Oh, I would say at least, Mr Schulman." A thought suddenly occurred as Hammond recalled the list of Nazi fugitives. "You mentioned Josef Conrad Schmidt among the list of people you're searching for. I understood that he died in forty-two?"

"Not according to Stanislav Paslov. He did some more checking, and now believes Schmidt is alive. He asked me to tell you. He also told me that you rescued Schmidt's young daughter."

Hammond sat open-mouthed, his mind racing.

"Yes I did, but is Paslov sure? I mean about Schmidt being alive?"

"I believe so, yes, but none of us can be certain of anything these days." The old man carefully studied Hammond's features "Mr Hammond, it is clear to me that you are either an exceptional liar or you know nothing of any of this, unlike your friend Mr Carpenter. Either way, I can see that I am wasting my time in questioning you, and so I will thank you for your time and the coffee, and apologize for having inconvenienced you."

The old man finished his coffee and gingerly climbed to his feet. Hammond viewed the relative frailty with concern.

"It was no problem, I assure you, and it was good to meet you, Mr Schulman. I'm sorry I couldn't help you in your search, but you must take care of yourself." The look of puzzlement demanded explanation. Hammond continued to lie. "I don't personally know these people, Mr Schulman, but I do know them by reputation. These are dangerous men, and many of them face the death penalty if caught. They have nothing to lose in killing you, or anybody else who tries to expose them or hand them over to the authorities. You must be careful."

Puzzlement suddenly broke into a smile.

"Oh, I see. You think me too old and weak for the fight." The old man massaged his knee. "It is nothing of importance, Mr Hammond, only weary bones, and in this battle I have God on my side and the odds in my favour." It was Hammond's turn to look puzzled. The old man saw and nodded. "Odds, yes, I believe that is what you call it."

"I'm sorry. . . odds?"

"Yes, Mr Hammond. Six million to one. I believe these are exceptional odds."

The old man chuckled at the blackness of his own humour as he shuffled out of the coffee shop, leaving Hammond to consider a wealth of possibilities, and two in particular.

42

As a man of breeding and refinement, Davis Alan Carpenter enjoyed many acquired tastes. Among other things, he was known to be a connoisseur of the delicate flavours and therapeutic properties to be found in Oolong tea. Carpenter could identify the age, region, cultivar and approximate degree of fermentation of the revered Chinese and Taiwanese leaf in a single tasting, and would comment on depth, complexity, balance, finish and finesse, much as if he were sampling a majestic Burgundy or first-growth Bordeaux.

After years spent hunting through a city better known for its wide variety of coffee shops, Davis Carpenter had finally found a tea room where he could not only try and buy his favourite tea, but also have it prepared to his precise specification. He had demanded, and the proprietor agreed, that the brew presented would be no less than the third and no more than the fourth steeping, be precisely controlled in terms of brew temperature and quantities of leaf to water, and served in a spotlessly clean two-ounce tasting cup.

Where Oolong tea was concerned, as with so much in Davis Carpenter's ordered life, when not travelling, he adhered to a strict routine. Each Saturday morning, at eight-thirty precisely, he would begin the journey from Woodley Park to the Silver Samovar tea-rooms on an otherwise largely-residential section of 13th Street. Upon arrival, he would sit at an especially-reserved table in the front window before ordering up his regular weekly tipple.

When an inquisitive waitress had once asked why he always reserved that particular table, he haughtily explained that Oolong's beauty lay not only in the nuance of each brew's delicate aroma and flavour, but also in its colour and clarity. The appreciation of such a thing of beauty demanded controlled storage, strict adherence to the agreed brewing process, and the natural light of day.

With tasting complete, and assuming that week's offering had met with his approval, the purchase of a precious four ounces of the black-dragon leaf would then be made.

But there was more to Carpenter's weekly pilgrimage to the Silver Samovar than met the casual eye, and more to its proprietor than a simple man looking to eke a living by educating Washington's coffee-drinking philistines in the ways of the cultured leaf.

Victor Sokolov was a White Russian émigré who had fled to the United States with his parents following the Bolshevik revolution. After spells in New York and Philadelphia, the Sokolov family had finally settled in Ivy City, one of the poorer parts of Washington D.C., where they kept themselves to themselves and scratched a modest living. His father taught cello, part time, to the precocious children of Washington's wealthy. His mother worked evenings as a dishwasher in a local restaurant.

When his elderly parents died within six months of each other, Viktor Sokolov moved out of the family's rented apartment, and bought both the tea shop on 13th and the apartment above. Both properties were paid for with proceeds from the sale of three pieces of original Gustav Fabergé jewellery, which his mother had kept hidden through all those years of struggle and deprivation.

Why she hadn't sold the pieces during all those years of hardship, nobody knew, but that didn't stop the rumours from growing and spreading. Some suggested she had stolen them from the late Tsarina Alexandra some months before the Bolsheviks took over and the Sokolovs fled Russia. Others claimed the Sokolovs had themselves been Russian aristocracy, hiding away from Bolshevik vengeance in underprivileged Ivy City.

But, with the notable exceptions of Davis Carpenter and a section of the staff at the Soviet Embassy on 16th Street, nobody knew the truth, and if they had they probably wouldn't have believed it, because Viktor Sokolov was in fact a deep-cover Soviet agent.

While his premises had indeed been paid for with items of Fabergė, claimed as family heirlooms, the pieces in question, and their forged bills of sale, had actually been shipped to the Embassy on 16th Street via diplomatic pouch. From there they had been passed to Sokolov, who had 'washed' them through a specialist auction house, with the successful bidder being a member of staff from that exact same building on 16th Street.

Apart from their initial meeting, when Carpenter had specified his precise requirements for the tea, Sokolov rarely spoke to Carpenter and Carpenter rarely acknowledged Sokolov. That morning, however, Viktor Sokolov personally dealt with the purchase, and that had worried Davis Carpenter.

Back in Woodley Park, Clara Carpenter hadn't greeted him when he returned from his Saturday morning pilgrimage. As he hurried to the kitchen, to check his purchase, he saw her sitting and reading in the lounge. When he walked in she looked up.

"What is it? No, don't tell me: they short-changed you by half-an-ounce of tea?"

Ashen-faced, Davis Carpenter shook his head and held a finger to his lips as he passed her the scrap of paper, retrieved from inside his bag of tea. Scrawled across the paper, the words *'They are watching you'* brought a look of alarm to disrupt the more usual contempt.

"No, darling; it's just that I gave him a hundred. He only gave me change for fifty."

The message to his wife was clear. Someone, somewhere, was listening to every word of their conversation. Clara got to her feet, pointed to the telephone handset and whispered,

"They fixed a fault on the line yesterday."

Carpenter's heart was racing, but he kept his self-control.

"I'll have to have a word with him," he said, "but let's not spoil the day. When all's said and done, it's only money. Look, it's lovely out. Why don't you get your hat and coat and we'll take a stroll over to Lamont. I have a book to return and we could both do with the fresh air."

While his wife hurried away to change into a pair of flat shoes, Carpenter ran through the instructions. Whenever a situation became critical, or too dangerous for the use of possibly-compromised dead-letterboxes, he would be contacted through the tea shop.

When contacted in this way, he and Clara were to immediately visit the public library on Lamont Street. Once there, they should separate. She was to peruse the drama section, on the ground floor by the stairs, and, if she saw anyone she knew, intercept and engage them in small talk for as long as possible. He was to make his way upstairs, to biographies, and look at the shelves from P to R, until a librarian appeared with the second volume of Hendrick's account of *The Life and Letters of Walter H. Page*.

He would find his instructions slipped into section sixteen. To the great amusement of his contact at the Soviet embassy, section sixteen was entitled 'Dark Days For The Allies'. To that same official's increased amusement, it began with a letter sent by Page to the founder of the Council on Foreign Relations: 'Colonel' Edward Mandel House.

Following a twenty-minute stroll, laden with tension but devoid of incident, they arrived at the library. She made her way to the busy drama shelves. He returned his unread copy of *Strange Interlude*, and then headed upstairs to the all but deserted section on biographies.

Only one other person stood studying the biographies and seemed glued to section P to R. He was a short man, in his late thirties, wearing a lightweight tweed jacket and carrying a brown trilby hat that he constantly fed through his fingers as he browsed. When the man finally wearied of section P to R and moved across the walkway to an adjacent section, Carpenter breathed a sigh of relief and took his place.

He scanned the shelves, looking for the space where Page's life and letters would soon be returned, then gave an involuntary start. It was already there.

He suspiciously eyed the stranger before picking up the book and thumbing through.

There was no section sixteen, with its 'Dark Days for the Allies' and letter to Edward M. House. Davis Carpenter began to panic.

From across the walkway, the man with the trilby hat had obviously seen Carpenter's feverish search and look of concern. He smirked, and nodded to the book as he called across.

"That is Volume One. I think you will find Volume Two more interesting." When Carpenter realised his mistake, the man wandered back. "You were followed."

"Who by?"

The smile was back as he mischievously corrected Carpenter's grammar. In direct contrast to Carpenter's panic-stricken state, he seemed to be enjoying himself.

"By whom. . . By your old friend Gerald Hammond. No, do not look, you will not see him, and do not worry. If we remain here, people in other areas of the library cannot see us, and if we keep our voices low they cannot hear us. We chose this location with great care.

"As for your friend Hammond. . . I need to know if he is working alone, and on his own initiative, or as part of a team. You are going to have to find out, my friend."

"How do I do that?"

"I think perhaps you should invite him for tea."

"I'm sorry?"

"Tea, at the café on 13th Street, tomorrow morning. It is all in the instructions. If he is working alone, tell Sokolov that you do not like your tea, and want to try a different brew. Oh, and make sure you sit at your usual table."

Carpenter's mind was a jumble of concern.

"They only keep that table for me on Saturday mornings. What if it's not free?"

"It will be."

"What if he is? Working alone, I mean?"

"That will be unfortunate for him."

"And if he is working with the FBI, or with other people?"

"I am told that Leningrad is very beautiful at this time of year."

Carpenter's jaw dropped. He had been about to babble a string of questions when a librarian appeared, a tall, thin, and austere-looking man, wearing horn-rimmed glasses. He was pushing a trolley filled with books. The missing Volume Two was perched on top of the pile. Carpenter assumed the librarian was working for the Soviets, but said nothing and stepped aside when he arrived.

The librarian replaced the volume and moved on without comment. The man with the trilby had taken the opportunity to disappear. Carpenter nervously scanned his surroundings, then snatched up the book and thumbed through until he found section sixteen.

There it was, a single leaf of lined notepaper, pressed between the pages. He slipped the unread instructions into his pocket, replaced the book and hurried downstairs to find Clara.

****

Hammond received the call late that evening. Carpenter used a public telephone. He kept the conversation brief. He needed to talk privately to Hammond, and would be at the Silver Samovar tea rooms on 13th Street at 9.00 the next morning. Hammond should come alone. It concerned Carlisle's death. It was important that Hammond spoke to no one else.

Hammond tried a question, but the line went dead. He hung up the phone and then sat quietly assessing Carpenter's words.

Until the phone call, he had been certain that Carpenter was Beria's mole. He had been on the verge of telling Zalesie, but hesitated because of a tiny nagging doubt at the back of his mind. It was the thought that he could be mistaken, the worry that he had come to the wrong conclusion, or been misled in some way. This latest development only increased that uncertainty. It didn't make sense, or did it?

Had he been duped all along, just as he had been duped by Gabriel and Allum, and so many others? Was Carpenter the mole, or had Hammond been guided to that conclusion by the real mole? Was all this just another Lavrenti Beria conjuring trick?

Carpenter claimed to have information on the death of Carlisle. Maybe he also had information on the Los Alamos spies. Maybe he had discovered something about the real mole. Maybe Carpenter was innocent. Maybe he had somehow been set up. Or maybe he was as guilty as sin, and just wanted to trade.

Who was the man Carpenter had spoken to in the biographies section that morning? What had they talked about? Hammond had been following Carpenter for three days. He wanted to be certain before handing him over to Zalesie, but he'd seen nothing to implicate his State Department boss, other than that one brief and possibly chance meeting in a public library. Hammond hadn't followed the man from the library that morning. He had stayed with Carpenter, believing that to be the best course of action. Now he was beginning to question the wisdom of that decision.

He switched off the light in the lounge, moved over to the window and looked down on the street below. It was almost midnight, but the street was still busy. That was good.

He didn't bother to scan for watchers. If they were good enough to follow him to his apartment without him seeing them, they were good enough not to be seen now. Hammond knew surveillance techniques better than most. The real pros never gave themselves away.

Hammond could spot an old friend avoiding him from three hundred yards. He could scan a sea of faces for an assassin's mask, and be sure to find it. He could pick out a plain-clothes cop on surveillance duty among a throng of people on the busiest thoroughfare. However, if he was the subject of a major Soviet surveillance operation, there could be as many as twenty or thirty people watching him, maybe more, and they would possess a far higher level of expertise than the average plain-clothes cop or cold-eyed assassin.

He had no choice. He had to assume that Carpenter was the mole, and they were out there watching him, waiting for him to make a move. He had to assume they had wired his apartment for sound, just as he had wired Carpenter's. There would be no physical evidence; there never was. . . No tell-tale pieces of wire left carelessly strewn, no unusual click on the line when he made a phone call, no strange interference on the radio, no sinister stranger lurking in the shadows opposite his apartment.

A voice in his head told him to call Zalesie, and then leave him and his dark-suited vigilantes to their grisly task, but he couldn't do that. He had to know what Carpenter wanted to say. This wasn't an official enquiry which would eventually lead to arrest and trial. He had to be certain the man was guilty of betraying his country before making the call that would undoubtedly end Davis Carpenter's life.

As Hammond considered his predicament, he remembered the words of a former Naval Intelligence officer he had met during OSS training. They had never rung truer than now.

The hard-bitten lieutenant-commander had likened espionage to a game, played by a group of short-sighted assassins in a huge darkened room full of secrets, with each man groping in the darkness with the fingertips of one hand, and carrying a knife in the other. The trick was to keep moving and searching, quickly and quietly and cautiously, or you would give away your position to the other assassins. Whenever you found a secret, you slipped it into your pocket and moved on. Whenever you found another assassin, you killed, quickly and silently, and similarly moved on. Any hesitation or undue noise could, and more than likely would, prove fatal.

Hammond knew he had already waited too long. But then he considered the instructor's words again, and a thought suddenly struck.

He picked up the phone and called for a cab, then headed downstairs to wait. The cab arrived within minutes. The driver was middle-aged and unshaven. He looked bored. Hammond gave him the address of the tea shop on 13th Street, and then sat back, idly watching the passing streets and late-night revellers as the cab sped across town.

When they arrived at The Silver Samovar he told the driver to wait, then got out and walked over to the shop. He peered into the darkened café, but could see nothing more than a dozen or so tables with chairs stacked on top.

His gaze left the café and wandered along the tree-lined street, with his mind alert and his peripheral vision working overtime. If he was right about Carpenter, they would be watching his every move. He couldn't allow them to realize what he was actually looking for.

It was then that he saw it; to his left, through a gap in the trees. It was a sign in an upstairs window, an advertisement in more ways than one. It could be the answer. It had to be the answer. If it was, it confirmed everything. If not, he could be in a world of trouble. Either way, he'd find out later that morning.

He climbed back into the cab and told the driver to take him to the nearest phone booth, then back to his apartment. The driver stopped on Vermont. Hammond made his call. When they got back to his apartment, he gave the driver a twenty and told him to keep the change. Then he held out a hundred.

"You wanna earn this?"

The driver rubbed a whiskered chin. His eyes widened. He suddenly didn't look bored.

"Sure. . . How?"

"Nothing difficult. Just pick me up here at eight-thirty tomorrow morning, and take me back to the same place."

"And that's it?"

"That's it. . . Just one slight difference, but nothing that should worry you."

"What difference?

"I'll tell you when you get here: tomorrow morning, eight-thirty."

The driver glanced at his watch.

"You mean, this morning at eight-thirty."

"That's right."

The driver shrugged and nodded. Hammond tore the bill into two pieces. He gave the driver one, and held up the other.

"You get this in eight hours. Don't be late."

The driver mumbled something about always being on time, and then drove off. Hammond climbed the stairs to his apartment. Once inside, he locked and bolted the door, drew the curtains, and then went looking for a street map.

43

The cab driver returned five minutes before the agreed time. He sat waiting. Hammond, dark-suited and smartly-dressed, came down at 8.30 precisely. He slid into the rear seat and gave the driver his instructions.

"Head for the café on Thirteenth, but when you get to Logan Circle I want you to take the turning before Thirteenth; that's north on Vermont. Once you've turned into Vermont put your foot down. Take a left on T and a right on Twelfth. Once you've turned into Twelfth, find some parked cars and pull up, but only long enough for me to jump out. Then you get lost in a hurry, and go spend your money."

"Somebody's gonna be following us, right?"

"That's right."

"What about the lights on the Eleventh crossway? That's a bad turning."

"Until you get to the circle there's no problem, take your time, but after that you run every light. If they're red, so much the better. It's Sunday morning; the streets are quiet. Anyway, that's why you're getting the hundred."

"What if whoever's following you comes after me?"

"They won't."

"You're sure of that?"

"Yeah, I'm sure. When they get close enough to see the cab's empty, they'll double back and try to find me. You probably won't notice them anyway."

Whatever the cab driver might have thought on that particular Sunday-morning drive over to Logan Circle, he didn't seem bored. For all of his obvious unease, he drove steadily, his eyes continually flickering between the road ahead and the rear-view mirror.

As they approached the circle, he asked if Hammond wanted him to go around twice. Hammond said no. He didn't want to give them any reason to close whatever gap they considered wise. He leaned over and dropped the second half of the hundred-dollar bill on to the front passenger seat, and then told the driver to put his foot down.

A few frantic seconds of lurching and tire squealing later, the driver drew the cab to a halt on 12th. Hammond slid out of the nearside door. He kept low and slammed the door shut behind him before creeping around and behind one of the half-dozen or so conveniently parked cars. The driver took off. Hammond stayed low and out of sight. He didn't peer out to see the two cars that sped along the street a few seconds later. If it was them, he didn't want to take any chance they might see him. If it wasn't, it didn't matter anyway.

He waited a few more seconds, then crossed the street and headed down the alleyway leading to 13th Street.

He checked his watch. It was 8.50. He left the alleyway and crossed the patch of waste ground separating the backs of the houses on 12th from those on 13th. He saw them, a little farther along: two dark-suited and belligerent-looking hoods, standing by the rear door of one of the Victorian house on 13th. They were smoking cigarettes, talking in muffled tones, and shuffling their feet. One of them saw Hammond. He mumbled to the other. The other looked up. Hammond nodded a greeting and kept walking towards them. When he got close to the picket fence that marked the properties' boundary, he asked,

"Has he arrived yet?"

The man on the left looked unsure. The other shook his head.

"No, not yet. It should be soon."

Hammond nodded and lit a cigarette, then turned his back and began looking around, as if he'd been sent to help. The trick worked, because they watched him for a few cautious moments before returning to their conversation.

When he heard them resume talking, he dropped the cigarette and pulled the HDM, then swivelled around and put two bullets into the man on the left. He realigned an inch, and put two more in the one on the right, then vaulted the fence and moved closer. They were both down and looked finished, but this wasn't a game with rules and conventions. He made certain with one more apiece.

He knew who they were, and why they were there. He knew they were Russian, because he'd asked the question and they'd answered in that same language. And he knew why they were there; assassination squads were the same the world over.

Despite there being four rounds left, he loaded a fresh clip and then tested the door handle. It opened noiselessly. He peered around the door and then stepped inside. Another quizzical face greeted him. The man was standing by the front door, at the far end of the hallway. When he saw the silenced automatic, he reached for his. Hammond shot him twice and watched as the twin impacts sent him sprawling against the door.

A voice from the floor above called out in Russian. It asked what the hell was going on down there. Hammond answered in Russian, loudly cursing, and saying that he had tripped on the mat. The voice told him to keep the noise down, and added that it was nearly time.

Hammond took the stairs three at a time, and then moved towards the bedroom at the front of the house. A fourth gunman stood guard at the open door. His reactions were slow. Hammond shot him twice in the head at close range. A fifth man stood in the bedroom. He was looking out of the open window with his back to Hammond, and holding a Mosin-Nagant 1891/30 with scope and silencer fitted.

When he heard the commotion and spun around, Hammond could see he was a big man, muscular and thick-set, but with a surprisingly small head for such a large frame. His clothes were threadbare and dirty. His barrel chest had strained the tattered open-necked shirt to such an extent that one of the buttons hung at the end of a thin thread of cotton. Another was missing altogether. He looked warily at the levelled HDM. Hammond recalled a photograph on an FBI sheet, and recognized him immediately.

"The FBI told me you went back to Moscow."

"They are fools. Sasha Gromyko went back to Moscow. I stayed for you."

Demidov squeaked his contempt for Hoover's finest. Hammond nodded and asked,

"The signal. What is it?"

Hammond watched Demidov, quietly assessing his chances of raising the rifle and getting off a shot before Hammond could pull the trigger. They were slim to none. Any chance the assassin might have had to kill him was gone. Hammond knew that, and from Demidov's shrug of resignation, it appeared he knew it, too.

"The awning. When it is time, the café owner will raise the awning."

Hammond glanced out of the window and looked down on the tea shop opposite. The shop's distinctive brown and black striped canvas awning had been lowered. That was inventive. With the awning lowered, whoever sat at the table would be unable to see the upper windows of those houses on the other side of the street, which effectively hid any sniper from his target until the very last moment. With the awning raised it offered the same clear field of fire through the trees that he had seen the previous night. It also left the morning sun directly behind the shooter and directly in the eyes of his target.

"Clever." He inclined his head in a gesture of respect for the assassin's meticulous preparation, and then asked, "Beria's orders. . . Was it to be only me, or both?"

"Both."

"Yeah, that's what I thought."

Demidov misread the signs. He showed two rows of yellow teeth as he shrugged and grinned. Hammond grinned back, and then shot him twice in the chest.

Acute shock flitted across the killer's face as each bullet found its mark. He staggered and dropped the rifle, but didn't go down. Instead, he snarled his hatred through the agony and moved to pick up the fallen weapon. As his eyes fixed on the rifle and his hands reached out, Hammond shot him again, this time through the top of the skull.

The assassin took one more step, his thick, blunt fingers still reaching for the rifle, but it was only gravity and the original madness that gave his corpse any momentum.

Vladimir Demidov was already dead.

****

By the time Hammond arrived at The Silver Samovar, it was well after nine. A smug-looking Davis Carpenter was the restaurant's only customer. He was sitting at his regular table by the window. Hammond sat down opposite.

"Sorry I'm late. I had to meet with a contact; old friend of Alan Carlisle."

"Who?"

"Nobody important. It turned out to be a dead-end. So what did you want to talk about?"

Carpenter eyed him cautiously for a moment. He seemed satisfied that all was well, because he smiled his usual smug smile before speaking.

"I wanted to know why you're following me."

Hammond surveyed the smugness and answered truthfully.

"Because I think you're Beria's mole in the State Department."

Carpenter's expression didn't waver.

"And why would you think that?"

"The report you wanted me to write, on the Paslov fiasco."

"What about it?"

"How did you know about the meeting in Frankfurt with Carlisle and Paslov?"

Carpenter shrugged.

"I don't remember. I suppose you must have told me."

Hammond shook his head.

"No, I didn't. If you remember, I refused to talk about any of it. It annoyed the hell out of you. I told you I would only talk to Carlisle."

"Well, then he must have told me."

"No. Marcus Allum told Chambers that he and Carlisle had specifically not told anybody, for fear of causing unrest in the department. Even Daniel Chambers was nose-out-of-joint.

Carpenter shrugged again, seemingly unfazed by the inquisition. Hammond knew why.

"And how did you know about Heinrich Müeller's defection? Carlisle didn't know about it until Paslov told him in Frankfurt. Nobody knew. Even Marcus Allum didn't know."

"Who told you I did?"

"A man called Alfred Schulman."

Carpenter's previous smugness quickly graduated to open contempt.

"He's just a crazy old Jew. Nobody can believe anything he says."

"Alfred Schulman is a little bizarre, but he's a long way from crazy. I just want to know why. Why did you sell us out: me, the girl, the old woman in Dessau, Carlisle, the cell in Magdeburg, and to Beria of all people? You were always such a fervent anti-communist."

Davis Carpenter turned his contempt on Hammond.

"I still am, and more than you could possibly understand." Hammond frowned. Carpenter sneered. "You think you know it all, don't you? You know virtually nothing."

"What do you mean?"

Contempt graduated to boastfulness as Carpenter dropped a bombshell.

"Remember that time in Rouen, when you came for me?"

"What about it?"

"I didn't crash-land the Lysander; they didn't force me down. I flew over there to warn them." Hammond looked blankly back. Carpenter explained. "About D-Day. About the landings being at Normandy, not Calais. . . I flew over there to tell them."

"You were working for the Nazis?"

Carpenter had become visibly animated. He clearly needed to share his guilt, and equally clearly believed that Hammond wouldn't be around long enough to divulge any secrets.

He claimed to have invested heavily in Germany before the war, and said that one of his largest investments had been in the German wine and spirit industry, a partnership with Joachim Ribbentrop. When Hammond asked if he meant von Ribbentrop, he scoffed at the ennoblement of his former business partner.

"No, not von. He adopted that title, pretentious fool. Joachim Ribbentrop was no more aristocracy than you or me. He was parvenu, cash rich and class poor, but in the beginning he had the ear of Hitler and that meant money for all of us."

Carpenter blamed the outbreak of war. He said Ribbentrop foolishly persuaded Hitler that if Germany invaded Poland, Chamberlain would sit still. But Ribbentrop reckoned without Churchill. They all reckoned without Churchill. Britain and France declared war before he had time to pull his investments. Davis Carpenter lost a fortune.

"So I risked my life, and killed so many, saving a man who didn't need saving."

"Oh, you did more than that, Gerald, much more. When you killed everyone in the Rouen Gestapo headquarters that night, you also killed the information I'd given them. The report was never sent. By the time they had re-staffed, found the report, passed it up the chain to Müeller, and he'd checked with Ribbentrop, it was too late: the invasion was underway. Without knowing it, you probably saved D-Day from being a disaster. Well, you saved some lives, at least. They should have given you a medal, but then people always said that about you, didn't they?"

"And what about all those thousands of Allied lives you risked?"

"It was a rash decision, Gerald. You know all about that, surely? You don't think about consequences, you just do what needs doing, and I never did agree with D-Day. Oh, I helped plan it, I didn't have a lot of choice, but by opening a second front we played right into Stalin's hands. He could never have gobbled up the territory he did without that second front."

Carpenter puffed his chest. He seemed almost proud of his betrayal, but when Hammond asked how he came to be working for Beria, pride became anger.

He talked about Heinrich Müeller and said the former head of the German Gestapo had betrayed him. He said when Müeller defected to the Soviets he took names with him, presumably as collateral. Carpenter's name was at the top of the list. He said Beria called and told him all about it, when he was over at Camp King.

"Can you believe the nerve? He telephoned me at my hotel, left me with no choice."

"And turning on all of your friends and allies didn't concern you?"

"A minor twinge of conscience, I suppose, but nothing to trouble me unduly. You see, I was at the tribunals when they showed that film about the Holocaust and the atrocities. It turned my stomach. I hadn't realised just how barbaric the Nazis had been. The thought of betraying people like that didn't seem so inglorious after I saw that film. I just wish I'd known from the beginning. If I'd known, none of it would have happened."

Hammond shook his head in disgust as he viewed Carpenter's only sign of remorse.

"Isn't it all a little late for regrets?"

"Perhaps. To tell you the truth, I'm glad it's finally over, but then, I expect that's what they all say. So who else knows about all of this, Gerald? Who are you working with?"

There it was, that same old familiar and unnecessary testament to truth.

"Why should that matter?"

"I suppose it doesn't really. I was just interested to see if you'd worked it out by yourself."

Hammond knew why Carpenter had asked the question, but wanted to play out the charade, and so lied and said he was working alone. Carpenter took a sip of tea, pulled a face of distaste, and called out to where Sokolov stood patiently awaiting his cue.

"Viktor. This tea is terrible. Get me another brew, would you?"

Sokolov apologized, and rounded the counter to collect Carpenter's cup.

"I'll make another." He looked at Hammond. "Can I get you anything, sir?"

Hammond shook his head. Sokolov nodded and carried away the tea. He returned holding a heavy metal handle and muttering something about the place needing more light. As Sokolov attached the handle and began winding in the awning, Carpenter said nothing. He just sat quietly, watching and waiting for Vladimir Demidov to do what he did best.

But then, nothing. No crash of glass, no shattered skull, no blood and matter spraying across the café; no dead or dying Gerald Hammond sprawled across the floor.

A further thirty seconds of tension-loaded silence elapsed, and still nothing. Davis Carpenter finally tore his eyes away from the face before him, then squinted through the sunshine and up at the window opposite.

The sign in the window that had advertised 'House For Rent – Immediate Occupancy' was gone, and the window closed. Hammond knew that without looking, because he had taken down the sign and closed the window before he left. For a few puzzled moments, Davis Carpenter sat looking up at the window, but then understanding must have finally dawned, because he closed his eyes for a moment, before turning the stare on Hammond. When Carpenter finally spoke, it was in a voice weary with resignation.

"I should have known. You always were the best."

Hammond signalled through the window to the row of black Cadillacs that sat waiting farther along the street. When he answered, it was without any hint of triumph or elation. He just felt sad and angry about so many lives being lost, and all for stupidity and greed.

"If it helps, he had orders to kill us both. I'm sorry, but these people are here for you."

He had felt sorry for so many people, but Carpenter wasn't one of them.

As Zalesie's men poured in, Davis Carpenter slumped back in his chair.

"Zalesie?"

"Otherwise known as Josef Conrad Schmidt."

Further realization suddenly cleared the features of despondency.

"But of course. I should have guessed who he was. When that weasel Kube turned up at Camp King, I should have guessed the others wouldn't be far away."

"So what did you do with Carlisle's evidence on Manhattan?"

"The basement incinerator. I'm sorry, Gerald."

Hammond nodded and posed one final question.

"So, why did Beria give you up? He did give you up, you know, and he did order Demidov to kill us both."

Carpenter slotted the final piece into the puzzle.

"When I told Schulman about Heinrich Müeller, Beria was furious. He said he'd taken months to turn Müeller, and I'd let it slip in one stupid moment of panic. That was when he checked the balance sheet and found my liability outweighing any asset. I knew then he'd give me up when it suited him, but there was nothing I could do. I had nowhere left to go."

As Carpenter climbed to his feet, Hammond turned away and stared out of the window. He was thinking of the promise he had given to the old woman in Dessau. He wouldn't actually pull the trigger, but he hoped that his part in Carpenter's downfall would suffice. Carpenter leaned over and placed a hand on his arm.

"One last request: even I'm allowed that, aren't I? Look after Clara for me, would you, Gerald? Don't let them get to her. She never knew enough to damage anyone."

The apparent show of gallantry took Hammond by surprise.

"An act of decency, from you?"

"Decency has nothing to do with it. I just hate the thought of her lying alongside me in my grave, nagging at me for eternity. Thinking about the peace and solitude of it all, is the only compensation I have left to me."

The gallows humour failed to elicit a smile. Hammond merely nodded.

"Do you want me to give her a message, or explain anything?"

Carpenter shook his head.

"There's no need. She knows. We both knew this was how it would end. It was only a question of when."

44

Hammond watched Davis Carpenter standing motionless at the nearside rear door of the Cadillac, silently waiting until they opened the door for him. With this final and pointless act of bravado made, he smiled weakly at Hammond before climbing into the car. When the Cadillac finally left the curb and sped away, it seemed almost an anti-climax.

"Can I offer you a lift?"

"Mr Zalesie. It's a long way from Connecticut, and you're up early."

"I thought I would take the time to rue an old and untrustworthy colleague's passing, and offer my thanks to the arrival of a new and hopefully more honourable one."

They stood in silence as the Cadillac melded into the distant traffic. Each man harboured his own thoughts and memories of the man who had been Davis Alan Carpenter. It was Zalesie who finally broke the shared moment of remembrance and regret.

"You two went back a long way?"

"A few years; not that long, I suppose. For all of that, I honestly thought I knew him."

"We are none of as we appear, Mr Hammond."

"No, Herr Schmidt. We none of us are."

The German allowed the briefest of smiles to lighten the moment.

"I see you finally removed the blindfold."

"It was becoming uncomfortable. So, tell me. Who are the Children of Etzel? You?"

There was no hesitation in the answer.

"No, Mr Hammond, just a foolish tale we sometimes told our children."

"So these people; they don't exist?"

"They did, in the mind of a megalomaniac long ago, but it died with the Reich."

"I wish I could be sure of that."

"Would you like me to give you my word?"

"What, as a proud Lithuanian descendent or as a gentleman?"

"Touché, Mr Hammond."

They eyed each other briefly and warily. Hammond posed the critical question.

"So, the blindfold's off. Does that mean I'm in that danger you spoke of?"

"Not from me."

"And so you've caught your spy in the State Department. Now what?"

Conrad Zalesie sniffed contemptuously.

"Now we wait for human nature and the fourth estate to take their individual courses. Tragic tale, can't say too much for security reasons. Betrayed his country, security services closing in, couldn't live with it, death before dishonour. Poor man, a hero gone wrong. Damn Soviets, we just can't trust them."

As Hammond watched the Machiavellian brain seemingly conjuring newspaper reports from thin air, he held no doubts. The press would print whatever Conrad Zalesie and the rest of the inner circle at number fifty-eight wanted them to print.

Zalesie went on. He said most importantly the papers would warn of the lurking danger that America now faced, and roundly damn an expansionist Soviet Union. Their storylines would tell of how easily an otherwise honourable man had become enmeshed and corrupted, but the underlying theme would be of an American nation no longer able to trust her former ally from the wrong side of the great political divide.

The German looked hugely pleased with himself as he finished his predictions. He said it was the perfect opportunity to get more of the right messages to the American people.

Hammond recalled his conversation with Marcus Allum in the New York hotel. That evening he had thought Allum cynical and undemocratic, but now he knew. Allum had been so right about so much, and he had been so wrong about everything. He studied the self-satisfied look on Zalesie's face, and posed a question he already knew the answer to.

"And the official position will only serve to confirm the lies?"

"But of course."

The German gleefully reeled off the anticipated statements: Thank God we got to him before he gave too much away. Thank God we have an army of dedicated men and women keeping America safe for decent Americans.

Hammond recalled another conversation. It had taken place in a sleazy Washington bar, not an upmarket New York hotel, but it had held the same familiar theme of harsh reality shattering naïveté. As with Allum before him, everything Morton Simmonds said that evening had been true. Hammond knew that now.

"Which was just what Beria wanted all along. Deflect all the attention away from the reason behind the death of Alan Carlisle, and take everyone's mind off the possibility of spies in the Manhattan Project. That was what you wanted, too, wasn't it?"

True to his naïveté, Hammond had sought confirmation. An elated Zalesie seemed in the mood for talking.

"Stalin will overrun Europe if we let him, and from there the tentacles will reach out. We cannot rely on another Pearl Harbour to disrupt the isolationists for a second time. We have to shake America from her complacency, and we have to do it before it is too late."

"Even at the risk of nuclear war?"

"Don't believe the scaremongers, Gerald. The world has seen the power of nuclear weapons with its own eyes. That power now lies in the fear it evokes, not the devastation it causes."

"You hope."

"No, I believe it. I truly do. And so, what now, Gerald, for the two of us?"

"I was thinking about your man Dawid Gabriel, about something he once said to me."

"Gabriel belongs to Marcus Allum. He's not my man."

"Whatever."

"So, what did he say to you?"

"He told me they were unbeatable. . . The Folks at Fifty-Eight."

Zalesie stood musing over the title.

"The Folks at Fifty-Eight. I think I rather like that."

"Yes, but I was also thinking about these other people, these people you claim don't exist; these Children of Etzel people."

"What about them?"

"I was just thinking. Wouldn't it be the darndest thing if the cancer that had so chronically infected our democracy, the cancer Dawid Gabriel said was unbeatable, had itself become infected by an even more malignant cancer?"

Zalesie smiled an enigmatic smile.

"Does it matter?"

"Does what matter?"

"The political philosophy we choose. They all come from the same tree, you know. Does it matter which branch we shelter beneath? Did you know the man who started the Council on Foreign Relations was a Marxist?"

Hammond shook his head.

"Oh yes, House, Edward M. Wilson's alter ego. So, what does it matter: Marxist, Fascist, a New World Order, or the Old World Order? It all comes down to one simple premise. A governing elite, ruling whatever parts of the world are worth ruling."

"So the world becomes a collection of oligarchies?"

"But it already is, Gerald. Can you not see that?"

"And Bolshevism. Isn't that just another branch to shelter beneath?"

Hammond thought he had spotted a flaw in the argument. Zalesie merely nodded.

"Bolshevism possibly, but the gulf between the rhetoric of Lenin and the reality of Stalin is as vast as the Russian Steppes." Another enigmatic smile followed. "And even the hardiest of growth can always benefit from a little judicious pruning."

"And what of democracy, our democracy? Is that an irrelevance, or just a casualty?"

Zalesie was clearly in his element.

"In a way they're all forms of democracy, representation of the people by revolution or ballot, apathy or ignorance. When any regime falls, all that changes over time are one or two personnel of the ruling elite. Or do you believe that Roosevelt and Byrnes and Marshall and Dulles and Rockefeller and Morgan, and all those backwoodsmen who sit up on the hill, see themselves as anything other than ruling elite?"

"Maybe I just like the idea of preserving an illusion of democracy for all us poor ignorant ordinary fools down here. Maybe I don't like the idea of an American government that constantly lies to the American people."

"All governments lie, Gerald. Those that lie the best are those we trust the most."

As Hammond listened to Zalesie's words and finally conceded the unpalatable truth of it all, he felt so many conflicting emotions; so much sadness and regret, so much anger and frustration. He stood dejectedly on the sidewalk, considering the extent of his own naïveté and impotence. Zalesie changed the subject.

"So, how would you feel about taking over from Carpenter?"

"On recent history, that wouldn't seem like a job with too many prospects."

"All tasks in life are like life itself, Gerald. They are what you make of them."

"Possibly, but there's already enough resentment from the last time you promoted me over so many heads. This time you'll probably get an outright mutiny."

"You won't be there for long, and I'm sure we will somehow survive. If we are ever to defeat Lavrenti Beria, we will need to put more passion into this new Central Intelligence initiative, with or without Mr John Edgar Hoover's blessing.

"There will be some major changes and expansions occurring over the next year or so, Gerald. I'd like you to be part of them. I'd like to get you into

439

E-Street, and if you are going to be effective, you are also going to need positioning at a senior level."

"We're going back to E-Street? Makes you wonder why they canned OSS."

"You wouldn't be the first to say that."

"And a promotion at the State Department, no matter how undeserved or premature, can mean the recipient shuffling across at a senior level without raising eyebrows?"

"Yes, something like that, but not undeserved. You sell yourself short, Gerald. You've done some fine work recently."

Hammond thought carefully before answering.

"So I'd become your man in Central Intelligence. You know, I'm not sure I want that. I'm not sure I want any of it. It's all a little too sordid, and the people involved are all a little too tainted."

Conrad Zalesie continued to smile that same enigmatic smile.

"What are you going to do if you don't accept my offer? Go back to that insurance company? Spend your days answering the telephone and filling out meaningless forms? Or maybe walk away from it all. Put your feet up and watch the grass grow. Struggle from week to week to pay the rent, and forever regret the chances you didn't take."

"At least I'll sleep at night."

"No you won't. . . None of us do."

Hammond knew the truth of that. He looked across to the house on the opposite side of the street from the Silver Samovar and remembered the five men he had so ruthlessly killed there. As he thought about them, he also recalled the last words of Marat Reznikov. Maybe celestial cognizance comes to us all in the moments before death. Maybe the Russian had seen both of their fates. Maybe there was a hell, and maybe they would meet each other there.

Zalesie followed the direction of Hammond's gaze and seemed to read his thoughts.

"We are each of us on journeys to hell, Gerald Hammond. We chose that destination many years ago. All we can do now is enjoy the ride."

As the German wandered back to his car, a movement farther along the street caught Hammond's eye. He looked beyond the remaining Cadillacs and bodyguards, and saw her there. She had climbed out of Zalesie's Mark-Three Phantom and was now standing on the sidewalk, her hair cascading over her shoulders and glistening gold in the morning sunshine, her head angled and lips smiling as she gently mocked his amazement.

She was wearing a simple black cocktail dress and high-heeled shoes. They made her appear taller and more sophisticated than he remembered, and more statuesque than he remembered; perhaps even more beautiful than he remembered.

He recalled that night at the guesthouse in Dessau, when he had first seen her naked and shivering and bathed in moonlight, and suddenly realised just what she had come to mean to him. Suddenly everything was clear. Suddenly he didn't care about age differences or social conventions or chattering gossip. Suddenly he knew that he had to be with her, that he could never be completely happy without her.

He knew something else, too. With or without the lure of Catherine Schmidt, he could never have gone back to his former life of boredom and mediocrity and regret.

With one last glance at the house opposite The Silver Samovar tea rooms, Hammond followed his new and Machiavellian master to where the rear door of the Rolls remained open and a beautiful young woman stood patiently waiting.

GLOSSARY

ATLI

American Trading and Libertarian Investments. Weapons and military equipment manufacturer, importer, exporter and wholesale distributor.

Avenue Foch (84)

Joint wartime headquarters of the Paris Gestapo. Other was at 11 rue des Saussaies.

Bohemia and Moravia

Former Nazi protectorate, established in 1939, in what is today the Czech Republic.

Camp King

U.S. military base, north-west of Frankfurt. Used for debriefing of Nazis and defectors at the end of World War II. The U.S. admitted its presence, but denied its covert purpose. Became a counter-intelligence centre under Reinhard Gehlen. America closed Camp King in 1993, and returned it to the German government in 1995.

CFR

The Council on Foreign Relations: a high-level 'think-tank' attached to The U.S. State Department. Membership includes many of the most powerful men and women in the U.S. Considered the most influential force in determining U.S. Foreign Policy over the last eighty years. Headquarters: 58 East Sixty-Eighth Street NYC.

Chekist

Name derived from Cheka, the first Bolshevik state police and security force (formed 1917, under Felix Dzerzhinsky). Became a derogatory term for any Soviet security police, especially those of brutish disposition.

CIG

Central Intelligence Group. Took over from the OSS. Changed its name to the Central Intelligence Agency (1947). Initially operated out of a suite of rooms next to The White House. Later expanded into former OSS Headquarters at 2430 E-St. Washington D.C.

Covert Ops.   Secret Operations, untraceable to source i.e. deniable.

Enormoz   Code name for the Soviet espionage offensive against The Manhattan Project. Initiated in 1940. Personally supervised by Lavrenti Beria.

Fallschirmjäger   German paratroopers; part of the Luftwaffe.

Fort Hunt   U.S Army base in Virginia, used for interrogation and debriefing of Nazis and defectors. For many years the establishment was so secret that outside the intelligence community it was known only by a PO Box number (1142).

Gestapo   **GE**heime **STA**ats**PO**lizei (Secret State Police) Section IV of Reich Security. Hitler's political police force and part of the SS.

Gulag   **G**lavnoye **U**pravleniye Ispravitel'no-Trudovykh **LAG**erey I Koliniy (The Chief Directorate of Corrective Labour Camps and Colonies). Infamous Soviet penal labour camps. The Soviets operated a network of almost five hundred camp complexes, scattered across the Soviet Union.

Los Alamos   Area in New Mexico. Home of the Manhattan Project laboratory.

Manhattan Project   U.S. programme to develop, build and evolve the atomic bomb.

MGB   Soviet Ministry for State Security, formed March 1946; forerunner to the KGB.

MVD	Soviet Ministry of Internal Affairs, formed March 1946.
NKVD	Soviet Peoples Commissariat for Internal Affairs. Disbanded 1946. NKVD and its offspring the NKGB were forerunners to the MVD and MGB respectively.
ODESSA	**O**rganization **D**er **E**hemaligen **SS-A**ngehörigen. (Organization of former SS members) Post-war Nazi group that specialized in helping Nazi war criminals escape justice. The escape routes they, and other groups, set up were known as 'ratlines'. The most famous 'ratline' was said to operate between Bremen and Bari, via the Vatican.
Ogrodowa Street	12-14, Wartime Headquarters of the SS in Warsaw.
OSO	**O**ffice of **S**pecial **O**perations. Became part of the CIA in 1947.
OSS	**O**ffice of **St**rategic **S**ervices. U.S. World War II Intelligence Agency, disbanded 1945. U.S. Equivalent of British Special Operations Executive (SOE).
Petschek Palace	Wartime headquarters of the Prague Gestapo.
SMERSH	**SMER**t'**SH**pionam (Death to spies). Initially Red Army counter-intelligence branch. Transferred to Soviet State Security 1943. Officially disbanded in 1946, although elements remained in various guises until the 1950s.
Übermenschen	Superior beings in Nazi ideology; a term 'borrowed' from the 19th Century German philosopher Nietzsche.

Waffen SS   Waffen (armed) SS/SchutzStaffel (Guardian Squadron), Hitler's elite guard. Grew to nine hundred thousand strong during WWII. Responsible for implementing The Holocaust. Many of Nazi Germany's most infamous war criminals belonged to the SS.

Wehrmacht   Name given to unified German forces 1935-45 (Did not include the SS).

Werwolf   Name given to units chartered by Himmler, for an ongoing guerrilla war under SS-Obergruppenführer Hans-Adolf Prützmann. The units were largely comprised of Hitler Youth. The majority surrendered, following an order from Grand Admiral Dönitz, but a handful of the more capable and experienced fighters refused to surrender and took to the mountains.

1946 Characters, both real and imagined (U.S. unless stated):

Abakumov, Viktor S.   Russian. Head of Smersh 1942-46. Became Head of MGB. Infamous for torturing prisoners with his bare hands.

Allum, Marcus Thomas   Princeton graduate, Wall Street Lawyer, former OSS member. CFR member. Senior State Department member, in Office of Occupied Territories. 'Handler' of Kube.

Angleton, James Jesus   Yale graduate, former OSS member. Senior CIG member. Known as the 'mother' of Foreign Intelligence services in U.S.

Bentley, Elizabeth Terrill   Soviet spy/courier 1938-45, turned informer. Exposed two Soviet espionage cells in the U.S. The names she gave included no fewer than 37 Federal Government employees.

Beria, Lavrenti Pavlovich   Mingrelian. Soviet Deputy Premier. Head of all security and espionage services for the Soviet Union 1938-53.

Brusilov, Sergey   Georgian. MGB agent based in Leipzig.

Carlisle, Alan James   Princeton graduate. Senior member of State Department's Office of Occupied Territories.

Carlisle, Angela   Repressed socialite, wife of Alan.

Carlisle, Mathew   Princeton dropout, son of Alan and Angela.

Carpenter, Davis Alan   Yale graduate and State Department member. Member of wartime strategy team for invasion of mainland Europe (Operation Overlord).

Chambers, Daniel — Harvard graduate and Wall Street lawyer. Senior CFR member.

Demidov, Vladimir — Russian. Former Red Army sniper and bodyguard to Beria. Former Smersh team member. For many years the NKVD and MGB's top assassin.

Dönitz, Karl — German. Grand Admiral and Commander German Navy. After 1943, Hitler's designated successor.

Donovan, William Joseph — Head of the wartime OSS. Wall Street lawyer. Known as the 'father' of Foreign Intelligence Services in U.S. Only man to hold all four of America's highest military decorations.

Dulles, Allen Welsh — Princeton graduate. Wall Street lawyer and OSS member. Senior CFR member (Appointed CFR President in 1946). Later became the longest-serving Director of the CIA.

Frank, Karl Hermann — German SS-Gruppenführer. Succeeded Heydrich as Reichsprotektor and Reich Minister for Bohemia and Moravia. Audience of 5000 people for his public execution in Prague, 22nd May 1946.

Gabriel, Dawid — Former N.Y.C. Police Lieutenant, turned Private Investigator.

Gehlen, Reinhard — German. Former Wehrmacht Generalmajor and head of Eastern Front Intelligence Service 1944-45. Defected to the west in 1945 and ran a counter-intelligence service for U.S.

Gouzenko, Igor

Belarusian cipher clerk, based in Soviet Embassy Ottawa. Defected September 1945. Provided the first documentary evidence of Soviet espionage activities against the west, and of spies in the Manhattan Project.

Hammond, Gerald

Princeton graduate. Former OSS member and Special Operations team leader. Senior State Department member. Later joined the CIA

Harvey, William King

Indiana graduate. Senior FBI agent, assigned to head the White House purge. Later joined the CIA.

Heydrich, Reinhard

German. SS-Obergruppenführer. Deputy Reichsprotektor Bohemia and Moravia. Hitler's blue-eyed boy. The architect of The Final Solution (The Holocaust). Assassinated in Prague 1942.

Helms, Richard McGarrah

Williamstown graduate. Former OSS member and OSO chief. Senior CIG member. Later Director of Intelligence.

Himmler, Heinrich

German. Reichsführer-SS. Head of Waffen SS and Gestapo 1936-45.

Hoover, J. Edgar

First Director of the FBI 1935-72. Donovan's main rival for control of Central Intelligence.

Kube, Martin

German. Gestapo Kriminaldirektor in Warsaw and Prague. Head of Bohemian and Moravian Intelligence service 1942-45. Defected 1946. Established Czechoslovakian and Polish counter-intelligence service for the U.S.

Kurchatov, Igor	Russian. Physicist. Leader of the Soviet atomic bomb project, reporting to Beria. Tested the first device, a plutonium implosion bomb, on 29th August 1949, ten years earlier than western intelligence forecasts.
Levitsky, Ivan	Ukrainian. MGB agent based in Leipzig.
Metreveli, Sachino	Georgian. MGB Agent, based in Vienna.
Müeller, Heinrich	German. SS-Obergruppenführer Head of Section IV of Reich Security (Gestapo) 1939-45.
Orsini, Carmine	State Department and CFR factotum
Offie, Carmel	State Department; later joined the CIA
Paslov, Anna	Russian. Wife of Stanislav.
Paslov, Stanislav Ivanovich	Russian. Survivor, Mauthausen Concentration Camp. Regional Head of MGB 1945-48.
Radcliff-Hammond, Emma	Washington Socialite. Estranged wife of Gerald Hammond.
Reznikov, Marat	Russian. Commissar, assigned to the Dessau and Wittenberg areas of occupied Germany
Scholde Lara Therese	Austrian fashion designer and wholesaler, living in Vienna.
Schmidt, Catherine Louise	German. Daughter of assassinated Nazi spymaster.

Schmidt, Josef Conrad   German. SS-Oberführer Head of Bohemian and Moravian Intelligence Service. Assassinated, Prague 1942.

Schulman, Alfred   Jewish. Holocaust survivor (Mauthausen) turned Nazi-hunter; worked with Wiesenthal in Linz.

Simmonds, Morton   Princeton graduate. Senior FBI agent assigned to the White House purge. Later joined the CIA.

Souers, Sidney   Miami graduate. Former Rear-Admiral USNR and Deputy Director of Naval Intelligence. The first Head of CIG, 1946.

Sokolov Viktor   Russian émigré and Soviet agent.

Strand, Melody   Switchboard Operator Camp King, Frankfurt.

Strecker, Howard H.   Colonel. Officer in Charge debriefing section, Camp King 1945-47.

Strieder, Karl Edward   German. Oberleutnant. Former Luftwaffe parachute commander with the 1st Fallshirm-Jäger-Division. Became leader of an Austrian Werwolf partisan unit.

Stalin, Joseph   Georgian. Born Ioseb Vissarionovich Jugashvilli. Soviet Premier and General Secretary of the Communist Party 1922- 53

Travers, Alicia   Wealthy Washington socialite.

Truman, Harry S.   33rd President of the U.S. Authorised the use of nuclear weapons against Japan. (Hiroshima and Nagasaki August 6/9 1945).

Vandenberg, Hoyt Sanford   Lieutenant General U.S.A.F. Second Director of CIG 1946-1947 Considered a founding father of the U.S. Air Force.

Wisner, Frank Gardiner   Virginia State graduate. Wall Street lawyer, OSS member, and State Department chief. 'Handler' of Gehlen. Director of OPC (Office of Policy Coordination) which later became the espionage and counter intelligence branch of the CIA.

Zalesie, Conrad   Lithuanian exile. Head of ATLI. Senior CFR member. Conduit for all significant European defections to U.S. 1943-57.

Zalesie, Theresa   Wife of Conrad.